The Firebox Stalker

Additional books by author:

Firehouse Fraternity Oral History Series:
Volume I: Becoming a Firefighter
Volume II: Life Between Alarms
Volume III: Equipment
Volume IV: Responding
Volume V: Riots to Renaissance
Volume VI: Changing the NFD

The Newark Riots: A View from the Firehouse

An Eerie Silence: An Oral History of Newark
Firefighters at the WTC

Hervey's Boys: New Jersey's First Chinese Community
1870-1886 (And What Happened After That)

Fiction:
The Hand Life Dealt you
A-zou: A Woman Living in Interesting Times

Children's Fiction:
A Hundred Battles (YA)
A Broken Glass (YA)
Balancing Act (Middle Grade)

The Firebox Stalker

Neal Stoffers

Springfield and Hunterdon Publishing
Copyright 2018
www.newarkfireoralhistory.com

First Printing: 2018

ISBN: 978-1-970034-21-9

Springfield and Hunterdon Publishing
East Brunswick, NJ 08816-5852

Chapter One

"It is going down tonight," the young man thought as he stepped off the bus. The confrontation could be put off no longer. The only choice left was how to react. If all went as planned, he could affect the outcome. Then the contract on him would be withdrawn out of fear of the terrible cost. If not, his mother would be alone in this world and the mob would have taken another man she loved.

He inhaled deeply to calm his nerves, the steam from his breath billowing out into the moist air. The familiar grind of his leather soles on the damp concrete sidewalk was the only thing disrupting the stillness after the bus pulled away. It was already past eight o'clock in the evening. Majestic oaks, bereft of their summer foliage, lined the street. Remnants of the year's crop of leaves covered the storm sewer on the opposite corner.

That would not have happened when he was a child. Back then the people in the neighborhood cleaned up the leaves as they fell. A shower of spray was thrown onto the brick retaining wall on the corner when a car drove through the puddle created by the blocked sewer. At least the wall was being washed. It had not looked that clean since Dr. Kawolski had fled the neighborhood.

The deceptive warmth of a humid, late autumn night surrounded him. The trench coat he wore provided more than comfort and protection from the rain. Its pocket concealed a family heirloom, his father's police service revolver.

Taking another deep breath and nervously releasing it, the man started to review his plan while waiting for the light to change. How had he gotten himself into this situation? Why had the family not moved after his father had died? The neighborhood had already been changing by then. Drugs were becoming a major problem. Were they not why his father had been killed? A cop who had been trying to do his duty; the mob tiring of bailing out their soldiers after his father had arrested them. First was the attempt to discredit an honest cop. After they had become bored with that game, they executed him. Even though only ten years old, he had been amazed at how corrupt the Police Department had become. Enough of the brass had been bought off to squash any attempt to investigate the murder. It was more convenient and lucrative to let the story of a good cop gone bad stand. He had never trusted the Police again. For the first time in three generations, there were no cops in his family.

Questions, questions, he had nothing but questions. He needed answers. Too preoccupied with his thoughts, the light changing went unnoticed. It did not matter. For the past five years the young man had arrived home at the same time each night, walked the same route no matter what the weather. If anyone had so desired, they could have set a watch by him, always arriving on his front doorstep at six o'clock, very rarely even a minute late. Tonight he was over two hours late. In fact, he had not arrived home on time for the past week. His mother had eagerly asked if a woman was the reason for his tardiness. She had looked a little disappointed when he had replied, "No, mom. It's just the traffic." It was not a lie. The drug traffic had made him change his habits; punctuality could kill him now.

Lately, his mother showed her disappointment easily whenever the subject of women came up. How does a man explain to his mother that he is a failure with the opposite sex? The problem was women were so naive. They didn't see the world for what it was. For the first few years of dating, he thought the problem was immaturity. The girls involved were only eighteen or nineteen year old college coeds. Their daddies had protected them from the harsh realities of life. Understanding their naiveté made it easy to overlook their immaturity. However, as time went by it became apparent that the problem was not youth. There had been changes in society. The nurturing woman, such as his mother, had been replaced by the foolishly independent woman who did not appreciate the protective embrace of a strong man. Their determination to be equal to men made them blind to the dangers that surrounded them. All he wanted was a partner to protect and love.

Maybe it was best that none had been found. The mob would have gone after her first. The surprise was that they had not attacked his mother yet. If tonight's plan worked out, they would be convinced the price of such an attack was too high and would leave both himself and his mother alone out of respect. Decisive action would earn that respect.

Review the plan! Preoccupation with analyzing how this situation had come about was causing him to neglect that review. Touching the bulge in his pocket, he took in his surroundings. The neighborhood had changed dramatically since he had played on these streets as a child. The streets were now too dangerous for children. Drug dealers driving BMW's roamed where little boys had once thrown footballs.

The appearance of the streets had changed as well. Garbage cans were strewn about waiting for tomorrow's pick-up. As a child, the city had men pull trash cans to the curb from residents' yards. The mess that lined this street was kept out of sight until just before the truck came to pick it up. The stench and unsightliness was exposed for a limited time. Back then the residents carried their refuse cans back to their yards immediately after the Sanitation Department completed its sweep of the neighborhood. Now they sat at the curb until the evening.

A cat crossed the street and went up on one of the porches ahead of him. The size of the cat was amazing. It was just another sign of the area's deterioration. Fat cats were an indication that there was a rodent problem in the vicinity. His father used to say, "The cats are fat where the rats are at." The cat meowing and scratching at the screen door of the house he was now passing apparently did its share to keep the rodent population down.

These streets no longer made up a neighborhood. They were just avenues with a collection of domiciles facing them. At one time each family on this block was known to him. The single family homes that lined the street had become merely houses. They had ceased to be homes when they had turned into way stations in the busy lives of their inhabitants. That change had come about over the past decade. Neighborhoods had children playing on the street, their happy voices shouting "You're it" until the calls of their mothers sent them home. Now there were no children running on the street. If there were any parents on the block now, they just farmed out the raising of their children to others. All were too busy aggrandizing themselves to bother with kids.

The houses were not as rundown as one might expect. This was partly due to their inhabitants' worries about losing face and partly because time had not caught up with the neglect. In a few more years the buildings would begin to fall apart. Respectable people would not buy a house in this area. The candy store that had been frequented by the neighborhood children had become a haven for drug pushers. That was where he would have to be decisive tonight.

It was the mob's store now. The owner had gone bad years before. John might appear to be grandfatherly, but the young man knew better. The ruthless proprietor of the local candy store sold more than just candy. Even as a child, it was known that he was a calculating, greedy old man. His father had told him about the store owner. Other stores in the area would give a cop on the beat merchandise as a token of thanks. John had refused to even give a discount. When the two men had argued, the old man had complained to Police Headquarters and his father had been transferred. That was when the mob started its campaign against a good cop. That was also how he knew the old man was a member of the mob. Only powerful people could have a cop transferred. John needed only to speak with the Police brass on the take and his father was moved.

The young man stopped at the top of a small hill to collect his thoughts. John's Confectionery was at the bottom of the incline. Looking down the hill, he saw where the youths had pointed at him and then argued the night before. They had yelled in frustration "There he is!" surprised by his crossing the street a block earlier than normal. The week before the young man had overheard part of their conversation as he walked past them. They must not have realized his hearing was that sharp. "5:45. Okay, we'll get him tomorrow night." Why they had wanted to get him was a mystery until his mother had told him that someone had broken into John's. The police had stopped by to see if she had seen something suspicious on one of her walks. Mom had not seemed the least bit worried, but the young man knew what that meant. All the cops in the neighborhood were on the take. The store owner suspected him of having something to do with the break in. He knew enough from his father to realize the old man had put out a contract on him.

For the past three days, his routine was purposely varied. He wanted to buy time to think. A quiet man who never bothered anyone, the thought of violence made his stomach turn. A confrontation would be avoided if at all possible. That would give the mob time to discover they were wrong.

A car parked at the bottom of the hill told him the stakes had been raised. The nose of a white luxury car was clearly visible jutting out into the crosswalk. The young soldiers of the mob who hung out on the corner had been reinforced by a mob officer. What to do? The plan, review the plan!

It was a simple one. Too complex a plan was destined to fail. Ignore them unless they approached in a threatening manner. The first phase called for him to try to talk his way out. As long as there was room to maneuver he would talk. Only if they reached for a gun or tried to force him into a car would phase two go into effect and his father's revolver be drawn. It was important that a distance be kept between him and the mobsters surely waiting at the bottom of the hill. If things got too tight, the gun would be forced out. His father had always said, "Never pull out a gun unless you intend to use it." If the gun came out it was going to be fired. He steeled himself with one more deep breath, tapped his pocket, and began to walk down the hill.

No one had seen him yet. Maybe it was not too late to turn around and go down another street. If the mob had a little more time they would find out he had nothing to do with the break in. As the last thought passed through his mind, one of the soldiers came out of the store and looked up the hill. A large smile spread across his face. The thug became very animated and rushed back into the store. It was too late now. The die had been cast.

Three young men came rushing out of John's as the young man approached the bottom of the hill. All three were dressed in suits. One ran to the driver's side of the limo; one walked over to the rear passenger's door; and the third waited with a smile for him to reach the bottom of the hill.

Why were they doing this? Laughing at him as he walked into their trap; waiting patiently for him to deliver himself. They must think this would be easy. The Police would not even look into the matter. They had not investigated his father's murder and he was a fellow officer. A simple, quiet man would vanish. No one but his mother would notice. These thugs expected him to quiver, beg for his life, and then die quietly. Determined not to leave the world in such an ignoble manner, he resolved to go down with a fight.

His heart was pounding as he reached the bottom of the hill. Flaws in his plan were now evident. To take on three thugs at once was a loser. He might be able to get one or two shots off, but his father's service revolver was twenty years old. The mobsters in front of him surely carried the new 9mm pistols. He would be dead before the obsolete revolver could discharge three times. If he tried to run across the street they would shoot him in the back and leave. No one would have seen anything. The neighborhood people were all cowering behind their doors. Even if someone heard the shot and looked out a window, the Police would ignore them.

These thoughts rushed through his mind in an instant. In that time the one thug waiting for him had moved to within arm's reach. He had not been decisive. His window of opportunity was already closed. He watched in horror as the man in front of him reached into his jacket for a gun.

Everything was now moving at an accelerated pace and yet his mind saw it as if in slow motion. The driver started the engine as his accomplice opened the car door and beckoned him to step in. If he entered the car he would vanish as completely as Jimmy Hoffa. The man reaching for his gun almost had it out. All choices had been reduced to one. He would leave this miserable world with a fight. Reaching into his side pocket, he pulled the old revolver out.

Chapter Two

Frank Helms quietly opened the bunkroom door of the old Vailsburg firehouse. A length of 3/4 inch rope was draped over his shoulder. After softly closing the door, he knelt down and crawled along the linoleum floor to the rear pole hole. A polished two inch brass pole went through the middle of two hinged wooden doors at the bottom of a three foot wide circular opening in the floor. Frank lay down on his stomach, gently opened one of the doors, and lowered one end of the rope to the apparatus floor. Several pairs of eager hands reached up for it as he began to inch along the floor toward a bed at the other end of the room. Heavy snoring could be heard coming from the bed. The young Newark firefighter struggled to contain his laughter.

How could anyone sleep through this racket? It was a question the firefighters assigned to Six Engine would have to answer over the next few months. Company closings and a realignment of Battalions had moved Six Engine from the Fourth to the First Battalion. Now whenever one of the Vailsburg companies needed manpower, Six would be the company drawn from to fill the gap. Everyone who worked with him on Springfield Avenue and Hunterdon Street knew there would be many more trips to this western edge of the city. No one was happy about that prospect; all firehouses were not created equally.

The most glaring point of difference between Vailsburg and "the hill", the area of the city served by his company, was the amount of work. The Burg was a stable residential neighborhood where firefighters who had put their time in at busy companies could spend their last years on the job. The few fires fought out of this house were battled with brain not brawn. It was not a firehouse for young firefighters.

Frank had grown up using the men stationed in this firehouse as role models, Scout Masters, and mentors. Jim Burr, his captain for the night, was his father's best friend. A former member of Six Engine, Captain Burr had advised the young firefighter to put in for that company. Frank had never regretted following that advice.

Because one of the guys had taken a personal day, Frank had already missed a working fire in an abandoned building. There had also been a couple of runs to the projects, but they did not matter. Walking up twelve flights of concrete stairs in a building filled with smoke from burning garbage was not why he loved his job. Since the effort to move along the floor quietly made the going very slow, Frank had a lot of time to think over the night's events. This bunk room was huge compared to Six's. That's what happens when you stuff three companies into one house. At least his wife would appreciate the extra rest he would get tonight. Chingli was always upset when Frank came home exhausted after a night in the firehouse. She had been happy on the phone after being convinced that the Burg was not that busy.

"Are you sure?" she had asked, "Sometimes I don't trust you with your simple explanations. There always seems to be something left out. You don't have to protect me."

He had let the veiled accusation slide, remembering how she was when alone at home. With a year and a half of experience dealing with her, Frank was beginning to get a feel for his wife's moods. She was unusually nervous tonight. "Walk gingerly," a voice in the back of his mind told him. Her next sentence changed the subject entirely and almost led to a fight.

"Can you transfer to this firehouse?"

"Why would I want to transfer to Vailsburg? It's too slow," he had responded without thinking.

"Why do you have to fight fires? You come home exhausted and smell like smoke and, and you get hurt too much. If you are going to go back to school, wouldn't it be better to go to a slower house? You can study better there can't you?" she had said in a soft, almost pleading voice. Alarms should have been set off in his head by her tone, but the atmosphere of the firehouse had deadened his senses. Too much *yang*, not enough *yin* would be the Chinese explanation for his stupidity.

"Then how come so many guys make captain out of Six Engine? You have to study for promotion on this job, my dear," Frank countered. "Don't worry about my studies. I studied for my BA while at Six Engine. I'm sure I can earn my MBA there also."

"You did not have a wife when you studied for your BA," she pointed out in an edgy voice.

"What does having a wife have to do with how I can study in the firehouse?" he asked, still not realizing the conversation was in a downward spiral.

"Having a wife does not matter to you, is that what you are saying? You think you can go to work and have fun like a little boy and if you get yourself hurt or . . . or worse and I don't matter, right?! Or don't you intend to go back to school? You promised me you would get your MBA and leave that crazy job. You mean you're not going to leave the Fire Department?!" Her voice had begun to rise, finally setting off the alarm in his head.

"No, my love that is not what I meant," he said reassuringly. "Our plans have not changed. I intend to get my degree and then leave this job. I didn't study Chinese for four years just to sit in a firehouse. Right now, though, we have to eat, so I'll stay on the job. The safest place to be on this job is in a young company that knows what they're doing," Frank tried to say the last sentence in as calm and authoritative a voice as possible.

"Okay, if you're so sure, but I'm still scared. I'm all alone here. You're the only one I have. I should have known better than to fall in love with a foreign devil. Why didn't you just leave me alone?" she finished in a teasing tone.

Leave her alone! While they were dating it was hard to tell who was chasing whom. This was not the time to point that out to his little scheming China doll. His answer was in Chinese and appealed to her Buddhist upbringing. "*Qian shi de guanxi*, my love." It was a debt from a past life.

As he crawled along the floor, Frank continued to review the conversation with his wife to see where it had gone wrong. American women were confusing enough; how did he fall for a Taiwanese girl? A woman of Byzantine complexity who was always two steps ahead, but not necessarily in the right direction. The manipulative ploys that came from her sometimes left his head spinning. The biggest mistake he had made so far in dealing with his wife was to tell her that if something mattered to her, but did not matter to him, then she won by default. Fewer and fewer things mattered to him.

His analysis of how the conversation had gone wrong pointed to the natural camaraderie of the firehouse. This had caused his guard to drop momentarily. Women! You always had to be on your toes or they would twist you into a pretzel. Taking a deep breath and holding it for a second, he tried to get his head back to where it was before Chingli called. Relax and enjoy the respite from the hectic in and out of the hill. The night had been interesting so far. After the welcoming banter, the guys had turned to the serious business of dinner. Unlike meals on an average night in Six Engine, they had eaten without interruption. Then Andy Roanoke had made the mistake of bailing out on the clean up after the meal.

A miserable cold had sent the senior firefighter up to bed shortly after he finished eating. He should have just stayed home, but none of the old timers did that unless they couldn't walk. Not that the younger firefighters were much better. Even though their labor contract allowed firefighters 365 days of sick leave, few of the men took advantage of the benefit. Between concerns for their reputations and the need to work a second job, most of them felt obliged to report to work. There they would crawl into a corner of the bunk room and ride it out, getting up to jump on the rig when an alarm came in. The only hazard to this arrangement was the playful atmosphere that permeated a firehouse.

By now Frank had reached the bed where Andy was snoring contently. He worked quickly, silently tying the rope around the bed's legs. After it was secure, he crawled back to the pole hole and eased the excess rope down through the doors. Then he backed off and waited for the show to begin. As the rope went taut a phone rang downstairs. When this was followed by the click of the joker circuit on the alarm console, Frank knew they had to hurry. An alarm of some sort was about to be transmitted over the telegraph system.

Andy's bed rocketed across the room before the house bells began to sound. The sonance of snoring was abruptly replaced by an unmanly shout. Frank watched Andy sit up, his mouth wide open and a confused, shocked look on his face. The shout stopped when the bed crashed into the metal piping that surrounded the pole hole. Bells immediately filled the quiet void that followed Andy's awakening. The bells sounded nine times in quick succession before the box number came over the system. A signal nine was being dispatched.

That would mean only half of the four engines and two trucks normally sent to a fire box would respond. It was probably a pulled box and so a false alarm. Frank slid down the front pole, but not before the senior firefighter had seen him.

"I saw you Frank Helms, you little red ass," Andy shouted as he eased out of bed.

Frank hit the pad at the bottom of the pole and stepped toward Twenty-one Engine. His boots were standing on the floor beside the rig. As he slid his feet out of his shoes and into the boots, he heard Andy's coughing travel across the bunk room floor. The elder firefighter slid down the pole while Frank reached for his turn-out coat.

"What goes around comes around, Frankie boy," Andy said with a smile. Frank knew it wasn't an idle threat. Andy had worked for years with a couple of the guys at Six Engine. They would like nothing better than to join in a little practical joke to make the time between alarms go faster.

A shout came from the watch room as Andy walked to Twenty-Six Engine, "Everyone goes. Signal Nine, Varsity Road and Eastern Parkway." The sound of other firefighters coming down the poles from upstairs, walking briskly down the stairs, and coming through the kitchen door filled the firehouse. All were moving toward the three rigs on the apparatus floor. None gave any indication that they had something to do with Andy's ride across the bunk room. Frank chuckled as he thought about what Andy had said. What goes around comes around in the firehouse.

Overhead doors started to go up and the doors to the trucks were slammed closed. Three diesel engines kicked out black fumes while the house bells continued to sound. Frank moved toward the door controls, but was waved off by one of guys from Truck Twelve. "We'll get the doors, kid." He went back to Twenty-one Engine and climbed up into the jump seat behind the driver. The rig pulled out of quarters a moment later while a second round of bells began to ring in the house. They stopped on the firehouse apron for a moment so the Captain could clear the road ahead with the siren and air horn. The rig pulled away and out into traffic. Since Twenty-one was first due on this box, Twenty-six Engine waited until they were clear of the apron before following. Twelve Truck brought up the rear after starting the doors on their way down.

It took less than three minutes for Twenty-one to reach the top of the hill on Varsity Road. As the apparatus began its descent down the small incline, Frank could see what he considered a familiar scene. A body was lying in the middle of the street at the bottom of the hill. This happened in the center of the city, but not in Vailsburg. By the time Twenty-one reached the corner, Frank had already counted three bodies. He could see there was little chance of reviving the young men lying on the ground. They had all suffered gunshot wounds to the head. Brains and blood had formed pools around each body.

Frank stepped down from the rig and heard the Captain ask headquarters to have Police and EMS respond. They began CPR on the victims immediately, although all knew it was futile. As he labored over the young body beneath him, Frank could only think "This is another one for Ray." One of his best friends was a homicide detective. Life had left this young man when the bullet had passed through the front of his skull and exploded out the back. Ray would have the job of finding the killer.

Chapter Three

Ray Friedrick responded to his old neighborhood from the West Precinct. Since the firehouse on Springfield Avenue was located along the route to Vailsburg, he made it a point to swing past it. Passing by the firehouse where his two friends worked was a habit of his. Since Frank had left the Police Department to become a firefighter, Ray had been on the defensive. It became necessary for him to keep track of Six Engine. When the gang got together, tales of busy nights responding to fires would be spun until his inevitably comment of "Every time I passed that firehouse, the rig was just sitting there." After that, the subject usually changed. The rig was not in quarters as he drove by so there was no way for him to quiet down the firehouse chatter the next time they got together. Something told him there was a reason to get together in the near future, but right now the homicide detective was clueless as to why.

Normally when he drove to Vailsburg, Ray went to visit his parents. They lived a short distance from the corner where the shootings had reportedly occurred. Typically, his biggest worry when in this neighborhood was how to answer his mother's incessant questions about Stacey Romanov.

"She's such a nice girl; when are you going to get serious with her? Nice girls don't wait around for long, you know," was what she had warned the last time he was home.

"We've been serious for a few years now, mom," he had answered. "What makes you think Stacey would want to change our relationship?"

"All girls want to change their relationships to something more permanent."

"Mom, Stacey just moved to her own place and is enjoying her independence. I doubt she wants me to get in her way or mess up her apartment," he had said, hoping to end the conversation.

As always, his mother got the last word in. "Stacey would like nothing better than to settle down and raise a family with you. I understand a woman's heart. You, my son, don't. That's how she's kept you to herself all this time." She ended with that all knowing feminine chuckle that made his father give up trying to reason with her. The subject had then changed to a break-in that had occurred down the block at John's candy store.

"What is this city coming to? Who would want to burglarize an old man's candy store? I just don't understand," she had said in an exasperated voice.

"It was probably some kids trying to be funny, mom," he had answered reassuringly.

"I don't find it funny at all," his mother had opined in no uncertain terms. The subject had changed after that and the incident was forgotten. "How is she going to react to this?" Ray wondered. Petty robbery was one thing, multiple murder was quite another.

Stacey came to mind again as he tried to sort through his feelings. His mother was probably right about her. The perky blonde was the only sane part of his life lately. Spending too much time investigating the worst that man can do to his fellow man was not conducive to a healthy mental outlook. Maybe Gloria could help. Frank's kid sister was Stacey's best friend. Then there was Jack. The thought of asking Stacey's brother for help brought a smile to Ray's face. Little Miss Independence's older brother was Mr. Non-committal himself. There was something about the Romanov family that made any romantic connection with its members seem hazardous. How could he pop the question to a girl who has an older brother like Jack as her example? His friend never wanted to break the ladies' hearts, but he inevitably did. For a firefighter who was known for pushing his luck, the boy showed a surprising cowardice when it came to committing to a woman. It was a funny peculiarity for a friend to have, but not very comical when it looked like a family trait and you were involved with his sister. What if Miss Independence turns me down? This was not the time to think about it, although thinking about Stacey did clear his mind.

Stacey Romanov was two years younger than Ray. An athletic blonde with seemingly limitless energy and an inquisitive mind, she was his mother's ideal daughter-in-law. The only complication as far as mom was concerned was that her son had to ask the girl to marry him. The two women got along famously. Ray was caught in the middle of their feminine ploys continually. When he had opposed

Stacey getting her own place, his mother had come down on him hard. "What's the matter? Are you afraid she might become too independent for you?" Mrs. Friedrick had guessed. Not about to miss an opportunity to point out his hesitation to commit himself wholeheartedly, his mother reminded him, "You haven't made any permanent commitments to her, so she can do as she pleases." Mr. Romanov was not thrilled with the idea of his daughter moving out either, but Stacey's mother thought it was wonderful. The men were voted down by the ladies. Now she had a cute little apartment that she called her "place" and there were four murders right down the block from his parents' house. Ray turned onto Varsity Road at Dr. Kowalski's old house and slowed down a little. This was not the time to dwell on personal problems. His mind had to be clear for the investigation ahead.

As the car came over the crest of the Varsity Road hill, Ray could see a fire engine, a couple of squad cars, and the coroner's van at the bottom of the incline. Responding to a murder investigation on John's corner would have been his last guess of what he would do tonight. After parking the car and walking down to the squad cars, he saw Frank talking to one of the patrolmen by a white limo on the corner.

"What are you doing in this sleepy part of town?" Ray asked as he extended his hand.

Frank grabbed his friend's hand. "I got detailed to Twenty-one Engine for the night, missed a working fire so far."

"Missed a fire? Aren't you lucky? You're getting paid the same and you don't smell like smoke, not bad," Ray said.

"You're a real comedian tonight, aren't you?" was the fireman's reply.

Captain Burr walked over to them as they finished their little sparring act. The three men considered each other to be part of the extended family of Vailsburg. None were happy to be dealing with the events of the night.

"Ray, how are you doing?" the Captain asked when he reached the two men.

"Mr. Burr . . . I mean Cap," Ray fell back on childhood habits for a moment, but quickly recovered. "I could be better, but this goes with the job. Can you tell me what you found when you arrived on the scene?"

After getting preliminary statements from Twenty-one Engine, the detective took Frank aside for a more detailed briefing. "I need details, Frank. What can you give me?" Ray asked knowing his friend would have noted more than the others. Frank had the training and experience from his days as a police officer to pick up on details that might seem unimportant to others. Once a cop, always a cop, no matter what happened.

Finishing with Frank, he began questioning the patrolmen on the scene. Then he spoke with the men from the coroner's office. Other homicide detectives arrived and started working with him to begin unraveling the puzzle of exactly what had happened.

Twenty-one Engine pulled away from the scene shortly after giving their statements. "I'll phone you about Stacey's party," Frank had called to him from the rig as it was leaving. "Damn, I forgot about that," Ray thought, thanking God that his friend had just reminded him. If he did not have something special for Stacey's thank you party, she would disown him. That would solve his problems the hard way.

A television news van pulled up while Ray was jotting down the information obtained so far. He finished the last of his notes before speaking with the news reporter. There was very little information to give the press. No eyewitnesses because so many of the elderly couples in this neighborhood vacationed in Florida at this time of the year. No one was home in the immediate vicinity. Speaking with people further up the block had only produced vague descriptions of a car backfiring. This was not an area of the city where people were accustomed to hearing gunshots.

The preliminary investigation had produced the identity of the victims, their occupations, and a curious thank you card that one of the young men was apparently in the process of taking out of his pocket when he was shot. Not much with which to start a murder investigation.

A reporter approached the detective as he was finishing writing in his notebook. She was young, tall, and thin reminding him of a model more than a news reporter. There was something different about her, but he could not afford to look too closely. Gawking at a woman while conducting an investigation was frowned upon by the department. "Excuse me. I'm Kathy Stanley from Eyewitness News. Could I speak with you about what occurred here tonight?"

"Well, Miss Stanley, I'm the one you would talk with, but I can't promise you anything concrete at this time," Ray began with his standard line to the media.

"That's alright. Can I ask your name?"

"Detective Ray Friedrick."

"Detective Friedrick, what do you know so far?"

"At the moment I can say we have four victims with gunshot wounds to the head. Three are young men from this neighborhood who had just started a limousine service. The other is an elderly man who was the owner of the confectionery store behind us," Ray began, trying to keep the frustration out of his voice. He had watched the boys grow up. They were only a few years younger than him. John had been an icon in the area for decades. It was tougher speaking with the media when you knew the victims personally.

Adding to his frustration was the elusiveness of any motive for the shootings. More often than not a crime scene made sense. That was true for 90% of the homicides he investigated. Who shot their girlfriend or stabbed their husband. Another 8% were tied to other crimes or accidents. Drugs were a big factor in those cases. Robberies gone awry accounted for a number of them also. The other 2% were true mysteries that took an extraordinary amount of good police work to solve. A few were never solved. This had the makings of a frustrating case. He had gone over all of the obvious motives in his mind a dozen times. None added up.

"We have ruled out robbery as a motive." Ray began to go down his list of the obvious motives for Miss Stanley. "There is no indication of this being drug related. The young men have no previous record. They had just started a limousine service. There was nothing found on them or in the limousine that might explain why they were targeted. The proprietor of the store has been in this community for over fifty years. There is no evidence that points to why he would be targeted. The only unusual occurrence in the vicinity prior to tonight is a burglary in the store about two weeks ago, but there is nothing to indicate that the two events are connected. So, to put it in a nut shell, Miss Stanley, we are stumped at the moment."

"Detective Fredrick - - - "

"Friedrick."

"Yes, I'm sorry, Detective Friedrick, you said the young men had just started a limousine service. Do you know when that was?"

"They have flyers in the car which indicate it was to have started tomorrow." was the curt reply for the detective.

"Then they never actually started the service?"

"Apparently not."

"Who was the first person on the scene, sir?"

Ray hated being called "sir", but he knew better than to let that effect his response. "The Fire Department responded to a pulled fire alarm box at eight ten."

"The Fire Department? What did they find when they arrived on the scene?"

"They reported finding the three young men lying in the street with gunshot wounds to the head. The firefighters called for EMS and the Police as soon as they arrived and then began CPR on the victims in the street."

"What of the store owner?" she asked.

"It was not until the second company arrived on the scene, that a search was made of the candy store. It was during that search that the body of the store owner was discovered," the detective answered as flatly as possible. Kathy looked at her watch and asked if there was a supervisor on the scene. Ray gladly pointed out a Sergeant behind them. A few minutes later, he watched as lights came on and the reporter went on the air.

"Thank you, Roger. I'm on the scene of a bizarre shooting in a quiet, tree-lined neighborhood. This is the type of neighborhood I normally enjoy reporting from. The homes are kept impeccably clean. The lawns are manicured. Even the refuse cans are neatly placed at the curb for tomorrow morning's pick-up. It's the type of neighborhood where the preferred pet is not a large watch dog but an overfed cat. In fact, the only crime reported in this area over the past six months was a break in at the candy store behind me about two weeks ago. As neighborhoods go this is an exceptionally quiet one. Most of the residents are retired. They raised their children here, but the children have long since gone to college, married, and started families of their own. Yet, tonight it was the scene of a horrific shooting. This is what we know so far."

"Around eight o'clock this evening three young men and the owner of the store behind me were shot and killed on this corner. The young men had recently started a limousine service. You can see the limousine behind me. Actually Bob, flyers the police found in the car indicate that the service was to have begun tomorrow."

"At ten minutes after eight the Fire Department received an alarm from the fire box on the next corner. When the companies arrived they found two men lying on the sidewalk and a third lying in the street on the other side of the limousine. Firefighters called for EMS and Police. They then began CPR on the victims. It was not until a second fire company arrived that the store owner was discovered inside. The gunman was quite thorough. Two of the victims were shot in the head and died instantaneously; the third was apparently first shot in the chest and then finished off execution style with a bullet to his head. The owner of the store was found cowered in a corner, shot in the head. There was really no hope of reviving the victims. Unfortunately for the investigation, the people who live in these corner houses were not home at the time. Police have no witnesses and very few clues."

She paused for a moment, apparently listening to a question.

"No, Roger. Although one of the officers on the scene theorized it may have been the killer who pulled the fire box after shooting the victims."

After another pause, she completed her report.

"No, they're baffled at the moment."

The bright lights went off while Ray walked to his car.

Chapter Four

Chingli was wearing a light blue silk robe when Frank arrived home. The long jet black hair he loved so much was in a bun on top of her head and the eyes that could instantly flash anger from across the room were puffy. In spite of the fatigue apparent in these windows onto her soul, they reflected the heartfelt smile on her face. The morning sun streaming through the kitchen window added to their beauty, making the dark brown irises sparkle. Stepping into the small apartment, Frank saw breakfast was waiting for him.

He was more rested than normal after a night at work, but when Chingli commented on it his only response was a grunt. He did not want to talk about what had happened at work. Frank gave his wife a peck on the forehead and then carried his bag of dirty firehouse clothes to the bedroom. They had only lived in this apartment a short time, but it was already a home. It was a skill learned from his parents. No matter what the configuration of his living space, people commented on its comfortable "homey" feeling. A wife had only added to that coziness.

Glancing at the living room as he walked through, Frank could easily see his wife's influence. The decor of the room was a true mix of the Orient and the Occident. A handmade rug with the Chinese character for happiness covered the wooden floor. The white of the walls was broken up by lithographs of the French countryside. These had appealed to the part of his wife that had invested so much into the French language. A Chinese silk painting adorned another part of the wall and books in Chinese, English, French, and Japanese were displayed on shelves. The couch and love seat were nothing extraordinary, but in a corner of the room stood an unusual silk screen he had purchased in Hong Kong a few years before.

As far as Frank was concerned, the central focus of the room was the scrolls of Chinese calligraphy written by her great uncle. He tried to read their words of wisdom at least once a day. One stated that in order for a moral man to be born into the world he must have three educations. The second admonished the viewer to have nine thoughts. These would lead to one becoming a *zhunzi*, a superior man. When asked by others what these scrolls meant, his response was simply "think before you do."

Most of the furniture in the room had been picked by Chingli because his bachelor pieces were not what one would call "presentable." She could tell you where each piece had been purchased and how much it had cost. The only furniture she could not do that with was the bookcases and television stand he had made. These were also the pieces she bragged about the most, much to his embarrassment.

"Don't take too long or our breakfast is going to be cold," she called from the kitchen.

"I'm just putting these clothes into the hamper." he answered while continuing to walk toward the bedroom.

Last night's conversation was going through his mind. It was going to be hard to leave the job. The camaraderie of the firehouse could not be matched anywhere. Then there was the feeling you get when fighting a working fire. What was going to replace that, exporting computers? Maybe he could talk Chingli into opening a consulting business on the side while he stayed in the firehouse. And maybe she would try to change his gender with a butcher's knife. That was not going to fly. His wife may have been born in Taiwan, but her temperament sometimes resembled a Sichuan firebrand. He had told her last night that he had not studied Chinese just to sit in a firehouse. Fighting fires was a young man's job. Better to get out before the winters became unbearable and the summers burnt away whatever survived the cold. Taking a deep breath and acknowledging the wisdom of acceptance, Frank walked to the kitchen for breakfast with his bride.

They sat down to an all American breakfast of omelets and toast with orange juice. She was trying hard to be an American wife when making breakfast. Since he loved Chinese cooking for dinner, an unspoken agreement had been reached between them. They ate American in the mornings, then whatever Chingli wanted to eat the rest of the day.

The firefighter was thankful for his mother-in-law's insistence that her daughter attend cooking school. He loved the dishes that came out of their little efficiency kitchen and Chingli was inspired by his exuberance. Lately his bride had begun to branch out beyond what they had taught at the Weichuan Culinary Institute in Taipei. Since coming to America, Italian food had become her distraction. The neighborhood Frank grew up in was half Italian, so he had a fairly educated palate when it came to the cuisine of Italy. Her spaghetti sauce or "red gravy" as it was called in the old neighborhood had impressed him. After this success, she became more adventurous, experimenting with different dishes and enjoying herself immensely. You could not have guessed from her enthusiasm that she had grown up with cooks and nannies taking care of her every need.

Frank found himself washing dishes after breakfast as she talked about what they could do that day.

"Since you are not too tired, I thought we could go shopping. There are some good sales at the mall. If we go today we could save a lot of money and you would not have to be with the crowds on the weekend," she said energetically.

It was amazing to Frank how quickly his wife had become Americanized. Everything had to be bought on sale. It required an enormous amount of research on Chingli's part because she would not even entertain the idea of purchasing anything without getting the best price possible. He had already pointed out to her that she probably expended more energy with her research than she would have if she haggled for the merchandise in Taiwan. This made no impression on her. In the end, the shopping habits of his wife had become one of those "he did not care and she did" issues. Surrendering to a drive to shop that was obviously superior to his hatred for that activity; Frank now let Chingli have her way.

"How much time do you think it will take to buy everything you want?" he asked in a resigned tone, absently putting the last of the dishes into the dish pan. Her answer brought his attention back to the conversation. His focus had to be on what was being said. Chingli's mastery of English was well beyond the point where one could listen with half a brain.

"To buy everything I want? A lifetime," she answered with a laugh, "But today we only have to buy a few things."

"Do we have to buy or do you want to buy?" Frank teased back.

"If you want to have something nice for Stacey's party, we have to buy."

Stacey's party was the following day, so he could not disagree with the use of "have."

The conversation had stayed away from what happened at work the night before, which was fine with him. Since Chingli had said nothing, Frank had no intention of bringing it up. If she had not watched the eleven o'clock news, there was a chance the subject would not come up. No need for her to worry. Her next question blew Frank's supposition about her missing the evening news out of the water.

"When did you take back from the shootings?" she asked in a matter of fact voice.

Frank dropped a cup with that question. Trying to change directions and get out from under the question, a feeble attempt was made to tease her about English. "When did we take back? You mean take up?"

"Up, back, you know what I mean." she said with a triumphant smile on her face.

"Oh, about ten o'clock," he answered as casually as possible.

Her voice was light when she asked the next question. "Were you not going to tell
me?"

"Well, I saw no reason to worry you. It was a once in a lifetime thing," he answered flatly.

"As I said last night, you don't have to protect me. What would you call not telling me? A lie of . . . of . . . omission, that is what you always say, isn't it?" her speech had such a ring of victory to it that Frank could only laugh.

"Touche, my wife."

"*Qu'est-ce que cest, touche*?" his wife asked in the language she had studied for nine years.

He should have known better than to use a French expression with her. "Well, it's a term they use in fencing when a point is scored."

"Fencing, how can you score a point with a fence? I know scoring points in sports and that men say they score with women, but a fence? You never told me about a fence."

Knowing better than to laugh, Frank briefly explained the sport of fencing to his wife. She chuckled at herself and then commented on how strange a language English was, before returning to the original subject of his "omission."

"Where did this take place?"

"On Kerrigan Boulevard and Varsity Road," was the answer given. He knew it was another lie of omission, but one that could easily be defended. The name of the street changed north of Varsity Road to Oakland Terrace. His parents still lived on that street. Chingli would flip if she found out the murders had occurred a block away from her in-laws.

"You said this was a slow firehouse. Is that true or were you trying to protect me again?"

Happy that she had not asked for more detail about the location of the shooting, Frank jumped at the chance to change the subject. "I never said I wanted to protect you. It was you who used those words. This is the firehouse that protects my parents. We pass it sometimes when we go to visit them, remember?"

"You mean the one by that big church?"

"Sacred Heart, yes. It's just down the road form Seton Hall. Jim Burr was my Captain last night." The last sentence was meant to turn the subject away from the firehouse. It succeeded.

"You mean Uncle Jim? I like him. At our wedding he told me about his experiences in China. After all those years he still remembered the meaning of the double happiness on the napkins," she remembered with a smile. "Are you going to be with him again tonight?"

"No, tonight it's back to the center of the city for your hubby. I have to call Jack to see if they want me to pick up dinner, then we should go shopping if you want. I'll have to leave about four thirty."

Frank finished the dishes and dried his hands. Chingli went to the bedroom to change while he called his friend.

The day went smoothly enough for the young couple. Chingli picked out a couple of nice plants for Stacey's apartment. "We should give her something alive, so she will not be alone," Frank's wife had said with a hint of sagacity in her voice.

"I wouldn't call plants company," he teased.

"Life is life. Just because it cannot talk doesn't mean it is not life. It is also important for the *feng shui* of her home. You don't want her to have bad luck do you?"

"No, I wouldn't think of it," Frank answered as he picked up a potted plant and carried it to the car. With two plants in the trunk, they drove away. By the time they arrived home it was four o'clock. He quickly carried the items they had bought on their outing into the apartment and began to get ready for work.

"You don't have to be in work until six o'clock. How long does it take you to go there? Twenty minutes? Why are you in a rush? Can't you sit and talk to me for a few minutes?" The questions followed each other in quick succession.

Her husband took a deep breath before he said anything. "Chingli, you know we relieve each other early. I have to pick up dinner, so that means leaving that much earlier," Frank said quietly,

37

knowing from the sound of her voice that she needed to talk. "But, I don't have to leave right now. I'm just getting ready."

"Can we talk for a little?"

"Sure," was the reluctant answer. His reluctance did not go unnoticed.

"Really? You don't sound like you want to," she snapped back.

Trying to sound more enthusiastic, he put effort into changing his voice before answering. "Okay, kid. What's on your mind?"

"When do classes start?" was her first question after they had both sat on the living room couch.

"Not until the spring semester, after the holidays," consciously avoiding the fact that he had not even settled on which school he would attend.

"But that's months away!" she complained. When he tried to answer, her held her hand up. "How long will it take you graduate and leave the Fire Department?"

"It may not be that simple. I have to land a job after I graduate. We can't just walk away from this job, Chingli. It is a good paying job that can give us everything we need," he said in what he felt was a reasonable tone. "There is . . ."

His wife exploded before he could finish. "You don't want to leave that job, do you? You lied to me! All you can think about is yourself and your pride. I'm supposed to just sit home and have your children and . . . and . . . , " she had started to cry while she was screaming at him. Now she reverted to the language of her childhood and began to curse him.

"Where did this come from?" Frank wondered, shocked by how quickly the conversation had deteriorated. He reached for her trying his best to give some comfort, but Chingli pulled away and turned her back on him.

When she began talking again it was in a quiet voice. "You still don't understand. There is nothing in America for me, but you," she said in a whisper. "If something happens to you what do I do? I am alone here."

"Why do you keep saying you're alone? It's not true! You are not alone! You have my family and our friends"

"I do not! They are your family and your friends, not mine! If we were to get divorced they would hate me!" she stated emphatically.

Frank had seen too many nasty divorces to deny the truth of what she said. He could only go back to the beginning of the discussion and try to reassure her. "What are you afraid of? Nothing is going to happen."

"What am I afraid of?" she cried in a forlorn whisper while looking at the ceiling. "Haven't you been listening? You can't say nothing will happen. You went to a shooting last night. You go to fires and shootings all the time and you don't care. Do you stop and think maybe I could get hurt in this building or could get shot on . . . on some wild corner in the middle of the city? No!" She shouted the last word at him. Her voice turned into a shrill, mocking yell. "You just want to prove you're macho, just want to have fun fighting fires. And you expect me to sit with a smile on my face and say 'Okay, honey.' I won't do it! You said you were going to leave that job. Leave it!"

Frank was totally unprepared for the onslaught he was now facing. They were not in a position for him to leave the job even if that was what he wanted. The more hysterical his wife became the more defensive he felt.

"You knew what you were getting into from that first tutoring session." he pointed out, referring to the condition of his hands the first time he had tutored her in economics.

She had come to America after meeting him in Hong Kong. Frank had been pleasantly shocked when he saw her in economics class. Chingli was having trouble with English and he was studying Chinese, so it seemed a natural alliance. A date was made to meet in the library and go over the week's lessons. He showed up with his hands wrapped in bandages because of cuts received while fighting a fire the night before. To him it was part of the job. She had not seen it in the same light.

"I did not love you then," she replied sadly. "I never knew it would be like this; just sitting home waiting for you. Why can't you quit? Third uncle is waiting for an answer about that job he offered you. You could just study at night."

"No! I will not fall back on 'Taiwan aid.' I got through undergrad work by myself. I'll get through graduate school the same way," he replied without any hint of compromise in his voice.

"*Zhenme jiao ao*," she said mockingly.

"Excuse me?" he asked even though he knew the meanings of the expression. How she translated it would tell him whether or not this argument was winding down.

"So proud," she said with resignation in her voice.

"Or so stuck up, right my wife?" he asked in a conciliatory tone.

She turned around, gave him an impish smile, and leaned her head against his chest.

"It's only for a few more years then we'll leave this behind and start a new life. It will be ours together," Frank promised. "*Je taime bau caoup, mon cheri*," he whispered to her using the little French she had taught him. I love you very much, my love. They sat quietly for a minute, at peace, not wanting to break the spell.

"Why don't you call mama tonight?" Frank suggested from the bedroom as he put the last of his clean uniforms into his sport bag.

"I called her last night," his wife replied from the living room.

"Did you discuss your worries with her?" he asked, coming out to her.

"Yes," Chingli answered reluctantly.

"What did she say?"

"You know what she said. The same thing she always says. *Jia ji sui ji, jia gou sui gou*,'" was the frustrated answer. If you marry a

41

chicken, you follow a chicken. If you marry a dog, you follow a dog. "She's right. You two must have been together in a previous life," she commented with a wry chuckle. "Will you be extra careful for me tonight? I know I sound like a superstitious Chinese woman, but I don't think what happened last night was a once in a lifetime thing."

"I'll be extra careful, my wife, but remember no one is shooting at firemen. We just get called afterwards to help patch them up. Now I have to get dinner," He leaned over and kissed her on the head, then picked up his clothes and left. She remained seated, staring at the plants they had bought for Stacey. The door closed quietly behind him leaving her alone once more.

Chapter Five

Frank pulled into the supermarket parking lot at twenty to five. He would have to hustle. Even if everything went smoothly, it would be after five before his foot stepped into the firehouse. Getting a cart and walking in through the automatic doors, he began reviewing the list Jack had dictated to him over the phone: chicken cutlets, eggs, tomato puree and paste, green beans, pasta, Italian bread, butter, and garlic. The rest of the seasoning and the bread crumbs were in the kitchen cabinets at work. Green beans would be the first of the items checked off the list because they were right at the entrance.

As he was sorting through the fresh green beans, Frank heard a familiar voice call from behind him. "Frank Helms, how are you?"

"Well, look who's here," Frank said with surprise after turning around. He had not seen Dan O'Brian in years. "Long time no see. How's your mom?"

"Her health isn't that great," Dan answered quietly. "She's getting older, but she's still a feisty thing. Hey, I heard you got married to some exotic oriental beauty."

"Well, she's oriental and I think she's a real doll, but exotic? I don't know. Since I've been handling her I've uncovered an international conspiracy. Women the world over act the same, they're all crazy. If you want to keep your sanity, keep your distance." Both men laughed.

"I wish it was that easy," his old friend said with a smile. "But we're not programmed that way. In the end, women are irresistible to men and men are irresistible to women. Kind of keeps the species going, if you know what I mean."

"Yes, I know. We have very little to say in the matter," Frank answered in frustration. "Like they say, 'You can't live with them and you can't live without them.' I call that the misery paradox."

"Frank," O'Brian said in shock. "I'm surprised at you. You've become a pessimist."

"Sorry Dan. Just been having a hard time lately."

"What's the problem?"

"She's nervous," Frank answered lightly.

"That's what you get for taking a wife, Frankie," Dan said with a laugh. "They're all nervous. You'll get used to it."

"You sound like someone who has resigned himself to being manipulated by a wife," Frank pointed out. "You're not planning to make any changes in your tax filing status are you?"

"No, no. Right now I have to focus on my mother. I'm all she has," Dan said with resignation. "Really wish life had worked out differently and I had connected with someone. Mom needs a daughter-in-law to talk with and give her a hand. I try, but I'm not a woman. "

Frank chuckle with his old coaching buddy, Dan was not the luckiest of men when it came to the fairer sex. Even though the two had not seen each other in quite a while, he had heard about Dan's hard luck with women from mutual friends. They had told him of a few close calls, but no one worth a lifetime commitment. Feeling bad for his old friend, Frank tried to reassure him. "Don't kid yourself, Dan. You don't want two women living under the same roof. They either fight like cats or scheme against you."

"I'm surprised you would say that after marrying an Asian girl. Isn't a Chinese daughter- in-law supposed to take care of her husband's folks?"

"Traditionally, they do, but things are changing fast," Frank said with a sigh. "And don't take that to mean there was peace in the household. Women are women. They also hate seeing a man unattached. If my wife gets hold of you, she's going to try to find you a mate."

"They say every pot has a lid," Dan chortled. "If she could find me a filial little China doll, you never know. I might go for it."

"Careful," Frank warned. "China dolls aren't as pliable as you might think. In fact, they are the ones who turn up the heat and melt you down. Then they remold you into what they consider to be a proper work of art."

"Don't all women do that?"

"All try, but Chinese women seem to bat those dark brown eyes and succeed where others have failed."

"Is this an autobiographical analysis?" Dan queried.

"I'm still resisting. Frustrates the hell out of her," Frank laughed while glancing at his watch.

"Are you still with the Police Department?" Dan asked changing the subject.

Frank shook his head no. "I switched to the Fire Department."

"You're kidding? What happened?"

"It was just easier on the Fire Department for me. I never got used to making an arrest, only to see some lawyer reduce the charges to nothing. You still doing the brokerage thing on Wall Street?" he asked, finally remembering his friend's job.

"No, now I'm into the analysis end of the deal. Work for the same house, just different function."

As the two old friends were chatting another young man approached them. "Excuse me," he said, "I couldn't help overhearing your name. Are you Gloria Helms' brother?"

"That should take you down a few notches, Frank. Now you're known as Gloria's brother." The three men laughed.

"With a sister like her, I wouldn't say he was taken down a notch at all," the newcomer responded.

"Careful mate, that's his little sister you're referring to," the stock analyst warned lightheartedly.

"My little sister can more than take care of herself these days. I only feel for the poor bastards she steam rolls," was Frank's response.

This was turning into too long a conversation. It was already a quarter to five. He had to pick up the rest of dinner, check out, and get to the firehouse. Arriving late with the fixings for dinner meant a late meal and some very unhappy campers.

"I'd like to stay and chew the fat guys, but I'm on my way into work," he said as lightly as possible.

"Oh, we can't keep you from protecting the citizens of Newark," the newcomer said. "I just have a quick question for you. When's there going to be another firefighter test?"

"I don't know for sure. The list in effect right now won't run out for another year, but if you're interested I'll just keep Gloria informed. You can ask her."

"You sure you want a job like that?" Dan asked. "You just spend a lot of time chasing false alarms after the bars let out."

"Oh, I don't know. Didn't you see today's paper? The Fire Department was the first to arrive at that shooting last night," the newcomer pointed out. "Someone apparently shot these guys and then pulled the fire box, either that or these guys pulled the box and then someone shot them."

"Now that sounds like a good idea," the stock analyst said seriously.

"I see nothing wrong with shooting people who pull false alarms," the newcomer replied.

"I think the two of you are pushing it a bit," Frank interjected.

"Nah," the two other men said together laughing.

Frank put the groceries into the trunk of his car and then jumped into the driver's seat. His commute had at least another ten minutes and it was already five o'clock. They were going to bust his balls the rest of the night for being late with dinner. Excuses like an argumentative wife or running into an old friend at the supermarket were not going to fly.

He felt bad for Dan. It seemed his friend was trapped between a rock and a hard place. Mrs. O'Brian's health apparently did not allow her son to get out and play the field. It's hard to meet a good woman when you're home taking care of your mother. Then there was his sister's friend, whose name had not even come up. How could he have a conversation, albeit a short one, with a friend of Gloria's and not get his name? The poor guy had asked for info about the next test. She was going to ask who wanted the information and big brother was not going to know. Gloria would then be added to his list of angry females.

Women, they were impossible to understand and impossible to live with. They say men don't understand them, but what about women understanding men? After two battles with his wife in less than twenty-four hours, Frank was glad to be going to work.

Chingli had needed comfort and a chance for her fears to be heard. That was understandable, but what about those little technicalities like getting to work on time? If he had suggested that tomorrow morning was a more appropriate time to discuss their future, she would have exploded. There was no way to avoid getting out of the house late without causing a war. Of course, everyone but Jack would understand. Whenever a woman started making noises about Jack changing, he high tailed it out of the relationship.

This brought to mind something Chingli had said the other day. She thought Gloria was making a play for Jack. His sister had known Jack since they were kids. Why was she suddenly trying to entrap him? Because she was a female and all females instinctively know that they can capture and change any male they choose. Those were Gloria's words which had been proven true countless times as evidenced by the poor souls she had mauled. He never knew how to react to having a man-eater for a sister, a nice man-eater, but a man-eater all the same. Poor Jack, if Gloria has her sights set on him, it was going to be a battle royal, with no way to be certain who would be the victor.

The neighborhoods he drove through had gradually changed while all of this went through his mind. Quiet tree lined middle class streets had become blocks of crowded working class apartment buildings before giving way to the abandoned buildings, vacant lots, and dilapidated housing surrounding Six Engine. After pulling into the alley beside the firehouse and parking his car, Frank gathered up groceries and clean uniforms and went in the door to the kitchen.

"Here comes firefighter death," Matt Hickerson called out as he walked in the door.

Jack poked his head in from the apparatus floor as Frank put the groceries on the table. "The Burg called and said they don't want you up there anymore. Said you were too much trouble; that you brought the Central Ward up with you."

Chief Gregor was sitting at the kitchen table sipping a cup of firehouse coffee. "Andy used some very choice words to describe what you did," he said with a smile.

Frank tried his best to have a shocked expression on his face as he responded. "What I did? Chief it wasn't like I acted alone. Dragging a rope across the floor and tying a knot were my only contributions. Andy should watch his back up there."

"Andy isn't the only one who should watch his back," Al Grili said from the doorway to the watch room. "You mess with the bull, you're gonna get the horns."

Frank could only chuckle. Al, Matt, and Andy had more years at Six Engine between them than he had on the face of the earth. It wouldn't take long for what went around to come around.

Captain Wagner came in as Al finished his warning. "You finally made it. I was beginning to wonder if they had waylaid you up there."

"Sorry Cap. I ended up in a discussion with my wife about the pros and cons of being a firefighter," Frank responded with a laugh. Things always looked different when among friends in the firehouse.

Everyone in the room began to laugh. "Let me guess," Captain Wagner said, "You were the pro and your wife was the con, right?"

"Now how could you guess that?" Frank asked facetiously.

"Don't even bother to ask," was the answer. "Did you get everything in or is there more?"

"I just need to get my turn out gear from the trunk of my car, Cap."

While Frank went out to get his gear, Jack came into the kitchen and began unpacking what he would turn into dinner. There was a surprise waiting for Frank when he carried his gear to the apparatus floor. The Ward LaFrance that was their normal rig had been replaced. A fifteen year old Mack pumper was parked in its place. There were no seats on this rig for the men not in the cab. Only the Captain and driver could fit up front. Everyone else rode on the back step. Plywood supported by angle iron protected the men on the back from any objects that might be thrown at them. A bar spanned the rear of the hose bed. This was held by anyone riding on the back. The only other added safety feature was loops attached to the bar. An arm could be slipped through these to help hold on whenever the truck went over any of the thousands of bumps or pot holes in the city streets. It was going to be an interesting night, but at least the weather was warm. Riding the back step in subfreezing weather was not his idea of a fun time in the city.

After putting his coat and helmet on the back step, Frank checked the mask assigned to him. This was sitting on the three inch hose in the hose bed. There were not enough working mask brackets in the compartments on the side of the rig for all the masks. Next he went over the nozzles on the three and four lengths of inch and a half hose carried on the rig. Then it was upstairs to change. At least he would not have to wash dishes tonight. He had picked up the meal. In the firehouse, if you picked up or cooked, you did not clean up.

The bell hit as Frank pulled his uniform pants on; nine bells and then four followed by seven, five, and two, the projects again. He leaped up the stairs to the bunkroom and slid down the rear pole to the apparatus floor.

Al was walking toward the front of the rig when Frank reached the floor. Something about the way the older firefighter glanced back told Frank to be careful. The doors started up and the Captain's door slammed while Frank stepped over to his boots. Al opened the driver's door and reached in to turn on the batteries. Something was not right. Normally, Al climbed into the rig before turning on the power. That was how he had taught Frank to start the rig. The momentary hesitation produced a quick jab from behind.

"What's the matter, Frank?" Matt shouted. "You afraid to ride on an antique? Let's go, all those folks in the projects are waiting for us."

Frank shook off his anxiety and plunged his foot into a boot. A white foam erupted out of the boot, running down the sides and forming a pool around it. The smell coming up from the frothy matter told him it was shaving cream oozing out around his leg. Al climbed into the cab with a satisfied grin on his face.

Matt let out a hoot and shouted, "Let's go, there's work to be done."

What should he do now? The doors were already up and Al was kicking the engine over. After a quick visual check of the other boot, Frank thrust in his foot. His toes jammed up against something for a second before the water balloon in the boot toe popped. He could feel the cool water rise to his ankle. Knowing there was nothing that could be done right then, Frank reached for his coat, threw it on, and climbed up onto the back step. Matt and Jack were already waiting, so Frank dropped his helmet on and pushed the button on top of the hose bed wall twice. Al released the clutch, propelling the rig out of quarters. Small clumps of shaving cream floated behind the truck as it headed down Springfield Avenue. Matt's face wore a content smile.

Chapter Six

When dinner was finished, Jack and Frank sat around the table talking. After the projects, they had responded to a car accident, had a couple of pulled boxes, and a garbage fire. Dinner had been interrupted twice, but only for the false alarms. Wagon sat on the bench next to Jack while he rubbed her ears; the little dog was content.

"Do you remember that crew of kids who hung out on John's corner? Vinnie Nicholas' kid brother . . . ." Frank asked.

"Yeah," Jack responded nonchalantly before he realized what his friend was trying to say.

"You mean they were the ones last night?"

Frank shook his head yes.

"Ah, no! You've got to be kidding," Jack moaned.

"It wasn't easy working on them. When we pulled up they were already gone. Doing CPR was frustrating. All we did was pump the blood out. I don't think there was much left in them by the time EMS got on the scene. Didn't even recognize them; too much damage to their faces from the bullets. Ray was the one who got their IDs from the flyers they had in the limo. He had to put up with more than we did, ended up talking to the news about it."

Jack just rolled his eyes and shook his head. "Who would want to pick on John and those kids? This is insane," he said, trying to make sense out of the senseless. "You're sure it was that gang? God, how could that happen up there?"

Both men sat quietly for a few moments, attempting to come to terms with what they felt was an invasion of their old neighborhood. Neither had lived there for a few years, but their parents were still there. The sense of security they had felt their folks enjoyed in that part of the city had been shattered with these shootings. Home was now besieged.

"The old neighborhood looks like it's changing," Frank began. "Funny, last night I didn't see it this way. My biggest worry was how Chingli would respond. Even with Ray showing up, it was more helping with an investigation than it was a crime occurring on my old stomping grounds. Now after telling you who got shot, I feel like home has been invaded."

"Yeah, I know what you mean," Jack said with a melancholy voice. "Funny, we both moved out a while back and yet we still consider mom and dad's place to be home."

"Of course you do," Matt interjected after walking in and overhearing the conversation. "In your mind, that is home. It's not some bachelor apartment where you make a pit stop between nights on the town. Although you should have begun the transition to creating a home with Chingli, Frank. You're moving onto the next stage in life. Some of us are still stuck in the mud of our youth, unable to make any commitments."

"Thank you father time," Jack responded. "Your insight has saved us a trip to the mountain top."

"And what were you going to do there, 'red ass', go skiing?" Matt replied sharply. "You may not appreciate it, but I'm just giving a little brotherly advice."

"You mean fatherly, don't you?" Jack shot back.

"Funny, 'red ass', real funny."

After hearing Jack referred to as a red ass again, Frank jumped in to try and distract his friends by asking a question about the term. "So Matt, where does the term 'red ass' come from?"

"What? Are you trying to do keep me off your protégé's case?" the senior firefighter laughed.

"The protégé doesn't need protection and his ass isn't red. If you want proof, I'll show you," Jack shoot back defiantly.

"Did you shave it yet, boy?" Matt responded, referring to an incident earlier in the year when one of the Chief's saw the junior firefighter chuck a moon. "Jack, the next time I see your ass, it better be shaved," was the warning he received that night. His pants had stayed buckled around his waist since then.

"The reason you young firemen are called red asses," Matt began as he turned to Frank, "is because you are like little babes on the job. If you've ever see a baby's rear end when it has diaper rash, you'll know what I mean."

Frank shook his head, satisfied with Matt's explanation and the shift in the conversation. Wanting to stay away from the subject of last night's shootings, he then turned his attention to Jack.

"Getting back to commitments or lack there of, Jack," Frank said. "Where do you stand now with female companionship? You've been without a 'main squeeze' for a little while now. Aren't you overdue?"

"Well, I have to admit that there is an interest in one particular woman, but it's more complicated than any relationship I've had before," Jack admitted grudgingly.

"Oh, that sounds bad, real bad," Matt chirped in.

"First you say I'm too immature because I won't commit myself, then you say it sounds real bad because there might be a chance I've found someone to commit myself to. Make up your mind."

"And who might this wonder woman be?" Frank asked.

"Well, that's part of the problem," Jack started before taking a breath. "Gloria," he blurted out.

The bell hit before Matt or Frank could react. One - four - three - three were quickly counted by the men. A full assignment which meant there was a good chance they had a fire. Captain Wagner came down the stairs while the three men went to the back step. Al came down the front pole, threw his coat on, hopped in the cab, and turned on the rig's batteries. The second round of bells ended before the radio on the rig came alive. "Attention Engines Seven, Six, Eleven, and Twelve, Trucks Eleven and Five, Battalion One and Deputy One, respond on a telephone alarm. Station one four three three, Thirteenth and Fairmont Avenues." A repeat of the transmission began as the rig started. Frank pushed the button on the back step to tell Al everyone was ready. The engine revved, throwing out a thick cloud of exhaust, and moved out of the house. As soon as the front of the rig was out of quarters the Captain hit the siren and air horn. The truck hesitated momentarily on the apron to be certain all the traffic had stopped. It then lurched forward on to Springfield Avenue, turning west with siren wailing and air horn blasting. Frank saw Chief Gregor coming down the stairs while his driver Don Longo pushed the button to open the overhead door in front of the gig.

They reached Fourteenth Avenue before Al's hand poked out the window of the cab giving a thumbs-up. "We've got a job," Frank informed the other two men on the back. They were bouncing down the street with their knees bent like skiers riding moguls. The Chief was following a couple of blocks behind. Between Fourteenth and South Orange Avenues the rig hit a bump that threw all three men into the plywood eighteen inches above their heads.

"Al's got to remember that bump or we're going to break our necks," Matt shouted above the siren after recovering.

"It wouldn't have mattered. He's pissed because he's driving," Jack pointed out.

Frank then noticed a glow in the sky off to his left. "It looks like it's already through the roof," he said pointing in the direction of the glow. He then grabbed his mask and, after hooking his arm through the ring on the hand bar, began to work it on to his other arm. Jack put his arm around Frank as soon as he saw what his friend was doing.

"Brother, you are one crazy bastard," Jack said after the mask was on.

"No, just desperate to get the tip. You both had jobs last night. I'm getting the tip if it kills me," Frank said with a laugh.

"Don't take your words too seriously. If Al had hit another bump like the last one, it could have done just that asshole."

"That's the last of the bad bumps until we hit Thirteenth Avenue."

"You never want to admit you did something stupid, do you?" Matt said shaking his head. The rig turned up Thirteenth Avenue before it hit another bump.

Fire was showing from the second and third floor of a three story frame building half way up the block. The guys from Seven Engine were stretching a line through the front door while the driver was pulling a three inch line off the back of the rig. Al stopped by a hydrant on the corner, opened his door, and handed wrenches and a double female fitting to Jack who had jumped off the back step as soon as the rig had stopped. The three firefighters from the back step pulled three inch and two and a half and three inch lines off the hose bed and wrapped them around the barrel of the hydrant. The rig pulled up to the back of Seven Engine after Frank and Matt had hopped on the back step.

Frank quickly looked at the building involved and the exposures threatened by the flames. What would Captain Wagner want? He reached for the four lengths, pulled a few loops of hose off, twisted the load so the top length rested on his shoulder, and began stretching into the building. Matt followed behind him after putting on his mask and pulling the rest of the line out of the bed.

The Captain was walking in ahead of them. Wagner trained firefighters to be independent and knowledgeable about what was required on the fire scene. If a man assigned to him could not learn to do that in a reasonable period, he was transferred out. A fire scene was not the place to baby sit a do-nothing firefighter. It was hard enough looking out for the guys who knew what they were doing. A firefighter's job was to aggressively advance a line to the seat of the fire. An officer's job was to make sure his men did not over extend themselves while doing their job. The captain of a fire company was a safety valve. Wagner's men knew that and implicitly trusted him because of it. The experiences of ten years as an officer had proven their trust was well placed.

After looking the situation over, Wagner turned to Frank and Matt. "The first floor looks clear and Seven is making the second floor with no problem. The third floor is ours. You took the four lengths right?"

"You trained us well, Cap," Frank answered.

"Don't forget Three Truck's out of service now. It looks like the fire is in the cockloft. So you'll have fire above you. You're not going to be able to put water on it until some truckmen get up there. We're going to have to wait for Eleven or Five Truck to get here before there's a hole in the roof. All that means slow and easy boys, okay?" the Captain reminded them.

"Don't worry, Cap. He might have a death wish, but I don't," Matt replied pointing at Frank.

"Death wish? Aren't we getting a little melodramatic in our old age?" Frank said as they entered the front door and began climbing the stairs to the upper floor.

Chapter Seven

As they stretched up the stairs Frank was continuing to size up the situation. Since Jack had been left at the hydrant, the Captain would want to give Al a hand getting the feeds connected. His initial size-up had told him they would have to get a second line into the building. The water from both feed lines snaking down the street would be needed to do that. Seven Engine had a feed from a hydrant on the other side of the fire building. Eleven Engine would probably also come in from that direction. Normally Four Engine would come in behind Six, but they had been taken out of service. It would be a bit of a wait for Twelve Engine, so Six would supply the only water from that side of the fire for the moment.

Frank knew the Captain felt uneasy about the situation. He had men already committed inside the building without a truck company to cut open the roof and release the superheated gases above them. They were going to the top floor and would need ventilation quickly or they were going to take a beating.

It would take less than a minute for them to call for water. Al only had time to break the lines from the hose still in the bed and get one hooked into the pump panel. There was no doubt Wagner wanted to check them, but knew they needed water more than anything. The realities of working for a city in a fiscal crisis forced the Fire Captain to trust his firefighters. They had no intention of letting him down.

Frank often wondered what went through his captain's mind when they were in situations like this. He had seen the look on

Wagner's face when one of them was injured. It was almost as if the Captain felt the pain himself, although it went beyond the physical pain. The emotional trauma obviously cut deeply into his boss whenever one of them pulled some bonehead move and got banged up. Just the thought of that look made Frank think before he committed himself to a building. He smiled to himself, realizing that it didn't slow him down. It only made him think. Pushing into the heat of a fire was just too satisfying. As far as he was concerned, if his ears did not feel the heat he wasn't pushing hard enough. Wagner knew this, which was why he always preached caution to his crew.

As he was climbing the stairs, Frank wondered how much longer Wagner could put up with everything that went with being responsible for his crew. With these thoughts came the realization that this crew probably wouldn't stay together much longer. Wagner, Matt, and Al all had enough time in to retire. Matt was already making sounds about leaving. It depended on how many men were promoted off the captain's list. Matt was in a sweat position. If they took as many guys off this list as the last one, he might just get promoted. That would probably mean a transfer out of Six and a few more years on the job for the senior firefighter. As far as Frank was concerned, all the expense and time invested in his education meant he would probably be the first to leave. It was only a matter of time. If Chingli had her way, that would be a very short period of time. That was frustrating because he loved his job. Don and the Chief were so far beyond the average twenty-five to thirty years of a firefighter's career, that it was a given they would retire soon. That would leave Jack as the senior man on the tour. He chuckled at the thought as he threw his face piece on.

Frank could hear Seven Engine moving their line into the second floor apartment. They had broken out the window at the top of the stairs. Looking out that window, he could see Al and the Captain working next to the rig. Jack was waiting at the corner hydrant in the background. Normally, Jack would not have been left at the hydrant. The next due engine would arrive quickly and supply water. Because of the delay caused by companies being taken out of service, their procedures would now have to change when operating in this part of the city. Before ascending to the upper floor landing, Frank saw Wagner pull down the short length of hose that was draped on top of the plywood mask cabinets. He knew they would have water soon. Al was working with a precision learned at countless fires. He was quickly breaking the three inch line and attaching it to the pre-connected short length. The two and a half would take more time because it required the extra step of connecting a double male coupling before being hooked into the panel. Matt leaned out the second floor window and yelled for water.

The call for water changed Al's priorities. He now moved to the pump panel on the driver's side of the rig and began pulling levers. The inch and a half hose coming out of the rear port jumped to life as water rushed through it. Captain Wagner hooked up the second feed line while Al turned the throttle out. A small cloud of diesel smoke appeared on the opposite side of the rig. Frank could feel the hose in his hands begin to fill. He climbed the last few stairs and crawled onto the third floor landing. As soon as the hose stiffened, he opened up the nozzle and began playing it off the ceiling. The heat forced him to stay low as he crawled slowly forward while feeling for holes in the floor. After the visible fire in the hallway was knocked down, the firefighter turned into the apartment doorway and hit a wall of heat.

Continuing to play the line into the burning apartment, Frank could feel waves of heat passing over him. When he turned to see where Matt was, the glow from the flames shooting out of the third floor windows appeared brighter. It was as if no water was on this fire. The angry roar of a working fire grew. Frank heard the sound of breaking glass as Matt took out the window at the top of the stairs. Determined not to back down from the fire, he tried to push in a little further to get at the seat of it. Knock that down and this fire was his. The sound of Captain Wagner's voice rose above the cacophony surrounding him. This was followed by the muffled shout of Matt calling through his face piece.

"Frank, back out! The Cap says to back out!"

Continuing to work the line off the ceiling, Frank began to move out of the apartment and back into the hallway. He knew not to take his time. If the Captain said move, he had to hustle. As he reached the top of the stairs, a piece of ceiling fell in front of him.

Frank heard a shout of "Get down!" then felt Matt's hand pull him down the stairs. At the same instant the cockloft exploded. They landed in a heap on the bottom landing, the hose wedged underneath them. The third floor had instantly become an inferno.

"God almighty!" Matt muttered through his face piece.

"You guys all right?" the Captain asked, not missing a beat. His voice undiminished by a barrier between his lungs and the smoke.

"Yeah, Cap," was Frank's muffled reply. He could feel a rush of adrenalin pulsing through his body as he shut down the nozzle and scrambled to get up. After getting back on his feet, the firefighter opened the line into the floor above. He started to climb the stairs again, but Wagner put a hand on his shoulder to stop him.

"We need another line up here," were the next words out of his mouth. Jack came up with the second line and a question from the Chief. "Is everyone okay?"

The low pressure warning bells on Frank's and Matt's air tanks began to go off a few minutes after Jack arrived. The Chief had ordered everyone off the stairs until the fire was darkened down by master streams from outside. The firefighters went down to change their tanks, so they could be ready when the interior attack began again. It was going to be a long night.

Chapter Eight

A ghetto mobile that is what the young man's father would have called the car he was driving. "You can't take a decent car into the ghetto. They'll ruin it.," was the reason given for the need to have such a car. It was appropriate to return to this part of the city to begin his work. The scum had spread from here outward, driving all respectable people before them. Eating away at the heart of the community like a cancer.

Some said the conditions surrounding him now had come about because highways had made it convenient to commute. Others said that there was no room in the nation's most densely populated city for returning veterans to begin families after World War II. The young man knew better. The cause of the city's decline was crime, immorality, and drugs. That had all begun after the riots. The bad elements within the community had been given free sway during that upheaval. Like Adam, they had tasted a forbidden fruit and had been addicted to its false sense of power.

The low lifes who preyed on the people of this neighborhood did so to feel empowered. But did not the predator depend on its prey? Those who stalked the elderly and weak of the community were too ignorant to realize such a deep truth. Wisdom and truth were not part of their makeup. Wisdom began with the fear of God. There was no fear of God in this neighborhood any longer. Fear was a useful tool for civilizations. If a man feared punishment would be the consequence of an action, he would avoid the punishment through restraint. Re-introduce fear into this environment and the behavior of those who lived in it would change. That was the hypothesis to be tested. Tonight he would begin his experiment to prove it. If this proved to be true, he would have the secret for returning the city to its pre-riot status. Before its center had become a burned out shell, when Springfield Avenue was a thriving business district filled with entrepreneurial spirit striving for the American dream.

It would be easy to return everything to the conditions that existed twenty years before. Put the fear of God into the rabble who prowled these streets and they would flee. As far as he was concerned, the fear of God was the fear of death. Kill a few of the petty hoodlums who formed the base of the criminal hierarchy and the whole putrid structure would collapse. One decisive person was all that was needed. He had been decisive the previous night and had sent the mob running for cover. They now had respect for him; that was obvious. There had been no retaliatory attack on him or his mother because of his decisiveness. He had been searching for an answer to so many questions in his life. Last night had been an epiphany and the answer to all his questions.

He would knock the base out of the criminal pyramid and the barbarians would flee. The city would return to its former splendor and he would be a hero! Life finally had a purpose. There had never been another time when he felt so alive; so empowered. For the past eighteen years his father's death had haunted him. That ghost had been banished and replaced by a mission to drive fear of crime from the city's streets. Those streets would be made safe for decent people by eliminating the bad elements. If those elements did not fear God, they would fear him!

As the car turned onto Sixteenth Avenue it slowed to a crawl. The time was just after two in the morning. Bars would soon be emptying their bowels of the drunkards and drug addicts. They were the petite criminal element on which everything else rested. If there were no drug addicts, there would be no customers for the substances that caused his father's death and ruined his neighborhood.

The streets were deserted. At this time of night they belonged to the cops, firemen, and EMTs. Respectable people did not go out this late at night. Other than civil servants, the only people who ventured out at this hour were the miscreants, thugs, and malcontents who stalked the honest, hardworking people of the community.

The young man chuckled to himself when he thought of the simplicity of his plan. A simple plan had worked last night. The key to improving the lives of the people in the city was to stay focused on their problems and have a simple plan. He was not hindered by the mentality of those who defended transgressors of the law, explaining away their malfeasance with excuses of poverty and desperation. Desperate people do desperate things only if they have no scruples. It had been said that revolution grew out of the barrel of a gun. Morality can grow beside revolution. He would show that by confirming the validity of his hypothesis. A man made his way to a telephone pole on the corner just ahead of the car. His pace slowed and he seemed out of breath. Upon reaching the pole, a hand moved up to the fire box attached to it.

The young man's heart rate jumped. This was the beginning of his crusade. Anger swept through him as memories of the shame felt after his father's death resurfaced. A death caused by the type of person who was pulling the fire box. Death would beget death. Eighteen years was too long to wait for justice.

As the box was pulled, the car leaped forward. The driver's right hand reached under the front seat. When it came up, the old police service revolver that had served so well the night before was held ready. He placed the weapon on the seat next to him so he could reach it quickly. A surge of adrenaline swept through him as he turned the car toward the pole. The young man began to roll the car window down before the vehicle came to a complete stop next to the pole.

The man who had pulled the fire box had a look of bewilderment on his face as the car came to a sudden halt beside him. This expression quickly gave way to one of relief. The driver of the car noted the changes on his prey's face. The first expression was attributed to fear of facing rival gang members. When the expression on the face of his quarry changed, the young man became enraged. It was obvious to him that the person had mistaken him for a police officer. Was the corruption now so rampant within the department that even a petty hood did not fear prosecution for pulling a false alarm? He wanted to shout that he was not a cop, that the police had disqualified him with a bogus psychological test. They had denied him his birth right because of their fear he would be an honest cop like his father. There was no time for that. If he did not strike quickly his game would bolt.

The man standing at the fire box began to move toward the car. The driver's face was covered with sweat which caused the man outside the car to stop momentarily.

Review the plan! They cannot get too close! You must be decisive! If you take out a gun you had better use it! These thoughts flashed through the head of the car's driver. Am I too late again tonight? I will not die without a fight! The gun came up as if it had a mind of its own. With the sound of his heart reverberating through his ears, the young man aimed the pistol at his victim. A look of astonishment crossed the face of the cornered quarry. This instantly changed to a mask of terror, much like that worn by the mobsters who had faced this gun the night before. The driver thought how sick the criminal element made him feel. They were so brave when wantonly attacking innocents, but if confronted by superior force they became whimpering cowards. Fear of death would make this city safe again. A feeling of power surged through the driver, flowing up his arm and into the finger that squeezed the trigger.

The first round pierced the victim's heart and drove him back. A second round was sent through his skull to make sure the miracle of modern medicine could not save him. Then the car pulled away at a controlled clip; its driver's rage slowly being replaced by a sense of supreme satisfaction. The street around the victim remained deserted.

Chapter Nine

The Captain sat writing in the company journal while his crew was cleaning the face pieces to their masks. Frank walked in as Wagner finished the last of the paper work that went with responding to an alarm.

"Cap, thanks for pulling me out of that top floor, if I had been blown down those stairs, Chingli would have probably been on the next flight to Taipei," Frank said with sincere gratitude.

"That's what they pay me the big bucks for, Frank. I sit back and make sure my firefighters don't go too far, too fast."

"And save them from their own stupidity," Frank added.

"Oh, how so?"

"I thought I knew how far I could push. All that was necessary was a few more feet of line and another minute. We would have knocked it down and then gone out to change our tanks. Everyone else could have started overhauling," Frank said laughing at himself. "Where all that fire came from is beyond me."

"I've been there. We had a similar job a few years before I was promoted. A couple of the guys got burnt pretty badly at that one. Just remember, on the tip you can only see the smoke directly in front of you, maybe a little red glow, but not much else. You couldn't see the way the smoke up around the ceiling behind you was acting and notice that there was no open flame in the cockloft," the Captain said, switching into the role of fire instructor. "If you had ever experienced a cockloft back draft, you would have bailed out before your grizzled old Captain had to tell you."

Wagner stood up and slapped the younger man on the shoulder. They walked out of the watch room. Everyone was sitting around the kitchen table. All seemed to gravitate to the kitchen after a tough job. Here fresh coffee would inevitably be brewing and the fire would be reviewed. What had gone right and what had gone wrong. How did they do it and how should it have been done. These informal critiques were one of the reasons Frank loved being at Six Engine. Chief Gregor never hesitated to share his view of the fire and his forty years of experience. The Captain used these same bull sessions to reinforce training.

Even if he had not enjoyed the review, going to bed was not considered. They all knew sleep was out of the question for the next hour. The bar crowd would begin pulling fire boxes in a few minutes.

"Chief, did you see the back draft coming, too?" Frank asked.

"Frank, I saw it coming when they put Three Truck out of service. No vertical ventilation means tougher fires," the Chief began in a matter of fact voice. "I'd like you guys to keep that in mind. If you have a good working fire and you don't hear saws cutting the roof above you, slow down a little. No one was reported trapped. No sense in getting hurt for a building that will probably be abandoned anyway."

"Cap, how did you see it coming?" Jack asked. "What can we look for to pick up on a possible back draft in the cockloft. They didn't teach us about it in the academy. You can't open a door and have air sucked past you in the cockloft. Hell, I never heard of a back draft like that."

"Jack, don't get too bent out of shape by this. In all my years on the job, I've seen this happen once before," the Captain responded reassuringly. "It is not going to happen every night, but the possibility is there. We're used to Three Truck getting the roof pronto in that area. Now the city fathers, in their infinite wisdom, put them out of service, so we have to adjust. We have to protect ourselves because no one else will."

"What about aggressively attacking the seat of the fire?" Jack asked.

"I said adjust not surrender," the Captain laughed. "Each fire is different. There are things they all have in common, but they each remain a unique event. Judge them the way I judge firefighters, each according to his merits."

"And that translates into be wary of yourself, my boy," Matt threw in a playful jab and then changed the subject. "Now, about what you said just before the bell hit, who is your new distraction?"

Jack looked up at the ceiling and cursed under his breath as Frank and Matt laughed.

"My new distraction is just that at the moment," he replied defensively. "I obviously couldn't just seek her companionship without the permission of her older brother."

Everyone around the table started laughing.

"Since when have you become chivalrous?" Al asked.

"Since his new distraction is the famed femme fatale Gloria Helms," Matt answered for him. Almost simultaneously, they all began to moan.

"Frank, are you going to allow this to happen?" Al asked lightheartedly.

"Well, I tried to warn him that she's a man-eater, but apparently the boy's not thinking with the right head," Frank teased his friend. "What I want to know is does the lady killer think he is a match for the man eater?"

"I have killed no ladies. That is a reputation given to me by those who are jealous of my success with the opposite sex," Jack began. "But do I think Gloria and I will get along? Well, we've know each other for a little while now . . ."

There were coughs mixed in with laughter and moans from his audience when Jack said this. All knew that Frank and Jack had grown up together; each with a little sister running after him.

"You know, I'm trying my best to answer a question and all I get is derision," Jack replied to the noise. After everyone quieted down, he continued. "As I was saying, Gloria and I have known each other for some time, so if we choose to start a more intimate relationship, it should work well."

"Woo, Frank did you hear that?" Matt piped in. "He said 'a more intimate relationship.' Are you going to let him get away with it?

Why, we don't even know if this cad's advances are welcomed by the man-eat - - - I mean the young lady."

When the laughter subsided, Jack addressed the question of how welcome his advances were. "I did not start this little game of flirtation. The lovely flower you boys are so intent on protecting fired the first shot across my bow."

"You think she's been coming on to you?" Frank asked.

"Yeah, it was subtle, but unmistakable," Jack turned toward Frank as he told him.

"You know, Chingli said something about it the other day. I have to confess to being totally oblivious to the whole thing. Whoever said big brothers should look out for their little sisters was foolish," Frank said ruefully. "Men never pick up on all those little signals women throw out. At least not until they've got us in their sights. Then it's too late."

"But the lady killer was supposed to be immune to feminine tactics," Al said with a hint of disappointment.

"Frank, I ask you again, are you going to let this happen?" Matt shouted in mock indignation.

"I seem to be doing a lot of this lately," Frank started, remembering the conversation in the supermarket. "I don't have to defend my little sister. She can more than take care of herself. She is quite capable of ripping a man's soul out. I will warn my friend, she has a very low opinion of the male of the species. Seems to think it's a wonderful game to attract them, distract them, and then dump them on the garbage heap of life."

Laughter filled the kitchen after Frank's warning. "I say we start a pool. Who will win the battle of the sexes?" Matt shouted. "Will it be the lady killer or the man eater?"

"And how do you know the battle will even be joined?" Jack shot back. "I haven't approached the young lady yet."

"You mean she might turn you down cold," Matt poked while laughing.

The red phone from fire dispatch rang before Jack could answer. Al picked it up as Matt turned to the Captain. "We're in service, right Cap?" he asked hopefully.

"Yeah, Matt, don't worry. We won't miss any work tonight," Wagner answered with a grin.

"Sixteenth Avenue and Seventeenth Street on a pulled box," Al repeated the information the operator gave him. The joker circuit clicked as everyone got up and walked through the kitchen doors to the rig. Coats were thrown on and feet slipped into boots while the door began its ascent. Al kicked over the engine as the bells began. The rig pulled out of quarters first, leaving the overhead door up. Don pulled the gig out before the Chief started the doors down.

There was no traffic on the streets as Al guided the rig through the flashing traffic light on Sixteenth and Bergen. Anyone on the streets at this time of night was probably returning from the corner bar. Most of the bar patrons in this neighborhood walked back to the three story wood framed tenement they called home. The crisp air would encourage them to move as quickly as they could. Frank stood with his arm passed through one of the loops hanging from the bar that spanned the back step of the rig. His back was turned to the wind while he chuckled at the prospect of his lifelong friend was making a play for his kid sister. He stood mindlessly watching the street recede as the rig advanced up Sixteenth Avenue. When they reached Tenth Street he turned around to see what they were rolling into. The darkness of West Side Park stretched out to the south as Six Engine stopped momentarily at the light on Sixteenth Avenue and Thirteenth Street. The last four blocks were covered at a moderate pace. There was no fire showing and no one standing in the street trying to get their attention. It was not until they reached Sixteenth Street that the body lying at the base of the telephone pole could be seen. Frank swore quietly under his breath.

Chapter Ten

"Engine Six to quarters." the Captain began.

"Engine Six."

"On the scene at Sixteenth and Seventeenth, we have a shooting victim on the ground. Have EMS and police respond and make it a three oh five."

"Received Six. Attention all units on station four four four six Engine Six reports a signal three oh five holding Engine Six. All chiefs in service. Oh two oh five hours."

Frank, Jack, and Matt stepped off the back of the rig and opened the middle side compartment. Inside were the E & J oxygen case and the first aid supplies. Jack reached in for the first aid kit. He handed this to Frank before taking the oxygen case out. Matt walked directly to the body along with the Captain. The sound of a fire engine had attracted attention to the corner. People were beginning to mill around the front of the rig, trying to get a glance at the body lying against the pole. Captain Wagner and Matt were crouched over the lifeless form when the two firemen reached them.

"It doesn't look good. Whoever hit this guy, hit him hard," then glancing over his shoulder at the growing crowd, Wagner made a quick decision. He turned back to face his men and quietly said, "Give him your best, you've got an audience."

"Understood, Cap," Matt replied softly. "We aren't doctors, so we can't pronounce anyway."

As Frank opened the first aid box, Jack took out the oxygen mask. The body had to be moved away from the pole before they could begin work. Without saying a word, Frank and Jack moved to opposite ends of the body and carefully lifted it. Matt followed with the oxygen case and the first aid kit. When the skull came off the pole, brain matter and blood momentarily poured out of the wound in the back of the head. There was no spurting of blood or any other indication of life. It was obvious to the firefighters that this man was beyond resuscitating. In spite of this, the body was placed gently on the ground and Jack began chest compressions. Frank had a feeling of *deja vu*.

Even though Six had only been on the scene for a minute, some of the people in the gathering crowd started to shout questions at the firefighters. Since the bars were beginning to let out, the tone of the gathering slowly changed. The questions were mumbled at first then shouted at the men bent over the victim.

"Where's the ambulance? You're just firemen. What do you know anyway? The brother's dying and all we can get in this city is a bunch of dumb firemen."

The Captain walked away from the crowd and called headquarters over the air again.

"Engine Six to quarters."

"Engine Six."

"Could you give us an ETA on EMS?"

"Cap, EMS said they will get to you as soon as possible. Right now they have nothing available."

"Six to quarters, have the Rescue Squad respond to this location."

"Received Six. Oh two oh nine hours."

Frank glanced up and noticed a little girl running down Seventeenth Street toward the scene. As soon as she was close enough to see what had happened she stopped short, put her hands up to her chin, and screamed. Before anyone could react the girl collapsed, her head audibly striking the merciless concrete of the sidewalk. In that instant things went from bad to worse.

Matt went to the girl while Frank and Jack continued CPR on the gunshot victim. Al, who had been standing by watching the rig to make sure no one walked off with anything, took a few steps toward Matt. The Captain quickly waved him back to the rig and went to help with the little girl. The situation was rapidly becoming volatile with the crowd growing larger and uglier by the minute.

"Where are the police?" Wagner muttered as he bent down next to Matt.

"I think you'd better call again, Cap. The folks in the neighborhood are getting antsy," Matt said as he checked to make sure the girl had an open breathing passage. After confirming she had no problem breathing, Matt took off his turnout coat, rolled it up, and placed it under the girl's legs.

"Engine Six to quarters."

"Six."

"Do you have an ETA on the police?"

"Negative Six. They can only say that they're backed up, but will get to you as soon as possible. Oh two ten hours, dispatcher one five"

Frank heard Wagner curse under his breath as he stood up. A working fire was more predictable than the situation they were in now. There was no telling what would happen with a crowd that just got out of the bars. Someone in the crowd began to curse their efforts. Something had to be done quickly or the crowd would turn on them.

He remembered what had happened a couple of years before when two angry teenagers had decided they did not like firefighters. After pulling a box, they had taken a swipe at Matt. By the time everything had cleared up, the police had five squad cars and a supervisor on the scene; Matt had been condemned as an "Uncle Tom"; and the two youths had been arrested. That had been a three hour ordeal. Everyone on Six had been there except for Jack. He would have to keep an eye on his friend if the taunting grew worse. With that experience in mind, Frank was relieved when Wagner decided to play it safe.

"Engine Six to quarters."

"Six."

"Give me the box for this location. Tell units coming in that there is a large crowd on the corner of Sixteenth Avenue and Seventeenth Street and they are not in a good mood."

"Received Six."

They could hear the alarm going over the air as the little girl began to moan. She was crying and calling "Papa, papa,"

"It's okay, honey," Matt said, "We'll get your dad. How do you feel? Can you sit up?"

The girl began to sit up, but when she saw the body on the corner she screamed "papa" and went limp. Matt, anticipating the possibility of another black out, caught her.

"I think that's her father on the corner, Cap," Matt said with a tight voice.

Frank noticed the Captain positioned himself between the little girl and the body on the corner, so she did not have a clear view of what was going on. Wagner then got back on the radio.

"Engine Six to quarters."

"Engine Six."

"We are going to need a second bus at this location. The daughter of the victim has fallen. Also could you push for an ETA on the police?"

"Received Six, we'll try the police again. EMS said they have a bus en route."

The girl woke up crying and muttering for her father.

"My friends are doing everything they can for your papa, hon, so don't worry. What's you name?" Matt asked, trying to distract his charge and gain her trust.

"Stella," she whispered.

"That's a pretty name. How are you doing, Stella?" Matt asked very gently.

"My head hurts a little, but papa . . . What happen to papa? And mama, are you going to help her?" she asked in a quiet voice.

When Frank heard this tiny voice his heart broke. Her father had been brutally murdered on a street corner. She had apparently stumbled onto the grisly scene out of curiosity. Now these pictures were going to play back inside her head for the rest of her life. This was not something a five or six year old should face, but life was often cruel. Sirens could be heard in the distance. Probably Rescue, but the other units would arrive in a matter of minutes.

As these thoughts were going through Frank's mind, Matt was gently questioning the girl about what she had just said. "Stella, why does your mom need our help?"

"She's going to have a baby tonight. Papa came down here to pull a fire box because the ambulance didn't come," Stella responded as she tried to see around the Captain. "He said the firemen would always come quickly, so he called you."

"We try to come quickly, hon, but where is your mom now?" Matt asked in a soothing voice.

"We live at 465 South Seventeenth Street, Newark, New Jersey," she replied with the cadence of first grader who had memorized her address.

As soon as Wagner heard all the information necessary, he lifted the radio up to his mouth again.

"Engine Six to quarters."

"Six Engine."

"Inform EMS that we also have a woman in labor at 465 Seventeenth Street."

"A woman in labor at 465 Seventeenth Street, received Six. Oh two eleven, dispatcher one five."

Sirens could be heard approaching from Sixteenth Avenue. A moment later the Rescue Squad pulled up behind the rig on the corner. Air horns and additional sirens were now clearly audible as the men from the squad went through compartments lifting out first aid supplies. Wagner stood up and walked over to the Rescue captain, while Matt positioned himself between the girl and her father. The firefighter kept up a chatty conversation about her school and the new baby, but avoided any mention of her parents.

The men from Rescue split up. Two went to help Frank and Jack while the other two went up the block to 465. Frank was relieved to see the squad. The guys from Rescue took over the resuscitation effort. He and Jack walked over to the rig, trying to put themselves between the crowd and the victims. The Chief pulled up as they got to the corner.

"Deputy One on the scene."

"On the scene at oh two twelve."

"Deputy One to quarters, any word on the police or EMS?"

"EMS said they will have one unit there momentarily, Chief. They can't give an estimate on the second bus. The police have squad cars and a supervisor en route."

"Deputy One received."

The crowd was growing larger as more of the neighborhood bar patrons were drawn to the activity on the corner, but Frank noticed that they had begun to quiet down with the arrival of other fire units. Nine Truck turned onto Sixteenth Avenue as the Chief finished his radio transmission. Eighteen Engine was less than half a block away and a patrol car could be seen in the distance coming up Sixteenth Avenue, so the members of Six began to breathe easier.

With the police on the scene, the crowd began to disperse. EMS arrived shortly after the first patrol car had pulled up. The body of Stella's father was quickly placed in the ambulance. One of the guys from the squad continued to help the EMTs with CPR as they transported the victim. Another ambulance arrived as the first pulled away. By now Stella was able to walk with the assistance of her new found friend Matt, who helped her get into the back of the bus. After stopping up the street to pick up her mother, the ambulance responded to University Hospital with the little girl, her mother, and her new baby brother. The last patient was delivered by the Rescue Squad a few minutes before EMS had arrived.

"What a night!" Frank muttered in an exhausted voice to Jack.

"God, I don't want to go through that again," Jack said, shaking his head. "Give me a working fire anytime. I thought they were going to jump us! And then the poor bastard's daughter has to show up. We're lucky we didn't have a riot!"

"My boy, you have to get used to this," Frank said chuckling. "They wouldn't riot because we're working on a shooting victim, not unless the victim was shot by the cops. They were just mouthing off."

"You should have been here when those two teenagers decided they didn't like firemen and began swinging at Matt," the Captain said as he walked up to the two firefighters. "That almost turned into a riot!"

"Matt told me about that," Jack answered. "If half of what he said was true, then this was nothing."

"It's all true." Frank said as they walked to the rear of the rig. By now all the fire units had taken up except for Six Engine and the Chief. Frank looked toward the squad cars on Sixteenth Avenue and saw Ray pull in behind them.

"Well, will you look who's here," he said to Jack while pointing to their friend.

"I'm going to have to talk with him," Wagner said in a tired voice. Frank knew talking about what they had seen was going to be tough. The little girl was the same age as the Captain's granddaughter.

Ray began this investigation by questioning Six Engine. It became apparent early on that there were no gang or drug ties to the victim. From what his daughter had told Matt, the man had pulled the fire box to get help for his wife. Robbery was apparently ruled out. He still had his wallet.

As the last of the crowd went home, Ray drove to University Hospital and Six Engine returned to their quarters. No one busted Frank's chops about what he had seen over the past two nights. Their thoughts were on the little girl and baby boy who were now without a father.

Chapter Eleven

Stacey Romanov parked her car up the block from the four story brick apartment building she called home. Walking briskly down North Sixth Street, she greeted her neighbors with a smile and lively hello. The trees lining the street were bare, so the evergreens along the walkway leading to the front door of her building were appreciated all the more. Her apartment was on the third floor of the fifty year old building.

Stacey opened the ornate iron and glass door that led into the foyer, stepped in, and gently closed it. The metallic clank of the latch catching reverberated off the white marble walls and stairs. She climbed the four steps energetically and stopped at her mailbox. After glancing at the mail, another ornate door was unlocked and she stepped onto the tiled floor of a hallway. The stairs leading up to her apartment were directly across from the door. These were climbed in the same manner as the four stairs in the foyer.

The petite blond called her apartment "my place" because it was the first place she did not have to share with anyone. She had lived in "her place" for about six months and had always felt secure. It was an ideal residence for a young single woman. The building was in a quiet residential neighborhood and was secure. The superintendent lived on the first floor. If anything went wrong in her apartment, Stacey could make a quick call to Mr. Lever. The super was a handy man par excellence. Leaking faucets, broken windows, or faulty light fixtures were all handled with a quick cheerful competence.

The advantages to living in this neighborhood were many. The commute to work was under an hour. Everything she needed seemed more convenient here than in the suburban neighborhood where her parents lived. Big brother lived fifteen minutes away, with mom and dad forty-five minutes up the freeway.

Life since relocating had been moving along at a comfortable pace. The position she had landed at a suburban research firm after graduation the previous year was promising. Yet, there was doubt in her life. That doubt was Ray. How do you get a man to commit himself to you without chasing him away? Even with Mrs. Friedrick gently prodding her son, the young police detective was balking at turning their *de jure* relationship into one of the more permanent *de facto* variety. Men! They wanted all of the benefits, but none of the responsibilities. That was for another time. Tonight would be the first time she entertained friends in her place. Everything had to be perfect. She took a deep breath and put the frustration about Ray behind as the key unlocked her door.

The door opened onto a cozy living room. The first things one saw when the door opened were oil paintings on the far wall. She had started collecting them after seeing Frank's apartment. They added a certain charm. Each of the four depicted the country side in a different season. Her favorite was the winter scene. It looked so peaceful with freshly fallen snow covering the ground and a farm house which looked so invitingly warm. Whenever she looked at it, memories of the muffled sounds of a snow shrouded countryside came back.

Bookcases were on either side of a television stand on the wall next to the door. These were filled with her favorite volumes. Stacey loved to read and did so unceasingly. Her taste ran the entire spectrum of the printed word. She had a leather bound set of books that contained stories written by noble prize winning authors. Just opening these books was a pleasure. Another set was called "The Library of America." The best of American literature was represented in these. History was a favorite topic of hers. The shelves were crowded with volumes concerning every age of human history, ancient through modern. She did not restrict herself to one area of the globe. Her library contained books dealing with all seven continents and everything in-between. The best of recent writings was also scattered among all of this. She was an unabashed lover of books; a quintessential bibliophile who felt most content when surrounded by them.

The hardwood floors on which the bookcases rested were covered with oriental rugs Chingli had helped pick out. A couch occupied the space under the oils, with a recliner resting between the two windows to its left. "With all of the sun this apartment gets," Stacey thought, "I really should have some plants to add a little green to the place." Writing "plants" on the list taped to the refrigerator door, Stacey glanced around the kitchen and then dashed into her room to change. Preparations had been completed with Gloria the night before. Tonight was for relaxing and enjoying the company of friends.

Gloria arrived before everyone else. She had picked up a bottle of red and a bottle of white wine for the women. Beer for the guys was already cooling in the refrigerator. Gloria asked Stacey about the note she saw on the refrigerator door when she dropped the white wine in.

"Plants?" she asked lightly. "What do you mean by that?"

"Oh, that's just a thought I had after I came home today," Stacey replied with a laugh. "I thought the place could use a little green in the living room where all the sun comes in."

"You're beginning to sound like my sister-in-law. Chingli might just give you some tonight. Says you have to have life in your space, something to do with luck," Gloria told her best friend.

"That would be appreciated," Stacey said. "How is Chingli adjusting to American life and your brother?"

Gloria shook her head a little and smiled. "I think she's having a harder time adjusting to my brother than she is adjusting to American life. There are some cultural clashes, but mostly her complaints seem to be part of the battle of the sexes. The biggest adjustment she has to make is being married to a fireman. She told me the other day that firemen in Taiwan are one step above shoeshine boys."

"You're kidding! That should take the macho pride out of our brothers," Stacey laughed.

"Come on Stace," Gloria said with more than a hint of sarcasm in her voice, "Our brothers don't have inflated egos."

"Gloria, those two were full of themselves when we were kids and they're still full of themselves."

"Don't look for an argument from me. My brother is totally oblivious to the entire situation," Gloria said shaking her head in seeming disbelief. "He just goes plodding through the day tripping over his maleness while she manipulates him into doing things the way she wants them done."

Stacey shook her head and then asked, "Does she find American men harder to change than Chinese men?"

"No, in fact she tells me that Frank is the most pliable man she ever met. He actually told her that if she cared about something and he really didn't, then she won by default." Gloria started to chuckle at her brother. "As if a man ever really cared about anything other than a warm meal and a warm body."

Stacey burst out laughing. "Gloria Helms! You have a very low opinion of the opposite sex."

"Why? Are you going to argue the point? They are basically selfish little boys who want to take their bat and go home when things get tough," Gloria stated in a very cynical tone.

"And we girls make fools of ourselves because we have a hard time living without their bats?" Stacey asked.

Gloria began laughing. After getting hold of herself, she said "That is not what I meant. Let me rephrase it. When they feel frustrated or threatened by us they want to take their ball . . ."

Stacey started to laugh again at her friend's choice of words. Gloria threw her arms up in exasperation and said, "Girl, you have a dirty mind."

"I do not, you just don't think before you speak."

"Don't you realize that they view the whole deal as a game? That's why I can't use those phrases to describe men's reactions. The language of the playground is used by them when they talk about relations with women," Gloria thoughtfully pointed out. "Think about it, 'I didn't get to first base with her'," she said in as deep a voice as she could muster.

"Or how about 'I scored with her'," Stacey joined in.

"And of course when you do become intimate, they go around like little roosters in the barnyard bragging about 'home runs', 'touchdowns', or 'goals,'" Gloria said acerbically.

"You mean like little cocks don't you?" Stacey asked before she lost control. Gloria's laughter mixed with hers.

After calming down a bit Stacey asked Gloria another question about her sister-in-law.

"You said that in Taiwan a fireman is one step above a shoeshine boy. That's a considerable step down the social ladder for a general's daughter isn't it? How is she taking that?"

"Oh, Stace, it's a shame. The girl is so in love with my brother that she's given up everything. Pride, home, family are all gone. It's a sin really because I don't think he realizes how much she's sacrificed," Gloria said, her voice now very serious. "You know we laugh at the fools men make of themselves over us, but we don't stand up very well either. Many a woman has been made to look like a clown by some skittish male who wasn't ready to settle down."

"Well, in the battle of the sexes, you are scoring quite a few points for us girls," Stacey told her friend. "But I think I'm a borderline fool."

"Don't worry Stace," Gloria answered reassuringly, "Ray just has to get up the nerve to ask you. Men are basically cowards when it comes to emotions. You have to lead them to the slaughter of their egos. They'll thank you later when they taste the steaks of married life."

"You have such a way with words, Gloria," Stacey commented with mock seriousness. "You make it all sound so romantic."

"Romance is a male concept," was the lighthearted reply. "We girls have to be much more practical than men."

"A male concept? We have turned into a skeptic haven't we?"

"I learned a long time ago that when it comes to women, men think with the wrong head," Gloria said in an assured manner.

"Since when have you adopted the language of the docks?" Stacey teased her friend.

"Language of the docks? I've never been near any longshoremen. Firemen and cops? Now I can tell you a thing or two about those fraternities," Gloria answered. "But the language I just used was mild compared to your comments about bats and balls."

"Not to mention cocks," Stacey reminded her.

"Not to mention roosters," Gloria poked back.

"Okay, you win, now a quick change of subject. Do you mind that I've thrown you and Jack in as a pseudo couple?"

Gloria smiled at the way Stacey phrased it and then shook her head no. Her mannerisms suddenly became coy when the question was asked, telling Stacey what she wanted to know. The buzzer went off announcing their quiet sharing time was over. Gloria checked her hair in the reflection of the microwave door while Stacey did a last minute check in the living room mirror on the way to the intercom next to the door. Stacey pushed the button and spoke into the intercom. "Yes, who is it?"

"It is your Romeo," the unmistakable voice of Ray replied.

This brought a light chuckle from Stacey. Pushing the button again she responded to Ray's remark with a poor imitation of Shakespeare "Oh, Romeo, Romeo, where for art thou Romeo."

Ray's voice came back with a hint of a Brooklyn accent, "Because that's what my mom named me. Now open the door."

Gloria was leaning on the kitchen door frame and shaking her head. "Is that the way you two always greet each other?"

"No, we're usually more passionate, love," her friend said with a poor British accent.

"Oh brother, he tries to sound like he's from Brooklyn and you want to sound like the Duchess of Windsor. What a couple."

Stacey opened the door and waited for her guests. The sound of voices came from the hall as Ray and Chingli made it to the top of the stairs. Frank and Jack followed behind with the leaves of two plants covering their faces.

Chingli's long black hair was hanging freely over her shoulders. A loose red silk blouse and blue jeans that complimented her figure reminded the girls why they felt threatened by "China dolls." Both knew that Chingli was much tougher than that stereotype, but men still reacted to her predictably. Frank did not always appreciate the attention. A smile was on her face even though she was a little winded by the climb. The men followed Chingli into the apartment carrying the plants before Stacey closed the door.

"Chingli, how did you know I wanted plants?" Stacey asked as she hugged her friend.

"A girl needs some company, something to breathe the same air she is breathing," was Chingli's response.

"They're beautiful."

"Yeah, they're great but they're not light. Where do you want them," Jack asked trying to sound annoyed.

"Over by the windows, guys. One on each side of the recliner."

Frank and Jack carried the plants to the windows and placed them next to the recliner. Stacey looked at them a second and then changed her mind. "Back them up, more toward the window," she instructed. After the plants were in place Stacey clapped her hands together under her chin and admired the new arrangement. "That's perfect," she said while spinning around to face Chingli. "Thank you. They add just the right touch."

Frank and Jack looked at each other and then simultaneously placed their hands on their lower backs. They began to moan as if they had injured themselves.

"Oh what's the matter? Did the big firemen hurt their backs?" Gloria asked sarcastically.

"You're not going to get any sympathy," Ray sighed. "They use you and then discard you after you've fulfilled your purpose."

Stacey could not let her beau get away with a statement like that. "You've got it wrong, deary. You men are forever throwing us women away after we get a few gray hairs."

"Stay away from that one Ray," Jack interjected, "It sounds like you have awakened the feminist in her. As you know, she can be very ornery."

"On this one, I think I'll take your advice," Ray said.

Chingli listened to this exchange between her friends with a questioning smile on her face. Gloria saw that her sister-in-law looked a little confused, so she walked over to greet her. "If you weren't my brother's wife I'd hate you," she said with a warm smile while gently taking hold of her hands. "You look great."

"I have to work extra hard," Chingli replied. "I knew there would be two beautiful women at this party to compare me to."

The men listened to this exchange and then began a poor imitation of what they considered female behavior. "You look great," Jack said to Frank who was still next to the plant. "I like the way that plant compliments your eyes."

"Why, thank you Jack. You know I brushed this plant for an hour to get it into shape," Frank quipped. "It was just a bad plant day; if you know what I mean."

Stacey shook her head and looked at the ceiling. "You guys don't understand what we girls do for you." She walked to her stereo while saying this and started a tape. The sounds of swing jazz added a melodic rhythm to the small gathering.

Jack laughed on hearing his sister's comment. "What you do for us? You've got to be kidding. Chingli already gave the game away. She has two other women at this party to worry about. Women don't dress for men. They dress to look good for other women."

"You, my brother, are a hard boiled cynic," Stacey said as she went toward the kitchen with Chingli and Gloria. "What are you boys drinking?"

"I guess she told you," Ray said to Jack before placing his order. "I'll have a beer, babe."

"And I'll have the same, baby sister," Jack responded.

"Make that beers all around, Stacey," Frank said.

"Ah, swing jazz," Ray commented on the background music. "You can always count on Stacey to have gourmet music."

His girlfriend stopped at the kitchen door and looked at him. "Gourmet music?" she asked. "Ray you are one sick puppy, but that's why I love you."

"She loves you because you're a sick puppy?" Jack said with a laugh. "I always thought she had a deranged view of the world."

"I'm deranged?" Stacey shot at her brother. "You introduced me to the sick puppy."

"That was before the hormones kicked in and he became ill," Jack replied. "When Raymond was a little boy he was sweet and innocent."

"Innocent!" Frank protested. "My boy lost his innocence the moment he took a breath of air."

"You know," Ray quipped. "I'm getting raked over the coals by my two best friends. Something is wrong with this picture."

"You're right, Ray," Frank said quickly. "We have no beer in our hands."

"Frank Helms, you were always so philosophical," Gloria teased her brother. "Come on girls, if we want them to be civil, we're going to have to give them a little beer."

The sound of the three friends talking followed the girls into the kitchen. They did not return to the living room quickly because they were having their own discussion in the kitchen. Gloria initiated everything with an unflattering comment on the attitude of her brother and his friends. "The machismo in that room is overbearing. Stace, I think you're going to have to air the place out after they leave."

They stood in an oblong room lined with walnut stained cabinets. A sink occupied the back wall while a white refrigerator was tucked in an enclave next to the entrance. This was the focus of the three women's efforts. Stacey reached in and began passing bottles of beer to Gloria. Chingli shared her view of American men as she accepted the bottles from her sister-in-law and placed them onto a tray that their hostess had left on the counter. "Oh, they're not so bad," she opined. "You should see Chinese men. They're so proud, so manly. Even when they make fools of themselves. Women can't say anything because it might cause them to lose face. So we just laugh behind their backs."

"You're kidding?" Gloria asked as she passed along the bottle of white wine. "I always thought they would be gentlemen. You know, scholarly, like a college professor. That's what the American stereotype of them is nowadays. But then I should know better than to listen to stereotypes. You are not the quiet China doll you're supposed to be. Was my brother surprised when he met the real you?"

"Oh, I let him know the real me before we really dated. No, he wasn't the least bit surprised. As for your idea of Chinese men, we Chinese have our own monsters," Chingli said with a faraway look in her eyes as he placed the wine beside the beer. "I remember seeing some men beat their wives in the street when I was growing up. My father would say it was none of our business unless it was a soldier. Then he would stop the soldier, but he did that because it went against the military rules. I never thought I would marry after seeing all of that."

Stacey had been letting the two sisters-in-law talk, but could not resist putting a question to Chingli after hearing her last statement. "Why did you decide on Frank?" she asked while closing the refrigerator and moving to the cabinets beside it.

The petite Chinese woman smiled coyly before answering with a devilish undertone in her voice. "I knew he would never hit me, even if

I hit him. And I could see he would be easy enough to mold into a good husband, so I set out to change him from an acquaintance into a tutor and then into a lover."

"Will you listen to this," Stacey said to Gloria while reaching into the cabinet for bags of snacks. "China doll? She's a scheming temptress who entrapped your brother." After placing the potato chips and pretzels on the counter top, she turned to Chingli and asked, "How did you do it?"

All three started laughing at the same time. "Talk to Gloria about how to get a man. She knows better than me."

"We already discussed that before you walked in with the macho crowd," Gloria told her sister-in-law as she reached into a cabinet opposite Stacey and retrieved two large bowls. "She's trying to figure out how to get Ray to pop the question."

"What question?" Chingli asked passing the bowls to Stacey who had been busy opening the bags of snacks.

"Oh, I'm sorry. Your English is so good sometimes that I forget you're still picking up," Gloria said with sympathy, stepping over to help the night's hostess fill the bowls. "'Pop the question', means to ask someone to marry you. Since no one has ever asked me, I can't tell her how it's done."

"I don't know if how I did it will help," she started, standing behind her friends as they completed their task. "But after I met him in Hong Kong it seemed to me he was a very unusual man. Did you know he shared a hotel room with a married woman in Hong Kong?"

Stacey was caught off guard by this news. "What? You have to be kidding," so surprised she stopped pouring the pretzels. "I didn't think Frank could be distracted that easily. He never struck me as the type who would have an affair with a married woman."

"Oh, he didn't," Gloria said as she completed filling her bowl with potato chips. "He just roomed with her to save money. They had double beds and he . . . How did he put it? . . . respected her vows."

"They spent the first night in a king size bed," Chingli informed her sister-in-law.

"What?" Gloria was shocked. "He never told me that. Did he tell you?"

"No, she did. She wanted to sell him to me."

"But you just met in passing," Gloria replied. "How would she know he was interested? I mean, he was sharing a room with a woman and wasn't attacking her. He could have been gay."

"Oh, Gloria, your brother can be so much like glass sometimes," Chingli said quietly. "It was obvious to both his classmate and me that he was interested. He couldn't keep his eyes off me. They were eating me up, as if he wanted to pick me up and carry me away. In fact, he was frustrated because there was very little chance we would meet again. I was flattered by his interest, but I was kind of mean, too."

"Chingli!" both women squealed in anticipation.

"Yes, I led him on. I said I was coming to America to study. He jumped at that and told me he went to Seton Hall and the Asian Studies Department was great and that there were a lot of Chinese students.

When he found out I went to Fujen University, which is a Catholic school, he overflowed and gave me his phone number and address. He really made a fool out of himself. Even took a picture of me, I'm sure so he could show it off in the firehouse."

"I remember that picture," Gloria recalled, closing the bag in her hands and placing it on the counter. "He was honest with mom and me when he showed it to us. But I doubt his ego would have allowed him to tell the guys in the firehouse the truth."

"Jack came home with some wild story about Frank rescuing a beautiful Chinese woman from some mean customs agents," Stacey told them before she started to laugh. Then she directed another question at Chingli while she placed her bag next to Gloria's. "Is that why you came to Seton Hall, to catch Frank?"

"Well, first I had to change him from an interesting man I had met in Hong Kong into a friend, then into a boyfriend, and then into a husband." Chingli said trying to take some of the romance out of her story. "That would only be if everything his friend told me was true, which I doubted."

"Was everything true?" Gloria asked.

"Yes, your brother is a - - - How do you say it? - - - a straight shooter. That's why I chased him, but remember I was coming to America to study, not get a husband," she pointed out, turning to pick up the tray with the drinks. "He seemed interesting, but I expected him to be like all the other men I had met. A paper tiger, not really what he appeared to be. He is the first real tiger I know."

"Oh, you poor girl," Gloria moaned. "You have it bad."

"Have what bad?" Chingli asked looking confused, her hands grasping the tray but hesitating to hoist it.

"The love disease."

"Have you ever had this terrible sickness?" Chingli asked with a smile as she turned to face Gloria, leaning back on the edge of the counter.

"I try to be more practical. You two are both starry eyed," Gloria told them. "One is so taken by my brother that she can't see his faults. The other is waiting anxiously for a cop to arrest her."

"Your brother's faults will all be corrected by the time I'm through with him," Chingli assured her sister-in-law. "My only worry is how to get him to leave his job before something happens."

"No comments from the girl who wants to be held in the custody of a certain police officer?" Gloria challenged while she leaned on her side of the kitchen cabinetry.

"What do you want me to say, Glor," Stacey sighed as she reached up into the cabinet for wine glasses. "I'm guilty as charged."

"Well, at least she's going after a cop," Chingli pointed out. "That's better than a fireman. Or would you think differently, Gloria?"

"What do you mean by that?" Gloria asked incredulously, folding her arms and attempting to look annoyed.

"Well, Glor. It is getting pretty obvious to everyone that you have more than a sisterly interest in Jack," Stacey said with a chuckle as he reached for a pretzel.

"Is it?" her friend answered defensively. "Is that why you asked if I minded being a pseudo couple before? Are you trying to set me up with your brother?"

"I don't get involved with my brother's romantic life. He breaks too many hearts," Stacey countered. "Do you think you can tame him?"

There was a little fire in Gloria's eyes, as if she was given a challenge that could not be passed up. "If I want to, I can teach him to heel," she said with conviction.

"Heel? What do you mean by heel?" Chingli asked hesitantly.

Gloria straightened up and put her hands on Chingli's shoulders as if to gently emphasize her meaning. "When you teach a dog to walk behind you, that's called teaching it to heel. To walk by the heel of you shoe."

Chingli started laughing. "English is such a strange language."

When all three girls had calmed down, Stacey asked Chingli, "Why do you think that Ray being a cop is better than Frank being a fireman?"

"Well, we went to that awards dinner. The one that gives awards to police and firemen," she began, appearing as if a weight was being lifted from her shoulders. "And I read the program. On the back was a list of policemen and firemen who had died in their line of duty. There were more firemen than there were policemen on that list. When I asked Frank about it, we got into a big argument. I don't like his job." The last statement was said very emphatically.

"Is that supposed to make me feel better?" Stacey asked. "My brother is a fireman and my boyfriend is a cop. Where does that leave me?"

"You're better off than me," Gloria said without thinking. "My brother is a fireman and the guy I'm interested in is a fireman, too."

"So, you admit to being interested in Jack?" Chingli teased.

"Oh God, what did I say?" Gloria said to herself as she turned red. "Is that how you got Frank? You changed the subject, so he dropped his guard - - - he didn't realize what he was saying?"

"Why are you blaming me?" Chingli asked. "I didn't eat my foot."

"You mean put your foot in your mouth?" Gloria asked.

"That's it." Chingli responded. "English!" They all started to laugh.

"We had better get out to the living room," Stacey reminded her friends, "or those guys will think up something really silly to do and ruin the whole night."

"Okay," Gloria agreed. "But before we go in there, what do you two think about my chances of getting Jack interested?"

"If I know my brother, he's already interested," Stacey opined. Chingli shook her head in agreement as they picked up the drink tray and the snack bowls then walked out of the kitchen.

Chapter Twelve

The girls set the trays of snacks and drinks down on two folding tables then sat on the floor in a semi-circle facing the men, who appeared to be content sitting on the couch. The smiles on their faces told the three women the boys found something funny. Reaching for some pretzels, Gloria asked "What have you guys been talking about? Something that can't be shared with us girls?"

"Just swapping jokes," Frank answered his sister.

"Jokes? What kind of jokes might they be? Can't share them with us?" she inquired.

"The words are not meant for innocent viewers during prime time," Jack told her.

"You consider us innocent?" Stacey laughed at her brother. "Don't you say all women are manipulative bitches? That doesn't make us sound innocent."

"Oh, my virgin ears," Jack exclaimed.

"It's been a long time since you were a virgin," Stacey shot back.

"I'd stay away from that," Ray warned.

"I agree, that's a loser," Jack conceded.

Stacey let the sibling rivalry go, instead turning the conversation to a subject more to her liking. "Chingli, I have never heard the full story of how you met Frank. Could you give us your version? I'm sure the version he told in the firehouse was off the mark."

"Now hold on, Stace," Frank said defensively. "Are you saying my story isn't true?"

"No, I'm just saying it's told from your point of view," she responded. "I want to hear how a woman views it." This would steer the conversation toward the subject of commitments and marriage. It should make for an interesting night.

"Well," Chingli began, "I don't know what Frank said in the firehouse, but this is what really happened. I was in one of the China Art Stores in Hong Kong shopping for a jacket to give a friend, but I didn't know how I could choose the right size. A couple walked past me and the young man was about the right size, so I asked the woman if she would lend her husband to me to act as a model," Chingli began with her eyes looking out blankly. "My pronunciation of model made it sound more French than English. The woman, Sally, heard me say model and asked if I spoke French."

"So they switched over to French, leaving me out in the cold," Frank pointed out. "I'm sure they began plotting my ruin from that point."

"Quiet, I'm telling the story," Chingli scolded her husband.

"Sorry, my wife." he replied with mock seriousness.

"She told me he wasn't her husband. I apologized and asked if she would mind if her boyfriend modeled for me. Sally told me he wasn't a boyfriend either, just a classmate. Since he was only a classmate, I spoke directly to him in French," Chingli continued, chuckling to herself.

"And I, of course, responded in perfect French," Frank interjected.

"No, you responded with an impolite stare. I should have slapped you for what your eyes were saying, but you were cute. Now be quiet and let me finish my story," Frank threw his hands up and pretended to be insulted as his wife continued her tale.

"I switched to that barbaric language, English, and asked this young man if he would mind trying on some jackets for me. To my surprise," she said feinting shock, "He started to bargain with me. If he acted as a model for my boyfriend, what would he get out of it?"

Gloria and Stacey made their enjoyment of the story obvious with the little sounds they made. Frank listened quietly and occasionally shook his head. His two friends chuckled at their friend's obvious discomfort and would have taken notes if they had the chance. This story was going to play well in the firehouse. Stacey knew Jack would see to that.

Chingli took a breath and then went on, "I told him it was not for a boyfriend, just a friend, but that I would give him *huaqiao* discount tickets, overseas Chinese tickets they give at the China Art Stores. He said the only thing he was interested in buying was dinner for me." The girls reacted to the last sentence with mock indignation. Frank just looked at the ceiling and muttered something about wishing he had been warned about this trial.

"I could not believe I understood his English, so I switched to French and asked Sally to translate for me. When she did I asked if this was an American custom. She said no, it was exceptional, but

Frank was an exceptional man." After hearing this, Frank began to turn red while his friends laughed.

"Of course, my poor husband did not understand any of this because it was all spoken in French. I asked Sally why she thought he was exceptional and she told me about their sleeping arrangements," Chingli mentioned mischievously. Jack and Ray reacted instantly to her statement.

"Hold it," Jack said gleefully. "What were these exceptional sleeping arrangements?"

"You mean Frank didn't tell you?" she asked innocently. "As Sally explained it to me, they were both a little short of money and so decided to room together. Sally was married, but she felt safe enough around Frank to suggest this arrangement. He was a gentleman the entire time they roomed together, even when they slept in the same bed that first night."

Jack and Ray began to howl. "A perfect gentleman?" Jack asked "How did you know the boy wasn't gay?"

"His manners were gentlemanly, but his eyes were very vulgar." she said, smiling at her husband.

"Frank, your eyes are rated X," Ray shouted.

"You better be careful how you look at me," Jack howled, "I'll slap you if your eyes get fresh."

"Who are you kidding," Frank shot back. "It would be the best offer you have had in a long time."

"Will you guys pipe down," Stacey demanded. "I want to hear the rest of this story."

"Oh, don't worry Stace," Jack reassured her. "I want to hear it even more than you."

When everyone had quieted down Chingli continued, trying to drag the story out as long as possible. Frank's embarrassment made the tale that much more enjoyable. She began again in an abnormally slow cadence, now looking directly at her husband. "So, I agreed to allow him to take me to dinner," Chingli continued. "Providing Sally came too."

"The wolf needed to be chaperoned," Ray said. "Did you require a guard the entire time you were in Hong Kong? Or did you come to agree with Sally that Frank was safe."

"Oh, he was safe, frustrated, but safe," Chingli could not resist putting in her true assessment at the time. Frank squirmed in his place as his friends enjoyed themselves. "This is turning into character assassination!" he said defensively.

"You ain't got no character to assassinate," Jack shot back.

Chingli looked puzzled and said something to Frank in Mandarin. Her husband answered her in that language. "No, it is not an assassination," she said switching back to English. "It is the truth. If you had no character I would not have chased you all the way to America so you could catch me."

The girls laughed loudly at Chingli's concise description of her romance with her husband. Jack and Ray joined in while Frank tried to regain some lost dignity by pointing out that he had made choices on his own and had not walked blindly into a feminine ambush. No one paid attention to his pleads, so he changed the subject.

"Did I tell you I ran into Danny O'Brian the other day?" he asked as if they were just beginning a conversation.

"No, how's he doing?" Jack replied, following his friends lead.

"Not too good. His mom's sick. Gave me the impression he spends most of his time caring for her."

"*Zhenme xiaoshun*," Chingli said approvingly. "Do I know him?"

"No, I don't think so," her husband responded.

"He's very filial," she said pronouncing each syllable of the last word carefully. "Is he married?"

"I warned him about you, my wife. He's expecting you to try and play matchmaker for him."

"I like him already. How come you haven't introduced him to me?"

"Just haven't seen him," Frank answered. "He's an old baseball buddy. Life got busy, so we lost touch."

"Oh, *bangqiu*," Chingli said using the Chinese word for baseball. "You played with him?"

"Well, he was one of the big kids. First he coached me; then we were teammates; and then we coached a little league team together. That's how we spent our summers."

Stacey began to giggle while Frank and Chingli discussed this. She could not help it after the talk she had with Gloria earlier. The subject of boys and their games kept popping up. Gloria started giggling when she saw her reaction.

"What's with the two of you?" Jack asked.

"Oh, we were just discussing baseball before you came," Stacey told her brother with a mischievous smile.

"Stacey!" Gloria chided her friend, a little too quickly.

"Well, we were, Glor," she replied with mocked seriousness, looking at her friend reassuringly. She had no desire to discuss their conversation with the boys.

"I used to play baseball when I was little," Chingli told the group. "I always found the Chinese translation of the name interesting. We didn't call it baseball because that doesn't sound right in Mandarin. Instead we called it *bang qiu*, bat ball. We played it all the time in Taidong."

As soon as Stacey heard the literal translation of the Chinese words for baseball she started to laugh. Gloria tried to control herself, but lost it when Stacey began laughing. Chingli looked at Frank with a puzzled expression. He just shrugged his shoulders and then asked, "What is with you two tonight?"

After they had calmed down, Gloria told her brother, "It's an inside joke." Stacey then began to comment on Chingli's translation. "I like the way you translate it better. It's more accurate. You need bats and balls to play. Bases can be anything, the tree, the rock . . . ."

"The backseat of a car," Gloria interrupted, breaking into laughter again.

"Gloria!" Stacey scolded. If she became any more brazen with her comments the guys would catch on and embarrass them both.

"And we all know how much we like bats and balls," Frank's sister continued, ignoring her friend. The two of them suffered another bout of laughter before gaining control and reverting to spurts of giggles. Their friends could only watch with a puzzled look on their faces. "Your sisters have a problem," Ray told his friends, shaking his head and chuckling.

Stacey walked into the kitchen to get another drink. After having a small cup of wine at the beginning of the evening, she had limited herself to soda. It would not be good form for the hostess to over indulge at her own party. Besides she had wanted to stay alert and enjoy her friends company. Everything had gone well. The guys had been good, no funny pranks or dumb jokes. They even helped clean up, although Ray had not jumped up willingly. Chingli had pointed out that one of the few advantages to marrying a firefighter was that they sometimes helped clean up. It was a rule of the firehouse which occasionally came into play at home. Ray reluctantly joined in the clean up effort after hearing that comment.

Chingli's story had been followed by a rebuttal from Frank, but the damage had been done. The poor man would have to live with the consequences once Jack spread the story in the firehouse. Would Ray pick up on the mood set by the romantic tale of their friends' courtship? Stacey doubted it.

Hearing the real story of how her friends had become a couple and the risks Chingli had taken to pursue her husband had broadened Stacey's respect for the diminutive Chinese woman. Where had she found the incredible strength required to fly half way around the globe to find and attract the interest of an acquaintance? How Frank had been manipulated into a relationship and then marriage remained a mystery. There was more to Mrs. Frank Helms than met the eye; that much was certain. Apparently, Chingli had seen what she wanted and had gone after it or him. "How am I going to get what I want?" was the question on Stacey's mind.

While opening the refrigerator door, she heard the sound of the television coming on. Then Ray called from the living room. "Stace hurry up. I've got a surprise for you." A surprise, what kind of surprise could he have that required the television to be on? Maybe he recorded a proposal and was going to play it back on the VCR. Doubtful, but a girl can always hope.

The late news was on when Stacey returned to the party, so much for a romantic tape. When she glanced at the television Ray was talking with a reporter on the news.

"Isn't that Kathy Stanley?" was the first question out of her mouth.

"Yes, it is. But I thought you would be a little more interested in the handsome chap she's interviewing," Ray replied.

"Oh, he's old news. Is she as cute as she appears on TV?" Stacey asked trying to avoid acknowledging Ray's existence on the picture tube.

"Is she an *ainoko*?" Chingli asked Frank.

"How am I supposed to know?" he answered. "Listen to the report."

"What's an *ainoko*?" Gloria asked.

"Will you listen to this," Ray said in exasperation. "I'm being interviewed about an important investigation and all you girls want to talk about is the reporter doing the interview. And you wonder why it took so long for us to give you the vote?"

"Careful, she'll throw you out," Jack pointed to his sister and warned his friend.

"*Ainoko*," Chingli answered her sister-in-law, "is the Japanese word for an Amerasian. It means child of love. In Japan it's a bit of an insult, but here it sounds nice."

Ray's picture vanished and the news reporter began to summarize the information about the case being reported on. "And so now the police have two shootings where the same gun was used. The only other thing these murders have in common is the fact that fireboxes were pulled in each insistence. Now they must determine if this is a coincidence or is there a serial killer, a firebox stalker if you would, on the loose in Newark. This is Kathy Stanley reporting from Newark."

"It sounds to me like my girl is trying to make a name for herself," Jack said with more than a hint of cynicism.

"We girls have to try harder than you boys to get the world's attention, big brother," Stacey shot back. "It is a viable theory, don't you think?"

"Well, you should ask your other half. He's the one investigating this case. As for me, it's a theory, but viable? Well, I don't know."

"Yes, it's a theory that is being pursued, but it's one of many," Ray answered before being asked. "It could also be a gun that was sold underground and used by two different people for different reasons. Fireboxes are pulled all the time for shootings, as the two firemen here will tell you."

"I know," Chingli said. "He tells me about it sometimes. Although lately I think he has been keeping secrets."

"I have many secrets my wife," Frank answered lightly. "You never know. One might walk up to me some day and say 'Hello, daddy.'"

"Then I will ask this child to take me to its mommy and Ray can figure out what happened to her," Chingli responded in kind to her husband.

"Uh-oh, isn't that assault, Ray?" Jack asked with mocked seriousness.

"Only if this phantom woman and child exists, which I can assure you they don't," he responded with confidence.

"Now how do you know that?" Frank shot back. "Everyone thinks they have my number. Maybe there's a darker side to me that has been kept from you. A side that existed before you knew me."

Jack started laughing, "When might that be? When you were four years old and the terror of your mother's sun parlor?"

"I have to get a new set of friends," Frank said to himself. "Everyone takes me for granted around here."

Chingli turned to Ray and asked, "Do you think this stalker is dangerous for firemen?" She had begun to look tense after seeing the news report.

Ray turned to her and answered in a reassuring tone, "I don't think so, Chingli. There is nothing to indicate this person doesn't like firemen. It could just be coincidental. I wouldn't worry too much about it."

"Do you think there could be a serial killer out there?" Stacey asked. She could see Chingli was having a hard time dealing with what they had just seen.

"I think it's a little early to begin speculating on whether or not we're dealing with a serial killer," Ray said in a tired voice. "That report was pure speculation. The press thinks the term 'serial killer' is fashionable right now, so they put that label on anything that has the least chance of becoming a 'serial.' It's much too early to determine whether or not the murderer fits that psychological profile."

"Chingli, a serial killer is the least of your worries," Jack interjected. "Didn't Frank tell you about what happened at that fire last night?"

Chingli turned to face him and answered, "No, he didn't. Could you tell me?"

Frank appeared to panic. Stacey hoped the beer wasn't beginning to talk. If Jack was going to say something Frank did not want shared it could ruin the night. All she could do was hold her breath and pray.

"Jack," Frank called out to his friend in desperation, "You don't have to try and upstage Ray. Cops deserve a little time in the limelight, too."

"You can have the limelight all to yourself, Frank," Ray groaned. "I want nothing to do with it."

Frank's feeble attempt to change the subject was transparent. Stacey could feel the party tip over the edge of a precipice and plunge into darkness. There was no way for her to retrieve the situation. Chingli appeared more determined than ever to hear Jack's story. "I want to hear what my husband is trying to hide," she said uncompromisingly.

"What makes you think I'm trying to hide something?" Frank asked. "Other than that little Filipino girl hidden in my locker, I am hiding nothing." The attempt at humor fell flat, as his wife pressed Jack for the story.

Stacey gave up all hope of saving the night when Jack made an obvious attempt to get out from between his friend and the woman he married. "Well, we had a fire in a three story frame and it got a little hot on the top floor. I had to come up with a second line to help him out."

She looked at Gloria and muttered "Oh, brother."

Chingli began to get agitated. "No! That is not what you wanted to say before Frank said something," she said adamantly. "I want to know what happened last night!"

It was very apparent that she would not back down on her insistence for the full story. Frank took a deep breath and explained to his wife what had occurred and why it had happened.

Chingli's face lost expression as she listened to her husband's explanation. By the time Frank completed his story her facial expression had become one of resignation. Her hostess began to hope that the evening could be salvaged. If Stacey could steer the conversation to something more innocuous than the firehouse, this would quickly be forgotten. How to get control of the conversation without upsetting Chingli? In the end, she realized it would have to play itself out.

"I understand. Did you rescue the person in the building?" Chingli asked Frank.

"There was no person, just fire," was the answer.

"Then why did you risk so much? What could you gain from putting out a fire in an old building with no person in it?" she asked unbelievingly.

Stacey cringed when she hear Jack jump in to answer for Frank. "That's the way it's done. We're not going to let someone else get our fire."

Chingli looked down at her lap after hearing Jack's comment. Her hands began to tremble slightly. "You think it's a game, a competition to see who can put the fire out first," she said quietly. Frank made a motion to Jack, while Stacey and Gloria sat silently. Stacey wanted to cry out to her brother in frustration, "Will you be quiet!" It was already too late. The damage had been done.

"Why do you want him to stop?" she asked angrily. "He's telling the truth, isn't he?"

"That's Jack's truth," was the reply. "He's still a red ass, still learning."

She shot back, "And you know all there is to know about fighting fires. You're the god of fire now! You think you can't get hurt, right?"

"No, that is not what I said or meant," he responded.

A steely expression came over her face as she stood up. "Thank you for being so honest, Jack. You taught me a lot tonight." Picking up her purse quietly, she turned to face Stacey. "Thank you for inviting me, I learned a lot."

"Chingli, where are you going?" Frank asked with an edge to his voice.

"Home, please don't bother coming back tonight. I may have to get used to being alone," she said bitterly.

Frank stood up and tried to calm his wife, but she stopped him before he could say a word. "I am not a child. There is no need to protect me. I just want to be alone to think about everything I have learned. I don't know if I can trust you anymore. What you consider important and what I consider important are two different things."

"What are you going to do?" Frank asked calmly, making no attempt to change her mind.

She switched to Mandarin and calmly said something, then smiled at the girls and quietly left.

"I can't believe she reacted like that," Jack said. He then turned to Frank, "Sorry about that, bro."

"How were you supposed to know she would fly off like that?"

Stacey couldn't believe how insensitive they were. She turned to face them and expressed her displeasure. "Will you listen to the two of you. You would think it was her fault. You men just don't understand how alone she is or what she gave up. If she were surrounded by her family, maybe she could draw strength from them, but right now she is totally isolated. Surrounded by people she didn't know until a year ago. None of them speak her mother tongue. How can you be so blind to what is going on?" She threw her arms above her head and let them come down to slap her hips as if to add an exclamation point to what she said.

Jack took the scolding from his sister in stride. Trying to add a little levity to a bad situation, he pointed to Frank and said, "But Stace, look at the quality of the material she got."

"Not funny, Jack," was all she said.

"She'll be back," Jack muttered confidently. "She's not going to walk all the way home."

"Don't let size fool you, Jack." Gloria told him. She then turned to her brother and told him, "She's not coming back, Frank. Does she have the car keys?"

"Yes, she made me give them to her. Otherwise I would have had to swear not to touch any beer. No drinking and driving, not even a sip," Frank said laughing forlornly to himself.

"You want to crash at my place or are you going to the firehouse?" Jack asked.

"Too noisy in the firehouse, besides you owe for that masterly performance that put my ass in the dog house." He then turned to Gloria and asked, "If she calls you, could you try to calm her down. Tell her I'm at Jack's and . . . well just tell her I'm at Jack's."

"Okay."

Stacey was fuming after everyone left. Ray had to put the news on. He could not leave things alone and just enjoy the night, had to show off. Now Chingli wasn't talking to Frank. Frank was miserable. Jack and Gloria missed an opportunity to make some kind of connection and she did not feel like even talking to Ray, what a wonderful party.

*　*　　*　　*　　*　　*　　*

Chingli closed the apartment door quietly, walked into the living room, and collapsed on to the floor sobbing. It felt as if the world were closing in around her. Happiness seemed to be poised just out of reach. Taunting her as it eluded every effort to caress it. Was she over reacting? Most firemen retired after decades of service. Why was she so fatalistic? Because Frank had attended two funerals for fallen firemen since she had come to America. When asked how often a Newark fireman died in the line of duty, Frank had told her once every three years as if that were a low rate. Who can I talk with about my fears? She looked at the clock and then walked to the phone. It was not economy time for overseas phone calls, but that did not matter. Frank can pay the premium rate.

"*Wei, mama. Gua she Chingli*. Mama, I almost lost him last night," she said sobbing softly into the phone.

"What? Is he all right? What happened to my Frank?" mama asked anxiously.

"He's fine, not hurt at all."

"*San ba*," mama scolded her daughter, calling her the Taiwanese equivalent of a Bohemian. "How can you frighten me like that?"

"Mama, I'm scared. I love him too much," Chingli cried into the phone. "He doesn't know how much I need him."

"*Aiyou*, how can you complain? You've been married only six months and you love your husband."

She had not thought of how her mother would view her problem. More separated them than a generation. The response coming over the phone made her slow down and think. "Didn't you love papa when you were married six months?"

"Love him? I hardly knew him. We met for the first time the day of our wedding. I did not have the choices you had. No, I did what a filial daughter was expected to do. Your father spoiled you."

"But I'm so alone here, mama," Chingli said, pleading for understanding.

"So alone? Does your husband beat you? Does your mother-in-law humiliate you?"

"No," she answered quietly. Frank's mother treated her like a princess. Always listening patiently, teaching her how to live in America, and supporting her when the pace of life became overwhelming. She never let the thought of domestic violence enter her thoughts. What she had witnessed as a child was sealed in the deep recesses of her mind. Frank was pursued because she felt confident he would not strike her. If she had doubted him, she would not have married him.

"You think you are different than other Chinese women? My marriage was arranged. I was sent to a strange house in a strange town. Your grandmother had to teach me to do everything her way because that was what your father was used to and I had to please my husband. She could be a very stern teacher. That is the lot of Chinese women. You must learn to eat bitterness. I have taught you this throughout your life. How is it you have forgotten? Do not disgrace your family. You must learn to eat bitterness!"

"Why?" Chingli asked in tears.

"Because that is the way of the world. What does your Christian God say you should do when you are scared and alone?"

"You don't understand. He could have been killed last night!"

"Could have, could have, he wasn't. You think I don't understand. What do you know? Your father was a pilot, he could have been killed anytime, but he wasn't. You must learn to stop thinking of all the bad things you fear might happen. *Pwa gei*, do not think such things or they might come true. Enjoy the love you feel for your husband today, instead of sitting in fear of losing it tomorrow."

Chingli spoke with her mother for a few more minutes, before she said goodbye. Just talking with someone in her native tongue made her feel better. Is it the lot of Chinese women to eat bitterness? Generations of women have been through much worse than the troubles she was facing. They had suffered silently. After thinking for a moment, Chingli came to a decision; she would not be silent. Maybe she was too Americanized, but she would not compromise. "I will either be happy or leave," she promised herself. Loneliness was better when it was chosen and much better than mourning.

Chapter Thirteen

Frank pulled into the alley next to Six Engine and parked the car. It had been a roller coaster of a week since Stacey's party. Chingli had called him at Jack's and invited him home at two o'clock in the morning on the night of the party. Her eyes were puffy when he had arrived home, but she did not want to talk. The following day, she remained strangely silent about their disagreements or why she had decided to allow him back. Instead they had discussed plans for graduate school and preparing for the interview at Pace University he had gone to earlier that day. The party had been on the first night of the seventy-two hours between tours of duty. She had two more days to fall in love with him again before he had returned to the firehouse.

Thank God there had been no other "stalker" shootings since his last night. Kathy Stanley's little theory about a serial killer had been sensationalism and was growing stale. Still, when Frank had left for work on his first day back in the firehouse, his wife had refused to look at him. He could thank Jack for that. She had been noticeably tense his two days on duty. The forty-eight hours between the days and nights of this tour were filled with discussions about when he would leave the Fire Department and where they would settle after he graduated.

Before he left for work tonight, she had confessed to phoning her mother after returning home from the party. Apparently, mama had calmed her daughter and given some advice that Chingli thought she could use. He wondered, was it that time healed her wounds or did her mother's advice give Chingli renewed strength to face this world of foreigners. Whatever it was, she had told him as he left tonight that she was going to try harder to adjust to his "lifestyle." Frank was not sure what lifestyle she was referring to, but he had not had time to talk about it.

His mental review of the week completed, he shut off the car engine and went into the firehouse. Clean uniforms were in his arms when he opened the kitchen door. Matt was sitting at the table and could not resist continuing the ball busting that had taken up so much of their time the last two days in.

"Nice clean uniforms for your first night in. Expecting some work tonight?" Matt began. "By the way, who washes the pants in your house?"

"Chingli, why?"

"Just curious. Since she obviously knows which of your buttons to push, I thought she might have you doing the laundry," Matt said in a matter of fact tone.

"No, I'm only allowed to wash the dishes," Frank answered with a chuckle. "She'd never allow me to touch clothes."

"Never, why is that? You screw up her clothes once?"

Frank put his uniforms on the kitchen table and sat across from Matt. "No, just the opposite," he began. "When she was an innocent coed at Seton Hall, she had hand washed two pure wool sweaters that were given to her as a present. These were then placed in a strange machine that is very rare in Taiwan. No one had one of these high tech contraptions when she was growing up," he chuckled to himself. "You know, I asked her how she would know since her nanny did everything for her, but that question was totally ignored. Anyway, the excuse for placing wool sweaters in a clothes dryer set on high heat remains national ignorance of a foreign machine."

Matt was laughing. "The poor little rich girl had never seen a clothes dryer before?" Frank shook his head no.

"Did she ask you how to work it?"

Frank nodded his head no.

"What were the results of wool sweaters in a clothes dryer?"

"Well, you won't find warmer sweaters anywhere. They have an extremely close knit. Of course, they'll only fit a five year old, but them's the breaks."

Matt nodded his head and then asked, "So, why can't you touch the clothes? Does she blame the reduced sweaters on you?"

"No, not at all. She would never blame me for her mistake. The woman does many annoying things, but denying responsibility is not one of them. No, her refusal to let me touch the laundry is based on the premise that if an intelligent, civilized woman like her can blow it, think of the damage a dumb foreigner like me can do."

Jack came in from the apparatus floor as Frank finished. "Look who's here, Mr. Manipulated himself," Jack shouted. "I still can't believe how your old lady blew your image of a man who thinks with the right head. She just wrapped you around her little finger until you put a ring on hers."

"You have to admit he's right, Frank," Matt said chuckling. "She decided on you in Asia and then came half way around the globe to claim her prize."

"Listen to the two of you," Frank said defensively. "How old were you when you got married, Matt? Eighteen, nineteen? You've got to be kidding. At least I held out until my late twenties. As for the wise ass over there, he doesn't know it, but I talked to my sister today."

At the mention of Gloria, Jack's smile became tense and his face began to turn red.

"Looks like he's nervous about what little sister told you, Frank," Matt laughed and slapped his knee. "Oh, it's going to be a fun night; I can see that."

"He should be nervous, but only because I know my sister so well," Frank told Matt before he turned to Jack. "Don't worry, my boy, she doesn't kiss and tell. All she said was 'It was wonderful.' but regional theater, Jack? Come on spring for some bucks and at least take her to Broadway. You're not going to impress her any other way."

Captain Wagner poked his head through the double doors from the apparatus floor. "Who's picking up dinner tonight?"

"Al, Cap," Jack responded. "He should be in any minute."

"Are we going to have enough for Captain Burr?" Wagner asked.

"Captain Burr? Is he abandoning his men to smell a real firehouse?" Jack asked with a light laugh.

"Will you listen to the red ass!" Matt said incredulously. "I'll have you know little boy, that Jim Burr was my first Captain when I came to Six Engine. He also taught the man who wears the bars in this company how to fight fires. Be real careful about what you think of guys from the Burg. Most of them are from Twenty Engine, Six Engine, or Twelve Engine." Matt then turned to face Wagner and asked, "Why is Jimmy coming down here, Cap?"

Before the Captain could answer, Chief Gregor walked into the kitchen. "He's acting Battalion Chief. Chief Heinrich had a class to teach tonight," Gregor told Matt. "Is there enough for him and Scotty?" He was referring to Scott Provost, Chief Heinrich's driver.

"If we need more, Chief, we'll go out and get it," Captain Wagner replied. "Jimmy Burr can eat with us any time."

Frank stood up as the Captain finished and walked toward the turnout locker room behind the kitchen. He still had to put his gear on the rig and check his mask. After everything was squared away on the rig, Frank went upstairs to change. Al was in the kitchen with the fixings for dinner when he came back down.

The conversation around the table as they prepared dinner centered around Frank's problems over the past week. At first Jack and Matt continued the banter of the past few days, then the conversation turned more serious.

"Chief, how does a man go about breaking his wife into the routine of the Fire Department?" Frank asked as he broke the broccoli apart, sounding genuinely perplexed. "I mean, she knew something of what this job was about before we married, but that doesn't seem to count anymore. It's like, it's all new to her."

"Well, Frank," the Chief began as he got plates down from the cabinets, "the God's honest truth is they never really get used to it. You boys have to realize that there is a fundamental difference between the sexes and how they each view the world. Chingli gets upset because she sees what might possibly happen. She's a woman and women deal in possibilities. What you do for a living doesn't bother you because you know that what might possibly happen probably won't. Men deal in probabilities. If you keep that in mind, you'll understand where she's coming from. Not that it's going to change much. I know guys who retired after twenty-five years because their wives insisted they not stay for thirty. It was retirement or divorce court."

"God, that didn't help much, Chief," Frank said after taking a deep breath. "I was hoping American women took it better and I could pick up a few pointers. The possibility of her hopping a plane to Taipei is going to turn into a probability if things keep going the way they are. My little empress is on the verge of demanding I quit the job and we both take up residence in the poor house." Then he raised his voice an octave and tried to imitate Chingli. "'It's better to be poor and together than rich and apart.' As if I'm going to get rich on this job."

"Did she really say that?" Matt asked while he stirred the linguine. "Ah, to be young and romantic again."

"Again? Who are you kidding?" the Captain asked as he completed preparing the garlic bread. "I've known you and your wife for over twenty years. One thing that never even crossed your mind was romance, at least not with your wife."

"African women can be extremely practical," Matt pointed out. "Bring home a pay check, help with the kids, and keep them satisfied and they're happy."

"African women?" Al shot back from the counter where he was cleaning the mess made while breading the veal. "Now I have to call you an African? You've got to be kidding. First you were colored then you were a Negro, then black, now you're African. You still look like the same kid who came on the job with me. Can't you make up your mind what I'm supposed to call you?"

"You can call me 'your majesty', peasant," Matt replied with a laugh.

"Why would you have a problem with that Al?" Captain Wagner asked. "Frank's big problem right now is with an Asian woman. Why can't Matt's problem come from an African woman?"

"And she can be just as big a pain as that little Asian girl," Matt sighed.

"You guys missed the most important thing he said," Jack jumped in with gusto. "'Keep them satisfied' is what the man said counts. So when's your old lady leaving you Matt?"

"Listen little boy. I'm not some inhibited European-American who knows nothing about what a woman needs," Matt exclaimed with mock indignation. "My old lady knows she has a good thing. She's going to hang around a long time." The whole room broke into laughter.

"So, Matt, since you have your wife under control, can you give me some advice on how to handle mine?" Frank asked with the hint of a challenge in his voice.

"Well, I don't know," Matt began, feigning an air of importance. "Since you've gone through the effort to climb to the mountain top, I'll try to pass on some wisdom. Ask away, any question you want."

"How do you keep her from getting so wound up when you walk out the door?"

"You don't. My old lady still gets uptight when she thinks about me at work. She just keeps everything inside," Matt replied seriously. "Although with this reporter going around making up stories, she's been hitting me with all kinds of questions, wasn't real happy with the answers either."

"You really have a special problem, Frank," the Chief pointed out. "Not only is your wife adjusting to a new country, new marriage, and the strange hours of this job, but you've got this reporter going around with her wild theories."

"Tell me about it. I tried to tell her that even if this stalker character does exist, and I doubt he does, he's not shooting at firemen."

"My wife didn't buy it either, Frank," Matt said. "But she's spent years putting up with me and my job, kind of resigned to her fate now." Everyone around the table shook their heads in agreement. Before anyone could say another word, the phone from dispatch rang.

Al had walked over to the table and sat beneath the phones during the conversation. He picked it up before it rang a second time. "The Hayes Homes, 242 West Kinney on a nine." was repeated into the phone. The members of Six Engine stood up and walked to the doors leading out onto the apparatus floor.

Don came down from the second floor as the door started up and the rig's lights went on. "What should I do with dinner?" he shouted above the sound of the engine starting and the rig doors slamming.

Matt leaned over from the back step of the rig to reply. "Al has the veal in the oven, the linguine is on the stove, and the garlic bread is ready to put in the broiler," he informed the Chief's driver. "Give it about fifteen minutes and put the bread in. Drain the linguine and add the gravy. We shouldn't be too long. It's only the projects." The bells began as he finished, then Al put the old rig in gear and pulled out.

Captain Wagner hit the siren and the air horn to clear traffic. Once traffic had stopped, the rig pulled into the far lane and headed down Springfield Avenue. It was no more than fifty yards before the old Mack had to turn onto West Kinney Street. 242 West Kinney was the first of a half dozen twelve story buildings which towered over the small firehouse diagonally across the street.

Chapter Fourteen

Al parked the rig in front of the concrete walkway that led to the building's doorless entrance. The usual debris of discarded furniture, burnt mattresses, and broken glass bottles was scattered about. After the rig stopped, Frank did a quick size-up of the building. They all knew project size-ups were different than those done on other buildings because they included a look for any obviously hostile individuals who might try to drop or throw something. There was nothing unusual on the roof or in the windows facing the street. Smoke was coming from the old incinerator chimney. The incinerators had been converted to trash compactors after Federal clean air regulations went into effect, but that did not change the number of times they responded to the projects for incinerator fires.

Frank went to get his mask from the side of the rig before stepping to the rear compartment that contained the tools needed to deal with project fires. He noticed the Captain glanced at the three of them before reaching into the front seat for the Halligan tool. Frank knew Wagner looked to see if they had thrown on their masks. One of his pet peeves was a firefighter in a smoky building unable to do his job because he did not wear a breathing apparatus. There was a time when firemen were expected to eat smoke, but those days were gone. The masks they wore allowed them to push deeper and faster into a fire building. This may have exposed them to a greater risk of over extending themselves, but a good officer monitored his men and the situation to prevent this from happening. A firefighter without a breathing apparatus would be left behind coughing and heaving up his dinner a floor below the fire.

Frank reached into the side compartment and grabbed the "project" bag. Inside the bag was everything needed to hook up to the standpipes in the building. All the fittings originally in the projects had been made of brass and so had vanished years before, sold for scrap metal by whoever could pry them free. Matt picked up a damp roll of inch and a half line. Jack followed with one additional length in case the closest connection was inoperable. The three firefighters met their Captain at the side of the engine. All four began to walk toward the building together.

"I wonder if they fixed the elevator," Matt said thinking out loud.

"They've only been out a couple of weeks," Captain Wagner reminded them. "It usually takes about a month to get an elevator fixed."

"You mean we're going to have to walk up twelve flights again?" Jack moaned. "I shouldn't have run this morning. My legs are going to be sore after this."

"Will you listen to Mr. Physical Fitness," Frank said. "He'll run ten miles a day, but can't climb a few stairs at work."

"Stick it where the sun don't shine," Jack shot back. "Twelve stories of stairs are not 'a few'."

"That's 168 stairs the last I counted." Matt told them.

"Is that why you're always so quiet when we climb the stairs here," the Captain asked. "You count the number of stairs you climb?"

"Only had to count them once in the past twenty-five years, Cap," Matt replied. "I'm quiet because climbing those stairs makes it hard to talk." They all shook their heads in agreement as they came to the opening leading into 242 West Kinney. There were no doors because they had been ripped from their hinges so often that the Housing Authority had stopped replacing them.

A group of teenagers was at the entrance to the building, standing around smoking and talking. When the firefighters approached a few of them began to complain. "They ain't cleaned out the 'cinerator in a whole week. Can't you firemans do somethin' 'bout it?"

The Captain responded in a fatherly tone. "No, son, we really can't make them clean it out. We can only complain about it being a health hazard. The Housing Authority is in charge of the building."

"Yeah, I know, but they don't do nothin' round here. Don't clean up the garbage. Don't fix the sinks. Don't fix the elevators. Nothin', why we payin' rent?"

The firefighters just walked by shrugging their shoulders. At least they got an answer to the elevator question; it had not been fixed. They would have to walk up.

The smell of urine permeated the stairwell, mingling with the odors of smoke and decaying garbage. It was hard walking up through the putrid smells while wearing turn out gear, masks, and carrying equipment. Matt had weighed himself on a shipping scale when they had inspected a factory once. In full turn out gear, his weight increased about thirty-five pounds. Added to this were the mask's twenty-four pounds and the thirty pounds from the hose. Dragging an extra ninety pounds up twelve stories while dressed in what amounted to a winter coat took its toll, especially since each also worn a helmet. Their bodies could not shed all the excess heat produced by laboring up the stairs through their necks and faces.

"What a smell," Jack complained.

"It'll make a man out of you," Matt taunted the junior man in the company.

"Thanks, but I think I want to go back to being an innocent child," Jack countered.

"Then you would miss all those lovely girls," Matt pointed out.

"Careful, Matt," Frank jumped in. "Don't give him any ideas about other girls. He's dating my sister, now."

"Who said I'm dating Gloria?" Jack said a little too quickly. "We're just keeping each other company."

"'Oh, but it was wonderful,'" Frank said mimicking his sister's voice. "That sounds a little more involved than keeping each other company."

"I have to talk to her about what she says to her brother," Jack muttered to himself.

"I've often wondered how people can live in this mess?" the Captain said quietly to himself. "Someone should do a sociological study on the effects of the projects on human beings."

"Anyone in the projects is desperate, Cap," Matt said. "I don't think they have a choice."

"Remember that lady the other night on Littleton?" Frank reminded them. "She said she was on a waiting list to get into the projects. There are worse places in this city to live than here."

"I can't imagine wanting to live here," Jack mumbled quietly.

By now they were on the third floor landing; all four firefighters were sweating. The chatter died down as the climb took its toll. Their pace of ascent had slowed considerably by the eighth floor. Sounds of boots on concrete stairs mixed with equipment hitting walls and reverberated up and down the stairwell. Darkness shrouded the stairs and landings where ever the lights had burned out. The black soot that clung to the walls from countless fires made the darkness that much more ominous. It also made it difficult to pick out the cockroaches. These were sometimes so numerous that the entire wall would appear to be in motion.

The legs of all four were tired and their breathing was heavy when they reached the tenth floor. Here masks had to be donned because the smoke was beginning to get heavy. Unique to the confined space of the projects, it was a putrid smoke produced by the burning of household trash. This mixture of plastics, paper, rotten food, and soiled diapers let off a blend of gases that could sicken the heartiest of souls.

Upon reaching the twelfth floor, the members of Six Engine quickly hooked up to the stand pipe and stretch a line to the compactor chute. There was no need for a nozzle, instead a bare hose butt was stuffed into the chute and the water was turned on. Frank had to use a pipe wrench to turn on the stand pipe because the stem had been broken by vandals when they had stolen the wheel.

"Don't lean on the walls, Jackie boy," Matt reminded him, his voice muffled by the face piece. "We already have company coming for dinner. There won't be enough if you bring home any uninvited guests."

"I have no intention of playing public transit for any cockroaches," Jack responded through his face piece. "No need to remind me."

The junior firefighter poked the hose into the chute, while Matt and Wagner checked the results of their work on the floors below. It was standard procedure that was followed a couple of times a day. Six Engine was first due at the Hayes and Scudder Homes and second due at the Stella Wright Homes. Each of these housing projects had twelve buildings with two compactor chutes per building. The Housing Authority did not have the personnel to adequately service the compactors, so backed up compactors were common. The one guaranteed way for the residents to clear out their compactor chutes was by dropping a match in them. Then the Fire Department had to respond to put out the fire.

The hose was draped over Jack's shoulder when he walked out of the building. The Captain, Frank, and Matt were a few feet ahead of him. Al was watching them from the side of the rig, waiting to roll the hose. The group of teenagers was nowhere to be seen. As Jack stepped out from under the small roof above the doorway, Al shouted a warning. The moment's hesitation from the yell saved him from being hit by a mop.

Laughter was coming from the roof of the building then someone shouted, "There, firemans, you can use that to clean up your funky firehouse."

They moved away from the building, threw the hose onto the back, and pulled away. Headquarters' acknowledgement of the Captain's radio report came over the speaker dangling above the back step as the rig drove down West Kinney Street.

"Engine Six."

"Received Six. Do you want us to notify Police?"

"Received, notify Police, Six Available at nineteen ten hours. Dispatcher one five."

Matt, Frank and Jack pushed off the back step as Al eased to a halt in front of Six Engine's quarters. Al had stopped in the west bound lane of Springfield Avenue, so the traffic on that side of the street was forced to stop. Matt stood in that lane with his hands held out facing the waiting cars, while Frank and Jack gingerly stepped out into the east bound lane and tried to halt any cars or buses heading for downtown Newark. A few cars ignored them entirely. Then an older gentleman allowed them to step out into his lane. Not until all the traffic had come to a complete halt, did Al pull the truck across the street and begin backing into quarters.

The Captain stood in front of the rig to direct Al into quarters. As they walked back with the rig everyone all began to relax. Frank sometimes wondered which was worse; the projects or stopping traffic. At least no one had pulled a gun or tried to run them down this time. Suburban firehouses were now built so the trucks could drive around to the back of the firehouse and pull into quarters. There was no need to stop traffic or back the rig into a bay that was only six inches wider than the truck.

Frank waited for the Captain so he could walk back in with him. Since the thought about how long this crew would be together had crossed his mind, the firefighter had wanted to ask his captain for an opinion.

"Cap, do you ever think of leaving the job?"

"Frank, I think about retiring all the time," Wagner replied as they strolled onto the firehouse apron. "Why do you ask?"

"It's just a thought that crossed my mind the other night while I was waiting for water."

"You do have the damnedest thoughts going through your mind when you're on some creaky stairs in a fire building waiting for water, don't you?" he laughed.

"Strange, isn't it?"

"Well, Frank. I don't think this crew is going to stay together much longer and I really don't feel up to breaking in a new one, but right now I'm having too much fun. I've got a crew made up of young bucks and old friends, all good people and good firefighters. The Chief and Don are like family and my wife understands me and my job, all of that and a paycheck, too. I figure I'll wait until the Chief goes, then think about it, even with the projects."

"Fair enough, Cap," Frank said with a chuckle. "I have to admit I'm jealous. The thought of leaving terrifies me."

"It terrifies me too Frank," Wagner sighed.

Chapter Fifteen

Al shut the rig down after backing it into quarters smartly. The firefighters stepped around the bumpers and walked to the back of the truck. Turnout coats were dropped on the back step, helmets placed on top of the coats, and boots lined up under them. The Captain placed his coat and helmet on his seat in the engine's cab. His boots were placed next to the stairs so when shoes were shed they did not end up in the path of the rig's wheels pulling out. More than one pair of shoes had been ruined because they were dropped too close to the side of a rig.

Matt started the door down as he passed by the controls. Now everyone divided up the small jobs necessary after a run. At this time of year, most of these were normally completed before they left the fire scene. When things began to rain down from the project roof, they always returned to the firehouse before they took care of them.

After changing the air tanks on their masks, Jack and Matt began rolling up the length of hose they had used in the projects. Al put the small rubber hose on the apparatus floor into the booster tank to top it off. Even though he had not pumped at this alarm, the tank leaked so badly he had to keep water running into it continually while they were in quarters. He then went to the far side of the rig and took the Captain's mask out of the compartment. The gauge on the tank read 2500 pounds per square inch, three hundred psi below the point where it had to be changed. Al carried the SCBA to the other side of the rig where he would have room and started to change the tank. Captain

Wagner walked to the watch room and sat at the desk to record the run in the company journal. Frank reached up for his mask, but Jack stopped him. "Go take care of dinner. We're hungry."

Excused from the minor chores that followed a run, Frank headed for the kitchen. Except for the broccoli, dinner was ready. He was going to stir fry the broccoli the way Chingli had taught him, that would take a few minutes at most. Maybe they would be able to eat before eight o'clock. They would need only wait for the arrival of their guests.

"What happened?" Frank was asked when he walked into the kitchen. The Chief and Don were sitting at the table looking up at the firefighter.

"Oh, some wise ass kids thought it was funny to throw a mop at us from the roof," he said as he retrieved the wok from a cabinet. "They said we could use it to clean up our 'funky' firehouse. Almost got Jack with it, but Al was being a good mother hen and gave a shout."

"Cap, you seemed to be reluctant to have headquarters call the cops," Don shouted toward the watch room facetiously. They all knew the Police would not respond to the projects because some kids threw a mop.

"Are you serious, Don?" Wagner responded. "They're too busy to waste their time on a couple of kids throwing something at us."

"That's not their only problem, Cap," Don said with a chuckle. "They could get jumped in those buildings real easy. They're not going to risk responding to some minor complaint when they know you're already back in quarters."

Matt, Jack, and Al walked in with the mask face pieces in their hands, lining up by the door to the bathroom off the kitchen. The room was too small for more than one man to use the sink. Al began washing the Captain's face piece while Matt and Jack waited. "Are we discussing our wayward youth from the projects?" Al shouted from the sink.

"What else?" the Chief responded. "You would think we would be used to it by now."

"I don't know if we'll ever get used to being abused for helping people out," Al said with a hint of anger.

"How many years you been doing this?" Matt asked. "Watch yourself my friend. You're going to drop dead of a heart attack if you can't take this. Either you get used to it or leave the job."

"I ain't gonna drop dead of a heart attack because of some kids throwing things, believe me," Al said as he stepped out and began drying the Captain's face piece with a paper towel. "And I'm not like Mr. Helms over there; I need this job until I retire."

Frank had been quietly stirring the broccoli until he heard Al's jab. "How did I get pulled into your little bitching session?" he asked. "I'm not having any problem accepting mops, brooms, golf clubs, stones, or anything else that's been thrown at us over the years."

"Golf clubs?" Jack asked as he walked out of bathroom and began drying two face pieces. "What are you talking about?"

Matt shouted from the sink in the bathroom. "You weren't here for that little battle. They didn't throw the golf club; a bottle is what they threw."

"A little bitch was swinging the golf club at the Chinese chef's head," Al finished for Matt pointing his thumb in the direction of Frank.

"I should have ignored the bottle, but that's ancient history," Frank said.

"Yeah, you're right about that," Matt replied as he walked out into the kitchen. "It would have saved us a lot of useless trouble that night. All of that hassle and then the cops just released the kid to her parents."

"Live and learn," was all Frank would say as he concentrated on cooking. Distractions could cause him to overcook the broccoli. He hated soggy vegetables. The guys took the face pieces back out to the rig and put the masks away while the Captain finished writing up the book and Frank labored over the stove.

Captain Burr came in as Frank was finishing up the broccoli. Scotty Provost walked in after Burr and stopped in the doorway between the watch room and the kitchen. He seemed hesitant to join in the chatter that began to fill the room.

Frank could understand why. Burr had spent years working with Captain Wagner, Matt, and Al out of this firehouse. The Battalion Chief's Aide probably felt like a cousin watching his uncle arrive home after a long business trip. The fact that the City had just closed his old company would only add to his ambivalent feelings. The scene unfolding before them would never be repeated for Scott Provost.

As he stirred the broccoli, Frank remembered a conversation with Scott a few weeks before. The Battalion Aide had told him how lucky he was to be part of Six on the first tour. When Frank had asked why Scott felt that way, the Aide had given him an analysis of each of the men assigned to Six.

"You're an interesting mix of guys," Provost had said. "evenly divided between the old school and the young bucks. There is Jack Romanov. No doubt about it, Frank. The boy fights fires with a lot of gusto, but little finesse. He's kind of like a young stallion that needs to be broken in properly. You guys do it right and he'll be a good solid fireman. It's up to the three of you. Don't ruin him with bad instructions and don't cut him loss too soon. I've seen more than one kid swagger into a busy firehouse at the beginning of his career, only to slink out a year later because he had been left on his own too soon. If the kid was lucky, there were no burns or broken bones involved. Only a bruised ego and some loss of nerve. Some guys got over it, others transferred to slower companies."

"He won't be cut loss too soon, Scott," he had replied. "The Captain's trained more than one firefighter in his time. Don't worry yourself about our red ass. We'll take care of him."

Scott had chuckled. "I'm sure you will," he had said and then had moved on with his analysis. "I'd place Matt diametrically opposite Jack. Matt Hickerson fights fires with a lot of brains and as little

150

brawn as possible. He was a pioneer of sorts, you know. Spent years as the only black man in this house. It wasn't easy at first. Back then there were few blacks on the job and a lot of animosity towards them. The guys here had agreed among themselves that they would accept him only if he could do the job. Matt proved all the doubters wrong. The black kids coming on the job now don't have to go through anything like Matt did, but some of them appear to be bitter anyway. It seems crazy sometimes. I think the lawyers are dividing the job with their law suits and consent decree. It just makes it more difficult for black firefighters to become part of the firehouse, although Matt probably wouldn't agree. But then he's a social reformer at heart and I'm just a working stiff."

"Well, Matt does think the consent decree is a good thing," Frank had told Scott, "but he also says the kids coming on today are expecting everything to be handed to them. Whenever we discuss this, Al points out that firefighting is an occupation where recruitment is done individually. Firefighters talk guys they know into taking the test, so there is no need for a consent decree. They just have to go out and recruit from among their friends and relatives. Matt doesn't take that well. He says the small number of blacks almost guarantees few blacks will try for the Fire Department."

"They both have a point," Scott said thoughtfully. "Al Grili is one of the old salts around here. To him the Fire Department comes first and anyone saying otherwise had better be ready to defend themselves. He's loud, proud, and would give a fellow firefighter the shirt off his back. His biggest challenge is dealing with you."

"Why would he have a hard time with me?" Frank had asked in surprise.

"Because you don't fit into any mold known to him. It's obvious to everyone that you love the job, but then you use your spare time and even your vacation to attend college. It wouldn't bother him as much if you were studying fire science, but studying Asia? That drives Al nuts. The old fart is more of a 'meat and potatoes man.' He doesn't understand the pleasure you might get out of seeking knowledge for the enjoyment of knowledge."

"Well, it's a little more down to earth than knowledge for knowledge's sake, Scott," Frank said with a chuckle. "I'm planning to move on eventually. I don't know if the Fire Department is a promising career anymore."

"Yes, I know," was the response to his confession. "I haven't finished yet. Then there is Frank Helms, the 'China man'. No matter what you say, I don't think you're long for the job. When you first came here, some of the guys thought you wouldn't cut it, probably why Matt took you under his wing. He had put up with nay-sayers once himself. You turned out to be a natural. It's almost obscene the way you love this job. It's going to be hard for you to leave, but since the City signed that consent decree with Justice, promotions are going to be a chap shoot. You're too ambitious to remain on the

Department. It might be better for you to move on to something else, although Al would get angry just hearing that."

Personalities, Frank thought as he turned off the stove. Every firehouse was filled with a unique mix of them. When the mix worked there was no better job in the world. Guys looked forward to going to work and wives claimed their husbands did not really work for a living. Work was not supposed to be that much fun. When the personalities clashed it was like being in a family on the verge of divorce. And that's what Chingli might ask for if he didn't get this mess straightened out. Maybe Scotty had a suggestion.

While Frank was deep in thought, Wagon leaped off the little carpet remnant that passed as her bed in the corner, ran over to Burr, and began jumping up and down, wagging her tail excitedly.

"I know, you missed me right?" Burr said to the little tan dog that had jumped up on him, leaning her two front paws on his leg. "Well, I missed you, too. Have you been good to the boys or are you still rolling in the garbage across the street?"

"She still in the garbage, Cap," Matt said laughing.

"So Frank told me the other night," Burr said looking up while he continued to pet Wagon. "How is everyone here doing?"

"We had a little run in at the projects, Jim," Wagner replied while walking into the kitchen from the watch room, "but nothing that unusual."

"Are you still looking for some respect, Al?" Burr asked one of the two members of his old crew.

"Me and Rodney Dangerfield, Cap," Al said with a laugh.

"You're not going to get any the way you smell now," Burr commented as he waved his hand in front of his nose.

"Ah, come on Cap, if we took a shower and changed after every run to the projects, we'd run out of clothes and look like prunes," Al protested halfheartedly. Jim Burr knew very well about the projects and the routine followed after responding to them.

The odor of project smoke was quickly overcome by the smell of stir fried broccoli and an Italian veal and linguine meal. Everyone sat around the table and tried their best to look at Frank impatiently. Jack and Al began drumming their fingers on the table top. Frank, ignoring their looks entirely, shut off the stove and pour the broccoli into a bowl. Then he walked over to the table and placed the steaming bowl next to the garlic bread. "Oh, were you boys waiting for me before you ate anything? You're all much too polite." There were a few less than polite comments directed at Frank, but everyone's interest quickly focused on the meal.

As they began to fill their plates, Jack turned to Frank and asked about the interview at Pace University. Everyone wanted to hear how it went. Frank did his best to tell the story in between bites.

"I don't think I'm going to get that scholarship because I won't quit my job," he began. "But don't tell my wife that; I'll tell her in my own way." The last sentence was directed at Jack. He reached for a piece of garlic bread and had another bite before continuing. "They said they could give me some sort of scholarship, which probably means I'll get a break on tuition."

"Does that mean you've decided on Pace?" the Chief asked.

"Well, NYU is too expensive and I'm told I shouldn't get my MBA from the same university where I earned my BA, so Seton Hall would be ruled out. Rutgers is an option, but they don't have any connection with Asia," Frank said, going through the same factors he had discussed with Chingli over the past few days. "Pace doesn't really have any connections with Taiwan, but Chinatown is right there, and they have some out reach programs to help the businesses in the area. Only thing is old Chinatown is all Cantonese, I'd have to go to Flushing to find a Mandarin speaking community."

"So, where are you going?" Al asked impatiently. "You seem to have reasons for not going to any of the schools you've talked about so far."

"I'll probably go to Pace," Frank told Al. "I need the MBA. If I can get experience by helping the small businesses in Chinatown, that's great. Everyone else does it with English, so I guess I can. If the people needing the help can write in Chinese, then we can jot notes to clear up any questions. But what I'll learn and the degree are what count."

"Why are you so concerned with the dialect they speak?" Don asked out of curiosity. "Isn't Chinese basically Chinese?"

Captain Burr jumped in because Frank's mouth was full. "Unless things have changed in the past 40 years, the folks in the north don't understand a word the people in the south say."

"Then why do they say the Chinese speak dialects?" Don asked.

Frank had finished his mouthful by now and so took over from Captain Burr. "Depends on what you call a dialect. Scholars think English is an Indo-European dialect. As far as I'm concerned, if I can't communicate with you, then I speak a different language. Since everyone writes the same way in China, people have this mindset that they must speak the same language, or so it appears to me. But then I'm just a dumb fireman who sees more similarities between the Latin languages of Europe than between the Sino-Tibetan languages of China. The Chinese see it my way. They say there are five major languages spoken by the Han Chinese."

"Slow down!" Al shouted. "This isn't exam week. Give me an example. I don't want to get into any scholarly discussions here."

"Now, how can the man give you an example, Al?" Burr asked. "He can only speak one of the languages of China."

"Never fear, Cap," Frank assured Burr. "My little China flower speaks more than one of those languages." He then turned to Al. "The easiest way to show the differences between two of these languages would be to count, say, one to five. In Taiwanese, which is just Fukianese transplanted from the mainland to Taiwan, one to five is *jit, neng, sa, she, go*. In Mandarin, which is based on Pekingese, it goes *yi, er, san, si, wu*."

"Not even close," Matt said.

Scotty just shook his head. "Who would have thought I'd be sitting in a firehouse in the middle of Newark listening to a conversation about the languages of China?"

Everyone laughed. "If you come to Springfield and Hunterdon you're going to run into all sorts of characters," Captain Burr warned him.

"You mean all sorts of strange characters, don't you?" Scott shot back.

"That's another way to put it," Frank responded, before changing the subject.

"Scott, you're an amateur psychologist. Maybe you can help me out. I'm having a little trouble with my wife. . . ."

Scott held up his hand and moaned. "You're talking to a man who's been through two divorces. Don't go any further 'cause you're wasting your time. I don't even pretend to understand women."

The men around the table laughed in sympathy. They were all just about finished with their meal by now. Jack stood up and began collecting the dishes. Wagon hovered near by, waiting for leftovers to be dropped. Her patience was quickly rewarded by Captain Burr. The little dog went over to her corner to eat the piece of veal given to her.

The Chief and Matt brought the rest of the dishes over to Jack. Everyone else leaned back to enjoy the peace of a quiet night. Dinner had not been interrupted by an alarm for the first time in two months. The entire city was strangely quiet. Matt felt playful, so he turned to

Scott and asked, "Could the department psychologist give us a profile of this stalker of Kathy Stanley's?"

Scott leaned forward, putting his arms on the table, and pointed at Frank. "There's the man you should ask about deviant personalities. He was a cop once, remember?"

Don could not pass up the opportunity to tease Frank about his previous occupation. "Frank left the cops years ago. He was never a real cop anyway. Why would he come to the Fire Department if he was?"

"I did my job well, thank you," Frank replied. "Well enough to receive a few commendations."

The flow of the conversation seemed to inspire Al to ask a question that Frank felt uncomfortable fielding. "So Frank, why did you leave the police and become a fireman? It couldn't have been the superior pay or benefits. The benefits are the same, but you lost the overtime for court. Was it because you realized that this was a superior calling?"

Knowing his answer would not sit well with Al, Frank took a deep breath before answering. "Why did I switch to the fire department? Honestly, because the hours and the time in the firehouse allowed me to study better."

Al had a tight smile on his face as he spoke. "That's a shame. This is the best job in the world and you just want to use it and then leave. If I didn't love you, I'd punch you in the mouth."

"I agree with you, Al," Frank responded. "This is the best job in the world."

Before he could say any more, Al jumped in. "Then why are you studying Asia? You should be hitting the books for promotion or at least helping Miss Stanley catch this stalker." The last part was said with a laugh. In the end, everyone knew that Al accepted Frank because he was a fireman, a good fireman, first. Everything else was secondary.

"Miss Stanley can catch her stalker without my help," Frank replied. "Since the guy exists only in her head, I'd say she had a real good shot of cornering the man. As for studying for promotion, well, I don't see it as being a given anymore. When I first took this job, I was told it was a young man's job and I should either go back to school or become an officer. School looked like a better bet."

The Chief had been sitting quietly listening to the conversation. Frank's last statement appeared to intrigue him. "Now, why do you say school is a better bet than studying for promotion? You're a good fireman and you obviously know how to hit the books. What's the problem?"

Frank was beginning to feel more and more uncomfortable with the way the conversation was going. The problem was the testing procedure would probably be challenged in court and changed. Scott had put it best. It would become a crap shoot. The City and State had agreed to alter recruitment and testing procedures because the racial make-up of the department did not match that of the City's population.

Civil Service would have no experience administering a new type of test and no one would know how to prepare because they did not know what would be on the test. How could he say any of this if front of Matt? Frank knew the debt he owed him. The senior firefighter had taken Frank under his wing when he had first arrived at Six. Much of what he knew about fighting fires came from Matt. Somehow it seemed disloyal to blame his plans for leaving on probable changes in testing procedures.

"They're probably going to change the test procedures, Chief," Frank began reluctantly. "No one knows what type of test it will be, so there's no way to really study. Besides, if the past is any indicator, Justice will have to be happy with the test results or they'll alter them or throw the list out." As soon as the last sentence was out of his mouth, Frank regretted saying it.

Matt jumped in immediately. "So, you're saying that the Consent Decree is forcing you off this job?"

"No! I did not mention the Consent Decree."

"You may not have mentioned it, but it was written all over every word out of your mouth," Matt said emphatically. "All book lists ever did was make sure only the guys who were invited into the good study groups got promoted. And you know no one ever wanted me in any of their groups. What difference does it make if you can remember which book said what, as long as you know what is the right way to do something?"

"Look, Matt," Al jumped in to defend Frank. He knew Frank had too much respect for Matt to discuss this subject honestly. Al and Matt had talked for hours about it and had finally agreed to disagree on the matter. "The kid wasn't around when they wouldn't let you into any study groups. He just wants to be reasonably sure if he decides to work for a promotion, he has a shot at getting it."

"I would have liked the same thing," Matt replied angrily. "But I wasn't allowed. Every man who got promoted off those old lists was in a study group. Every one of them, but I wasn't allowed in."

"But you're in a makeable position now, right?" Al reminded him.

"Yeah, twenty years later," Matt growled.

There was a moment of silence before he turned to Frank. "Look kid, I know you would make a great officer, but things happened on this job years before you came on. That decree is supposed to help make some of those things right. I love working with you Frank, but I can't lie to you. You've got a lot on the ball. Maybe you should take that job Chingli's uncle offered you and make room on this job for someone who doesn't have any other skills."

Before anyone could respond, the phone from the operators rang. Al picked it up.

"Six. Fifteenth and Tenth, got it." As he hung up the phone, he repeated the information from the operator. "Fifteenth Avenue and Tenth Street on a signal nine, pulled box."

The members of Six Engine stood up and headed for the apparatus floor. Don walked through the watch room, so he could lower the overhead door after the rig pulled out. As the door went up, Frank could see it had started raining. That explained why they had been able to eat straight through. Rain always kept the number of false alarms down.

The guys on the back step stood with their backs against the rig, protecting their faces from the rain and wind. Matt turned to Frank as the rig slowed for the light on Springfield and Bergen. "Look, Frank, sometimes I get wound up and say things that I really don't feel," he began apologetically. "My wife usually throws me out of the house when I do it, too. But, well you touched a raw nerve. I don't want you to leave the job. You and your crazy wife make life too much fun and I'd miss having someone who should have a Ph.D. humping hose for me," he finished with a laugh.

"Ph.D., huh," Frank said as a way of accepting the apology. "Doesn't Al say that stands for pile it high and deep."

All three of the firefighters on the back step laughed as the cold rain ran down their necks and backs.

Chapter Sixteen

The young man parked the car in a remote corner of a supermarket parking lot at the edge of the city, turned off the engine, and listened to the new tool that would help in his mission. A portable scanner sat on the front passenger seat of his ghetto mobile. This device would allow him to hear all the broadcasts of the Newark Fire Department. No firebox could be pulled without him knowing. Rain began to fall on the windshield as he leaned over to turn up the scanner volume.

It was hard to believe he was still alive. The mob had not attacked him even after three of its soldiers and one of its officers had gone down before the old police revolver under his seat. The predatory gangs from the center of the city had not tracked him down and the corrupt police, who must have been losing an enormous amount of money because of the decline in crimes that followed the beginning of his mission, were not pursuing him. The chances that none of these powerful forces could easily find and eliminate him were very remote. The only explanation for the failure of the evil forces in the city to silence the gun stalking them was divine intervention. God had approved this mission. With this enlightenment came an inner peace the young man had not known since his father's death. His mission was now a crusade which could not fail. The city of his youth would return. God had preordained it to happen.

The television news had reported the possibility that someone might be stalking the scum who pulled fireboxes unnecessarily. That was a beginning. The message had to get out to the public. Then he would be a hero, a crusader who was bringing peace and prosperity back to the city. That hopeful sign had died because there had been no executions for a week. Little could be done about that. If he were to complete his crusade, then appearances would have to be kept up. Work could not be missed or people would be suspicious. His time had to be budgeted so that he could function during the day and still fulfill the calling that had been given to him.

It took little thought to determine how to divide his time. Those known to him would benefit from the satisfaction of seeing the malcontents of the city fall before his gun. He would strike on Frank's tour of duty and in Six Engine's first due district.

Apparently the miscreants of the city did not like to get wet. There had been no alarms over the system since Six Engine had responded to the projects. Thinking about the radio transmissions he had heard when Six had called back into service only heightened the young man's anger. What kind of animal would attack firefighters after they had extinguished a fire in its den?

The rain was beginning to lighten up when the scanner came alive. "Attention Engines Six and Eighteen, Truck Nine, and Battalion One. Respond on a box alarm, station four four four six, Fifteenth Avenue and South Tenth Street. Twenty twenty-five hours. Dispatcher one five."

The young man quickly started the engine and began the drive into the center of the city. The riff raff had emerged as soon as the rain began to let up. It was doubtful that the culprit who had pulled this fire box would be in the area when he arrived, but these people were like roaches. If there was one in the area, there would be more.

Before the car passed over the Parkway, Six had arrived on the scene and called in a signal three hundred, a false alarm. The young man continued up Eighteenth Avenue, planning to circle the area around the last pulled box. As he crossed over the city line, another box came over the air.

"Attention Engines Six and Eleven, Truck Eleven, and Battalion One. Respond on a box alarm, station one four four six, Fourteenth Avenue and South Tenth Street. Quarters to Engine Six."

"Engine Six responding."

"Six responding at twenty thirty-three, Dispatcher one five."

He made a left onto Thirteenth Street. West Side Park was on the west side of the block, dilapidated tenements and vacant lots occupied the east side. It was a good street to take across town. The engine responded to the gas pouring into its carburetor, pulling the car quickly toward Fourteenth Avenue. The sound of Engine Six responding in the distance came clearly through the moisture laden air. Six would be on the scene momentarily; they probably had not reach Tenth Street when this alarm came over the air. The sound of their siren died down as the scanner came alive.

"Six on the scene."

"On the scene at twenty thirty-four."

"Engine Six to quarters."

"Engine Six."

"Signal three hundred."

"Received. Six Engine reporting a signal three hundred on station one four four six. All chiefs in service twenty thirty-five, Dispatcher one five."

If the same person had pulled both boxes, then they were walking toward South Orange Avenue along Tenth Street. He thought for an instant and then decided to continue along Thirteenth Street, figuring whoever it was would pull another box in the general area of Fourteenth Avenue and South Orange Avenue. South Orange Avenue would be too busy for anyone to pull a firebox without someone seeing them. Fourteenth Avenue would be his best bet.

The car slowed to a crawl after crossing Fifteenth Avenue. He was now a panther on the prowl for its meal. If that prey crossed his path, it would be devoured by the revolver now under his seat. At the corner of Fourteenth and South Thirteenth the car stopped. The young man scanned the area, trying to pick out anyone acting suspicious. The street seemed to be deserted until a man stood up slowly from the front stoop of a building between Twelfth and Thirteenth Streets. He staggered west along Fourteenth Avenue approaching the corner where a predatory angel awaited. Knowing that it would be suspicious if the car did not move, the young man glided across the avenue. After the drunk had crossed the intersection and continued up the street, the car's headlights went dim as it turned around.

The drunk was clearly visible under the street light. When he reached Fifteenth Street, the man stopped at the firebox on that corner, reached up, and pulled it. Then he shook his head from side to side, laughing to himself, and walked toward the stoop of a building. A car without its lights on pulled alongside him before he could sit down. The bullet entered through his smile.

The flash of red emergency lights warned the young man that there was no time for a second shot. The front of a fire truck pulling onto Fourteenth Avenue was visible as the young man turned quickly onto Sixteenth Street and sped away.

The scanner on the seat beside him came alive.

"Engine Six to quarters."

"Engine Six."

"Have the Police and EMS respond to Fourteenth Avenue and Fifteenth Street. We have a shooting victim."

"Fourteenth and Fifteenth, received. While you're there Six, check the box. It's coming over the circuit now."

"The shooting victim is next to the box. Make it a three oh five."

"Received, a three oh five for Engine Six at twenty forty-one."

The young man slowed down when he saw the reflection of Six Engine's lights recede. He did not want the police to pull him over. They might see a sign of God's calling on his face and put two and two together.

There had been no satisfaction in this kill. It was done too quickly. The rush of God's power he had felt in his previous executions had been cut short because Six had arrived on the scene. It was ironic that he had to flee from the men he was serving. Fleeing had made him feel both angry and embarrassed. It was a rather ignoble way to fulfill a mission, but a prophet is never welcomed in his home town. How could he let the world hear his message and still carry on his crusade? The people of the community could not know of his heroic efforts unless an effort was made to inform them.

After turning onto Eighteenth Avenue, the young man spotted a small boy walking through the drizzle, holding something very close to his chest. As he closed the distance, it became obvious that the boy was squeezing a loaf of bread as he walked with his eyes down cast. His mother must have sent him out in the rain because she felt confident the gangs would not molest a five year old. That was what this city had come to, mothers afraid to step out of their front doors for fear they will be mistaken for members of a rival gang. The bad taste of his last kill vanished as the young man saw this graphic example of the city's decline. He remembered why God had given him this crusade. The city would soon be a safe place for little boys to play and mothers to shop. Here was an opportunity to inform the community of God's will. He quickly pulled a ski mask over his head and parked the car under a burned out street light. The boy ignored him as he walked past. "Boy," the young man called out in a southern accent. The boy stopped, looked up, and then froze. "I ain't gonna hurt you, son. I just want you to give a message to your mama. Tell her to call the police and say that the firebox stalker is gonna make the city nice again for everybody. You understand?" The small child shook his head yes. "Okay, now you run home." With that the boy bolted, the loaf of bread still firmly pressed to his chest.

Chapter Seventeen

Chingli heard her husband's tired shuffle coming up the stairs to their apartment. She was sitting quietly on the living room couch, a red silk robe draped over her body. The morning news was on the television. Kathy Stanley's report about the occurrences of the previous night came on again just as she had hoped. The little Taiwanese woman waited patiently for the sound of Frank's key in the door then she picked up the remote and turned up the volume. The timing could not have been better. The sound of the reporter's voice could be heard when the door swung open. Muttering under his breath, Frank stepped in and closed the door softly. The reporter was signing off as he walked over to Chingli. She was sitting with her legs curled up. There was no breakfast on the table and no fire in her puffy eyes.

She picked the remote up from the couch cushion and shut the television off without looking at her husband. What would he say? Would he try to protect her from the truth again? Vowing to be calm, the Taiwanese woman quickly reviewed what mama had said last night.

"*Mama, gua she Chingli.*"

"Is my Frank all right?" were the first words her mother had asked.

Is her Frank all right? What about her daughter? Feeling helpless and frustrated, she had begun to cry. "Mama, he's at work again and I'm frightened. There is a murderer shooting people who use fireboxes and he only does this when Frank is working," Chingli had sobbed into the phone.

"Are you saying Frank is killing people?" was her mother's incredulous response. Chingli had laughed in spite of herself when she heard that question. "Mama, please, Frank would never hurt anyone, but this person might not like firemen."

"Might not like firemen? Who doesn't like firemen? Firefighting is not the most respectable of professions, but firemen are good hearted people."

"Mama! Your thinking is very old fashioned. You are the wife of a soldier." Switching from Taiwanese to Mandarin, Chingli said, "'Good iron is not used to make nails, good people are not used to make soldiers.' Do you think baba is in a disreputable profession?"

"Then you respect your husband's occupation, my daughter?" was the wizened response from her mother.

Finding herself trapped because she had defended Frank, Chingli had changed the subject of the conversation to her husband's future. "Does third uncle still want to open an American office?"

"What, do you think business plans are made and dropped over night?" Mama replied impatiently. "Of course he still wants to expand to America. He is waiting for Frank's answer before he goes any further. Uncle would prefer to have a family member in that office. It would be safer that way. Has Frank made a decision yet?"

"No," Chingli sighed. "He is still thinking of studying for an MBA, before he leaves the Fire Department."

"Didn't you tell me that he could study for a master's degree while he worked full-time for Uncle?"

"Yes, but he wants to do everything by himself."

"By himself? Don't family members help each other in America?" Mama asked in a confused way, "and what of third uncle? He is hoping Frank can help him. Chances of success are much greater in a foreign country if a foreigner is helping. Can't he be filial now and then go out on his own later?"

"I will try to talk to him today, explain that uncle is depending on him, but he can be so stubborn and so proud. I fear he doesn't want to leave his job because he is proud of what he does."

"Proud of being a firefighter when his education would allow him to use his mind instead of his labor? I think you are confused."

Chingli knew better than to try and convince her mother that Americans thought firefighting was a proud profession. "What should I do Mama? How can I convince my husband that it would be best for him to help third uncle and leave the Fire Department?"

Her mother thought for a moment before she answered. "Appeal to his ego. Men are so simple; all you have to do is convince him that not helping uncle would make him look very foolish. Men would rather die than look foolish. If that doesn't work then threaten to leave him. In America wives can leave their husbands so easily, he will give in."

The conversation continued for a few more minutes as they discussed how to convince Frank that it would be very foolish not to take third uncle's offer. After hanging up the phone, her night had been spent worrying and thinking. Could she leave Frank if that became necessary? She became angrier at herself each time she thought about the situation. "Why had I not just stayed in Taiwan? Why chase a man half way around the world?" Gloria had been right the night of the party. Love was a disease and she had it bad. Before meeting Frank, her life had been simpler and completely under her control. Now she felt vulnerable because her emotions were controlled by a foreign man.

After a restless night, the morning news had told her a little boy had been given a message about the firebox stalker. Now there was a name given to this insane person prowling the city. Did her husband know this? She took a deep breath in an attempt to clear her mind and control her frustration.

"How was your night?" Chingli asked in Mandarin. "Any more shootings?" she finished in English.

"Someone hit a drunk on Fourteenth and Fifteenth," Frank responded in a matter of fact tone.

"They shot him! They didn't 'hit' him!" she snapped back angrily.

"Easy, kid, that's what hit means here," he said chuckling quietly. "You asked about shootings, remember?"

"Okay," she answered with a little pout on her face. "I talked with mama again last night. Uncle still wants you to help set up a branch office in America."

Frank picked up his uniform bag and walked toward the bedroom, leaning over and kissing his wife on the head as he passed her. "Good try," he said continuing to the back of the apartment, "but we already discussed that subject. I want to do things my own way in my own time."

"Why are you so stubborn?" she asked impatiently. "In China, family always helps family. You won't lose face and you'll help uncle."

Placing the dirty uniform in the hamper, Frank called back to his wife, "I'll be helping him or will he be helping me?"

"Both and there is nothing wrong with that!" she spat.

"Everything will work out, don't worry."

"How can everything work out if you get killed?"

"So what did Ms. Stanley say?" Frank asked as he walked back into the living room, looking as if he felt a need for more information to avoid a useless argument.

"She said that fire companies heard the shot and saw the car leave the scene. Was Six Engine one of those companies?"

"We were the only company."

Chingli sat quietly for a moment, staring at the floor. "What kind of car was it?" she asked softly.

"I was on the back step, my dear," her husband responded in a calm tone. "Al and the Captain saw a set of tail lights go around the corner, that's all."

"Did you respond to the little boy, too?" she continued to ask questions and stare at the floor.

"Little boy?" Frank asked, as if caught totally off guard. "There was no little boy involved last night. A little girl last week, but no one other than a poor drunk last night."

"A man wearing a ski mask and speaking with an accent stopped a little boy and gave him a message," she continued to stare down, not wanting to look in his direction. Everything was under control now. As long as they discussed this subject, it was best to avoid eye contact.

"I didn't know about the warning. Were firemen mentioned?"

"No, they didn't say anything about firemen, just that a man with a ski mask said the firebox stalker is going to make the city nice again for everybody."

Frank chuckled bitterly. "Yeah, for everybody but the people he hits. That little girl's dad would have liked to share a nice city with his children." He dropped to the floor in front of his wife so she would have to look at him. Chingli immediately looked away from her husband, tears filling her eyes.

"At least this nut didn't threaten firefighters," he muttered under his breath. "Look we're both obviously exhausted. Why don't we go out for breakfast and then come home and get some sleep. We'll feel better with some food and a little sleep."

Chingli gathered the strength to look her husband in the eyes, their blue looking more like a dull gray from lack of sleep. Why did she love him so? Would it not have been better to have walked away from the crazy foreign devil she had met in Hong Kong? Even as the question passed through her mind, Chingli knew it was her destiny to walk through life with the man sitting on the floor in front of her. *Qian shi de guan xi.* It was a debt from a previous life that brought her to this relationship. He was the key to her happiness. Tears began to flow down her cheeks. "*Wo ai ni, Yang guizi Xian Sheng,*" she whispered to Frank.

"And Mr. Foreign Devil loves you Chiu Chingli *Xiaojie.*"

After breakfast they spent a quiet day, resting and avoiding any derisive subjects. The day passed quickly, too quickly for Chingli. When they got out of bed, Frank's immediate concern was to get ready for work. His wife sat on the edge of the bed reviewing the suggestions made by her mother the night before, desperately trying to think of a way to persuade him not to go in that night. When the phone rang, she jumped noticeably.

Frank picked up the phone. "Ray, what's up?" he said with a smile. "If it's okay with the Chief, I don't have a problem." Chingli did not like the sound of her husband's end of the conversation. Why would he need approval from the Chief to get together with his friend? If Frank's boss had to say yes, they were not discussing a friendly visit between friends. This was business and Ray's business was murder investigations.

"Don't drop the ball or you're going to get me in hot water."

She felt a little better after hearing the talk about a ball. Were they talking about a game? It must be played in water, but what kind of game is played in hot water? Then she remembered Frank talking about dropping the ball once when they were applying for her green card.

They had been waiting outside the Newark immigration office in a line that wrapped around the building. He had complained that Congress had dropped the ball when funding the Immigration and Naturalization Service. Why was he talking about playing with a ball when they had to wait for hours just to get forms? She felt the government was treating her like an animal and her husband was talking about sports. When he saw the confused expression on his wife's face, Frank had explained that "dropped the ball" was an expression. It meant that Congress had not done its job.

When Chingli remembered the meaning of dropped the ball, her heart began to beat a little harder. She did not understand what hot water had to do with anything, but it was not a game being discussed.

"Okay, I trust you. See you in a bit."

By the time her husband had hung up the receiver, Chingli was primed for battle. "What job are you afraid Ray won't do and what does 'get you into hot water' mean?" she asked coolly.

"Excuse me?" Frank asked, bewildered.

"What does Ray want you to do?" she went on, by-passing the English lesson. Frank hesitated a moment and then answered,

"My old sergeant would like me to stop by the precinct on the way into work."

"For what?"

"To talk about this stalker thing, I guess."

"No! You cannot," Chingli shouted. "You can't make up your mind, can you? Are you a fireman or a policeman?"

"I can make up my mind, thank you," Frank responded defensively. "I am a firefighter, but I am also a civil servant. Look, they don't want me to wear a gun, they probably just want information."

She swore in Taiwanese at him, before responding. "Don't want you to have a gun, is that supposed to make me feel better?" she snapped back. Then, in a calmer voice, she pleaded, "You will have no way of defending yourself, if they make you do police work."

"They are not going to make me do police work. That would be illegal," he reassured her. "I know how these things work. They might ask me to keep an eye out . . . to look closely at what happens in our first due area, that's all."

"Before you said this stalker is not shooting at firemen. He may not be, but I am sure he will shoot the police."

"I am a firefighter, my love, not a cop. It is against the law for a firefighter to do a cop's job. Don't worry," Frank said quietly.

"I am worried. Can't you go on sick leave?" Chingli whispered.

They had had conversations about sick leave before. She did not understand why any firefighter would not go on sick leave if he did not feel well. He had explained that there were unwritten rules of the firehouse. A man did not go on sick leave unless absolutely necessary because it was felt he was screwing his chief and the guys who worked with him. If a firefighter had a reputation for "throwing a shoe" too often, his chief would not take care of him. Any undesirable jobs were more likely to come his way; it would be more difficult to get personal time; and no one would trust him. On a job where trust was the glue which held everything together, those not trusted were ostracized. A man guarded his reputation on the Fire Department above all else. She had told him to marry his job, but leave her alone.

"I feel fine, my wife," he answered softly. "Nothing is going to happen. I'm just going to talk with a couple of old friends and then go to the firehouse."

The anger that she had held in check now took control. "How do you know what is going to happen?" she shouted. "I know why you won't go on sick leave. It's because of your reputation. You care more for your reputation than you do for me!"

"We live on my reputation!" he said a little too loudly.

"Why?" she asked unimpressed. "Won't the City pay you if you have a bad reputation?"

"Life depends on my good reputation. Guys will extend themselves further to pull me out because they know I would for them. They'll push to save a life because they know I'll be there."

"*Fang chou pi*!" she cursed. "I remember what Jack said at the party. You push even when there is only a vacant building burning just for your reputation."

"Look you are having a problem dealing with my job and I'm trying to help you solve it. Can't you see that it's all from the news media trying to make a story?" Frank replied, changing the subject. "This isn't about my reputation; it's about your getting used to the American news."

He was not listening! The news media had nothing to do with it. How could he be so selfish, so blind to her anguish? She was determined not to let him go without a fight. But how does a woman compete with a man's reputation? If her husband was so intent on fighting fires, then he would have to fight a major conflagration at home.

Over the past year, Chingli had studied her husband's weaknesses. Now she intended to squeeze him and make him feel wretched. Maybe she could not stop him tonight, but from this moment her goal was to force him off the job within a year. MBA be damned, he would work for third uncle or live alone.

She stood up and stared up at him, fury in her eyes. "My getting used to the American news? It is not," she screamed. "I am not the one with the problem. Go ! Take your precious reputation and get killed. I will take the insurance money and leave this barbaric country. They can send your pension to Taiwan. "

"Why can't you be more rational?" he asked exasperated.

"Rational? *Shenme yisi?*"

Reluctantly, he responded "Rational means well thought out."

She went ballistic on hearing his definition. "Who is not thinking? You want to go to work with a mad man killing people and calling you to clean up the mess and maybe even kill you," the Taiwanese woman shouted in cold fury. "*Shenjing bing.*" She turned and walked to the bathroom, slamming the door behind her.

Frank cursed her under his breath. There were no options left for him. Placing uniforms under his arm, he walked out the door of the apartment and locked it behind him.

Chingli sat on the edge of the tub, crying. What to do? Who could she call? Who would understand her feelings? She could not leave easily. He had the car.

Gloria, yes, Gloria would know. Drying the tears from her cheeks, Chingli stood up with renewed strength. Why had she been calling mama all this time? Her mother could not understand a foreign man, but Gloria knew her brother very well. She also understood how to manipulate men and how to squeeze them when necessary. Unlike Frank, her sister-in-law knew when to talk and when to listen, when to give advice and when to absorb a sister's anguish. After hearing the apartment door close, Chingli went to the phone.

Chapter Eighteen

The streets passed without being noticed. What does she want, blood? All of that talk and the problem was still there. Nothing had been solved because no viable solutions had been discussed. They had only talked with emotion, not with their heads. A solution to the problem of his wife always anticipating the worst was what he needed.

In the middle of the city by now, he drove past Six Engine and turned onto Hunterdon Street. After traveling a block the car turned onto Seventeenth Avenue. The West Precinct was on the corner of Seventeenth Avenue and Irvine Turner Boulevard. Frank parked the car and walked up the stairs. As soon as he walked in the door, his old colleagues began to bust his chops.

"Look who's here. Hey guys, one of Newark's bravest has come to see if Newark's finest want him back."

"We don't want him. He's been contaminated. Frank, did they really give you sheets and a pillow case when you graduated from the Fire Academy?"

"That's right, Tony," Frank shoot back. "But they were both flat sheets, none of that fitted stuff. We fireman know how to rough it."

Before anyone could respond to that remark, Sergeant D'Amico walked out of his office. "He can't chat with you boys now," D'Amico shouted with a smile, "his chief wants him in the firehouse ASAP. Come on into my office, Frank. Ray and I have been waiting impatiently for you."

Frank walked to the rear of the precinct, glancing around and waving to guys he knew. This building was in no better shape than the firehouses, although it was not quite as old. Budget constraints in the city meant no maintenance of buildings. It showed in the water stains on the walls from leaking roofs and the disrepair of the furniture cramped into the rooms off the hall. Ray was sitting next to the Sergeant's desk reading a memo when Frank walked in the office.

"You made it," he said, standing up and holding out the paper. "I thought you boys in the firehouse came to work early."

"We usually do, but Chingli went crazy on me again," Frank replied before glancing at the paper. It was a copy of a memo from the Mayor's office asking for information on Miss Stanley's firebox stalker. D'Amico sat behind his desk and motioned for Frank to sit across from him.

"So, when are you coming back?" the Sergeant began lightly. "There's no consent decree on the Police Department. You'd be a sergeant before you knew it. Think of the possibilities."

"You've got to be kidding, Sarge," Frank laughed. "Didn't you hear me tell the guys up front? They gave us sheets and a pillow case when we graduated from the academy."

"Yeah, and I visited you in the hospital the following year because you fell two stories when some stairs collapsed in a fire building," Ray interjected.

"Minor cuts and bruises, I was back to work for my next tour."

"You wonder why your wife has a hard time dealing with you? You are one sick puppy," Ray laughed, shaking his head.

"Will you listen to Mr. Homicide Detective," Frank shot back. "Who's the sick puppy around here, me or you?"

"Okay guys, enough," D'Amico ended the banter. "We have to get Firefighter Helms back to duty quickly or I'm going to have to deal with an angry Deputy Fire Chief." The Sergeant pointed at the piece of paper in Frank's hand and said, "You can see we have a problem. The Mayor is pushing for this to be solved pronto. He met with your Chief and my Chief and made it very clear this case has top priority. If people are afraid to pull fireboxes, you boys could end up with major problems. The Mayor also pointed out to my Chief that those boxes are used to report more than fires. They act as a communication link between the people on the street and the City."

"Sarge, do you think this stalker really exists?" Frank asked.

"What I think doesn't matter, but I'll tell you anyway," he began in a tired voice. "If there was no stalker before the news got hold of the story, there is one now. You know we get copycat crimes all the time. Whoever talked to that kid last night thinks of himself as the firebox stalker. Nothing else matters."

"Why do you want to talk with me?" the firefighter asked.

"There might be a pattern developing," Ray answered. "Other than the ones in the Burg, all of the shootings have taken place in Six Engine's district and while your tour has been working. Obviously, we want you to keep an eye out, but what we need is information."

"What kind of information?"

"Where are most of your runs?" D'Amico asked.

"Now you're going to get a firefighter's impression, Sarge. There's no guarantee I'm going to even be in the ball park. Can't you ask Fire Headquarters for an analysis of our runs?"

"There's no time, Frank," Ray stressed. "You know the general area you cover. We only want your company on your tour."

Frank thought for a moment, wanting to give the most accurate assessment he could. He could say where most of their fires where, but these shootings were not occurring at fires. He had never really thought about where they responded for the miscellaneous calls. Taking a breath, he gave his best answer. "The impression I have is between Sixteenth and South Orange and from Bergen west to the city line. That's where we get most of our work. When we pull out of quarters, we usually head west."

"That's a pretty big area to cover in detail," D'Amico said. "Can't you get more specific than that?"

After another moment of thought, the firefighter attempted to delineate a narrower area. "From Ninth Street to West Side Park and between Sixteenth and Fourteenth Avenues, that's the best I can do, Sarge."

"That helps, Frank," D'Amico said as he quickly jotted the information down. "Frank, when you get back to the firehouse, Miss Stanley is going to be there. I'd like to keep your role out of the news, so stay low and make sure you talk to the Chief before she gets to him. Don't want him to spill the beans either."

The three men stood up and walked to the front of the precinct. As the two younger men walked down the front steps, Frank began to shake his head. "Now I have a role in this investigation, do I?" he swore under his breath. "This is not good Ray. If Chingli hears this she's going to hop the first plane out of Kennedy, flipping me the bird."

"I don't believe she would ever be so rude as to flip you a bird," Ray commented lightheartedly. "Get on the next plane out, no doubt, but flip you a bird? I can't see it."

"She's got you fooled, too, does she?" Frank chuckled in frustration.

The two shook hands and Frank got into his car. He pulled away from the curb while Ray walked to his car in the precinct lot. Frank turned onto Irvine Turner Boulevard and gunned the engine angrily. Why had they called him to the precinct? The Chief or Captain should have been there. Just because they knew him did not mean he had the most relevant information. He was no longer a cop. Fire Officers dealt with the statistics Sergeant D'Amico had needed. The Captain recorded all the runs of the company and submitted quarterly reports to headquarters documenting their work. He would have been able to give the informed opinion needed by the police.

The firefighter turned west on to Springfield Avenue and pressed the accelerator down, climbing the hill briskly. Vacant lots and abandoned buildings surrounded the few dilapidated structures still occupied between Turner Boulevard and the firehouse. The projects loomed up on the south side of the street as he came to the light on Springfield and Livingston.

How could Ray and the Sergeant except someone who rode the back step and humped hose into buildings know where his company responded most often? All they could hope for was an impression. Even if the opinion of a particular blue shirt could be considered dependable, Frank was not that firefighter. For the past four years he had sat at the watch desk memorizing Chinese characters, studying Asian history, and writing research papers on everything from English literature to Daoist philosophy. A departmental statistician he was not. Now, a police task force was going to be mobilized based on information given by him. It would be comical if lives did not depend on it.

He took a deep breath to try and clear his head. Was he over reacting because of the argument with his wife? The defensive shouts that he was a firefighter and not a cop reverberated through his mind. He was a civil servant, sworn to protect the citizens of the city. Were they asking more than should be expected of a firefighter? The request was for information only. If there were better sources for the information, there was no time to tap into them. In the end, Frank realized his impression was probably sufficient for the moment.

He stopped for the light on Springfield and West Kinney. It was the last obstacle between the precinct and Six Engine. A news van could be seen parked next to the firehouse as Frank stopped for the red. A quick prayer for the strength to make it through the night passed through his mind. First a knock down drag out fight with his wife and now the woman whose reports precipitated that fight was waiting in the firehouse. If he kept the low profile Sergeant D'Amico had requested, maybe she would not notice him. Chingli would have to be dealt with in the morning. Holding off Kathy Stanley was the primary objective of the night.

When the light changed, the car turned up Sixteenth Avenue and into the side lot. He gathered his clean uniforms and went in through the back door of the firehouse.

Kathy Stanley was sitting at the kitchen table with her back to the parking lot door. Something about the way the reporter was sitting gave Frank the impression she was too comfortable. While her cameraman and soundman were talking in a corner away from the guys, Miss Stanley looked like she was right at home. Just seeing this annoyed him. She was at least partially responsible for his misery and now she was invading the last peaceful enclave in his life. Putting these feelings aside for the moment, Frank walked over to the Chief.

"Chief, can I talk to you?"

"Sure Frank," the Chief responded and then quickly added, "up in my room in a few minutes. Go get changed."

When Frank stepped onto the apparatus floor he almost walked into register forty-seven. The third tour had to change over again. They must have been in a good mood when they were relieved. At least Frank missed the antics of the sometimes cantankerous guys on that tour. Before going upstairs, his turnout gear was placed on the rig and his mask was checked. The Chief was waiting in his room when Frank walked up the steps from the locker room.

"Did you talk with Sergeant D'Amico, Chief?" the firefighter asked.

"Yes," the deputy replied in a tired voice, "and with headquarters. The Captain and I talked it over. Since you came in late, the best way not to raise suspicions is for him to request you write a report on why you missed the time blow. Just try to keep a low profile."

Frank chuckled to himself, liking the idea of fooling the news media. "That sounds like it'll work, Chief. I promise I'll look as contrite as possible."

"Don't get carried away," the older man pleaded as they both walked toward the stairs. "A low profile, remember."

By the time Frank and the Chief returned to the kitchen, Kathy Stanley seemed less relaxed. Frank hoped no one had insulted her. A hostile reporter would only add to his misery. All he wanted was a few questions that could be answered with a yes or no. Then the Director would be happy and they would be off the hook. Too bad he could not steer the interview toward the closing of companies, but that would take an obvious effort and the Chief had said to try and keep a low profile.

Captain Wagner turned to face Frank when the firefighter came in through the double doors. "Frank," he said in a stern voice, "I want a report on why you were late by our first day in."

"Okay, Cap," the admonished firefighter responded before slumping down on the bench across from the reporter. He refused to make eye contact, staring down at the table with a glum expression instead.

"Firefighter Frank Helms," Don began, "this is Kathy Stanley from Eyewitness News. Miss Stanley, the bad boy across from you is Frank Helms."

"Hello, Ms. Stanley," Frank replied, hissing out the Ms. "I will apologize beforehand. I've had a bad day, so I don't know what kind of interview I can give. I'd suggest you stick with the other guys around here."

"Oh, I'm sorry to hear that," Stanley countered. "Since you were the only one who responded to all the shootings, I was hoping you could give me more details."

Frank could not help showing his surprise at her comment. How did she know he had been detailed to Twenty-one the other night? Caution was called for tonight, that was obvious. His answers to her questions would have to be curt.

Stanley looked disappointed for a moment and then just blurted out a sentence that seemed to have no relationship to the supposed reason she had come to Six Engine.

"I've always felt that firemen have the best job in the world," she began awkwardly.

The firefighters chuckled nervously while her camera crew looked up at the ceiling in embarrassment. Chief Gregor signaled to Captain Wagner, trying to come up with a way to move the focus from Frank. The focal point of Stanley's interest slouched a little further down on the bench and muttered, "*Ni zenmo zhidao?*"

Kathy Stanley looked shock and then replied, "*Yinwei, wode baba shi xiao fang dui yuan.*" Frank's response was to stare at her.

"Hold on," Jack protested. "Could you two let us in on this conversation?"

"Oh, I'm sorry," Kathy apologized, turning a little red. "That was impolite, wasn't it?"

Matt laughed, "Don't worry; he does that to us with his wife all the time."

"You been hanging around my wife?" Frank shot back with a laugh, before reverting to quiet caution. He was beginning to have doubts about his earlier opinion of the reporter across from him, but it was better to be safe than sorry. Just because her old man was a firefighter, did not guarantee she could be trusted. The tension in the room began to dissipate with the laughter of the firefighters.

"Where did you learn to speak Mandarin?" Kathy asked.

"Seton Hall University, and you?"

"On my mother's knee. From what Matt," she said his name in a questioning tone. After he responded with a nod, she continued, "From what Matt said, your wife also speaks Mandarin?"

"Yes, among other languages," Frank responded.

"Where did she learn?"

"The same place you did, Mama's Knee U," Frank answered, laughing at his own joke. This brought moans from around the table.

"It's nice to see you two have a common interest," Al interrupted, "but we're still in service and have to get . . ."

"Dinner going," Kathy completed his sentence instinctively. She then chuckled to herself while blushing. "Firemen are all the same."

Frank was the only one who did not look confused. Everyone else became very quiet, not sure how to take her last comment.

"Sorry guys," he said as soon as he realized why they would miss her meaning. "You didn't understand the beginning of the conversation. Miss Stanley's father is a firefighter, but she didn't give me any other details."

"Actually, he's a Fire Captain in New Providence."

When the Chief heard New Providence he asked, "Frank, didn't you say you met the daughter of a Fire Captain from New Providence when you were on that study seminar?"

"Yes, Chief," Frank replied thoughtfully. "Her name was . . . ."

"Jenny Scott," Kathy finished his sentence. "She told me about a New Jersey firefighter on that seminar. Seems he was a trouble

192

maker, always expressing his opinion, even when it wasn't asked for. You're the culprit?"

"If I recall correctly," Frank replied in his defense. "Jenny said I should be a diplomat. Those girls from New Providence are so smart." This caused everyone to hoot loudly.

Frank ignored them entirely. "So my wife was right, you are an *ainoko*," he said before realizing that she might not understand that Japanese term. "That's Japanese for . . ."

"I know," she reassured him, "I speak some Japanese also."

"You learned that from your mother, too?" he asked hopefully.

"Yes, I did. Did you study Japanese as well as Chinese at Seton Hall?"

"No, I picked up a little at my wife's knee," Frank teased.

"Oh, brother," Jack commented. "If this goes any further, Frank, I'm calling Chingli."

"Is that your wife's name, Chingli?" Kathy asked with genuine interest.

Frank shot a look at Jack before relaxing. It did not matter if she knew his wife's name. In fact, it might help. He had to find out where Kathy's mother was from. She apparently spoke both Mandarin and Japanese, implying she was from Taiwan. If Kathy understood some Taiwanese, he could be sure her mother was from that island.

"*Li gong Daigee*?" the firefighter asked with a very poor accent. If she spoke Taiwanese, then she would be a perfect match for Chingli. Her father was an active Fire Captain and her mother would be Taiwanese. If he could somehow cultivate a friendship between this woman and his wife, maybe sanity would return to his life.

"*Tia bo, tia bo*," she answered waving her hand and laughing. "Mom never taught me Taiwanese. That she reserved for talking with her family, although I can scold you in it. Poor dad, he didn't speak anything but English, so he was left out whenever we went back to Taiwan."

"I know the feeling," Frank moaned. "I spent all that time and money studying Mandarin and then went and married a Taiwanese girl. When we went back to Taiwan after we were married, everyone in her family used Taiwanese when they talked to her. They were probably calling me all sorts of vile names and I never knew it."

"And it was all probably true," Al added.

"I never denied I was a vile person," Frank countered. "I just want to be told to my face, that's all."

"Okay, you're a low life, now how about dinner?" Matt reminded everyone.

Jack, Matt, and Al stood up to begin preparing the meal. When Frank tried to join them, Kathy looked at the Chief. "Frank, why don't you go out on the apparatus floor with Miss Stanley. She has a deadline I'm sure and the Director wants us to give our full cooperation."

"Okay Chief. I just follow orders around here," he replied. The last sentence was meant to assure the Chief that nothing about the assistance provided the police would be mentioned.

After Kathy asked Frank about what he had seen when responding to the shootings, she interviewed the Chief. "What has the Fire Department done to try to insure the safety of citizens who need to pull fire boxes and the firefighters who respond to these alarms?"

"Well, Miss Stanley," he replied slowly, "the Department has standard operating procedures that would naturally be followed on every response. Firefighters have not been threatened. In fact as far as I know, there have been no threats given that would imply you should not pull a fire box in an emergency. I would also like to point out that, if these shootings are connected to fireboxes, there were no fires in the area when the boxes were pulled."

The red phone rang as Chief Gregor finished. A moment later, the joker circuit clicked. The camera crew shut off their lights and equipment as Kathy stepped over to talk with them. A voice could be heard talking into the phone on the other side of the wall.

"Sixteenth and Seventh on a box," Don said as he opened the kitchen door.

"Is there a fire?" Kathy asked.

"We don't know yet," the Chief answered.

"Could I go with you?"

"I don't know about that. Why don't you follow if there's a job - - - a fire," the Chief suggested.

The guys from Six were now walking toward the rig. Al hit the button for the overhead door as he walked past. The bells started as the doors began up. Frank slipped his boots on and grabbed his turn out coat. The rig's doors slammed shut and the engine kicked over as his coat slid down his upraised arms.

"Listen to the radio, Kathy," he shouted while reaching for his helmet, "If you hear us call a fire, just go up to the light at the corner by the bank, hang a right and then a left at the next light. That's Sixteenth Avenue. Bergen Street is like First Street, so count up six blocks and you'll be at Seventh. If we have a job, you'll be able to find us from there." Finishing these directions Frank quickly hopped onto the rig. An instant later, the engine was out the door with its siren blaring, leaving a cloud of diesel exhaust behind.

They could see a glow in the night sky off to their right as the rig turned onto Sixteenth Avenue. When they reach Seventh Street, fire was blowing out of the second floor windows of a two and a half story framed building in the middle of the block. Al stopped the rig next door to the fire building and put it into pump. Frank had put his mask on and pulled up his boots in the jump seat as soon as he saw they had a job. He stepped down from the truck, reached for the three lengths of hose stored behind his seat, and flipped a few folds of it over his shoulder. Matt came around to back him up, pulling the rest of the hose out of its bed and dragging it behind Frank toward the front door of the building. Sirens could be heard in the distance over the roar of the engine.

Frank let the hose draped over his shoulder begin to peel off as he climbed the stairs. The remaining loops were dropped on the second floor landing and spread out. There was a space of about three feet by six feet from the stairs to the door of the fire apartment. He could see a glow around the edges of the door.

"Matt, tell Al to wet the line!" Frank called down the stairs. Then there was silence. He always marveled at the contrasts inherent in fighting fires. No more than fifteen to twenty seconds had passed since his ears were being assaulted by the wail of a siren coupled with the blare of air horns. Now he was crouched on the landing of a building abandoned by its occupants. The only sound discernible was the quiet crackle of flames behind the apartment door.

While he waited the few seconds it would take for the hose to fill with water, Frank reviewed the situation now facing him. The fire had vented itself out the front windows of the apartment. There were no reports of anyone trapped. Jack would be helping Al stretch to a hydrant, so they would probably have water before they drained the booster tank. Five Truck was first due here. That meant no repeat of what happened the other night. The roof would be vented shortly, although they would probably have the bulk of the fire knocked down before that. This fire was his; it would be a walk through. He chuckled after remembering that was what he thought the other night.

The sound of air pushing out of the cracked nozzle in his hand told him water was coming. The firefighter put his face piece on quickly, completing the well-practiced drill in seconds. Water sputtered out of the cracked nozzle as he walked to the door. One kick collapsed the hollow core door.

Working the stream off the ceiling, Frank pushed into the apartment. Matt fed line whenever he pulled on the hose, so the only work Frank had to do was fight the hundred pounds of back pressure on the nozzle. As the line moved into the fire room, the sound of water bouncing off the ceiling and walls mixed with the boom of a television picture tube imploding. The contrasts of a firefighter's world were never stronger. They had been preparing dinner ten minutes before. Now adrenalin raced through his blood. Jobs like this made him wondered if he would ever willingly leave the firehouse.

Chapter Nineteen

Don slipped in behind the wheel of the Chief's car while his boss handled the doors. After the car pulled out of quarters, the Chief turned to Kathy, "I probably don't have to warn you, but be careful. It's a tough neighborhood. I wouldn't want to explain anything to your father."

The two men in Kathy's camera crew shook their heads after the Chief pulled away.

"It seems they've adopted you, Kath. How did you pull that off?" her camera man asked.

"It's a long story, Jerry," she answered with a laugh. "Let's put it this way. They didn't have to adopt me. I'm already part of the family. I'm a fireman's daughter."

"I'd love to get some pictures of a good fire," he hinted.

"Okay, if you're willing, I'll tag along. Reporting on this story with a working fire in the background might add just the right touch," she said thoughtfully.

"A what fire?" her sound man asked.

"Let's get in the van, Max. I'll explain there."

After explaining what a "working fire" was to Max, Kathy relaxed for the first time since she had suggested to her producer that she interview the firefighters responding to the shootings. If she had come up with nothing, her credibility would have been lost. The producers knew she was a firefighter's daughter. They would have accused her of losing her objectivity. She had listened to her father preach about the importance of a good reputation to a firefighter. They were not the only ones concerned with their professional reputations. If this story crashed, her reputation would be shot.

As the van turned onto Bergen Street, the reporter was deep into a personal analysis. Had she lost her objectivity? Firefighters had been a fascinating study for her since she was a little girl. What type of person enjoys the challenge of fighting fires, and so many of them obviously did enjoy it. Over the years she had come up with an informal personality type most likely to succeed on a fire department. Firefighters the world over seemed to share certain traits. It did not matter whether they were stationed at the Yuan Shan firehouse near her grandparents in Taipei or at a firehouse outside London. Members of the fire service all followed the rules and regulations of their respective departments and yet retained a certain crass individuality. If you could gain their trust, they would do anything for you, but gaining their trust was not easy. Unless you had fought fires, you would remain an outsider, a guest of a very hospitable family, but still an outsider. The only possible exception to this rule was if you were the daughter of someone who had fought fires. Had the fact that she was a member of a fire service family distorted her objectivity? The reporter quickly came to the conclusion that it had not. This story involved the firefighters at Six Engine more than the police investigating the crimes. They were the ones rolling up to the scenes of these shootings. They were the ones who might roll into a dangerous situation.

The reporter moved onto an assessment of how the interviews had gone so far. The Chief had given a standard interview repeating what the city administration wanted to be said. She respected him for that. Then there was Frank Helms. She could not believe her luck. The one firefighter who had responded to all of these shootings was the same rouge that Jenny had told her about and now he was married to a Taiwanese woman. This was a gift out of the blue. Even if this story did not pan out, maybe she could get to know this couple. New Providence was too far for frequent visits and work took up so much time. It was difficult to have any kind of a social life.

The van arrived on the scene of the fire as the flames were beginning to darken down. They would never get the equipment set up before the fire was under control. It was too small a fire fought by a crew with too much experience. She walked over to the Chief as the last bit of visible flame was extinguished.

He turned to her after completing a radio transmission. "I'm sorry Miss Stanley, but it was only a little fire. Your crew isn't going to get good footage out of this one."

"There is no need to apologize, Chief," she reassured him. "Your firefighters did an excellent job. Now the people who live here will have something to salvage."

"They are going to be here for a little while," he informed her.

"I know salvage and overhaul, right?" she asked.

"Did you study for Captain with your father or just gain this knowledge through osmosis?" Gregor asked with a chuckle.

"Osmosis, Chief?" she replied. "No, mom couldn't help dad drill, so I was elected. Besides that I picked up a lot from listening to all those war stories told over and over again by him and his friends."

"You sound like you are tired of hearing fire stories."

"No, Chief. I didn't say that I was tired, just that I had heard quite a few stories," she corrected him. "As I'm sure you aware, no one can tell stories like firefighters."

"We do have that reputation, don't we," he laughed. "I'm going back to quarters now. Do you want to expand our interview or are you going home?"

"I think we'll go get a bite to eat and then come back, if you don't mind," she answered hopefully.

"If you want to hang out with a bunch of low life firemen, I have no objection," the Chief told her. "Providing you tell us what is on the record and what is off the record."

"That's the most reasonable offer I've had in a while, Chief," she replied cheerfully. "It's a deal."

When Kathy rang the bell to the firehouse on Springfield and Hunterdon, the men were finishing up dinner. Don let Jerry, Max, and her in through the door on Hunterdon Street. The smell of wet burned wood permeated the apparatus floor. She could see the guys had placed their spare turnout gear on the rig as she walked to the kitchen. Frank, Matt, and Al were still at the table eating the last bites of their meal. Jack was rinsing dishes at the sink and the Captain was writing in the watch room. Chief Gregor was nowhere in sight.

Wagner stood up and walked into the kitchen when he saw they had returned. "The Chief and I have been discussing your request to ride in the gig," he started. "The way we see it, if you sign the waivers the Auxiliaries sign when they ride with us, we should be covered."

"You're going to make a television reporter and her crew official buffs?" Al said with a laugh.

"She already knows more than the average auxiliary," Wagner pointed out. "The Chief said she learned it through osmosis when her father was studying. Isn't that right Miss Stanley?"

Kathy was laughing by now. She was to be an auxiliary firefighter; her father would love that. "No, Captain Wagner," she corrected him. "I told the Chief I didn't learn it through osmosis. I learned it by helping my dad study. I would ask the questions and he had to answer out loud. By the time he made Captain, I could go through the Fire Chief's Handbook, the NFPA Handbook, and assorted other books on building construction, supervision, and hydraulics with no problem. Then there were those books from Oklahoma State."

"IF-STA's," Al said as he shook his head in disbelief.

"That's it, IF-STA's," she laughed. "I liked those the best. They reminded me of some of my college textbooks."

"Ho, we have a ringer among us," Matt yelled jokingly.

"You helped your old man study for captain?" Frank asked. "How did you get dragged into that?"

"It was summer vacation after my freshman year. He needed a hand; mom couldn't help; and I was a little bored."

"She was bored, so she studied for captain!" Matt said incredulously. "It just ain't fair."

"I didn't study for captain," was her response. "How could I? I had never even seen a real working fire. I just helped my dad memorize some facts out of books, that's all."

"That's all it takes on this job," Matt said in frustration. "I've seen some real beauties wear gray shirts. Some guys are always checking for extension on the first floor when the fire is on the third." Everyone laughed.

"So, you got drafted because your mom couldn't help or because she wouldn't help?" Frank asked.

"Now that's an interesting way to put the question," she answered in surprise. "It was as much the latter as the former. My mother has had a hard time dealing with dad's job. You see my father didn't get promoted until relatively late in his career because he has a successful business on the side. It still drives mom crazy that he won't quit the Fire Department and concentrate on his business. Her opinion of firefighters is not very high."

Frank smiled when he heard her answer. Kathy suspected there was more to his last question than he was letting on. If she played her cards right, maybe his wife could become someone to talk to about the difficulties she was having with adjusting to being on her own so far from home. The past few weeks had been depressing. Hopefully there was light at the end of the tunnel.

By now Jack had finished with the dishes and had made his way over to the table. When he heard Kathy's explanation of her mother's attitude, he could only mutter, "This sounds familiar."

Kathy looked at Frank sympathetically and asked, "Is your wife having a hard time adjusting to American firemen?"

"A hard time would be an understatement," he replied.

Maybe she could help them as much as they could help her. The joker hit while she was considering this. A round of bells followed. Matt got up and went to the watch room to write in the company journal. Everyone else relaxed. Frank reassured her, "That's a box for Downneck. We wouldn't get it until at least the second alarm."

"Okay, but Jer," she said turning to her camera man, "you had better put your camera into the Chief's car. Max, what do you think, should you try to squeeze in with the two of us or follow with the van?"

Max thought a moment before responding. "I think I should follow in the van, Kath. If these guys end up at another fire and there's a shooting, we'll want to go to the shooting, no?"

Kathy admonished herself silently. Do not lose track of why you are here. The station was not after a story about a fire in Newark. They wanted a firebox stalker. "That's why I love you Max. You always keep my feet on the ground. You follow with the van."

Frank and Matt took their plates to the sink while their guests arranged the equipment they would need and signed the waivers Captain Wagner gave them. By the time the kitchen was cleaned up, it was ten o'clock. There had been a number of alarms since the end of the dinner conversation, but none for Six Engine. The red phone from headquarters rang at a minute past ten. Their short hiatus was over.

Chapter Twenty

"Headquarters to Engine Six."

Frank watched from the jump seat behind Al as Captain Wagner drop his hand from the air horn chain and picked up the radio mike. The roar of the engine that sat between the seats used by the firefighters made it challenging to hear what the Captain said, but the speaker above the engine compartment allowed them to hear what came over the air clearly.

"Engine Six," Wagner replied as the rig stopped for the light on Sixteenth and Bergen. There was no traffic, so Al turned the wheel hard and pointed the rig up Sixteenth Avenue.

"Six, we have several reports of a fire at 272 Ninth Street. There is also a report of a child trapped in the building."

"Six, received," Wagner responded. Then he turned to Al and shouted over the siren, "There's a hydrant in the middle of the block. Stop there," The he turned and shouted, "Jack take the hydrant, but get right back on the rig. If I remember right 272 is that three story brick we inspected last spring."

Al pointed to their left while the Captain was talking. Frank stood up, looked in that direction, and saw a glow in the sky. He reached down and pulled up his boots, then grabbed his mask. Matt, who had been standing the whole time while Jack was pressed into the jump seat, did the same.

"Engine Six to quarters."

"Engine Six."

"We have a fire."

"Received, Engine Six reporting a fire at twenty oh three hours, Dispatcher one five."

Al stopped the rig just beyond the hydrant. Jack wrapped the feed line around the barrel and jumped back on. Matt had slid into the seat, so Jack reached for the mask on the inch and three quarter hose stored behind the jump seats. He wrestled to get the mask on before the rig stopped. Al placed the rig just before the three story brick. Flames were coming from the second floor windows. A woman was standing in front of the building, screaming and pointing toward the third floor.

As they stepped down, a loud clunk told Frank the rig was in pump. Al looked at the speedometer to be certain the pumps were engaged, then jumped down and ran to the back step. He would be on his own for the first few minutes. There was too much fire for a child to still be alive on the second floor, but that would not stop the firefighters from trying a rescue. All three would be making the attempt with their captain. If the child was on the third floor, they had a shot. Al would get a feed line hooked up while the rest of his crew was stretching into the building. Then when Twelve or Eighteen Engine took the hydrant, they could give him water from their tank immediately.

As Wagner came around the front of the pumper, a woman ran over to him.

"My baby, my baby. You have to get my daughter out!"

"Can you tell me where she is?"

"She's in her bedroom. Help her, please!" the woman pleaded, crying hysterically.

"We're going to do the best we can. Where is her bedroom?" he asked as calmly as possible.

"In the back of the third floor, on the right side," the woman answered, calming down somewhat now that there was hope.

"How old is your daughter?" was the last question he had for the distraught mother.

"She's four. I tried to go back there and get her, but I couldn't breathe," she said.

"I know," the Captain reassured her. "You did the best you could. We'll get her out, don't worry."

Four years old, Frank thought as the Captain walked away from the mother; that meant she was mobile. If the little girl woke up, she would try to flee from the smoke. She could be anywhere in that apartment.

Wagner turned to his crew, who were at the side lays of inch and three quarter line. "Stretch two lines in. Try to keep that fire from getting control of the stairway. There's a little girl on the third floor."

Matt and Jack each grabbed a line, Frank backed up both lines as they stretched into the building. It was a straight stretch from the rig to the front door. Since the lines were still dry, Frank had no trouble dragging both out of the beds then flaking the excess out on the sidewalk and up to the front door. The fire was crackling angrily above his head as he pulled line into the front door behind Matt and

Jack. He noticed the fire was going up the back of the building on the way in. Frank pulled more into the front foyer and spread it out at the base of the stairs. He then leaped up the stairs as the Captain followed.

Figuring that it was such an easy stretch and the Captain was in position to pull hose, Frank squeezed past Matt and Jack and made for the stairs leading to the third floor. The door to the second floor apartment was closed. Only a thin fog of smoke hovered in the air around them, so they could coordinate.

"Cap," Frank shouted. "I'm going upstairs. Can you feed line for a few minutes?"

"Watch yourself Frank," his captain replied. "The fire's going up the back porch."

"I saw," he responded before turning to Matt and Jack. "Hold it back from the stairs and I'll get her out." Then he threw on his face piece and went up the stairs. The sound of the door below being kicked in and water flowing followed him up. Heat drove him down as he ascended the stairs.

The mother had said her daughter was in the back bedroom. He had to hurry because the fire was burning from the rear to the front of the building. When he reached the third floor landing, the firefighter saw the door to the apartment had been left open when the mother fled. While he stood in the doorway for a second to get his bearings, the scream of a small voice pierced the air. The girl was in the room he stepped into.

He stepped in quickly and moved toward the rear of the room. Darkness and smoke obscured his vision. As he began to move along the wall to his right, the quiet puff of a flash over came from the back. A quick glance told him time was running out. The rear rooms of the apartment were in flames. Using the light given off by the fire, he surveyed the rear wall and picked out his only hope. There was an open door between the fire in the back and the front room. The heat was beginning to build rapidly. If he could close that door it would give him a window of opportunity to complete the search. The girl was in this room somewhere; hopefully she had not tried to hide from the "firefighter monster" that had come in her front door. Frank crawled along the floor toward the open door.

When he reached the door, the firefighter hesitated for a moment. It opened into the rear of the apartment, so he would have to reach toward the flames to pull it closed. The light from the fire gave him a clear view of the door handle. Lying on the floor, Frank measured the distance to the knob, then quickly sprang up and slammed the door shut. That should buy him some time, but he paid a price for it. His ears took some of the heat now behind the closed door. The girl had enough strength to scream when he entered. If he found her quickly, she had every chance of making it.

Remaining close to the wall, the firefighter started a search pattern towards his left. Gloved hands moved over chairs, knocked over lamps, groped under tables, and finally came to a couch. His left hand was moving along the cushions of the couch when his right touched the now unconscious girl lying motionless on the floor. He quickly picked up the tiny body and moved across the room blindly in what he thought was the direction of the door; the sounds of the fight downstairs guiding him. Out of habit, Frank glanced back as he left the apartment. The fire had burned through the upper panel of the door he had closed moments earlier.

The little girl was limp in his arms as Frank rushed down the stairs. This was the second time in a week he had to contend with the emotional stress of helping a child. They were unable to help the little girl's father the previous week. The firefighter was determined to bring this girl through. Descending the stairs as quickly as possible without risking a fall, he emerged from the front door seconds after scooping up the lifeless body. As soon as he was in fresh air, Frank ripped off his face piece and leaned over to begin mouth to mouth resuscitation. The floor he had just abandoned was now completely involved in flames.

Al left the pump panel to help. He gently took the little girl out of Frank's arms and leaned over to continue mouth to mouth as he walked away from the fire building. Someone brought a cylinder of oxygen and other firefighters from the Rescue Squad wheeled a stretcher over as all fought for the girl's life. Her mother stood motionless, staring at the firemen and her child. The woman collapsed when someone shouted "She's breathing!"

Meanwhile, Frank went back into the building. The third floor was heavily involved and his crew was still fighting hard to gain control of the second. It had taken less than two minutes for this scene to play out. Now the work of gaining control of the fire could begin.

Chapter Twenty One

The old car turned onto Fifteenth Avenue from Twentieth Street. Its driver had been cruising around the area for about an hour. If his services were ever needed, tonight was the night. Six Engine was fighting their second fire since the first tour had come on duty and it was only ten o'clock. The least he could do was clean the streets of the hoodlums who would harass them by pulling malicious false alarms. Is that not the mission God had given him? To defend those who would protect the helpless of the city.

If the firefighters were not grateful, they would have pursued him last night. Six Engine was on the scene of last night's work so quickly. They must have seen his car fleeing, yet they did nothing. There was no other way to express their thanks. The choice not to capture the young man and bring him to the police was a sure sign of gratitude. Frank would have known better than to call the police. A former cop would know how corrupt that department had become. Is corruption why the firefighter had left the police? It must have been because he knew Frank Helms was an honest man.

Smoke from the fire on Ninth Street was floating across Fifteenth Avenue when the car reached Tenth Street. He stopped for a red light on that corner and looked in the direction of the fire. A glow was visible above the roof tops. The scanner came alive while the young man waited for the light to change.

"Deputy One to quarters."

"Deputy One."

"Do you have an ETA on EMS? We have a four year old girl in respiratory arrest."

"We'll call again, Chief."

"Deputy One received."

He felt sorry for EMS. They responded to clean up after his work was completed. That was inherently unfair. His father had always taught the young man to clean up after himself. Then from deep within him came a cry that his father had not cleaned up after himself, but this was suppressed. Even if life was a mess for the family after his father's death, it was not the police officer's fault. The department he had worked for had denied the debt it owed the family of a slain brother. Instead of comforting and aiding his mother, the police brass had dragged his father's name down. Making false accusations and fabricating evidence to support their case. The young man knew in his heart that his father was not corrupt. The police department had been and remained tainted. It had rejected his application for appointment out of fear. Fear that he would prove corruption existed and they would have to vindicate his father's name.

God demanded vindication! The son would be the instrument used by God to sculpt a new city free from crime and corruption. The citizens of that metropolis would then honor him and the memory of his father. He had not chosen this calling; he had only answered it. With these thought racing through his mind, the scanner came back to life.

"Headquarters to Deputy One."

"Deputy One."

"EMS said they will be there momentarily."

"Received."

"Twenty oh five, Dispatcher fifteen."

The sound of EMS responding up Fourteenth Avenue gradually grew louder as he turned north onto Tenth Street, the fire's glow continuing to light up the sky to the north east. A police cruiser was blocking Fourteenth Avenue, preventing the car from turning down toward the fire. Instead, the young man turned left and began to prowl westward on Fourteenth. He now knew where the police were, so he moved off in the opposite direction. His area of concentration tonight would be between Fifteenth and Eighteenth Avenues and from Tenth Street to the city line at Twentieth Street. There would be more than enough time. Six Engine would probably be at the fire for at least an hour. No need to bother them, he could complete his work well before they were back in service.

The car turned onto Fifteenth Avenue behind two teenagers. He watched them closely, slowing down to get a better look. When one of the boys turned around, the young man accelerated a little and turned down Fourteenth Street. How could he stalk them? If they were going to pull a fire box, it would be pulled when no one was in sight. He had the scanner now and so would be able to hear companies dispatched to a pulled box. He could circle around and catch them further down the block.

The job would not be completed next to the fire box, but that did not matter. After last night's work, the entire city was aware of his crusade. The news media would know who had completed the task. The scanner announced Engine Twenty-one had been sent out on a signal five. Over the past week or so the driver of the car had become familiar with Fire Department radio signals. A signal five was a single company response. Twenty-one was up in Vailsburg, they would not be responding to this neighborhood, so he could relax and stalk these youths without worry.

He turned onto Sixteenth Avenue and accelerated. Approaching them from Tenth Street would put his headlights in their eyes if they pulled a box between Fourteenth Street and Eleventh Street. The car pulled over beside a vacant lot next to the building on the corner of Fifteenth Avenue and Tenth Street to wait. It did not take long for the alarm to come over the scanner.

"Headquarters to Engine Twenty-one."

"Engine Twenty-one."

"Can you go in service as Six Engine yet?"

"We're on Eighteenth Avenue and Seventeenth Street right now."

"The box for Fifteenth Avenue and Twelfth is coming in."

"We'll take it."

"Received. Engine Twenty-one in service as Engine Six. Signal five for Twenty-one as Six. Twenty ten, Dispatcher one five."

The car moved away from the curb slowly, as the young man thought. Twenty-one Engine was responding to this alarm from

Eighteenth Avenue and Seventeenth Street. That did not give him much time at all. He had to be decisive! What should he do? His heart began to pound as he weighed the risks and benefits of completing the job. The crusade could be jeopardized if Twenty-one arrived before he could leave the scene. But if he did not hit these two young hoodlums now, the crusade would be forgotten by the criminal elements of the city. Those people lived life day to day. They did not care about yesterday's news. What should he do?

An inner voice told him, "Trust in God." If the situation presented itself, then God had ordained that the youths should die. Accepting this truth gave him an inner peace. The car turned west onto Fifteenth Avenue and the young man immediately began scanning the street for his prey.

The sound of Twenty-one's siren could be heard in the far distance. Time was running out. It was his responsibility to complete the mission God had given him. To fail tonight was to let God down. He now knew that there could be no compromise. No matter what situation presented itself his mission had to be completed. To answer a calling was not always easy, but those called must answer all the same. The car's high beams were switch on as his mind settled on a course of action. No matter how risky this kill would be, it had to be made. These animals would die tonight.

The two boys were standing on the corner of Fifteenth and Eleventh. One was looking at his watch, while the other stood looking silently toward the west. They were timing the firefighters! How quickly did they want the Fire Department to arrive on the scene of their little tasteless joke? Did they not realize how dangerous it was to respond too quickly in the middle of the city? Enraged by what he saw, the man reached under the seat for his weapon of vindication. The scum of the city would run before him; the good citizens would pay him homage; and the politicians would push him to become mayor. All that was necessary for this to come true was for him to be decisive. The adrenalin was pumping through his system as the car swerved toward the corner occupied by the boys.

The car came to a stop, its lights blinding both youths. Neither ran, they must have thought the car holding them in its headlights was an unmarked police car. The young man was infuriated by their supposition. He leaned out the window, tasting his anger and needing retribution.

His heart jumped as he squeezed off the first shot. The animal furthest from him fell. A second shot rang out before the other could flee. These were not clean kills. Since he was not confident of the kills, the crusader emptied his revolver into the two mounds lying on the sidewalk and then threw the car in reverse. He retreated back down Fifteenth Avenue and turned toward Sixteenth at Eighth Street, slowing to avoid drawing attention to himself. A feeling of satisfaction washed over him, as he placed the old police revolver back under the seat. Maybe it was not the cleanest kill, but the power he felt with each discharge of the gun made up for it. The sound of Twenty-one Engine responding could be heard in the background.

The window was rolled back up and the headlights were switched back to low beam. A moment later, the scanner crackled to life.

"Engine Twenty-one as Six on the scene, nothing showing."

"Twenty-one as Six on the scene, nothing showing at Twenty twelve."

"Engine Twenty-one as Six to quarters. Have EMS respond to Fifteenth and Eleventh Street. We have two shooting victims on the ground here."

The young man sat up straighter in his seat, proud of the job he had done this night. Proud that he was vindicating his father's name and bringing peace back to the city. The satisfaction felt was disrupted when he thought about the last two jobs. Fire Department response had been too quick both times. What would happen if the firefighters caught him on the scene and tried to detain him? Which took precedence, the desire to help lighten the firefighters' work load or his mission? The mission was a calling from God! If anyone tried to stop him, they would have to be sacrificed. Any fallen firefighters would be martyrs for the mission. The car turned west onto Springfield Avenue, its driver humming to himself.

Chapter Twenty Two

Gloria stepped out of Stacey's car and reached back in for her overnight bag.

"I'll see you bright and early tomorrow, Stace."

"It will be early, but you won't be bright, that's for sure. The way you said Chingli sounded over the phone, you have a long, hard night ahead of you."

"Even distraught females eventually collapse from exhaustion, don't we?"

"I don't know if I've ever felt the way she does right now," Stacey remarked. "She's a long way from home with nothing but - - - what does Frank call us all the time?"

"Foreign devils."

"That's it, nothing but foreign devils to talk to. Try to show her we sisters should stick together and it's the males who are devils."

"I'll teach her how to pull my brother's strings, so she can get what she wants," Gloria reassured her friend.

"Good, and when you're done, teach me how to pull Ray's."

"If you teach me how to get around Jack, it's a deal."

The two women laughed, before Gloria began to mount the steps to Frank and Chingli's apartment building. While Stacey drove off, Gloria rang the bell and waited for her sister-in-law to answer. It had already been an extraordinary night. Chingli had called in tears, swearing at her husband and pleading with Gloria to come and pick her up. In her anger, she had forgotten that Gloria did not have a car. They had talked for about fifteen minutes, before Gloria understood everything that had happened. She then suggested going to Chingli's. Stacey could join them and the three women could talk. Chingli had agreed without hesitation.

It turned out Stacey had what she thought would be an important date with Ray and so could not make it. She could drop Gloria off at Chingli's and pick her up in the morning. That left Gloria packing an overnight bag in a rush. Chingli opened the door herself instead of using the buzzer. She looked miserable. Her eyes were puffy and red. Her demeanor was dejected.

"Thank you for coming, Glor," she said as the two sisters-in-law hugged on the steps.

"You didn't doubt I would, did you?" Gloria asked in a consoling voice.

The Taiwanese woman shook her head no, then turned and walked into the hallway, motioning for her husband's sister to follow. They sat and talked over tea for a while, Gloria listening as Chingli tried to explain all of her fears and frustrations. She described the increasingly bitter arguments between Frank and herself over the past week, ending with the acrimonious blow out before Frank left for work.

"Why can't he see things my way for once?" she asked Gloria. "Why does he always have to do the proper thing?"

"Chingli, you wouldn't love him if he compromised himself," Gloria pointed out. "That type of man would not have gotten a married woman to room with him in Hong Kong. Would you have flown to America for him if he gave in that easily?"

"I still feel frustrated," Chingli said slowly. "I have decided that if he does not leave this job within one year, I will go home to Taiwan. Then he can decide what is more important, me or keeping this job."

"One year?" Gloria asked. "Are you sure? He can be very stubborn."

"I know," her sister-in-law replied, "But I am persistent and persistence usually wins."

"Persistent?" she chuckled at how well Chingli used English sometimes. "That's one reason he loves you so much, because you're persistent."

There was a moment of quiet while they both caught their breath then Gloria began to coach her brother's wife on how to manipulate him.

"Did you try to go soft on him?" she asked displaying the knowledge of a little sister.

"What do you mean go soft?" was Chingli's reply.

"You know, some tears, a little pouting."

"What is pouting?"

"Pouting is looking sad and lonely."

"What good would that do?" Chingli asked. "He knows I'm sad and lonely."

"Maybe, but that's in his head. You have to get his heart involved," Gloria coached. "He can't resist a pouting, crying female. As soon as I understood that, I could get him to do anything I wanted. Your husband has a hard time saying no to quiet, loving females. Remember, he got his own place, his own apartment, because he was so bad at resisting mom's requests that it was hard for him to study."

Chingli thought about what Gloria said for a second and then smiled. She muttered something to herself in French.

"What was that?" her sister-in-law asked.

"Oh, something I read in French class," the Taiwanese woman said with a smile. "It is from a letter written to Voltaire. How is it said in English? 'Women are never stronger than when they arm themselves with their weakness.'"

They both laughed. "It is so true," Chingli said. "Now that I think about it, Frank always gives me what I want if I ask quietly. But that is always for smaller things," she added thoughtfully. "How am I going to get him to change major plans?"

"Well, we're going to have to try some manipulation," her sister-in-law answered. "That means we have to make him change his mind without him knowing it. You told me before that your uncle had offered Frank a job. What is his reason for not taking it?"

"He wants to do it his way," she answered in a bitter tone. "without help from my family or your family."

Gloria shook her head. The stubborn streak Frank had as a child was still there. This was all coming about because of pride. She could picture Frank, Ray, and Jack acting like idiots at Frank's eighteenth birthday party, singing Frank Sinatra's "My Way" with beers in their hands. That picture alone was enough for her to agree with the Legislature's decision to raise the drinking age back to twenty-one. Men and their pride; may they all choke on it.

"Then we have to convince him of how foolish it is not to take the job offer."

"That is just what my mother said!" Chingli laughed excitedly. Then she calmed down and asked, "How do we do that?"

They had talked for forty minutes straight before taking a break and watching the news. Kathy Stanley had the lead story.

"It appears the firebox stalker has struck again here in Newark," the reporter was saying when the television came on. "Here is what we know at this point. Two teenage boys have been shot. One died en route to the hospital. The other is in critical condition at University Hospital. The firebox a block west of this corner was pulled at about ten minutes after ten. When the Fire Department pulled up to the firebox, it appeared to be a false alarm. Upon further investigation, the two shooting victims were discovered. This marks the fourth time the stalker has struck. At a news conference earlier today the Mayor, Police Chief, and Fire Chief addressed questions about the situation."

A picture of Mayor Andrews came on the screen. Chingli listened intently. Gloria matched her intensity; anticipating questions after the interviews were over. The Mayor gave a political answer in an attempt to reassure his constituents that everything was being done to solve the case. He then turned the press conference over to the Police Chief, who repeated his boss's assertion that every effort was being made to capture whoever was responsible for the shootings. Finally, the Fire Chief made an impassioned plea that the citizens of Newark not become so fearful of using fireboxes that alarms for fires would be delayed. None of these shootings have been connected with a fire, was the final statement from the press conference. Kathy Stanley came back on the screen live after the Fire Chief's statement.

"It is true that none of these shootings have occurred at a fire," she began to summarize. "When I spoke with the Deputy Chief on duty tonight, he expressed the same thought. The citizens of Newark should not be frightened to use the fire box system of the city to report a fire. In fact, the company that normally responds to this firebox was actually fighting a fire when the alarm was received. The firefighters rescued a small child a few short blocks from here at the same time these two boys were shot."

The news anchor, Bob Adams, asked Kathy a question after she had completed her report. "Kathy, how have these shootings affected the firefighters who are responding to them?"

"They are holding up very well, Bob. Although, I have heard implications that their families are having a hard time dealing with their husbands and fathers being so close to the work of an apparent madman. The firefighters themselves seem to believe they are not the targets. The only concern they have in the way of personal safety is any delay in an alarm because of the public's fear."

Gloria noticed her sister-in-law become rigid while watching.

"Do you think she is really an Amer-asian?" Frank's sister asked, trying to draw Chingli away from the news report.

"Is she an Amer-asian?" she answered with a giggle. "You're just trying to distract me. Your brother does the same thing."

"My brother does the same thing," Gloria muttered. "How about we shut off the news and just talk?"

"It doesn't matter now. We already saw what I wanted." Chingli shut the TV off with the remote and turned to face Gloria.

Gloria tried to come up with something to ease her sister-in-law's mind. After what was said the other night, how could she? If her brother was in work, his wife's worry was justified. Before she had a chance to say anything, the doorbell rang. Chingli jumped; uneasiness evident in her eyes.

It took a moment for Gloria to realize why her sister-in-law might be nervous. Frank was in the firehouse. If he were seriously injured or killed the department would send a chief officer to inform her in person. She tried to reassure the Taiwanese woman with a gentle pat on her knee while she said, "Don't worry. If there had been a firefighter hurt, the news would have said something." Then she stood up and walked to the intercom on the wall by the apartment door.

"Who is it?"

"Glor, it's me, Stacey," was the reply in a voice laced with emotion.

Now what could have happened to Stacey? Gloria thought as she pushed the buzzer. Her best friend came up the stairs slowly, visibly upset.

"What happened?" Chingli asked as soon as she saw Stacey.

"I hate him and his job and all the men on the face of the earth!" she replied vehemently.

"I take it your date with Ray went sour," Gloria said.

"Sour, sour! The preoccupied bastard barely paid any attention to me," the little blond told them. "He asked me to a late night dinner, just the two of us. That was so unusual for Ray, to want to do something romantic. The man's about as romantic as a Mack truck." The last words were spit out in anger. "'A late night dinner so we can discuss things,' that was the way he put it. We're having dinner and everything seems to be going fine. He's not saying that much, like he has something on his mind, you know? So I figure he's trying to get up the nerve to give me a ring. Then his beeper goes off and he has to call the office!"

"There was another shooting by a firebox," Chingli interjected. "Kathy Stanley told us about it on the news."

"That's probably it," Stacey sighed, exhausted from her rage and tears. "He came back and said he had to go in to work. I blew up. We had a quiet little argument while he paid the bill. I called him some not so polite names and he left. Thank God I had my own car. I wasn't going to take a ride from him. I'm fed up. Tomorrow he's going to get a very nasty phone call. Put up or hit the road. He can marry his job, just leave me alone." The last sentence brought on another round of tears.

The three women talked after Gloria and Chingli calmed Stacey down. By the time Stacey and Gloria left, they had decided to work together on their respective beaus. The plan was to force Frank to take the job offered by Chingli's uncle, make Ray ask for Stacey's hand, and get Jack to decide it was time to settle down with Gloria. All the members of this newly formed conspiracy agreed that it was a no holds barred fight between them and the men in their lives. None of the three had any intention of losing.

Chapter Twenty Three

Al turned the rig onto Hunterdon Street from Sixteenth Avenue and let it roll the fifteen yards between that corner and Springfield Avenue. The news van was parked on Hunterdon Street next to the firehouse. Captain Wagner hopped off the rig at the corner so he could open the side door. Frank, Matt, and Jack jumped off the rig and walked out into Springfield Avenue. There was no traffic at this time of night, but departmental procedures had to be followed.

The street was deserted. All that could be seen looking up or down the avenue was the flash of blinking traffic lights. The rig backed onto the firehouse apron in front of the Deputy's door. Engine Twenty-one was still in their quarters. As the rig was shut down, the overhead door in front of the Deputy's gig began to rattle, announcing the start of its ascent. All four men walked into the firehouse laughing.

"He said 'Here I go,'" Jack was saying, "then he went and I had to hump the line for him."

"I said 'Here we go.' Not 'Here I go,'" Frank answered defensively.

"Then how come you wouldn't give up the line?" Jack said pressing his point home. "I gave it to you when you came back up."

"I gave you the line!" was Frank's response.

"Yeah, after the fire was knocked down!"

"It was too hot to give up the line. I was taking the pounding, no need for you to take a beating too. I have to save you for my sister, remember?"

Jack swore under his breath. "What kind of excuse is that? You're full of it. Admit you got greedy."

"I didn't get greedy."

"No, he's been that way all along," Matt threw in.

"Will you listen to this," Frank shot at Matt. "I didn't see any magnanimous offer to give the red ass your line."

"Mag who?" Matt shouted with a laugh. "What's you talkin' about, boy? Besides he had his piece of the fire while you were upstairs."

Frank ignored him entirely. "Look, when you're in a position like I was in most guys around here won't give up the line until they run out of air or are ordered out of the building."

"Bull," was Jacks retort. "Just admit you hogged the line." Then he turned to Matt. "And I didn't really get a piece of the fire when he was upstairs. We had to protect the hallway, remember? I couldn't get too aggressive until he came down. Someone had to hang back and you weren't, so I did. "

"I never denied that I had the line for longer than usual." Frank said with a chuckle. "My only defense is that it was too hot to go around being polite and making sure everyone got a piece of the fire."

Kathy was sitting in the kitchen with the guys from Twenty-one when Six Engine walked in.

"It's good to see the arguments are still the same," Captain Burr said with a chuckle. Wagon was sitting at his feet, looking up at him and wagging her tail rapidly.

"Well, Captain Burr," Matt shouted enthusiastically. "Welcome home. I see the mistress of the house is treating you kindly."

"Of course she is," Burr responded while looking down at the little mutt between his feet. "You remember who rescued you from that nasty old fence out back, don't you girl?" The smell of smoke permeated the room as the members of Six Engine sat around the table.

"I hope you boys didn't have to cover for too much while we were gone," Matt said with a smile.

"We didn't even get here before we had to do some of your work," Captain Burr told the firefighter.

"You're kidding, what did you have?" Matt asked with genuine interest.

"Another shooting on Fifteenth and Ninth," Burr said in a tired voice. "Two teenagers, from what Miss Stanley says one was still alive when they got him to College Hospital."

Matt swore under his breath before he remembered Kathy was still there. Frank turned toward Kathy and asked, "Who responded from the Police?"

"Detective Friedrick and his people. The same cast as all the other shootings over the past week."

The guys from Twenty-one gave a quick description of what happened at Fifteenth and Ninth and then got up to leave. "Can't say it hasn't been interesting," Burr mumbled as he rose. "But we old men have to get our sleep, so we're going home."

"You better hurry or headquarters is going to be calling you," Al reminded them. "Engine Twenty-one as Engine Six, take a Signal 9 to the projects. Smoke reported on the twelfth floor."

"That will get us out of here quicker than anything else will," Burr laughed. "I'm not walking up twelve floors filled with compactor smoke if I can help it."

Al picked up the red phone and informed headquarters that Twenty-one was going out of service as Engine Six. He then followed the older men out onto the apparatus floor. After Twenty-one pulled out, he would have to back the rig into quarters.

"Just go up and get changed when you come back in Al," Frank called. "I'll hang down here 'til everyone's cleaned up."

"I'll take that as my cue to take a shower," Matt said as he walked toward the kitchen door.

"Kathy," Max said from the corner where he and Jerry had been talking. "We're going to go find some gas for the van."

"Okay, Max, I'll be finished by the time you get back."

When the doors stopped swinging, the Captain was in the watch room writing up the company journal and Frank and Kathy were in the kitchen. The firefighter knew he had a golden opportunity to learn something from Kathy about how her mother had handled the fire department. "Kathy, could I ask you a personal question?"

She seemed completely at home with them and answered without hesitation. "Shoot, or maybe I shouldn't put it that way," she chuckled after realizing what she had said. "No problem, Frank. What can I tell you? Where I studied? How much experience I have as a reporter?"

"No," he answered hesitantly. "Actually, I wanted to know how your mother handled your father's job."

Kathy started laughing as she answered, "Not well, not well at all. Why?"

"Just thought you might be able to give me some pointers. Your mom and my wife are both Taiwanese. How did your old man handle his wife?"

"There were times when my mother would get so wound up that I thought she would collapse. Dad tried his best to reassure her," Kathy began with a faraway look in her eyes. "But there was only so far he could go with that. Mom came here on her own. She had no family in the States and the Chinese community at that time was much smaller than it is today, predominantly Cantonese, and anyone her age was probably American born. So she was really dependent upon my father for everything. What made it worse was the obvious enjoyment he got from his job. Mom still doesn't understand that. I have to admit I don't either and I've made it a lifelong study. Did I tell you I had a habit of stopping in firehouses where ever I traveled?"

Frank chuckled to himself and shook his head "no" in response to her question.

"I've been in firehouses in Europe and Asia, talking to the firemen and trying to understand what kind of person enjoys going into burning buildings. Still don't have a clue."

"I think you have to experience it to understand," Frank said thoughtfully. He was encouraged by Kathy's openness. Her mother's experience in dealing with the job seemed to be made to order for Chingli.

"Well, then I don't think I'll ever understand because there is no desire in me to get my ears burned for a cheap thrill."

"A cheap thrill?" Frank asked, feinting insult. "Is that how you view Newark's bravest?"

"Bravest or most foolish?" she shot back with a laugh. "My mother always had a hard time choosing between the two."

"You know, talking to you could deflate a man's ego considerably. I was hoping a fireman's daughter would be more understanding."

"More understanding? Don't take anything I've said as a condemnation. It's not, but I still don't understand what motivates firemen. In my conversations with them, I've come up with an informal profile of what it takes to be a good firefighter. I am well aware that not all firefighters love their job the way my father does, but for those who do, it does take a certain personality to enjoy the risks involved."

Frank touched his ears lightly as he thought for a moment. It was an interesting conversation, but would it lead to the resolution he needed? He was pulling relationships, as the Chinese would say, in an attempt to steer this woman toward his wife. Getting an informed opinion of firefighters from someone who was not a part of that profession was a rarity, but he had to remain focused on his problem. If it was not solved, Chingli might be on a plane to Taiwan shortly. "Are my ears that noticeable?" he asked, worried about his wife's reaction.

Kathy leaned toward him as she looked. "Well, if you weren't so fair skinned, it might not be noticeable. They are a little red. Does your wife examine you when you come home?"

"With a magnifying glass."

"Then you're going to have to explain. I assume you anticipate a negative reaction."

"Very."

"Does she have anyone to talk to about this? I mean a Chinese woman she talks with often?" the reporter asked thoughtfully.

"Just her mother," Frank answered. "And she's in Taiwan."

"That's the road to bankruptcy," Kathy chuckled. "There's no Chinese community in the area?"

"There's a fairly large student population at Seton Hall, but most of them are outside born and have to worry about studying, so she doesn't bother them."

"They still do the *waisheng ren* routine?" Kathy asked in amazement.

"Are you kidding?" Frank laughed. "Her cousin came home with a boyfriend whose parents were from Hunan and her aunt had a real bad reaction. The poor bastard didn't know he wasn't Taiwanese. He had been born and raised there after all, but he didn't speak the lingo. That was the last time that cousin came home with a *waisheng ren*."

"Even after all these years, they still consider someone who doesn't speak Taiwanese 'outside born'?" Kathy said skeptically.

Frank shook his head yes before he pressed on with the issue most important to him. "So do you think you could shed some light on how I should handle my wife?"

"Do you think it would help if I talked to Chingli?"

"How could you have guessed?" was the enthusiastic reply.

Captain Wagner stepped into the kitchen from the watch room as Frank exchanged phone numbers with Kathy.

"Frank, I'm going up to get changed," he said flatly. "I'll send someone down to cover for you."

"Okay, Cap. Are we back in service yet?"

"After two working fires before midnight, I think the City can afford to give us a break until we're all cleaned up."

"As long as we don't miss any jobs, Cap, I have no problem with that," Frank replied lightly.

Kathy shook her head when she heard Frank's response. When he noticed the reporter's reaction, the firefighter could not resist questioning her. "And why are you shaking your head, Miss Stanley?"

"I'm jealous of your enthusiasm," she answered. He did not believe her, but accepted the white lie because he thought it would be better not to push the issue.

Frank came down after a shower to find Kathy had left and the two senior firefighters were sitting at the kitchen table talking about him. Since he had the down watch and could only lie in the watch room, Frank had no objection to Matt and Al keeping him company.

"Well, here he is," Al said as Frank sat at the table. "We can stop guessing now and just ask him. The Captain said you were getting very cozy with our guest while we were upstairs. You're too new at the marriage game and too loyal to even think of starting an affair, so what gives? You trying to fix her up with somebody or just exchanging notes on college?"

"I don't know anyone to fix her up with," Frank said with a smile. "And she doesn't know my plans, so that blows those two theories out of the water."

"Then why so cozy?" Matt asked suspiciously.

"Cause her father has been through the same thing I'm getting right now."

"I knew there was something you were digging for!" Al laughed to himself. "You would have really disappointed me if you were just chasing after a skirt, Frank."

"Please, I already have more than enough skirt for one man to handle," he responded in exasperation. "I got Miss Stanley to offer her assistance in calming my wife, although I'm not sure what she will say is going to help."

Al and Matt looked at each other and laughed. Matt leaned back and took a breath before plunging into a counseling session on women.

"You were smart to try and recruit a woman to deal with Chingli," he began trying his best to sound like a sage. "But it's always a gamble even when you know the woman you recruited. Now, you don't know what Miss Stanley thinks of firemen and you're going to bring her in to calm down your wife? Doesn't sound like a sure bet to me."

"Has the wise man chosen to humble himself and come down from the mountain?" Frank asked with a smile.

"Yeah, I'm down here to rub elbows with the low brows," Matt said in the accent of a boxer who had taken a few too many punches.

"Well, anyway," Frank continued with his worries. "I think I know her opinion of firefighters. She thinks we're all crazy."

Al started to laugh when he heard this. "You talked her into speaking with your wife and she thinks we're crazy. I'd say you've got a problem."

Frank put his elbows on the table and lowered his head until it rested in his hands. Swearing softly, the firefighter began to doubt the wisdom of inviting the reporter to speak with his wife. At least she did not speak Taiwanese. He would be able to understand the conversations and could attempt to counter any bad information.

"You're letting the situation get to you, Frank," Matt counseled. "It's tough making decisions that will affect you for the rest of your life. This job is for young men. Just ask my sore shoulders and aching back. You know, if you think about it, you're not the only one putting off a decision about the job. I should have transferred to a slower company years ago. The basic problem is the same. We're both avoiding change. Human beings hate change."

"But you don't have a wife declaring war because you're putting it off," Frank pointed out after raising his head.

"No, but I don't have a future in another profession. You've accomplished a lot over the past few years, Frank. And you did it all with the intention of leaving the job," Matt countered.

"It's not that easy," was the frustrated response. "There are no guarantees."

"There are no guarantees around here either," Matt reminded him. "Look, Chingli would be happy if you left the job, right? Why don't you just take that job her uncle is offering? She's just going to make you feel miserable until you do anyway. Besides, with the City closing companies, there are fewer spots for captains. Your chances of promotion get worse with each company we lose."

"It's not about promotions, it's about a job. This is a good job. Leaving the firehouse is not that easy," Frank started. "Look, you might think my Mandarin is good, but I don't think I speak well enough for business. Besides, I'm a civil service cripple with no real experience in the private sector."

"You're a kid," Al interjected. "How can you have a lot of experience doing anything?"

"Didn't Chingli say your accent fooled people over the phone?" Matt asked.

"An accent and a working vocabulary are two different things. And they taught me Pekingese. I sound like I'm from northern China, not Taiwan. All of her uncle's business associates are from Taiwan."

"So, you sound like you're from northern New Jersey, big deal," Al said with a laugh.

"It sounds to me like you're making excuses so you don't have to leave the nest," Matt said, obviously agreeing with Al's assessment of the problem. "Maybe Chingli is good for you, like the mother bird forcing its chicks to fly."

Frank was tired. He had spent the last few weeks continually bombarded with questions about his future. His only relief had been the firehouse. Now, with even this safe haven gone, the pressures exploded. "Why are you pushing me to leave?" he asked angrily. "You want my spot for the consent decree?" As soon as the words were out of his mouth, he regretted saying them. Matt deserved much better.

There was a moment of quiet before Matt answered in a very controlled manner. "If I thought you were serious, your buddy Ray would have to figure out whether what I did was justified or not."

"Sorry, Matt," Frank said sheepishly. "I've been having a hard time at home. We had a big blow out before I came in tonight. It's getting to be a regular occurrence."

"I know, kid," Matt answered quietly. "Your old lady's been putting you through a lot and I know it's not easy making major changes. Like I said, I should have left this house years ago. Look at the Chief and the Captain. Between pension contributions, union dues, and the cost of their commute, they're paying to stay on the job. You got to take a couple of steps back, Frank. Take a look at what's out there and make some kind of thoughtful decision."

Al and Matt stood up and started to make their way upstairs. Just before he stepped through the door, Al gave Frank one more thought to ponder. "Remember, kid, the City doesn't care. You're just a number to them. That little China doll you have home is probably going to bury you at a real old age. The trick in life is to be happy. If you ain't happy on the job anymore, then maybe you should go."

Chapter Twenty Four

Frank climbed the stairs leading to his apartment with trepidation. He was not married long enough to be feeling this way. Whatever happened to the honeymoon? The thought of talking to dad crossed his mind, but was quickly rejected. His father would advise him to listen to what Chingli was saying and then try to find a compromise. They were down to basics already; how could they find room for compromise? It was either leave the department now or after earning an MBA. There were no other choices. The only bone of contention was the timing.

The firefighter pushed all thoughts of the future out of his mind after reaching the door to their apartment. All these questions receded into the background. Only one question now mattered. How was his wife going to react to his ears? These were now very sore. Thank God he had some burn cream left over from the last time this had happened. Frank took a deep breath before putting the key into the door. It did not matter. He was too tired to fight. Besides, today could not possibly be any worse than yesterday and he had muddled through that nightmare. Turning the key, the firefighter gently pushed open the door. His hopes now rested on Chingli and Kathy Stanley hitting it off. Hopefully, his wild card would not turn on him and become a trump for Chingli.

As he stepped into the dinette, Frank remembered what Al had said the night before. "If you're not happy on the job, maybe you should leave." The firefighter was happy with the job; it was home that was the problem. Chingli was sitting on the couch with her legs curled up when her husband opened the door.

"Are you talking to me this morning?" Frank asked with a boyish grin.

"I guess," his wife responded coyly. "You didn't go to that shooting last night, did you?"

"No, we were busy fighting a fire. You watched Kathy Stanley's report?" he asked while walking toward the bathroom. The cream for his ears was in the medicine chest above the sink.

"Yes," Chingli answered without looking at her husband.

The firefighter carried his dirty clothes past his wife quickly, hoping she did not notice the redness of his ears. The effort was really a waste of time. Chingli would notice soon enough, but Frank just wanted to begin the day with as little excitement as possible. After the bathroom door was closed, dirty uniforms were dropped in the hamper. The cream was then retrieved from the medicine cabinet and applied very gingerly to his sore ears. From what could be seen in the bathroom mirror, the burns were only a bad first degree. In a couple of days things might clear up. Satisfied that his ears did not look too bad, Frank opened the door and went out to face his empress.

Chingli watched very closely when her husband came out. His effort at keeping a distance between them was obvious.

"What's the matter?" she asked playfully. "Are you afraid I'm going to hit you?"

"Why would you ask that?" Frank replied with a strained smile.

"Because you're so far away. I promise to try and be nice."

The firefighter could see there was no way to hide his ears, so he decided to gamble and lay it all out on the table. "Well, my ears got a little singed last night at that job and I didn't want to worry you."

"Singed?" she asked not recognizing the word.

"Yes, burned, but just a little," he answered hesitantly.

As soon as she understood what her husband meant, Chingli turned cool. Looking down at the floor she asked without emotion, "What happened?"

"Didn't Kathy Stanley tell you?"

She shook her head "no", so he began to explain. "We had a fire in a three story brick with a little girl trapped on the third floor. Matt and Jack held the fire while I went to the third floor to search for the kid. It got very hot, but I couldn't back down because there was a little girl up there. I was her only hope."

"Now that you said that, Kathy Stanley did report that a child was rescued from a fire a few blocks from the shooting. Did you save the child?"

"Yeah, I got her out. She's going to be fine," he said with a grin.

Chingli stood up and walked over to her husband. Tears began to fall down her cheeks as she reached out to hug him. "I'm proud of you," she whispered. "For a life, burned ears are not bad."

"Hey," Frank whispered reassuringly. "Everything will be okay."

"When you are safe, then I will be happy," was her reply.

"I found out she is an *ainoko*," he said, trying to cheer her up.

"Who is an *ainoko*?" Chingli asked, puzzled.

"Kathy Stanley. Her mother is from Taiwan and her father is from Rhode Island."

"How do you know that?" his wife queried, confusion drying her tears.

"Oh, that's not all. It gets better," Frank said with a laugh. "Her father is a fire captain in New Providence."

"*Fang chou pi,*" she replied in disbelief. "You're making it up to tease me. How do you know?"

"Miss Stanley told me, herself," he said barely able to contain himself.

"You met her?" Chingli asked, before she became suspicious. "I thought you were at a fire. Her report came from where those two boys were shot."

"She was in the firehouse when I got there," he said before realizing it could lead to questions about the precinct. That was a subject best left buried.

She hesitated for a moment, as if making a decision not to bring up anything controversial and then asked, "What was she like?"

"I've forgiven her for complicating my life."

"Complicating your life? What do you mean by that?" his wife asked genuinely curious.

Frank slowed himself down; doubting Chingli would react well to his blaming Kathy Stanley for all the troubles they had been going through since the reports on this stalker had first aired. He chose a playful, but safe course instead. "Since you first saw her, the question has been 'Is she an *ainoko*?' It took me a long time to answer it."

"Are you sure that's what you meant?"

"Yes, honest," he answered as genuinely as possible before changing the subject. "Would you like to meet her? She said she would like to meet you."

"Why would she want to meet me?"

"I don't know. Maybe she wants a foster mother. Rhode Island is too far away to drive home every night."

"What kind of mother?"

"A substitute mom," he answered playfully. "You know, someone to step in and take her mother's place for a little bit."

"And you can arrange this?"

"She requested it. Even gave me her phone number for you."

"That might be fun," she answered. "Maybe Mrs. Stanley could tell me how to handle American firemen."

"Handle American firemen? You seem to be doing a good job of it now," Frank said cheerfully, shaking his head. "Okay, now we're both tired and hungry. Which do you want to do, eat or sleep?"

Chingli chuckled and reached up to pull the hair pin out of the knot of black silken hair on top of her head. Her hair fell to the middle of her back, but she quickly pulled it over her shoulders and draped it down her chest. Frank stood mesmerized as his wife dropped her robe to the floor. Chingli's beauty seemed to swirl around him causing the details of the apartment to fade. The sheen of her dark hair covered her breasts as if teasing him. He remembered how even the Chinese commented on how black her hair was. The thought crossed his mind that Confucius had been right. Women were the root of all evil. Men could be driven insane by the tiny creature who stood before him. "Should I make breakfast first or do you have some energy left for me?," he heard her say. It took a moment to realize he was required to give her an answer.

"I think I could muster up a few extra breaths for my lady." he replied quietly. "I showered before I left the firehouse, but if you want I can rinse myself off again."

"No," she said breathlessly. "I don't want to wait. Besides then your hair will smell like smoke and ruin the mood. Save the shower for in between."

"In between?" Frank asked with a smile.

"You're going to be a busy man today, Mr. Helms."

"Am I?" Frank asked as he gently picked up his love and carried her to the bedroom.

****

"How about I make you some breakfast?" Chingli asked as she snuggled up against her husband.

"Well, if you go through that effort now, I'll have to take you out to dinner tonight."

"Okay, we can go see Gloria. She's working this afternoon."

How did Chingli know Gloria was working today? The way his wife had jumped on the opportunity to see his sister made Frank suspect he was being set up.

The couple arrived at the Rendezvous at seven o'clock. It had been a peaceful day. They had both slept soundly after breakfast, rising around two o'clock for lunch. The weather had turned cooler, so Frank's ears felt better when they finally set out for dinner. Chingli went into the restaurant to stand in line while Frank parked the car. When he walked in, Chingli was sitting in one of the chairs provided for patrons who were waiting for a table. Glancing around the bar off the waiting area, he saw Stacey sitting there. Gloria would be getting off in a few minutes. Stacey was probably there to pick up her friend. Before he could get her attention, a young man approached Stacey and began a conversation.

"Look who's sitting at the bar," Chingli said to her husband, pointing at Stacey.

"Yes, I noticed," Frank said with a smile. "Where's Ray?"

"Oh, he's not here," Chingli said. "They had a big fight last night. Stacey isn't talking to Ray right now."

How did Chingli know that Stacey had a fight with Ray last night? Feeling more uneasy than ever, he decided to hazard a question. "And what was this fight about, my well informed wife?"

"Oh, the usual," Chingli replied. "Is his job more important than their relationship? When is he going to make a commitment? You're familiar with all the topics."

Knowing better than to take the bait on those topics, he steered the conversation toward the young man instead. "He's the kid who wanted me to tell Gloria about the next test."

"Oh, you know him?"

"No, don't even know his name. Just met him in the supermarket that once," the firefighter answered. "I'll be right back."

Chingli smiled to herself as Frank walked toward Stacey.

Frank knew that Chingli and Stacey had talked last night. Is his job more important than their relationship? Ray was at the shooting last night. Probably was on a date with Stacey and had to leave. That would explain the job-relationship part of Chingli's comment. Hesitant to make a commitment? What was Ray doing? He admitted without hesitation that Stacey was the ideal woman for him. If he could muster up the nerve to ask, Stacey would jump at becoming his wife. That was obvious to everyone but Ray. As he approached Stacey, Frank debated how to get information for Ray without appearing to do so. He decided banter would work best.

"Anastasia Romanov, the Grand Duchess herself," he said in a cheerful voice before he bowed at the waist.

Stacey looked at the ceiling and turned red. "Frank Helms, do you have to shout my name so the world can hear?"

"A thousand pardons, your grace," he continued with his teasing. "But yonder empress wishes me to pay my respects."

Stacey looked in the direction Frank had pointed and saw Chingli. She smiled and waved at the Taiwanese woman. Then she turned to the young man who had been speaking with her and changed her role to that of the little sister. "Art, this is my adopted brother, Frank Helms. You'll have to forgive his rudeness. He's only a fireman and so has forgotten everything I know his mother taught him."

"Art and I already know each other," Frank informed her. Art was his name. Now he could tell Gloria and get off that hook.

"Yes," the young man replied. "I met Gloria's older brother the other day in the supermarket."

Frank moaned at being called Gloria's older brother, but Stacey did not pay attention. She appeared to be a little tense, although he could not be sure why.

"Did you?" Stacey responded with what appeared to be false enthusiasm. "And what did the two of you talk about, the fresh fruit or the canned goods?"

"Well, I asked him about the test for firefighter. Then I believe the conversation revolved around what to do to people who pulled false alarms." Art said with a chuckle. He then pointed his finger at his head like a pistol and pretended to pull the trigger. Stacey shook her head, apparently not surprised by Art's response.

"Can I ask why Frank referred to you as the 'Grand Duchess?'"

"Because he has a sick sense of humor," Stacey said with a nervous laugh.

"You see Art," Frank interjected, "Stacey or should I say Anastasia shares her name with one of the last czar's daughters. You remember that line from that Stones' song 'Anastasia screamed in vain.' The girl doing the screaming was Grand Duchess Anastasia Romanov. As I'm sure you are aware Miss Anastasia Romanov sits before you."

"You're kidding?" Art asked excitedly. "You have royal blood?"

Stacey leaned her elbow onto the bar and rubbed her temples while looking at the floor making it obvious to all that she was not enjoying this conversation. After a deep breath, her head came up and she faced Art. "No, we're not from the royal Romanovs. Strictly peasant blood sits here. But my grandfather was a czarist sympathizer of sorts, so he thought it would be nice to give me the same name as this duchess although, for the life of me, I can't understand why. As I understand it she died in the basement of some farm house in Siberia. Not a fate I want to share."

Gloria walked over to save a deteriorating situation. "Frank, your wife is waiting for you. She says she's hungry and they have a table for you." Gloria then turned to Stacey and said a little nervously, "I'm ready when you are Stace. I have to hustle if I'm going to meet your brother on time."

Looking relieved, Stacey quickly stood up. "It was nice meeting you Art, but I have to get Miss Helms home or my brother will kill me."

"That would be a shame," Art answered with a chuckle. "But I'll probably see you around, until then, farewell, your grace."

Stacey responded with an awkward smile and hurried to follow Gloria who was already walking toward the door. Frank now found himself alone with Art. He was surprised by his sister's rudeness. She had not even acknowledged Art. Jack would not be upset if his date was a few minutes late. Why were they using that as an excuse to brush Art off? Maybe Gloria was thinking of Ray. But then why was Stacey so nervous around this guy? Although, after Frank thought for a minute, he had to admit the boy did seem a little strange. The pistol to the head routine was definitely off the wall considering the events of the past week and a half. Everything told the firefighter to keep the young man standing beside him at a distance.

"Well, Art," he said with a false cheeriness in his voice. "I have to go join up with my bride. I'll be seeing you around."

"Oh, you will, Frank," Art shot back. "I listen to you boys all the time on the radio. You might see me at a fire some time, you never know."

"Okay, at a fire then, *ciao*."

Frank walked away feeling uneasy. This was only the second time he had spoken with this character. Both times had left him with a feeling that this guy was not all there. The conversation was still running through his head when he reached Chingli.

"What was the matter with Gloria?" his wife asked as Frank sat down.

"It showed from all the way over here, did it?" he replied thoughtfully. "I don't know. Not like Gloria to act that way. She ignored this guy entirely and hustled Stacey out the door. And Stacey seemed very nervous around him, too."

"Oh, you're just trying to keep Stacey from talking with other men," Chingli laughed. "If Ray can't commit himself, the girl has a right to find someone who will."

"No, really," Frank answered defensively. "That's the second time I talked with him. The boy is strange."

"If you say so," she said with a sigh. "Now, how about we order? I'm hungry."

Chapter Twenty Five

Throwing her coat on as she jogged toward the exit, Stacey hustled to catch up with her friend. Gloria was out the door and into the parking lot before she reached her.

"What's the rush?" she asked breathlessly. "You know him, don't you?"

"Know him?" Gloria replied. "Did he tell you that? I waited on him a few times, but I can't even tell you his name."

"Art."

"Excuse me."

"His name is Art," Stacey informed her friend. "And he knows you as 'a tall red head.'"

Gloria shook her head. "Is that supposed to make me feel better?"

Stacey had expected some kind of negative reaction, but nothing quite like this.

"You've spoken with him then," she stated.

"Have I spoken with him?" Gloria said thoughtfully as they walked across the lot. "I've spoken to him, but not really with him. What did he say to you?"

"What did he say?" she laughed sardonically. "What didn't he say? My God, Gloria, you wouldn't believe what came out of his mouth." From the look she received, Stacey knew there would be nothing new in her story. Gloria's reaction to Art was getting her more nervous than had his stories.

"What did he tell you he did for a living?"

"Oh, he's done this before?" Stacey queried.

By now they had reached the car. Stacey unlocked her door, tossed the keys to Gloria, and slipped into the driver's seat. After they were both settled in, Stacey started the engine and backed out of the space. Her passenger waited until the car had begun to roll forward before voicing a challenge.

"Tell me the story and see if you can shock me."

The car stopped at the entrance to the lot and waited for traffic to clear. Its driver took up the challenge while leaning over the steering wheel looking for an opening.

"I get the feeling you've been through this with him, but I'll try to impress you anyway. I got here a little early and so sat at the bar waiting for you," Stacey began. She continued the story while driving through the post rush hour traffic of early evening.

****

The bar was crowded with patrons waiting for tables. Stacey made herself comfortable on one of the stools by the restaurant entrance. When approached by the bartender, she smiled and told him she was waiting for Gloria. Her friend's work place was frequented by young couples and college students. The lighting was subdued and the decor was rustic. Prices for the standard Italian - American fare were reasonable and the food itself was not bad. All of these factors helped make the Rendezvous a busy establishment any night of the week. Looking to see if she knew any of the people waiting for seats, Stacey noticed a young man who seemed to be looking directly at her. She quickly averted her gaze, but noticed out of the corner of her eye that he was making his way toward her.

"Hi, my name is Art. I was watching you from across the room and was wondering if I could buy you drink."

Art was a tall handsome man with a slim physique. She was flattered that he found her attractive. It had been a couple of years since Stacey had flirted with a man. How much of her edge had she lost since committing herself to a relationship with Ray? The thought of Ray and commitments made her angry. The perky blond decided to accept Art's offer with a small qualification. "A glass of white wine would be nice, but I have to warn you. I only came to pick up my friend. She's a waitress here."

"She is? What's her name?" he asked enthusiastically. "I'm here often and know most of the waitresses."

"Gloria," she answered hesitantly

"Tall, thin, reddish hair."

"Yes, you know her?" Stacey answered feeling more comfortable.

"Well, I wouldn't say I know her. She's served me occasionally," he replied quietly.

"Do you have a thing for tall, thin redheads or is your memory that good?"

"I'm good with names and faces," was the response.

"I am jealous. I sometimes have a hard time remembering my own name. What do you do for a living?" she asked, going with what she thought was the natural flow of the conversation. "Being good with names and faces would serve you well as a cop or detective or - or maybe sales." The last comment showed that her skills at flirting were rusty. A cop or detective? It was a struggle to come up with the afterthought of "sales." That was Ray's influence. Right now, she hated it.

The suggestion that he should be a cop or detective seemed to rock the young man momentarily. A shadow crossed his face. For an instant he almost frowned and had a faraway look in his eyes. The smile quickly returned, but the momentary lapse left Stacey with the uneasy feeling that Art was giving a show of bravado in spite of some hidden pain.

"Well, you're close enough," he answered a little too stiffly. "I'm not a cop, but I do work for the government."

She put the uneasy feeling off with the rationalization that she watched the news too much. Gloria always said she was paranoid. Even after his momentary lapse, Art appeared to be a pleasant, personable young man. His answer was said in such a way that it piqued her interest.

"What do you do for the government?"

"I work for the CIA. I'm a clandestine operative. When I started I was a Southeast Asian expert, but that was during the Vietnam thing. Now I work in the Soviet section. I specialize in cases dealing with the gulag."

As soon as Stacey heard these claims she began to laugh. Art was no more than thirty years old. He could not have been involved in Vietnam. This was going to be a fun glass of wine. After last night, she needed to laugh a little.

"No, but really. What do you do?" she asked with a smile.

He seemed to become a little agitated when she asked this question again. His answer was curt and to the point.

"That is what I do."

"Is this some kind of joke?"

"No, does my occupation bother you?"

Now she began looking for a way out. He was either carrying a joke too far, was a nut, or thought women were dumb enough to believe him. Chauvinist, prankster, or quack, Stacey knew she did not want to share a glass of wine with him. She decided to play along to give him one more chance before she closed the door.

"I can't say that it does. It is a little hard to believe. I mean, you're a little young to have been in Vietnam." She was hoping he would burst out laughing and say he liked a woman who could play along with a joke.

"I was one of the sewer rats," he said with a straight face.

"The what?" was her astonished response.

"Well, not many people know it, but during Nam the CIA recruited ten to twelve year old boys. They trained us in clandestine operations and sent us into the Vietcong tunnels to gather intelligence," he answered proudly.

"You're serious?" Stacey was now getting nervous. He could not possibly be serious. If he was, then the young man standing in front of her was a certified lunatic.

"As serious as a heart attack, my dear," Art answered flatly. Changing his voice to a lighter, friendlier tone, he then asked, "Now, what kind of wine did you say you wanted?"

The car rolled to a stop at the traffic light by South Orange town hall. Its driver turned to her passenger and finished the first half of her story. "That was when your brother showed up," Stacey finished telling Gloria. Her friend, who had been sitting quietly the entire time, chose the natural break in the story to provide what background she knew.

"You actually said he should be a cop?" she asked shaking her head.

"Well, I can't remember exactly what I said, but it was something along those lines. Why?"

"From what I know, he applied to the Police Department; passed all the tests and was about to be appointed, but then failed the psychological test. After that something seemed to snap in him. He's been offered all sorts of jobs. FBI Director, Secretary of State, and now he's a CIA operative. Anyway, after he fell off the deep end, I started giving him a wide berth."

"That was the weirdest conversation I have had in a long time. I felt like I was in the Twilight Zone with this guy." The car turned up one of the side streets as its driver finished her explanation. "I have a real bad feeling about this guy, Glor," she added in a worried tone.

"God, he really shook you up, didn't he?" Gloria responded with surprise in her voice.

"He makes me nervous."

"Well, how's he going to find you? You never come here without me. So, stay away for a while. You won't be missed and you won't miss it. I'm certainly not going to tell him your name or address," Gloria reassured her friend.

"He already knows my name," Stacey replied flatly while she applied the brakes for a stop sign.

"You told him your name?"

"No, I didn't. Not even my first name, your brother did that."

Gloria looked at the roof of the car and closed her eyes. "Why did he tell this joker your name?" she asked in a tired voice.

"He knew him. This is the guy who asked about the firefighter test. So, Frank went right into his Grand Duchess routine."

"Oh God," Gloria moaned. "So, Arty boy knows your full name and your parentage, isn't that great."

"My parentage?" Stacey asked with a laugh.

"But of course, your grace. Are you not the daughter of Czar Nicholas?"

Stacey muttered a curse as she turned the car onto Gloria's block.

"Calm down, girl," her friend reassured Stacey. "He's weird, but probably harmless."

"Probably, but I wish I had followed my father's advice and gotten an unlisted number. You don't know this guy's name?"

"Well, you just told me it was Art, other than that, no. He always paid in cash, so I never saw his credit card. Besides, I didn't want to get to know him after he turned weird; before that he was too quiet," Gloria finished as Stacey pulled the car over in front of her apartment house. "It'll look better in the morning. Hey, maybe you could play this up for Ray and get him jealous. That might push him off square one and get some kind of commitment out of him."

"We'll have to discuss it with Chingli. I think she was the one who gave Frank the push to come over and talk to me. Ray will hear about this very quickly through the old boys' network, believe me!"

Both women laughed then Gloria stepped out of the car and closed the door. She gave her friend one last wave, before she turned to hurry into her apartment to get ready for Jack. Stacey leaned over the passenger's seat as she pushed the button to lower the window. "Say hello to my brother for me," she shouted, teasingly. Gloria laughed and shook her head "yes" as she reached the door. After a quick wave, the door closed and Stacey drove off.

Two days after leaving Gloria at her doorstep, Stacey stepped into her apartment from work carrying her briefcase and a small bag of groceries. Frank had obviously spoken with her beau the previous day because Ray had apologized the night before. The good old boys' network could be manipulated as easily as the boys who were part of it. Now to direct her cop toward the commitment she desired. Chingli had given herself a deadline with Frank and his job. Should Ray be held to a time schedule also? Doubting she was as good as her Taiwanese friend at bending men, Stacey decided against any personal vows. Certain that if she were patient enough everything she wanted would come true, she focused her attention on the present. After the briefcase was put down and the groceries stored away, she walked to her answering machine to see if anyone had called.

The first of three messages was from Ray confirming the time he would pick her up tonight. The familiar voice of her boyfriend was followed by a male voice that took her a moment to recognize. The context of the message more than the sound of his voice told Stacey that Art had found her.

"Anastasia, I was hoping we could get together for that drink I owe you. We could discuss your situation before it becomes too dangerous. I'll call again."

The next message was also from Art, although he sounded more distressed in it than in his previous one. His fantasy world had begun to intrude into the real one.

"Anastasia, your grace, we must get together to discuss your escape. Please remain at home so I can contact you before your father's enemies find you."

As soon as she had realized whose voice it was, her heart had jumped. Since Ray had called to apologize, the conversation with Art had been put completely out of her mind. His messages sounded more psychotic than the stories he told the other night.

The young woman quickly picked up the phone and punched numbers in nervously. "Gloria, he called," she said into the phone with a hint of nerves in her voice.

"Who called, Stace?"

"The nut, he must have looked up my number in the phone book."

"Take it easy, Stace, and tell me who you're talking about."

"Art, you know, the weirdo who hangs out at the Rendezvous."

"Oh, my God, you're kidding?" she asked in shock. "Did you talk to him?"

"No, he left two messages on my machine," Stacey replied a little more calmly.

"Two messages? What did he say?"

"First he wanted to get together for a drink so we could discuss my situation. Then he wanted me to stay home so we could discuss my escape before my father's enemies find me."

"What enemies does your father have?" Gloria asked.

"He must be trying to protect me from the Bolsheviks, the commies."

When Gloria heard Stacey's theory, she became very quiet. "This wacko thinks it's 1917 and the Russian revolution is in full swing," Gloria muttered. "He wants you to stay home so he can contact you?" Before she could say anything else, Stacey panicked.

"Gloria!"

"Calm down, Stacey," she said in a controlled voice. "Let's take this one step at a time. We have to determine if he's going to pursue this any further. Why don't you meet me at Jack's apartment? We can talk to him about it and call Ray. You can call for your messages from there every now and then, so we can monitor your phone."

"I didn't tell Ray or Jack about this."

"I told Jack the other night, although I don't know if he remembers it."

"Okay, you want me to call Jack?"

"He's not home," Gloria said with a chuckle.

"Oh? And where might my older brother be?" Stacey asked with anticipation. "Do you need a ride Gloria Helms, or do you have someone to take you?"

"As a matter of fact, I have my own private service that provides me with a ride to the destination we just discussed any time I want it, providing he's home."

"He's there now isn't he," Stacey squealed with delight. "Now we just have to get Frank on track and our triple entente will be a complete success."

Stacey found it hard leaving her place. In her mind she realized that she was not leaving for long, but her heart told her she was being driven out. That was what made it so difficult. The feeling of abandoning her home and fleeing for an unknown period made her feel like a refugee.

Was she over reacting? Maybe Gloria was right and she did watch the news too much. In the end, what drove her out was a sixth sense telling her Art was not harmless. What was it about him that made her nervous was still unclear, but until the dust settled she did not feel safe in her place.

Chapter Twenty Six

When Stacey arrived at her brother's apartment, Gloria and Jack were waiting for her. The drive over had been used to think through the problem she faced. In the end, the paramount emotion felt was no longer fear; it had turned to anger. She was angry at herself for getting so nervous about a young man who was apparently a pathological liar. Either that or he was genuinely psychotic. One or the other, there was nothing to indicate he was violent, so there had been no need to leave her apartment. What Art had done may have been annoying, but was not threatening. Intent on only staying a short while to discuss her "panic attack", Stacey knocked on her brother's door. Gloria let her in.

She stepped into a sparsely furnished, bachelor's apartment. There were only three chairs. If anyone else was coming, someone would end up on the floor. Jack's place was really the antithesis to hers. When people came to her place, they usually commented on how it felt like a home. Walking into Jack's was like walking into an army bivouac. The thought of a temporary base camp for some chaotic operation was what first came to mind.

A partially melted dome light from a fire truck sat on top of one lamp. Pictures of fires and copies of fire service magazines were scattered about. Shelving was made up of cinder blocks and pine boards.

The kitchen remained impeccably clean, but not from any effort on the part of the firefighter who would have cooked there. It was clean because it was never used. Stacey knew her brother ate only take out food at home. His most nutritious meals of any week were prepared in the firehouse. In so many ways, Jack was the stereotypical bachelor. Could Gloria tame such a wild mustang? She knew if anyone could it was her best friend.

"If it isn't the Grand Duchess herself," Jack chuckled as his sister stepped in. "Now you have the CIA attempting to protect you? We've moved up in the world since 1918, haven't we?"

"Moved up?" Gloria said sounding confused. "How could you have moved up from being the ruling family of Russia?"

"In 1918 the United States wasn't really that interested in what happened to the Czar in that Siberian farmhouse cellar," Jack informed her. "From what you told me of this nut, the CIA now wants to rescue the Grand Duchess."

"How does that line go in Star Wars?" Gloria asked herself out loud. "'Who's the fool, the fool or the fool who follows the fool?' So Jack, who's the nut; the nut or the nut who believes the nut?"

"I never said I believed him," Jack answered defensively.

"Then don't encourage the charade." She then turned to Stacey. "Ray's on his way over and we also called Frank, since he's talked with this guy, too. He and Chingli will be here in a bit."

"But we aren't going to turn this into a party," Jack reminded everyone. "I have to be in work tomorrow morning."

"Oh, is tomorrow one of the two days out of the week you have to get up with the rest of us?" Stacey asked facetiously.

"Will you listen to little miss bright eyes," was the sarcastic response from her brother. "Yes, besides watching the sun rise our last night in work, I have to show up for work tomorrow. They get particular if you only report for duty when it's fun. Someone has to clean up the firehouse."

The doorbell rang as Jack finished. Gloria went for the door while Stacey put her coat on a chair. She knew this was not really the time to tease her brother, but he deserved it after that remark about the CIA. Ray walked in with a worried look on his face. "What was he worrying about?" she wondered. "Making a commitment or the messages on my machine?" Gloria did not follow behind the homicide detective.

"Frank and Chingli were right behind me," Ray said.

"Good, then we can sort through this thing real quick and come up with a battle plan," Jack replied.

"You two seem to have everything in hand," Stacey said with a little more annoyance in her voice than she had meant to show. She could see the men in her life were now going to become overbearing and over protective. She silently cursed her panic attack. The three stooges would soon be together. They would then undoubtedly revert to the insufferable teenagers all men are when they feel a female they know is threatened. Ray looked surprised by the tone of his girlfriend's voice.

"Don't pay attention to her Ray," Jack reassured him. "She's been ornery since she walked through the door."

"Excuse me?" Stacey shot back. "There is no need to apologize for me, Jack Romanov."

"Stace, shhh," Jack said, putting his index finger to his mouth. "We can let everyone settle in and then you can tell us what happened and what you think should be done."

At that moment, Gloria walked in with Frank and Chingli, so Stacey bit her tongue. The girls sat in the three chairs, while their respective beaus dropped down to the floor next to them. After everyone was seated, Jack asked his sister to describe what had happened. She gave an abbreviated version of the conversation with Art and concluded with the content of the phone messages.

"Is this guy a prankster?" Ray asked.

Gloria told him what she knew of Art and his mental condition. With this background, the group began to discuss what, if anything, could or should be done.

"I'll dig a little at work," Ray offered. "But that isn't going to help tonight. You don't know this guy's last name?" he asked Gloria.

"I didn't even know his first name until Stacey told me."

"Frank, did he tell you who he was?" the detective asked.

"No, Ray. Both times I spoke with him, we had nameless conversations. He knew mine from overhearing Dan O'Brian call me, but he never offered his."

"Do you think Dan would know him?" Jack asked.

"I don't think so. He didn't react as if he knew him, but I could always ask."

Stacey could see this little pow-wow was going to turn into a long drawn out affair unless she stopped it. But how could she stop it without sounding like a hysterical female who had suddenly come to her senses. Maybe Art had left another message that would give them some clue about his intentions or who he was.

"Why don't I call and check my machine," she suggested. "The last message implied Art intended to call back."

"Go for it, kid," Ray said enthusiastically. "Anything more would help us make a decision."

Swallowing the urge to tell him she was the only one who had to make a decision, Stacey got up and walked to the wall phone in the kitchen. While punching in her number, she overheard the discussion in the next room.

"Could we have him arrested?" Chingli asked.

"For what?" Frank replied. "He hasn't made any threats. The boy wants to protect her."

"Frank's right," Ray pointed out. "Besides, we don't know his name or where he lives."

"How can you protect Stacey if you don't know him? Maybe she could spend the nights somewhere else until you find out," Chingli suggested.

"I could probably find out at work," Gloria said. "Someone must know him. He is a regular customer and the gossip had to come from somewhere, but that's going to take a day or two."

Stacey punched in the access numbers for her answering machine quickly. She had to get back into the conversation before the three heroes decided they knew what was best for her. The women's comments would only make Ray and company feel they had to smother her with protection. What Jack said next almost made her hang up the phone.

"I have a suggestion. How about I stay over her place for a few nights? I can just crash on the couch until this all blows over."

Both Gloria and Chingli started talking at once. "No, no," they agreed before Chingli gave way to Gloria. "I don't think so Jack," she said with a mischievous grin. "If little Miss Independence wants anyone to stay at her place, you are not the one."

"I don't know if Stace wants anyone intruding right now," Ray answered halfheartedly.

Stacey was listening to her answering machine with one ear and the conversation in the next room with the other. She did not like what was going on in the other room, but the message on her machine said the crisis was over. Quickly hanging up, she marched into the living room and triumphantly announced, "He left another message. You'll love this. He's been ordered out of town on a top secret mission that is related to my cause. He can be reasonably sure of my safety for the period he'll be gone. Then he said to take heart, God is watching over our crusade."

"No, he didn't say that," Jack laughed. "Your crusade? What is your crusade?"

She gave an annoyed look to her brother and answered, "How am I supposed to know what his crusade is?"

Feeling that the last message put the problem of Art to bed at least for the night, Stacey went to pick up her coat. She had to be in work in the morning and there was no dozing in front of a television waiting on an alarm for her. Lab technicians had to be conscious when they worked.

"I can say it hasn't been fun," the little blond said to her friends. "Now I have to go home and get some sleep. So, if you'll excuse me, good night and thanks for the effort guys." The thanks came from her heart. She had felt threatened and her friends had come to help her.

"Hold on, Stace," Ray protested. "Just because this guy left some halfwit message doesn't mean this is over. Sit down and talk."

"Ray, I have to get up in the morning," his girlfriend objected.

"Just humor me for a few more minutes, so I can sleep tonight; or do you want me to stay at your place?"

Chingli looked triumphant when she heard this. Gloria sat watching Stacey with an expectant smile on her face. The reply Ray received quickly put a damper on their enthusiasm.

"I'll give you a few minutes, babe," she said wearily.

"This nut has made no threats?"

She shook her head "no."

"He claims to work for the CIA and wants to rescue the Czar's daughter," the detective continued, summarizing the situation out loud. "Gloria is working on a last name. I'll see if I can get any info from the personnel investigation. But the best thing we could do is approach the man and request he lay off."

Frank and Jack shook their heads in agreement. Stacey remained quiet. There seemed to be little harm in the three of them talking with Art. After his friends agreed to this Ray went on. "The security in your building is pretty good. Do you feel safe going home?"

"If I didn't, all three of you clowns would be spending the night on my living room floor," she said emphatically.

"Clowns?" Frank protested. "Try to help out a friend and you turn into a clown."

"You're the one who started this, Frank Helms," Stacey shot back, silencing the firefighter. "You and your sick sense of humor. There is a time and place for levity. If you men could just get that concept down, the world would be a better place."

"You mean duller, don't you?" Jack asked, coming to his friend's rescue. Stacey gave him an impatient stare and then picked up her coat. She was determined to get out from under the three stooges before they became unbearable. Walking toward the door after giving Ray a peck, she played her last card in an attempt to make sure Dad did not hear about this little panic attack.

"I didn't have to teach you that concept, Jack. You're already under the tutelage of an experienced instructor, right Glor?" she said at the door. "By the way, Jack, have you talked to Mom recently?"

Jack would easily pick up on what she was implying. If their mother found out about Gloria, he would have no peace. The firefighter looked at his sister as if waiting for the other shoe to drop.

"No need to tell Dad about my little panic attack is there?" she asked in a bargaining tone.

Jack must have felt her description of the reaction she had to Art's calls was accurate, because he did not hesitate. She knew he would consider the deal offered too good to walk away from. "I don't see why we should trouble Dad with it. You already have three clowns on the case."

"Then I'll go back to my little haven, *ciao-ciao*."

Stacey had to work late the following day. When she finally returned home there were several messages on her machine. Ray called confirming he had received her message changing the time they would meet. The next message was from Jack saying her "three clowns" were going to try to talk with Art before she met Ray. The third was from Ray saying they had spoken with Art, who had apologized for frightening her. He claimed it all was an inside joke that she had enjoyed the night they had met.

An inside joke! That was a typical male response. The three stooges had probably believed him, too. What was it about the y chromosome that made sick humor so important to men? She did not have the time to think about it. Ray would be arriving any minute to pick her up. What could she wear tonight that would really bother him? Stacey went to her closet to pick out something to show her beau women had their own way of teasing.

Chapter Twenty Seven

Frank placed the dishes around the small table in the dinette of their apartment. He stopped to think for a second before putting the flatware in place. How does it go? Were knives and spoons on the left or the right? Remembering the arrangement at the restaurant the other night, the firefighter completed setting the table. Gloria would have known instantly and laughed at him for being ignorant of how a table should be set. But then their mother taught that skill to her daughter. She never bothered to enlighten her son on the intricacies of polite table settings. Frank had spent his childhood learning to behave in a civilized manner once the table had been set and the food had been served. Before then he had always been chased out of the dining room for fear he would break something.

Was that all a feminine ploy to keep men dependent? He laughed at the thought. If it was, the girls were off the mark. The only ones who cared how the table was set were the ladies. Unfortunately, Kathy Stanley was a lady. His stomach turned a little just remembering the gamble he was taking. Would Miss Stanley turn out to be his ace in the hole or Chingli's trump card?

"You don't want me to put out any chopsticks?" he asked his wife playfully.

"Chopsticks for meatballs and gravy," she answered seriously, showing it had been considered. "No, we're eating Italian, so we'll eat the way the Italians do."

"How much time did she say she had?" Frank asked. His wife had spent twenty minutes on the phone with Kathy, happily chatting as if she had found a long lost sister. Reminding himself of that only made him more nervous.

"Oh, she has a couple of hours at least," Chingli reassured her husband. She was standing in the kitchen at the stove stirring a large pot. The smell of fresh red gravy filled the small apartment, making Frank's stomach growl when he was not doubting the wisdom of the evening. The firefighter would have preferred a fully involved three story frame to this little dinner party.

Chingli's enthusiasm for meeting the reporter had begun to grow after she had time to think about it. His wife was no longer lukewarm on the idea. Frank now feared she would do him bodily harm if he suggested they cancel. It was not just the phone call. Before they had left Jack's the previous night, the two sisters-in-law had talked privately. Gloria was apparently all for it and must have pointed out some advantages he had not even considered, because Chingli was absolutely bubbly when they left. He had asked why she was so happy. Her reply was a simple, "Because everything is working out the way we had planned."

The ringing of the door bell interrupted his brooding. The time for doubts was over. Now the contest of wits would begin. The expression "Let the best man win" crossed his mind, but the opponents were not men. If a tie could be pulled out of this, he would consider himself lucky. The only way a man won was by walking away from the relationship. Frank was not about to do that and he knew there would be no way to negotiate a victory. His wife always escalated beyond the point he felt was necessary for any particular issue. The knock down drag out fight over how the toilet paper should be put on the holder came to mind. If she were willing to go that far for toilet paper, how could he hope for a victory tonight? Resigning himself to a hard fought stalemate, the firefighter rose to open the door. Chingli quickly removed her apron and smoothed the dark red dress she was wearing. Kathy wore a business outfit that would obviously record well for a news broadcast. In her hands was a bottle of red wine.

"Hello, Kath," Frank said as the reporter came in. "Let me introduce my wife Chingli."

His wife smiled, pushed right past him, and gave Kathy a big hug. How westernized she had become still amazed Frank. In China you bowed. You never threw your arms around a new acquaintance. The way the two women addressed each other told the firefighter the battle may have already been lost. Their conversation was conducted in Mandarin with Chingli calling Kathy *mei-mei* or "little sister". The reporter willingly referred to his wife as "older sister", *jie-jie*.

"I smell something wonderful," Kathy said to the cook. "I haven't had homemade gravy since I left Rhode Island."

As he closed the door, Frank knew he was in trouble. What did these two women talk about for those twenty minutes? He was supposed to be introducing them, but was already two steps behind.

His suspicions were immediately aroused when Kathy inserted the English word "gravy" into the middle of her Mandarin statement about what most Americans call spaghetti sauce. His excuse for referring to this sauce as gravy was growing up in a neighborhood that was half Italian. What was hers and how did she know Chingli would understand?

"You have to tell me how mine compares to your mother's," Chingli insisted.

"Ho, what are you two talking about?" Frank interrupted, now totally off balance. "Her mother's gravy? You told me your mother was from Taiwan."

"Oh, she is," Kathy replied with a chuckle, switching to English. "But my father's parents were from Italy, so mom learned how to make grandma's red gravy. Oh, the Sunday dinners we used to have."

"Your name is Stanley and you're half Italian, half Taiwanese?" Frank muttered, shaking his head.

"Welcome to America," Kathy laughed. "Why don't you tell your husband how I got my last name, *jie-jie*. I'll put the wine in the kitchen."

The reporter stepped into the kitchen as if she were a member of the family. What was more amazing was the lack of protest from his wife. Now Chingli was going to tell him why her new found friend walked around with an English name when she was really Italian. Kathy was not going to be his ace in the hole. The two women were getting along too well.

"Well, it was like this," Chingli began, in Mandarin. "When little sister's grandfather came to Ellis Island his name was Sanelli. When he left, it was Stanley. They didn't know how to change it back to their original name, so they decided to begin their new life in America with a new American name."

"My mother still can't understand how they could do that," Kathy said walking back from the kitchen. "In China, there is nothing more sacred than your family name; but dad thinks it's funny."

"Okay, let's eat," Chingli said enthusiastically.

"First let me look at your dress," Kathy insisted, gently placing her hands on Chingli's shoulders and turning her around. After taking a step back, the reporter sighed.

"I have to get back to Taipei and pick up some *qipaos*. I outgrew all of mine in high school and just never had a chance to pick up any more when we visited my mom's family. Is this how you trapped your husband?" she asked, moving her hand up and down as she pointed at the dress.

Chingli giggled and looked at Frank. "No, he was easier than that. I just smiled at him and he couldn't take his eyes off of me."

Frank turned red while the two women enjoyed their little joke. "You have to teach me that smile," Kathy said as they walked into the dinette for the meal.

Before they sat down, Kathy glanced at Frank's ears. "Your ears don't look too bad, Frank. Has your lovely wife been treating them with a little TLC?"

"What is TLC?" Chingli asked.

"Tender loving care," Frank told her, before answering Kathy. "Yes, those lovely, delicate hands of hers slap them every chance she gets. That way, I won't have to go back to work for a while."

"Men and their jokes," his wife complained to the reporter. "I help him put cream on, but now he has given me an idea. Maybe if I do slap his ears he will stay on sick leave a little longer. Then Ray can catch this stalker and I would have one less worry. Right now, he intends to go back to work."

"I would not go on sick leave my wife," Frank protested, in an attempt to keep the subject away from his return to duty. "I would go on injury leave."

"There's a difference?" Kathy asked curiously.

"Yes, sick leave is for those laggards who stay home because they have a runny nose," the firefighter replied. "Those of us on injury leave were hurt doing our job."

"Of course, I should have remembered," the fire captain's daughter said with a laugh. "Doing your job, like falling on the ice while shoveling the sidewalk in front of the firehouse, right?"

"You, Miss, have a jaded view of the world," Frank said with mock indignation. "Are there no heroes left for you?"

Kathy looked at Chingli before she responded to Frank's pomposity. "Must I remind you Firefighter Helms that you are speaking to a fireman's daughter? You're going to have to come up with something better than 'injury leave' to impress me."

Chingli laughed at Kathy's remarks. Frank sat down to dinner with the feeling he was at a decided disadvantage. The Chinese half of Miss Stanley had connected with his wife. A feeling of doom closed in around him. This little gathering was turning into a major snafu and there appeared to be little that could be done to salvage the situation.

The conversation after they finished dinner centered around the events of the past two weeks and what the future held. Frank tried to change the subject to how Kathy's mother had adapted to being married to a firefighter.

"Did your father ever face anything like these shootings," he asked her.

"I really don't know," the young woman replied. "Dad never talked about the firehouse when he was home. I picked up his stories from being around him and his friends at picnics or parties. He never talked about his experiences with her because she told him not to. Mom could never handle the stories and probable embellishments that go with a group of firemen drinking beer. After watching that fire the other night, I think I understand a little better why she didn't want to hear the stories. Although, I was impressed with the way Chief Gregor orchestrated the entire scene. But I have never had a desire to follow in my father's foot steps and I don't understand why anyone would want to do that job."

Frank almost panicked. He had to change the direction of the conversation quickly. Laughing a little too loudly, he attempted to focus on her description of firemen getting together. Chingli just shook her head, obviously sympathizing with Kathy's mother.

"Now, why would you put it that way?" the firefighter asked. "Embellishments and firemen drinking beer, it sounds like you're a little skeptical about the accuracy of the tales you heard."

"Dad would tell me afterwards whose story was close to reality," she informed him. "Not that all the stories were meant to be taken as factual. As I got older, I could pick out the tall tales from the attempts at exaggeration, but Mom never could. So, she stayed away and tried to talk Dad into finding another occupation."

Her mother had tried to talk her dad into leaving the job! If he played this right, maybe Frank could show Chingli that there was no need for worrying. Another Taiwanese woman had faced this situation and had found ways to cope. He glanced at his wife quickly, but could not read her reaction, so he decided to push on.

"Why didn't your father leave the job?"

"Well, you have to remember, that was a different era," the reporter began. "Dad had met my mother while stationed in Taipei at the firehouse for the American military base. When they met he was already a firefighter with no other skills to speak of. He was a kid, a draftee, on an adventure. Instead of sending him to Vietnam, Uncle Sam sent him to Taiwan. After spending some time there, Mom walked into his life, wore a dress like your wife is wearing tonight, and captured his heart," she finished laughing with Chingli.

"You both have a very low opinion of the opposite sex," Frank pointed out, still unsure if this little story would help out his cause.

"Why?" Chingli asked. "Do you deny men can be easily trapped by the right woman?"

"You're interrupting Kathy's story," Frank pointed out. "But the key word you just used is 'right'. The right woman can easily trap a man. But only because he wants to be captured by this 'right' woman."

"Point made," Kathy conceded. "Anyway, Dad was a kid who had no college education and no specialized training other than firefighting. After marrying mom and returning home, he took the test for fireman in New Providence. Mom wasn't impressed with the job, but thought they could start a business and then he would resign."

"Did they start this business?" Chingli asked, seemingly thankful the conversation was in Mandarin. Frank was working to keep up. Kathy's Mandarin was spoken with an American accent and had a smattering of English words thrown in, making it harder for him to understand. Chingli appeared to have no trouble at all with their guest's speech.

"Yes, they did," was the response, "but Dad never got around to leaving the department. Seems there was always some reason to stay on the job just a little longer. It's still not a good subject around our house, but they've learned to gloss over their differences."

"So, your mom has accepted your old man's job?" Frank asked for emphasis.

"Accepted it?" she asked thoughtfully. "No, she has never accepted it. She only accepted the fact that he never had the opportunity to get a college education. On the other hand, I never had the opportunity not to get one," the reporter finished with a laugh.

It had sounded so good until that last sentence. Her mother had adjusted to being a fireman's wife. There were ways to cope with being married to a firefighter. Even if you were an immigrant married to an American and the only member of your family in the States. Kathy's father had started a business on the side. They would do the same. A consulting business to help American companies expanding into Asia. For a moment anything was possible. Why did she have to bring up education? Damn!

Chingli was laughing with Kathy. "I know what you mean. It is hard being Chinese. You have to study and study. The tests in Taiwan are very hard and determine everything. What grammar school and middle school you attend. Whether or not you will attend high school and go on to university, attend junior college, or vocational school."

"Yes, my mama told me," Kathy replied. "She couldn't go to junior college or university because my grandparents couldn't afford to send her to tutoring schools after school, at least not while sending my uncles. When she came to America, she saw everyone had to go to school until they were in high school and that all you had to do was work hard and you could go to college. This was heaven, and no little girl of hers was going to miss out. I was going to college if she had to kill me!"

The two women burst out in laughter, while Frank sat smiling silently. His hopes for a draw had crashed and burned. Kathy was Chingli's trump card. The fleeting dream of retiring from the Fire Department and concentrating on his already successful consulting firm was gone. How can he use the Chinese emphasis on education to support his desire for earning an MBA before resigning?

"You sometimes take the opportunities in America too lightly," Frank interjected awkwardly. "Of course, I had an additional advantage of being a fireman. The hours I worked allowed me to earn my degree while working forty-two hours a week. Think of the opportunities if I go on for my MBA."

Kathy continued to chuckle as she replied lightly in English, "Oh, Frank, are you kidding? Do you know where trade with Asia is going? You can write your own ticket now."

"He doesn't have to go to Asia, *mei-mei*," Chingli informed her. "Asia is coming to him. My uncle wants to expand and wants Frank to run the American branch of his company."

"Frank, what a wonderful opportunity!" was the energetic reaction. "You could leave the job tomorrow, no need for advanced degrees. My father always said, 'Degrees are nice, but they can't beat experience.'" The reporter's pager went off as she unknowingly crushed his last hope of salvaging something from the evening.

Frank glumly helped Chingli clean up after Kathy had left. His wife was in an expansive mood. The way she chattered on about Miss

Stanley made it obvious the Taiwanese woman felt she had finally made a friend outside his circle.

"What was the name of your old friend?" Chingli asked. "The one who was so filial."

"Dan O'Brian?" Frank asked. "Why do you . . . Hold on. I know what you're up to, my wife. How do you know Kathy is even interested in a relationship? Did she say anything to you?"

"No, but I think she seems lonely."

"You do?" he said with a laugh. "Well, I don't know if Dan is looking for anything right now. He has to take care of his mother."

"We really have to make an effort to go home with Kathy and meet her parents," Chingli suggested, changing the subject as she bubbled with excitement. When Frank gave a nonchalant response, she turned to him and said, "You didn't really think her parent's experience had anything to do with us, did you?"

With that he realized the battle had been lost before it had begun.

Chapter Twenty Eight

Stacey opened the front door to her apartment building quietly. It had been a long day, especially after the past two nights. She walked up the stairs slowly, thinking about her date with Ray the previous night. Dinner had gone well. No calls from the office pulling him away. His attention was focused on her. They had discussed the past few years and their relationship. When the subject of commitments came up, he had been quite defensive. Did the last few years not count as a steadily deepening commitment on his part? After she had conceded that he had shown a level of attachment to her over the course of their relationship, he had asked what more he could do to convince her. She had looked him straight in the eye and said what Chingli probably would have said if given the opportunity, "Give me a ring to put on my left ring finger."

Ray had looked shocked at first, but then started to laugh. "Who taught you to be so blunt?" he asked.

"Who taught me?" she asked herself out loud. It was a fair question. No one had sat her down and said, "If you want it Stacey, you're going to have to go after it." Her rapid evolution from polite shyness to matter of fact bluntness was not taught overtly. Probably her biggest influence over the past few weeks was a certain Chinese woman who had seen what she wanted and gambled everything to get it. This sudden realization gave her a feeling of peace. Knowing the source of her knowledge always made her more comfortable. She looked at her beau and gave as honest an answer as possible, "I guess you could say Chingli, but it was taught by example not through advice."

"Well then, my love," Ray had said as he reached for his wine glass. "Here's to Mrs. Chingli Helms, who came all the way from China to keep us together."

Stacey really could not remember the rest of the night. It was a blur, partly because she had cried so much over the course of the evening. Her co-conspirators had been called when she returned home. Then there were phone calls to her mother and her future mother-in-law. It was after two before she finally got to bed and even then sleep eluded her. Ray had to work tonight, so it would be her night to catch up on sleep.

The light on her answering machine was flashing. After putting her things down, Stacey went over and pushed the replay button. Gloria's voice came from the speaker. She was obviously upset.

"Stacey, Art was in before. He was very irrational. The manager had to call the police to escort him out. Stace, he kept ranting and raving about a Bolshevik conspiracy and the Grand Duchess. Why don't you go stay at Jack's tonight? I'll call you back, bye."

Jack came on next, "Stacey, your low flying aircraft crash landed at the Rendezvous. They had to throw him out. Why don't you come over here for the night? You can have my bed and I'll sleep on the floor."

Frank's was the next to last message. "Stacey, this is Frank. Talked with Jack a minute ago. Nix the idea of going over to his place for the night. No need to suffer through that. Why don't you come here? Chingli has been dying to have a sit down talk with you since you demanded Ray give you a ring. Give us a call back, okay."

She recognized the voice of the last message immediately. "Your imminence, I have received approval for our evacuation plan from headquarters. The situation in the city is very fluid, but I fear the reds will prevail. We must move tonight. Prepare yourself as best you can. You must be ready to flee at a moment's notice."

Stacey stood transfixed, staring at the machine. Her heart was bounding and her palms were sweaty. What were her options? Picking up the phone, she called Ray at the West Precinct. The pleasure of saying she was his fiancé for the first time was lost to her. She was too nervous to remember what had changed since last calling him at work.

"Detective Friedrick," he answered with curt professionalism.

"Ray," she said breathlessly. "Art called again. They threw him out of the Rendezvous ranting about a Grand Duchess and now he called me."

"Did you talk to him?"

"No, he left a message on the machine. He said he has to rescue me tonight. Frank and Chingli offered to have me stay at their place. I think that's what I'm going to do, but how do we stop this guy? I can't go on worrying about some nut all the time. Isn't there some way you can arrest him?"

"Right now our problem is getting you to Frank's," the detective said. "I don't want you going out alone. You're safe in your apartment. Keep the door locked and wait for me to get there. I'll call Frank and Jack and have them meet me. If this guy rings your door bell, call dispatch and request a squad car, got it?"

"Got it," she repeated, feeling much better. "Careful coming here, babe. He's not beating the door down."

"Don't worry about me," he reassured her. "Just don't open the door."

Hanging up the phone, Stacey walked over to the door to lock the dead bolt. Then she went to get ready for an overnight stay at Frank and Chingli's. As soon as her nerves were under control, anger filled her. When will this guy quit? He should be locked up as a psycho.

Packing her overnight bag really brought home the fragility of a "normal" life. Three days ago, her only problem was convincing Ray to pop the question. Then she had a conversation with a quack. The following night was the strategy session with her friends to figure out how to deal with this character. Tonight she was packing a bag and leaving her home until they could get this guy arrested. Last night was the only

"normal" night of the week. That is if you called demanding someone ask you to marry him normal. If Stacey had not lived through this week, she would never have believed it. The phone rang as she finished packing. Hopefully, that was Chingli telling her Frank was on his way over. She walked out of the bedroom, picked up the phone, and said a hesitant hello.

"Your grace, I hope you have prepared, I will be at your place momentarily."

Stacey stood frozen for a moment and then exploded. "Why don't you leave me alone?" she screamed into the phone. "Go away! I'm not your grand duchess! Just, just go away or I'll have you arrested!"

"I understand you're under intense pressure and can't talk now. You needn't fear. It will end tonight. I am confident I can affect a rescue quickly. Take heart; it will soon be over."

There was an abrupt click. She wanted to throw the phone to vent her rage. Tears were streaming down her face as she tried to understand what the lunatic on the phone had said. "I can affect a rescue quickly. I will be at your place momentarily." Fear overpowered her rage. "Oh my God," she whispered to herself. She then picked up the phone and dialed Jack. He was the closest.

Jack answered the phone in an obvious rush. "Jack," Stacey sobbed into the phone when he picked it up, "he called again. He's going to be here momentarily. I'm scared, Jack. Hurry!"

"On the way, kid," he answered quickly. "Just don't open the door for anyone but us."

She hung up and called police dispatch. Her struggle to hold herself together failed as soon as the police operator came on the line. "Hello, my name is Stacey Romanov," she began, telling her story to the operator as clearly and concisely as possible. The operator assured her in a business like tone that a car would respond quickly. Stacey ended with a pathetic whimper, "Please hurry."

She paced the floor by her door. It was impossible for her to tell how long it had been since Art had called. What does the word "momentarily" mean to a man whose mind is back in 1918. She jumped when the buzzer went off then said a quiet prayer while pushing the intercom button. "Jack?" Her legs almost buckled when she heard the reply.

"Your highness, come down quickly. There's not a moment to lose."

"Go away!" she shouted, then released the button and prayed, "Please Lord, don't let anybody open the door for him."

As she completed her prayer the sound of a gunshot reverberated through the hall. The crack of the gun took her breath away. She began taking quick, shallow breaths which caused her head to spin. "Have to calm down or I'll hyperventilate and pass out. What to do? I'm trapped!" What had been her personal, private space was being invaded by a mad man. Was her place going to be her tomb? Where could she go? How long would it take to open the window and climb out onto the fire escape? Even if she succeeded in doing that, he would catch her and then Ray would not know where to find her. How could she resist a mad man who towered over her? Stacey felt she was going to choke on the frustration and terror building in her. With no place else to go, she fled to the bathroom. There she locked the door and crouched down in the tub.

Her sobs almost drowned out the distant sound of sirens. Please let it be the Police responding. These sounds were blocked when he started pounding on the door.

"Your highness, can you open the door?" He pounded for an instant longer and then shouted, "Stand back from the door. I'll shot the lock off." This was followed a moment later by the roar of a gunshot. Art tried to force the door after this, but apparently had only noticed one of the two locks on it. She heard another shot explode into her apartment and then the sound of the door flying open.

Stacey held her breath out of fear she would give herself away. She heard him stepping into her apartment, grinding pieces of the shattered door into the wooden floor of the entrance way.

"Your eminence, quickly, they're right behind me. We must flee."

That was when Stacey heard it, the sound of feet rushing up the staircase. Jack! Did he know Art had a gun? Oh, God no!

"Jack, he has a gun!" Stacey shouted, not knowing where she found the courage to warn her brother. She loved him too much to let him walk into a trap. After that shout, Art began trying to open the bathroom door.

"Go away!" she screamed between violent sobs. "The Grand Duchess orders you to go away!"

The sound of a gunshot exploded in her ears with such violence that her head began to swim. She could see where the bullet had pierced the door and ricocheted off the floor. It had missed its mark. The lock was intact. Stacey curled up in a fetal position with her arms covering her head. A second shot reverberated through the tiny room. This time the lock was destroyed. The spent bullet cracked the mirror on the wall across from the tub. She could see Art in the mirror. His image was split in two by the cracked glass. He would have her now.

"Your majesty, the time has come. We must flee or die together."

Stacey looked at her tormentor. His blue eyes were piercing and wild now, his hair disheveled. Sweat covered his brow and ran down his face, dripping onto the black sweat suit he wore. All she could do in her terror was whisper, "Go away."

"Freeze! Police! Drop the gun now!"

Terror so gripped her throat that she could not shout a warning. Art remained motionless except for the arm holding his gun. He slowly, almost imperceptibly, raised this arm. The gun was pointed directly at her. Stacey only had the strength to cover her head with her arms and lower herself into the bottom of the tub. "We must flee or die together," is what he had said. The police had arrived too late for her. She could hear Art apologizing to the Grand Duchess. If she were to die because of her name, then her last act would be to renounce it. She defiantly raised her head and with tears running down her cheeks shouted, "I am not Anastasia!"

What the young woman witnessed next seemed to occur in slow motion. Art had raised the gun to his temple. "I am sorry, your grace." Stacey covered her head again, not wanting to see this hapless man's blood splattered over her bathroom floor. She stayed cowered in the tub as a last shot rang out. The sound of the gun dropping to the floor was followed by that of Art's body sliding down the wall. It was not until she heard his quiet crying that she looked up. He was clutching a gunshot wound in his left shoulder. A cop cautiously walked over to Art, stepped over him, and kicked the gun further into the bathroom. Jack slipped by the two and picked Stacey up out of the bathtub.

The cop turned to the siblings and asked, "You alright, Miss?" She shook her head then Jack walked toward the living room.

"You better call EMS. Tell them we have one suspect with a gunshot wound to the shoulder," the officer in the bedroom called to his partner.

Ray and Frank came through the door as Jack reached the living room. They both knew the officers who had responded and could not thank them enough. By the time EMS was carrying Art out the door, Ray had introduced his fiancé to the cops on the scene. Stacey, in turn, had informed everyone in her building that she was now engaged. Shortly after the police had left, Kathy Stanley showed up with a camera crew.

"Kathy," Frank greeted her. "Long time no see. Are you here to apologize for sabotaging my future at dinner?"

"Frank Helms, what are you talking about?" the reporter asked, genuinely perplexed.

"Nothing, nothing," he responded, seeing she did not understand. When he noticed all his friends looking at him strangely, he muttered something about an inside joke.

"I don't want to hear any more inside jokes, Frank, please!" Stacey pleaded. She was proud of herself for having held up so well during the questioning of the detectives. Ray had hovered close by to add his silent support, making it that much easier to tell her story. Frank and Jack had cleaned up the bathroom as soon as the police had given the okay. They were now trying to figure out a way of securing the door until it could be replaced. The superintendent of the building was working with them.

Kathy appeared surprised to see so many of the people involved with the stalker story collected in the same place for this story. "Detective Friedrick, could I ask you a few questions?"

"Please, Kathy," Ray said. "Just call me Ray. I won't hear the end of it if I'm the only one you address by a formal title."

"Okay, Ray," she answered with a smile. "My boss heard some chatter over the police radio. Did this guy really think he was rescuing a Grand Duchess?"

"Apparently, yes," Ray responded. "You see Stacey shares her name with the daughter of a Russian Czar. The suspect connected the names and imagined himself taking part in the Russian civil war."

"He is psychotic enough to imagine this? Do you think he is psychotic enough to be the stalker?" she asked, speculating.

"We are looking into the possibility," he replied. "The gun used tonight was the same caliber as that used in the firebox shootings. The lab will run some tests on the gun and give us an answer in a day or so."

"Okay, that answers my only question," the reporter said as she put her pad away. She then turned to Stacey. "You must be Stacey, Chingli told me about you. From what I heard as I walked in the door, congratulations are in order."

Stacey beamed as she thanked the reporter. By then the door had a temporary lock installed, so Frank picked up Stacey's overnight bag and everyone began to move out of the apartment. They had decided earlier that she would spend some time at Frank and Chingli's. Whether or not she would move back home, to her future in-laws, or in with Ray was not yet decided. All Stacey wanted right now was to sleep in a secure home.

The door to her place made a grinding sound as it was closed behind them. The bullet holes in the wood told Stacey she could never live in her place again. Silent tears coursed down her face as the temporary lock clicked shut. A chapter to her life closed along with the battered door.

Chapter Twenty Nine

Chingli and Stacey sat at the table in the dinette talking over a cup of coffee. The guys were at Stacey's place straightening up and picking up some of her things. The lab technician had taken a couple of days off to try and get her life in order. After a conference with her co-conspirators, it was decided that she would take her future mother-in-law's offer and stay at the Friedrick's. Chingli had pointed out that staying there would keep the pressure on Ray to buy a ring and plan the wedding. The three had spoken with Stacey's mom and Mrs. Friedrick, both of whom agreed. Stacey would move in a few days, but needed to get back to work tomorrow. Work meant getting clothes and make-up from her place and Stacey still was not up to going back. Her "three clowns" volunteered to do the manly thing and retrieve a list of things for her.

"Do you think they can get everything you asked for?" Chingli asked her house guest.

"No, of course not," Stacey replied. "If they can accurately bring back half of what is on that list, I'll be happy. I don't know about Frank, but neither Jack nor Ray know the difference between foundation and mascara."

"Frank only knows that it makes women prettier," the Taiwanese woman laughed. "He always says, 'I don't know what you are doing, but you look great.'"

"He always was a little corny."

300

"I don't think it's corny," Chingli countered coyly. "I think it's nice."

"You are right, Chingli," Stacey said with a sigh. "Maybe Ray will get around to being as 'corny' as Frank."

"How far do you think Gloria wants to go with your big brother?"

Stacey thought for a second before answering. "As far as she possibly can, the girl has always had a thing for Jack. Since we were kids, really, but she knew it would be suicidal to try to capture him too soon. Whenever we talked about it, Glor always said he had to get tired of the dating game before she would go after him."

"How did she know he wouldn't fall in love before she tried to get him?"

"She didn't. Her attitude was if he is foolish enough to fall for some other girl, that's his loss," Stacey answered with a laugh.

"Looks like my sister-in-law knows your brother very well."

Both girls enjoyed a laugh at Jack's expense before the conversation turned more serious. Chingli admired the little blond in front of her for the strength she had shown two nights before. If she could learn to be that strong, then maybe Frank could have his dream of an MBA. Mama had said Chinese women must learn to eat bitterness. She had sworn to herself that Frank would leave the Fire Department or she would leave him, but oaths were dangerous. Did she know her husband and herself well enough not to fear defeat? Unsure of the answer to that question, she wanted to have more than one way out. What was the basis of Stacey's strength?

"How did you get through that night?" Chingli asked. "You said that you were lying in the tub, terrified. But when you thought you heard Jack running up the stairs, you found the courage to shout a warning. Where did you find the strength?"

Stacey smiled shyly, appearing embarrassed by the compliment. After staring at her coffee mug for a second, she raised her head and shook back her hair. "Jack has always been there when I needed him," she answered quietly. "We've always been close. I don't know if what I found was strength or courage or just realizing I would be unable to face the world without my brother there to help me through. In the end, it wasn't courage that allowed me to shout that warning. It was love." A tear escaped from her eye as Stacey completed her explanation.

Chingli sat quietly for a moment. Did she have that much love for Frank? Could she sacrifice everything to ensure his safety? Fearing where that road might lead made her hesitate to go down it. Those thoughts should be put off to another time. When life was back to normal and she had quiet time to think. The chaos of the past few weeks had left her nerves raw and her mind spinning. She remembered what was written by *Sunzi* in the Art of War. "If you know your adversary and you know yourself, then there would be no need to worry in a hundred battles." To know herself and her adversary would require time to analyze the situation. Before then she would have to survive on her wits.

Stacey recovered quickly and brought the conversation back to the original subject, their conspiracy.

"How do we stand with Frank and your uncle's job?" she asked expectantly. Chingli had hinted that there had been a change.

"I have recruited a new ally," she replied, leaving her dark thoughts behind.

"You're kidding!" was the excited response. "Who?"

"You met her the other night," Chingli said triumphantly. "Kathy Stanley. I think Frank insisted I invite her to dinner to get support. But the two of us spoke over the phone and found we have so much in common. We chatted and she told me a little about her family. By the time she got here, Frank knew he wouldn't get what he was after. How does he do that?" she thought for a second and then lowered her voice and raised her arms as if holding onto an anti-aircraft gun. "Boom, boom, boom. Crashed and burned." Both women laughed loudly.

Frank, Jack, and Ray returned with most of what Stacey had asked them to retrieve. She organized her things while Chingli poured them tea. The men began to talk about going into work. Their hostess was not happy with the prospect of her husband going back to the firehouse, but had resigned herself to it. When Jack and Ray started to discuss the stalker, Frank tried to change the subject, but the two bulls he had as friends were too busy stampeding through the China cabinet to notice. The only one who took note of his efforts was Chingli.

"Why don't you want them to talk about this stalker?" she asked her husband, annoyed that he seemed to think these thoughts would not cross her mind.

"I didn't say anything about not discussing the stalker," Frank replied innocently. "I was just trying to see if we - - - we could maybe plan to get together and figure out when we can move Stacey."

Chingli was doing her best to remain polite, but her husband's efforts at protecting her from the truth infuriated her. Stacey had come out of the bedroom by now and overheard Frank's feeble attempt to explain away wanting to avoid the topic of the stalker.

"Ray," Stacey asked. "Have they found out whether my psycho was also the firebox stalker?"

"He remains a suspect," the detective replied. "Because of the type of weapon he used and the statements he made in front of Frank and Stacey. The lab results came back negative on the gun he used, but that doesn't mean he isn't the stalker. There have been no stalker type killings since he was arrested and the weapon used at the fireboxes could have been ditched anywhere. Right now, he's undergoing psychiatric evaluation to determine whether or not he fits the profile of a serial killer. Even if he is the stalker, we have a long way to go before we can prove it."

"Damn," Jack chuckled. "You got more out of him than Kathy Stanley ever did."

"That, my friend, is a prepared statement drawn up just for our little inquisitive reporter."

"Then I can tell her," Chingli asked teasingly.

"Please, let Ray handle the official answers for Kathy," Frank pleaded with his wife.

Chingli had tears in her eyes as Frank walked out the door with his friends. She had promised herself not to cry in front of the men. As the door closed, tears began to flow freely. Stacey gave her a hug and some reassurance that things would return to normal soon. When she suggested that Art was the stalker, Chingli gave her a little smile. Wiping her tears, the Taiwanese woman said, "Thanks for being here Stace, but I don't think Art's the one." She then took a deep breath and asked, "What do you want to eat for dinner?"

Stacey thought for a moment and the suggested they go to the Rendezvous. They could meet Gloria, eat, and plan their next move.

"Are you comfortable going there?" Chingli asked, surprised.

"There's an English saying, 'If you fall off a horse, you have to get right back on it, or you'll never get on a horse again.' Something like that anyway. Want to go?"

"I'm a game," Chingli replied, trying to use one of her husband's expressions. Stacey chuckle and patted her on the back. "Good try, but you don't need the 'a'. It's simply 'I'm game'."

They both laughed as they went for their coats.

Chapter Thirty

Frank and Jack walked into the firehouse to find Kathy Stanley was in ahead of them. Her camera crew was nowhere in sight and the rig was out of quarters. Wagon jumped up from Kathy's feet to greet the firefighters. As Frank leaned over to pet the company mascot, he noticed the reporter look at her hands and grimace.

"It comes off with soap and water, Kath, don't worry," he assured her with a grin. "A little love can be a very dirty affair around a firehouse, can't it Wagon?"

"Don't you guys ever wash that dog?"

"Do you hear that Wagon?" Jack said sounding hurt. "The lady thinks you should take a bath." Upon hearing the last word, the little tan mutt's tail went between her legs and she crept away to hide under the table. Kathy was shocked at Wagon's reaction to the word "bath." Jack had emphasized the word, but not in that harsh a tone.

"Does she always react that way to a bath?" she asked.

"Don't use that word too much," Frank requested. "You'll have her shivering in fear like it's the Fourth of July. Two things the little lady dreads are being washed and firecrackers."

"Then make sure she never goes to Taiwan during Chinese New Year," Kathy said with a laugh. "Everyone gets a bath to begin the New Year and then they set off thousands of firecrackers to frighten away the evil spirits. At least that's why they did it in the old days. Now it's more for fun, but just as loud."

"You hear that, Wagon," Jack said as he leaned under the table and picked up the frightened dog. "If you're real bad and keep going across the street to roll in the crab shells, you'll end up in China on the New Year. But, right now you're a good little girl, so you don't have to worry. You want a cookie?" The firefighter put the dog down and walked to a cabinet. Wagon followed closely behind with her tail wagging furiously.

Frank turned to Kathy with a smile on his face. "You were here when they pulled out?"

"Yes," she replied. "I think they went to the projects. The Chief and Don are upstairs, so we girls were just hanging out waiting for the rest of the first tour to come in."

"Everyone else is in?" Jack asked as he made Wagon jump for her treat.

"Everyone but Al."

"And might I ask why you have honored us with your presence again, Miss Stanley?" Frank teased.

"Because everything happens when the first tour is working," she said in a tired voice. "At least that's what my boss thinks."

"Can I ask you something, Kathy?" Jack asked. "Why is it that your reports never include the fact that the City just closed down companies?"

"Because my bosses are not interested in the Fire Department unless there's a major fire or a death. Something that they think will make the public watch our broadcast."

307

"We almost got roasted the other night because Three Truck was put out of service. Don't your producers think the citizens of the City should know they and their firefighters are at greater risk?" he asked, getting annoyed just voicing the question.

"I'm sorry, Jack," the reporter said, "but there is nothing I can do. I've tried to put a spotlight on the Fire Department with the stalker shootings. When the editors get hold of any recorded interviews, they always slice the Fire Department and broadcast the Police. Sensationalism is and always has been a part of news reporting. Whether it was increasing newspaper circulation in the nineteenth century or increasing viewers of news broadcasts today, the overall goal is the same. Enlarge your market share. My bosses send me out to cover a story on a serial killer. I weave the Fire Department into the coverage because you have responded to every shooting, but my bosses are like yours. They assign a task and want that task done. I put myself on the line to bring you boys into the story those bosses assigned to me."

"Thanks for the effort, but we're losing levels of safety here," Jack said in frustration. "We'd appreciate it if you mentioned something about that or you might have to cover a firefighter funeral."

Frank had listened to the exchange quietly. Now he turned to his friend and said, "Jack, I think you're preaching to the choir."

"Yeah, you're right," Jack said quietly. "Sorry, Kath, I just get frustrated sometimes. I'm going upstairs to get changed, Frank. Entertain our guest and try to convince her I'm really not that bad."

Jack walked out of the kitchen through the double doors leading to the apparatus floor. His friend turned to the reporter to apologize.

"Jack's only been on the job a couple of years. These are the first companies he's seen closed, so he's not used to the idea yet. Give him time."

"I understand, Frank," she said with a smile. "Remember, I'm the choir."

"I wonder if you are," he said with a wry smile. "After your performance with my wife the other night, I suspect you are a double agent."

"I didn't help your situation much, did I?"

"Well, now my wife has someone she considers a friend who was not part of my circle when we met. That's a plus," he said thoughtfully. "But you didn't exactly encourage her to accept my job or my plans for the future."

"And how did you expect me to do that?" she asked curiously.

"I thought you might be able to tell her about how much your old man loved the job and how your mother had come to accept that."

"Then I would have had to lie," she informed him. "She never accepted the job, only the necessity of him having it. As far as my dad loving his job, it never came up in the conversation. That was your slip up, not mine. Although, I would have had to say I didn't understand why he loved it if she asked me."

Frank took a deep breath. If she did not understand why a man could love this job, how could his wife ever understand?

"Didn't your father ever try to explain to you why he loved his job?" he asked hopefully.

"No, Frank, he never did. As I told you the other night, he never talked about work around my mother. I only overheard the stories of bravado at picnics. They never explained why someone would love the job."

"Do you go to work to do a job or to get the job done?" he asked, seeming to change the subject. "There's a subtle difference between the two."

Kathy thought for a second and then shook her head in agreement. "Yes, there is. If you show up to do a job, then you accept limitations of, say, job description. You do what the job calls for. If you show up to get the job done, then you are willing to go beyond the job description so long as it will help finish the job."

"Bull's-eye!" Frank shouted, hoping this understanding would help explain how a man could love being a firefighter. "Men who love this job come to work to get the job done. They know that their efforts can make a difference. That little girl we got out the other night, she's a difference. You see, fighting fires has a definite immediacy to it. The job has to get done. There is no room for slacking off. Doctors are not the only ones who bury their mistakes. If you give your all, you can see results. You can see a little girl whose mother thought she was dead comfort that woman. It's not a job you will get rich doing. The rewards are intrinsic. You feel them in your heart. Does any of this make sense to you?"

Kathy had been sitting quietly, as if mesmerized by the firefighter's speech. "Of all the explanations I've ever received over the years from firemen around the world, none has expressed a man's love for this job quite as succinctly as you just did. I can't say it gives me an understanding of why men rush into vacant building that are burning, but now I think I have a clearer understanding of what makes you guys tick," the reporter said thoughtfully.

"How about you try to explain how we tick to my wife," he said hopefully. "She already seems to have more trust in your explanations than she has in mine."

The sound of a siren came from Springfield Avenue. Frank walked to the watch room and leaned out the door to press the button for the overhead door. The rig began to back in as he climbed the stairs to get changed.

Chapter Thirty One

The car turned onto Sixteenth Avenue and slowed to a crawl. He had been cruising the streets for the past hour and a half. Six Engine had responded to the projects twice, but there had been no false alarms. The weather was apparently keeping the malcontents of the city indoors. They did not have what it took to brave the elements and do an honest day's work for a fair wage. How could he have expected them to come out on a cool autumn night? Passing Camden Street School, the young man could see the end of Sixteenth Avenue ahead. The little firehouse Six Engine rode out of was on his right. A news van was parked beside the firehouse on Hunterdon Street. His car eased to a stop at the corner of Hunterdon and Springfield. The Hayes Homes loomed up across the street on the left.

His father had told him these had once been nice, before those people moved up from the south. They had come with no skills, looking for work in Newark's factories during the war. Industry fled the city afterwards because of their presence. There could be no other explanation. Newark had been a thriving industrial city prior to this wartime migration from south of the Mason-Dixon Line. Then came the slow decline as business fled. Business knew before everyone else that it was time to move onto greener pastures. Pastures with a skilled work force, not one made up of farmers from Appalachia. The Appalachian migrants simply went on welfare.

Now there had been three or four generations on welfare with nothing to supplement that but selling drugs. Dad had laughed when he told stories of how they used to keep these people in line. A voice in the back of the young man's head reminded him that his father was usually drinking when he bragged about the beatings he gave people. That meant he spoke of these matters frequently because the cop was a drunk.

No! His dad was an honorable man trying to help the city deal with the flight of the middle class. The pressures of dealing with this occasionally required something to help him relax. Then why did mom say she wanted a divorce? The scene had been played through his head countless times, but was just a recurring nightmare. It had never happened. His folks had been happily married. The car remained at the stop sign, its driver frozen as images of the past flashed across his mind.

"Your friends were here and they weren't happy!" his mother had screamed. "They know you're singing. They got a contract out on you. I don't want them carrying it out here, so leave!"

"You ungrateful bitch!" his father had yelled back as he slapped her across the face. "I did it for you!"

"No you didn't! You did it for the money and then you drank the money away!"

His father cursed her and raised his fist to strike again when a little boy jumped at the drunken man.

"You can't hit my mother!" the young man yelled in the idling car next to the Springfield Avenue firehouse. His eyes were open, but they did not see the bar across the street. The past had taken control.

He was reliving that night of so many years before. A car passing along Springfield Avenue brought him back to reality.

"No, that did not happen," he thought even as his hand reached up to rub the scar on his temple. Quickly pulling the hand down, he muttered "That is from a fall off my bicycle. Just like Dad had told the emergency room physician who had stitched it up. Dad did not lie. He was a good, honest cop." The images were just from that nightmare.

Turning right onto Springfield Avenue, the young man glided past the firehouse and then accelerated. The nightmare was replaced by thoughts of his last kills. These gave him a feeling of satisfaction. The streets were deserted because the riff raff feared the firebox stalker. The crusade was succeeding. Criminals are all cowards. That was why they went after the little people of the city. Maybe another low life would be eliminated tonight. This thought brought back the feelings of his flight from firefighters the last night he had been out. What if they arrived earlier? Can he shoot the men he is campaigning to help? The contradiction involved in answering this question made his head spin. Then he heard his father's voice as if the cop were sitting in the car.

"Come on boy, you started it. Don't be a coward, finish. Get up so I can kill you. At least I'll be proud of you then, get up!"

No, it had not happened! He touched his scar once more while applying the brakes for a red light. Without the distraction of driving, the nightmare took hold again. He was in the family car with his father, leaving the hospital. A strange man approached with something in his hand. After his dad saw the man, he tried to start the car quickly. The engine whined, but would not kick over.

"Won't start without this," the stranger said, taking a last drag on a cigarette and then throwing it angrily to the ground. He held up an engine coil.

His father appeared to be in a panic, sweat began to run off his brow. All attempts to start the engine ceased as he cursed under his breath.

"Time to pay," the man was now leaning up against the car looking down at the cop. "We know you've been singing. After all we did for you. They already picked up some of our guys. You're the only one who could have fingered them. You sang like a canary and now they're locked up. Time for the canary to go to sleep."

The sound of a car horn from behind startled the young man. It was a bad night. He prayed to God to take these dreams away from him and vowed to complete his mission. Pushing the gas pedal down, the car moved briskly away from the light. After traveling west for a short period, it turned onto Tenth Street and slowed to a crawl.

Why were these flashbacks haunting him tonight? No, they were not flashbacks, just a recurring nightmare, one that would soon be put to rest. He pulled the car over beside a garbage strewn vacant lot and put it into park. Images came flooding into his mind as soon as the need to concentrate ended.

"But, the kid," his father had whimpered.

"You don't want the kid to see? Take a walk kid," the stranger responded with a nonchalant coldness.

When the boy looked at his father he saw tears streaming down the man's face. "Go on, son," he said with a terrible sadness in his voice. "Go, Dad loves you."

"But I don't want to go, Dad," the boy had responded angrily.

"Get out of here before I give you another shot on the other side of your head!" his father had shouted furiously.

"Hey, that's the way you always treat your kid?" the strange man said in disgust. "I'm doing him a favor."

The boy had run as fast as he could, determined to find a police officer. After turning a corner, he heard a shot. This was followed by the sound of a car pulling away. He stopped and cheered, knowing that his father had only been acting, that he had surprised the stranger by pulling his service revolver and shooting him. The boy quickly ran back so his father could see him and not have to go around the block to pick him up. He stopped short as soon as he saw the family car still parked where his dad had left it. The boy approached the car cautiously and saw his father leaning forward, a red spot on the side of his head.

The young man sat in the car crying quietly. "Daddy," he whispered. "I should have never left you. If I had stayed he wouldn't have shot you." None of them would have had the nerve to shoot a man in front of his son. Then he heard his father's voice harshly accusing him.

"You were a coward! You should have jumped the gunman. Instead you ran as fast as you could to save your own skin!"

"No, pa!" the man shouted in the idling car. "I ran to get help. You told me to run! I am not a coward!" Becoming conscious of his surroundings, he put the car in gear and began to roll toward Sixteenth Avenue. This crusade proved there was no coward in the car.

His father had died because he had wanted to protect the citizens of the city and prevent its decline. If the police officer had lived, he would have held the city together. Now the son would do what the father had been prevented from accomplishing. The city will be cleansed so what happened to his father could not happen again. The results were already evident. Not only had the streets been deserted by the criminal element, but business was beginning to come back to the city. Had not the mayor announced today that this entire area was slated for redevelopment? Private money was going to be invested to provide housing and stores for the good people of this neighborhood. He knew his crusade had been a crucial element in the decision of private business to invest in this city. The timing of this announcement proved it.

The crusade would move forward. It was all that mattered, all that made life worth living. That is what he would tell the mayor when they honored him for bringing the city back from the brink. This was a mission given by God; it was impossible to turn away. Only the question of the firefighters remained. The crusade must not fail. It had been ordained by God.

If the Fire Department arrived on the scene too quickly, firefighters would have to die. Then his father would know he was not a coward, that he had the strength to complete the mission. It was his father's mission. The young man could not let him down again, not after a lifetime of failures. Now Dad could be proud, would turn to God and say, "I told you the kid could do it. That's my son." When Frank and his friends met his father in heaven, they would learn of the crusade and understand. They would feel proud of him and honored to have fallen for so worthy a cause. The realization of this truth gave the young man peace.

Content now that there was a purpose to his life, he pressed on the accelerator lightly and listened to the fire scanner in the passenger's seat. The car turned east on Sixteenth Avenue and began another large circle around the neighborhood its driver had chosen to patrol that night.

As the car approached Littleton Avenue, a woman rushed to the telephone pole on the corner and pulled the firebox. He hesitated for a split second because a woman had pulled the box. God made no differentiation between male and female sinners, all were condemned! The car leaped forward and swung onto Littleton Avenue, stopping next to the woman standing by the firebox. The now familiar rush of killer adrenalin was surging through his system as the car window came down and the gun was thrust out.

"No! He set my house on fire!" she screamed while dropping to a crouch, one arm wrapped over her head, the other pointing toward a vacant lot. The young man looked in the direction she was pointing and saw a man standing there defiantly laughing.

"That's right, bitch, you tell the world," the man shouted angrily. "You gonna throw me out? No, I'm gonna burn you out! Nobody messes with me!"

The stalker felt a special kind of disgust for the type of man who would assault a woman. This thought was followed by a voice inside his head shouting, "You mean like your father!" This only enraged him more. Throwing the car into park, he stepped out and leaned over its roof, desperately desiring the satisfaction of the gun's recoil. The sound of its discharge filled the cool night before the target could react. The animal went down in the middle of the lot.

Unsure if it were a clean kill, the young man decided to walk into the lot and finish his work. When he reached the carcass, it was evident the beast was mortally wounded. Another shot discharged to the head finished the job. A scream pierced the air as this second bullet exited the gun. He had forgotten about the woman! She could jeopardize the crusade! If firefighters could be sacrificed, then women were not immune. He started back to silence the witness.

The woman quickly fled in panic to her house. Fire now had control of the rear porch. Sirens could be heard in the distance. She looked toward him and then ran into the burning building. He thought it was a courageous, rational decision on her part. Certain death was pursuing her.

The young man jumped into his car and drove it to the front of the fire building. He could hear Six Engine responding even before the scanner came to life dispatching them. There was very little time to chase down his prey and slay it. The car screeched to a halt in front of the building and he jumped out. She was not in the doorway. Seeing the fire was spreading rapidly, he decided to leave his prey to burn. Six Engine pulled up to the firebox as the stalker ran back to his car.

The crusade was now in grave danger! If the firemen saw him or extinguished the fire before it had done its work, he could be identified. A decision had to be made instantly. The mission was sacred. The young man had already dealt with the paradox of possibly killing those he was trying to help. His personal feelings did not matter. An old friend like Frank Helms might have to perish. The benefits of this crusade for the citizens of the city were too great. It could not fail.

These thoughts solidified his resolve and forced him into action. The old police service revolver was raised and aimed at the rig standing at the corner. A single shot disturbed the night. It pierced the front windshield of the fire truck. Sure this would slow down the firefighters the young man jumped into his car and quickly drove off. There was no need to determine if any of the firefighters had been hit. The bullet was guided by God. If He called his old friend that night, then Frank would be delivered into the Lord's loving embrace.

Chapter Thirty Two

"It has been a topsy-turvey day here in Newark. Earlier Police Department sources informed me that a possible stalker suspect had been arrested last night after he assaulted a young woman. The man was obviously psychotic, believing he was rescuing a Russian duchess from the Bolsheviks. The type of gun used and the man's psychological state caused the police to think they finally had a break in this daunting case. They were awaiting the test results from the gun used last night before making any announcements. The results came back negative and now, as if to confirm those results, there has been what appears to be another stalker shooting.

Adding to their frustration, the pressure to find the person responsible for these crimes has climbed a notch. Prior to this evening the targets appeared to have been people who had pulled fire boxes where there was no fire. Tonight, people pulling a box for a fire and the firefighters responding to that alarm have become targets.

This is what we know so far. Shortly after ten o'clock, a fire alarm box was pulled on the corner of Sixteenth and Littleton Avenues for a fire at 159 Littleton Avenue. When the Fire Department arrived a bullet pierced the windshield of Engine Company Six. The bullet passed through the cab of the truck and out the back without striking any firefighters. However, the Fire Captain and firefighter in the cab were slightly injured by flying glass."

Stacey reached for the remote control and shut the television off. Chingli was sitting on the couch staring at the now blank screen. Her jaw was tightly clenched and tears had started to stream down her cheeks.

"I have to leave," the Taiwanese woman said quietly. "I have to leave or he might get killed because of his stupid pride."

Her friend sat quietly for a moment. Chingli continued to stare at the blank screen with a determined look on her face.

"Do you think he is going to stay out of the firehouse if you leave?" Stacey asked softly.

"I don't know what to think," was the quiet reply. "Remember you told me it was love that gave you the strength to warn Jack the other night? I am going to use the strength love gives me to force Frank off his job. This crazy person is shooting at firemen now!"

She could no longer hold back her emotions after verbalizing that fact. Crying freely, Chingli struggled to explain her reasoning. "You had to shout a warning to save Jack. This is my shout to save Frank. If I cannot save him, I don't want to be here for the phone call that tells me I lost him."

Stacey leaned over to give her friend a hug and waited patiently for the crying to stop. When the tears had dried, the lab technician suggested they call Gloria.

"Is she going to help me leave her brother?" Chingli asked skeptically.

"We can talk about what is best. Gloria knows her brother."

Stacey went to pick up Gloria; the two women returned to Chingli's apartment shortly after midnight. After listening to her sister-in-law's plan, Frank's sister gave a qualified approval.

"You have to allow him to find you, but not too quickly," Frank's little sister advised. "Where can you stay that would be easy enough for him to find you, but hard enough for him to have time to think everything out?"

"Mom and Dad's house is no good," the Taiwanese woman pointed out while the other women agreed.

"No, it can't be any one of the three stooges parents' homes. Do you have any friend in the area?" Stacey asked.

"No, no one but the two of you. I haven't talked to my room mates from Seton Hall for a long time. With school and then the wedding and everything there was no time - - -," she stopped in midsentence and smiled for the first time since watching the news. "That might work."

"What might work?" her two friends asked in anticipation.

"Kathy Stanley. I think she might help me."

"How are you going to get hold of her?" Stacey asked. "Do you have her number?"

"Yes, I can call her at home or at work," Chingli answered with confidence. "She is part of our group now, remember."

Chingli spoke with Kathy in Mandarin, so Gloria and Stacey had to ask what was discussed.

"She said that she was waiting for me to call. It seems Frank tried to talk her out of reporting what happened tonight. I hope he doesn't sleep all night," the Taiwanese women spat the last sentence out angrily, remembering her husband's attempt to protect her from the truth. "I can stay at her apartment. The only thing she wanted me to do was call my mother in case Frank decides to call Taiwan. Kathy doesn't want Mama to be worried."

"Okay," Stacey began. "We'll pack our things first then we'll drop Gloria off. How do we get to Kathy's?"

Chingli held out a slip of paper covered with Chinese characters.

"As long as you can read it," Stacey said with a laugh, "I'll get you there."

It had taken less than an hour to call Taiwan, get their things together, and drop Gloria. Chingli sat quietly as Stacey turned into the Queens Mid-Town Tunnel. The roads were empty, so the drive had been easy. It had been a silent trip because both women were too tired to talk. Chingli began to review what her mother had said as the car entered the tunnel.

"Mama, they're shooting at firemen now," she had whispered into the phone. "I can't take this. Mama, I'm leaving him." This pronouncement was followed by silence.

"Mama!"

"*Sanba*, I hear you my daughter. There is no need to scream in your mother's ear," her mother had admonished. "Why are you leaving my Frank? What will that achieve?"

324

Chingli had hesitated a moment, shocked that mama had not supported her. "It will wake him up," she had replied bitterly. "He will know that I can leave him."

"Gunshots did not wake him up?" was the skeptically response. "Have you spoken with him since these shots were fired?"

"No!" she spit out vehemently. "I do not want to talk with him!"

Her mother did not say anything for a heartbeat. Then she began to ask the questions Chingli had been avoiding asking herself. "Why, are you afraid he might persuade you not to leave?" The doubts this question raised cut deeply into her resolve. Mama's next questions rocked her daughter. "Do you not think you are deciding too quickly? When were these shots fired?"

Chingli did not want to answer the last question. To do so would make a response to the first one needless. Her mother waited quietly. There was no way around the queries. "Tonight," was the quiet reply given. How she hated it when mama caught her acting impulsively. Why had she remained silent when her daughter announced she was going to marry an American fireman?

"Tonight?" was the wry response. "How do you know these shots were aimed at Frank?"

"They were fired at his fire truck," she said angrily. "He was driving. Mama! The bullet passed between him and his captain. He could have been killed."

"But he wasn't," her mother said calmly. She then changed the subject to Frank's future. "Have you talked with him about uncle's job? Have you tried to show him it would be foolish not to take this job? I think you will get further if you remain home and talk to your husband. Where will you go?"

This final question allowed Chingli to change the subject without answering the harder questions that preceded it. "I have met a new friend. She is the television reporter who has been covering this story. Her mother is from Taiwan." The last sentence had the desired effect.

"Is she Taiwanese or outside born?"

"Her mother is Taiwanese, but Kathy cannot speak Taiwanese. We use Mandarin when we talk."

"You are going to her home?"

"Yes," Chingli informed her mother with determination in her voice. Her resolution to leave was strong once again. Mama's questions had bent that resolve, but the thought of Frank stubbornly insisting this stalker posed not danger to firefighters prevented a break. The bullet had passed between him and the Captain! Her husband would feel foolish when he came home to an empty house.

"Can you give me her phone number in case uncle has some news for you?"

Chingli told her mother Kathy's number knowing that she would talk with the reporter before they arrived at her apartment.

It had been hard to leave after she had hung up the phone. Mama had only acquiesced to her leaving. She had not given any support. She had needed her mother's support because of the empty feeling in her heart. Over the past eighteen months Frank Helms had supplanted

Mama as her anchor in life. There had not been a day without him. There had not been a moment when he was not on her mind. Now she could only reach inside herself for the strength to leave, even if it was only for a short time.

The doubts had returned to haunt her as soon as the phone's receiver had been hung up. Was she right? Would her husband's love be strong enough to compel him to find her? What if he rejected her? Could she live in America without him? Why had she not just forgotten about Frank Helms after Hong Kong? Confucius had said that women were the root of all evil. He was wrong! Men were evil incarnate!

Mama did not understand. Gloria, Stacey, and Kathy understood. Their little entente was the only thing keeping Chingli sane. Realizing how isolated she was, Chingli broke down and began to cry silently. Stacey noticed and reached over to squeeze her shoulder.

"Don't worry. It'll be all right," she reassured her passenger. "I know Frank Helms. In the end, he has the strength to swallow his ego and do what is sensible. When Frank gets home and finds you're not there, he'll take a step back from himself, analyze the situation, and see his future is with your uncle."

"Do you think so?" Chingli asked, putting aside the hurt of her mother siding with Frank. "I only want us to be happy. How can he be happy working in an old firehouse filled with cockroaches and flies?"

"You have such a picturesque way of describing the firehouse," Stacey pointed out with a chuckle. Chingli laughed through her tears.

"Thanks, Stace, I big time owe you," the Taiwanese woman said.

Stacey smiled. "Owe me big time? No you don't. If I get a ring on this finger, I'll be the one who owes."

The two women sat in a comfortable silence for the last few blocks of the drive.

Stacey parked the car across the street from the address Kathy had given. The reporter opened the door and began walking to the car before the engine stopped.

"I just got off the phone with your mother," she said to Chingli with a tired smile. "She wants you to call her as soon as you get here."

Chingli took a deep breath and gave an exhausted smile. Sometimes Mama was so predictable. "Kathy, how can I call her?" she asked. "It is more than a toll call."

"Don't worry, older sister," Kathy replied affectionately. "A sister always supports a sister. You will probably have to listen to my problems before the night is over."

They walked into the reporter's apartment and sat around the small table in the kitchenette. Kathy started water for coffee as the three women caught their breath. She broke the silence with a question for Stacey. "Do you have to work today?"

"I was supposed to go back today," she answered forlornly. "I haven't been in to the lab since my apartment was invaded by the Twilight Zone. But I don't think I'll do anyone much good today. When I get to Gloria's I'll just call and explain to my boss. He's been a sweetheart for the past few days. He'll let me slide one more time, I'm sure, but after the coffee I have to dash."

The hot coffee seemed to give Stacey the extra boost she needed to face the drive back across the Hudson River. After she left, Kathy and Chingli began to discuss what had happened and what options were opened.

"Do you have the strength to stay away from him?" Kathy asked quietly.

"I think, but it is hard," her guest replied. "It was so much easier before him. Why can't I just leave?"

"Because you have learned to love him," the reporter answered. "You'll never be the same. Unfortunately, men do that to us girls."

"Yes, they do," Chingli said with a sigh. "What makes everything even worse is the way my mother seems to side with him all the time. She never asks how Frank is. She says 'How is my Frank?' I sometimes wonder if I married him or she did. If I complain she reminds me that her marriage was arranged. The other night she told me how lucky I was because we have only been married six months and I loved him. 'I hardly knew your father when we were married six months.'" Both women were laughing when she finished. "I get the same type of thing from my mother, although she was more of a rebel," Kathy said thoughtfully. "She did marry a foreigner and move to an uncivilized country, after all."

"She was brave," Chingli pointed out.

"She was head over heels in love is what she was, poor little Taiwanese girl. She didn't have the education or language training you had. Her family came into money because they were farmers who owned land in the right place. All of my cousins ended up in college and with high paying professions, but my mother made it through high school and that was about it."

"Does your mother have brothers?"

"Yes, as a matter of fact she does. They went to college, but they were younger. My grandfather had hit it rich by the time they could go to college."

"Or is it that he wouldn't waste his money educating a girl," Chingli asked provocatively.

Kathy stopped for a moment before answering. "I can't say for sure. Mama never spoke about her disappointments with me. Only her hopes for my future and how I had opportunities she never had."

"Do you ever get the impression that you are living the life she wants you to live and not the life you want to live?"

Kathy started laughing at the question. "No, not quite, although it's not from want of her trying. She gives me advice freely and often. I moved here as much to put a little distance between her and me as for the job opportunity. Don't get me wrong. I love my mother dearly, but she has her way of doing things and I have mine. If she were me then she would be married to a nice young man I knew in college and would have dropped out without finishing her degree. He has forgiven me and we're still friends, but I don't think mama has forgiven me yet."

"Then you are here in New York all alone? How do you do it?" Chingli asked, realizing that without the emotional support of Frank, she would have fled back to Taiwan.

"Oh, I get by," Kathy replied shyly. "It isn't easy. There are sleepless nights and I don't have the advantage that you do. There is no time difference between New York and Rhode Island. If I called home on those nights, my mother would be down here the next day."

"Do they ever stop trying to teach us how to live?" Chingli asked in exasperation.

"Not as far as I can see. At least not Taiwanese mothers," her hostess responded with a sigh.

"Do you have someone you're interested in?" she asked, trying to prolong the conversation and delay the inevitable phone call.

"You mean romantically?" she replied coyly. "No, not right now, I'm trying to establish a career. If I get all flustered with a man . . ."

"It would make your life perfect," Chingli finished with a laugh, remembering Frank's friend Dan. Maybe when this was all over, Kathy would like to meet him.

"You sound like my mother!" the reporter scolded her guest. "And now you have to call yours. You've been putting it off, haven't you?"

"We both knew that from the beginning of our little chat," the Taiwanese woman said with a chuckle. "I'm just so afraid I will be wrong and she will be right. Then she will say nothing to me about how I made a mistake. She'll just move onto another subject, but I'll know that a master teacher has given me a lesson that I am expected to remember forever. She will not allow me to make the same mistake again. If the subject comes up, Mama will say 'You have learned that lesson already. Let's not go over it again.' And I will feel like a little girl who has received her mother's scorn."

"I can understand how you feel," the reporter said sympathetically. "My mother has a habit of showing her displeasure by simply clearing her throat. The sound is different when she is annoyed than at any other time. I still respond to that sound. It drives me crazy." After pausing to sigh, she asked, "What does your mother want you to do?"

"She doesn't want me to leave Frank," was the tired reply. "She said if I am not with my husband I can't persuade him to take uncle's offer. But, Kathy, if I stay with him he won't leave that job. He'll keep putting off the decision because he loves fighting fires. It's fun for him! The little boy doesn't want to grow up! If I make it obvious what the cost of staying on the Fire Department will be, maybe he will wake up. Do you think so?"

"I don't know what to think. My mother could never get my father off the job, but he never had the opportunity your uncle is offering," the reporter then looked at the kitchen clock. "You're going to have to call soon. It's already mid-afternoon in Taiwan."

"I know, I know," was the reluctant reply. "I might as well get it over with. She can only yell at me over the phone."

"*Wei, mama. Gua she Chingli*," she said without energy.

"You are at Kathy's now?"

"Yes."

"Uncle needs some information so he won't lose face when he offers Frank a salary. What is his salary as a fireman?"

Chingli was trapped. She did not know her husband's salary. Whenever he had tried to tell her, she had put him off. Now she would have to confess this to her mother. They were not more than a few sentences into the conversation and already Chingli felt defensive.

"I don't know," she replied sheepishly to mama.

"You don't know?" was the shocked response. "You mean you make your husband do the tedious work of family finances? Men don't have the patience for that my daughter. Why do you not do what a good wife should?"

"I don't understand American money, Mama," she said defensively. "After I learn I will do what should be done."

"We can discuss that in a few days," her mother said nonchalantly. "Uncle needs to know a salary that will persuade Frank to leave the fire department. I will have to tell him an approximate. Can Frank get to this place called 'Port Newark'?"

"I think so. It must be in Newark. That's where he works now."

"Have you talked with him tonight?"

"No."

"Be strong, I will be there to support you and my Frank. Don't worry."

When she hung up the phone, Chingli knew in her heart that her mother was coming to America. There had been too many hints for that not to be true. "I will be there to support you and my Frank." She meant here in America!

Chingli wanted to call back and shout "Don't you dare!", but knew it would be futile. Her determination had been learned from Mama. Now she would be under her mother's tutelage once again. Can a daughter ever really escape from the lessons of her mother?

Chapter Thirty Three

Frank walked up the stairs leading to his apartment with a bag of dirty uniforms thrown over his shoulder. Was it possible to feel more tired than he felt at that moment? He doubted it. The exhaustion seeped down to his very soul. Lack of sleep was not its cause. He felt as if his emotions had been dropped off a cliff. The free fall was about to end with a sudden stop. The firefighter touched the bandage on his face and wondered how to explain it to Chingli without an explosion.

In the end, there would be no need for an explanation. His wife would have watched last night's news. Kathy did a good job of reporting the events that led to the small cuts on his face. As soon as Frank opened the door, his wife would know what had happened. How to keep the impending explosion to a subatomic blast was the question he had been pondering all morning. If only the world would leave them alone, they would be able to work through their disagreements.

Over the past few weeks, nothing had gone right. The outside world kept intruding with its problems. How could he think about the future when the present demanded all his time? Swearing quietly under his breath, Frank unlocked the apartment door and pushed it open. Remembering days when his wife greeted him with a warm smile and a warm breakfast only made what he was about to face that much harder. He stepped into a strangely silent apartment.

It was unusual for his wife to sleep in, but Frank was sure she had kept Stacey up to all hours discussing the news report. Stacey had said she was going into work this morning. She must have been exhausted. The firefighter walked quietly through the living room, not wanting to disturb his sleeping wife. A quick glance at the corner where Stacey had stored her things told him something was wrong. Throwing his uniforms into the bathroom, he opened the bedroom door with a sinking feeling in his stomach. The room was empty. Maybe they had gone out for breakfast. Even as this thought crossed his mind, Frank knew it was not true. Stacey had taken her things when she had left. The firefighter walked over to the closet and looked for Chingli's overnight bag. Where could she have gone?

"Gloria," Frank said to his sister's answering machine, trying to keep the annoyance he felt out of his voice. "Can you tell me where my wife is?"

The next phone call was to Ray. Since Stacey was with Chingli, maybe Ray had an idea of where they could have gone. "Ray, Chingli's gone," he informed his friend. "I think she took off with Stacey. Any idea where Stacey is?"

Ray swore into the phone before answering. "She said she was going into work. I'll call her there and get back to you."

Where else would she have gone? He doubted Chingli would have fled to his folks' house, but she might just to embarrass him. Frank thought for a minute before calling his parents. How to find out whether his wife was there without letting Mom know that she had walked out? Deciding to make it a casual call to see how things were back home, Frank took a deep breath and dialed. Mom answered and immediately began grilling him on his future.

"Have you made a decision on leaving the Fire Department yet?" she asked with an edge to her voice.

"No, Mom, nothing definite yet."

"I really wish you could leave. Did you see the news? They said this kook is shooting at firemen now."

"Yes, I heard," he answered in as neutral a voice as possible.

"How's Chingli taking this?" his mother asked in a concerned voice. "She seemed upset the last time we talked."

"She's still upset, but everything will work out."

"Well, if you're sure. Your father said if you want to come over and crunch numbers to see what is best, he's available."

"Okay, when I get some numbers from her uncle, I'll be over to discuss things."

"You seem very tense, dear. Is everything all right?"

"Nothing to worry about, Mom," he replied a little too quickly. "I have to go now. See you soon."

Three phone calls and still not a hint as to where his wife might be. His head was humming with the possibilities. Could she have gotten hold of a ticket to Taiwan? Not very likely at three in the morning, but he went to check the dresser where she kept their passports just in case.

After confirming the passports were still in their proper place, Frank called Jack. Maybe he had some ideas about where Stacey would go or where Gloria was. Jack answered with a groggy voice.

"Chingli's gone. Where's Gloria?"

"What?" his friend snapped out of his stupor. "Where did she go?"

"I'll be damned if I know," was the frustrated response. "Do you know where Gloria is?"

"Gloria? No, as far as I know she's at home. She worked last night. Why?"

"I think Chingli would ask Gloria for advice before she took off. And my little sister wouldn't hesitate to give it to her."

"Did you call Ray?"

"Yes, he's calling to see if Stacey is at work," Frank said unenthusiastically. "I left a message on Gloria's machine and called my folks, but nothing so far."

"How did your mother react to her little Chinese princess leaving?"

"I didn't tell her," he said with a dry chuckle. "That would have turned into a long conversation."

"Tell me about it," Jack said with understanding. "Look, I'll call my mother and see if Stacey is there. Then I'll come over to your place and we can work out a battle plan."

From Jack's reaction, Frank knew he must sound like he was about to go over the edge. What other options did he have? Chingli remained so dependent on him that there were few places where she could go. She had distanced herself from the Chinese community at Seton Hall, instead concentrating on building a life for the two of them. Now that she needed time away from him, her choices were severely limited. Why couldn't she just throw him out of the house like any other woman? Then he would at least know she was safe. The phone rang as he finished this thought.

"Stacey's not at work," Ray said. "Her boss said she called and said she hadn't slept all night, so she took a vacation day."

"Do me a favor," Frank said. "Call your mom and see if Stacey dropped her things there or something. Just keep it quiet and find out if they are with her or not."

The sun had moved to the other side of the building and Frank still did not know where his wife was. After ruling out all the obvious places she might have run to, he had come to the conclusion that she was either with Gloria or Kathy Stanley. His sister had not returned his phone call and there had been no sign of her when they had driven past her place. The number for Kathy had been under a magnet on the refrigerator. It was no longer there, so he could not call to confirm Chingli was with her. Was his wife so efficient that she would remember even that small detail? He knew the answer before finishing the question.

Jack and Ray were sitting across the table from him. They had spent the entire day helping Frank try to locate his wife. Everyone was tired and frustrated. They would all have to leave for work in a

339

few minutes. When the phone rang Frank jumped up, knocking over his chair in an agitated rush to answer it.

"Gloria, do you know where she is?" he spat out impatiently.

"Do I know where who is?" Gloria asked her brother. He had a feeling that she had been home for a while, but had refused to call right away. It would be just like his manipulative sister to let him stew in his own juices for a while.

"Don't get cute with me," he said coolly. "Do you know where she is?"

"Frank, you have to give her a little time to calm down," Gloria began to lecture. Her brother just cursed and slammed the phone down. This was one of the most difficult periods of his life and his sister has to start giving unwanted advice. It was obvious to him that the girls were working together to make a point. He had to control himself or they would play him like a hooked fish. The apostles were not the only fishers of men.

Jack picked up the phone and called her back. "Glor," he said in a calm voice, "I'm sure you know where Chingli is. Your brother is going off the deep end. Just tell him she's safe."

"Okay," she answered in a matter of fact tone. "Of course she's safe."

Frank lost control and grabbed the phone from his friend. "You know where she is then?" he snapped in an accusative tone, regretting it instantly. He was very exposed and knew she realized it. Was she going to play with him a little more or give him what he demanded?

Gloria apparently decided it was not quite the right time to let her brother off the hook. She taunted him one more time. "Yes, but I don't know if I should tell you."

"She's my wife!" he shouted through the phone.

"Frank Helms, I'd suggest you get control of yourself and take a step back. You'd see how much of an ass you really are. Time to grow up, big brother. Don't you see the gold you have in your hand? Take the job her uncle is offering or the whole world is going to think you're the biggest fool."

He slammed the receiver down again, too furious to deal with his sister. Take a step back. There was no doubt in his mind he looked foolish, but it was not the question of a job offer that gave him that appearance. His wife and his sister were playing him like a fool. Gloria had pushed all the right buttons. The doubts that had been eating away at him since Chingli's uncle offered this opportunity had been verbalized. That did not solve

his present dilemma. He had to get information from Gloria, but was too angry to speak with her. Jack re-dialed Gloria one more time.

"Look, we have to get into work. Just tell him where she is so he can concentrate."

"I have no problem with that," she said with a laugh. "He's the one who keeps hanging up. Put him on the line."

Jack put his hand over the receiver and turned to Frank. "You have to keep your cool, my boy, or we're going to be late."

Frank shook his head yes and took a deep breath before taking the phone. "Where is she?"

"She's at Kathy's."

"Kathy's?" was the response. "You mean Kathy Stanley's? Where the hell does she live?"

"I don't know. Chingli wrote the directions down in Chinese and you weren't there to read them."

"Who drove her?"

"Stacey, of course," Gloria answered, seeming to enjoy revealing another layer of their conspiracy.

"Stacey," Frank said in a tired voice. "What's going on here? It sounds like you girls are scheming against me."

"That's only part of it," she said with a laugh. "It's a conspiracy so immense you would have a hard time grasping it."

"What?"

"Goodbye Frank, Chingli is fine. It's you I'm worried about." She hung up the phone, leaving a dozen questions darting around his mind.

"Well, at least we know where she is," Jack said trying to sound optimistic. Before either of his friends could answer, Ray's beeper went off.

"Good timing," the detective said with wry chuckle as he reached for the phone. "One mystery solved and now another surely beckons."

"Another mystery beckons," Frank said shaking his head. "Ray, you are one sick puppy."

342

Ray's phone conversation was short, but obviously to the point. When he hung up the phone, the detective was animated. "We've got him!"

"Got who?" the two firefighters asked together.

"The stalker," their friend replied. "That woman you pulled out of the building last night, Jack. She gave us a composite sketch of the stalker. We should have him by the end of the night."

"God," Frank moaned in relief. "Not a day too soon. Now this story can stop haunting my life."

"You're not through with this quite yet, Frank," Ray said quietly.

"What?" Frank said sounding confused. "Now, hold on. I'm a fireman, not a cop. I turned in my police badge and my weapon a long time ago."

"If what the Sergeant thinks is right, we're going to need you. He thinks the stalker is your old coaching buddy, Dan O'Brian."

Chapter Thirty Four

The young man heard sirens in the distance while he sat in the living room reading the paper. They were not the electronic sirens of the police or EMS. These were clearly the old mechanical sirens still used by the fire department. When the crusade was completed and the mayor had stepped down in favor of the city's savior, one of his first acts would be to modernize the equipment used by the fire department. The trucks that responded to the city's fire emergencies were clearly obsolete, but he had to be realistic. The procurement of such complicated equipment took time. One thing that could be done during the first days of his administration was to place the companies that had been closed back into service.

The sirens seemed to be getting closer. Where were the firefighters responding? The scanner was on, but no alarm had been transmitted and none of the Vailsburg companies had been sent out. The sirens continued to get closer until it seemed they were on his block. Flashing red lights suddenly filled the living room windows as the scream of the siren reached a crescendo and then began to die down.

"Danny," his mother called from upstairs. "A fire truck stopped in front of our house. Do you smell smoke?"

"No, Mom," the young man replied putting down his paper and looking out the window. He could hear his mother coming down the stairs. She walked into the living room as the door bell rang.

"Did you call the fire department?" she asked her son with a puzzled look on her face.

"No," was the perplexed reply.

If they had been the police he would have thought the mission had been betrayed. Why would the Fire Department come to his home? Maybe they had discovered the purpose of his crusade and had come to thank him. Then he would no longer have to wrestle with the paradox of last night. These men would understand the importance of his mission and appreciate its benefits for themselves and the city. With these hopes flashing through his mind, the young man rose to answer the door. Frank Helms greeted him with a serious look on his face.

"Dan, did you call the fire department?" the firefighter asked with concern.

"No, Frank, we didn't. What's going on and what are you doing up here?"

The last question seemed to make his old buddy nervous. "Oh, I'm on detail. One of the guys on Palm Street is on vacation." Frank told him before responding to the rest of the question. "Headquarters received a call saying someone had set fire to your house".

"Set fire to our house?" Mrs. O'Brian whispered in the background.

"Hello, Mrs. O'Brian," Frank said with a quick smile. "Fire Headquarters received a phone call saying that. Could we walk around the outside to make sure everything is all right?"

"Please do, Frank. Who would say someone set fire to our house?" she muttered to herself.

The young man stood silently, realizing that either the mob or the city gangs had found him. The crusade was in jeopardy! They were warning him to stop or his home would be set ablaze. What to do? This was only a warning. Whether it was the mob or city gangs, both had felt the power of the crusade. The respect his adversaries had for the crusader was shown by the indirect warning. If he wanted to protect his mother and her home from possible harm, then the mission would have to end.

This option was instantly rejected. It was not his mission. It had been given to him by God. He could only rest if the Almighty gave some sign showing the crusade was complete. No matter what the risks were, the mission took precedence. All else could be sacrificed.

"It's probably some sick person's idea of a prank," he told his mother. The young man had borne the weight of his calling by himself from the beginning. His mother did not need to carry any of the load. He would continue as before.

"Well, I'll go tell my Captain," Frank said. "Then he can inform headquarters and see where we should go from here."

Frank walked back to the rig and spoke to the man on the passenger side of the truck. Afterwards, he and another firefighter walked around the building. Their inspection complete, the firefighters reported back to the fire truck. Frank then made his way back to the front door.

"Dan, headquarters says they have the voice of the caller on tape. If you could come down to the Arson Squad office, maybe you could identify the person who called."

The young man became more suspicious. There had been no radio traffic. How could Frank or his Captain know what headquarters said without a radio transmission? "Did they know that before you came, Frank?" he asked. "I haven't heard any radio traffic since before you arrived."

The young man thought Frank hesitated for a moment. His mother did not like the question and made her displeasure obvious with her movements. She had always thought Frank was a nice boy. That was in the past and did not matter now. The future of God's crusade was at stake. Frank may have been one of his mother's favorites when they were children, but that did not mean he would understand the mission. There was no time to explain. His old friend could turn on him out of ignorance. His mind cried for caution while waiting for Frank's answer.

"You sure there was nothing over the air?" Frank asked. "Headquarters must have the mixer off. I'll have to tell the Captain when I get back on the rig. If you can't hear it over a scanner, then the rest of the department can't hear it either. No one will hear us if we need help."

The young man had known in his heart that his old friend would not betray him. Frank had fled the corruption of the police department. There was no need to doubt his loyalty.

"Danny, you should go," his mother advised. "It could be the mob trying to burn us out. Maybe you can recognize the voice. It could be that man who was with your father last."

"I think it would help," Frank added. "With all of these firebox shootings, everyone is nervous about crank calls."

This assertion caught the young man off guard. He had not expected the firefighter to even mention the subject. His reply was a reflex reaction that voiced what he had hoped would be the firemen's view of the situation. "Why would you guys be nervous? I always thought the shootings were an attempt to help the firefighters."

"Help us?" Frank asked incredulously. "That's a novel way of looking at it, Dan. Maybe you're right. If you can identify this voice, they might be able to find this guy and determine whether he's a hero or a goat."

"How do you know it's a man?" Mrs. O'Brian asked.

Frank seemed to stumble for a split second before he blurted out, "I don't know, Mrs. O'Brian. It's just a habit of speech to say he or him."

The young man's suspicions were aroused once again. These were quickly dismissed as nerves. He would go with Frank, but would bring his gun in case someone wanted to betray his friend.

"Okay, Frank," he said in a calm voice. "How about we take my car?"

Frank pulled on his turn out coat as he answered. "Dan, you don't want this smelly thing in your car," he said with a grin. "We'd probably be overcome unless we drove with the windows opened."

The young man chuckled at his friend's comment. There was no denying that the heavy black coat smelled. The amount of soot on the coat was shown on its blackened yellow reflective strips. It would take quite some time to air his car out if his friend wore that coat in it. The thought of taking the ghetto mobile crossed his mind, but was instantly dismissed. He could not be certain Frank had not seen that car the other night. Then an idea crossed his mind. Impulsively, the young man blurted out a request. "You think I might be able to hitch a ride on your truck?"

The firefighter smiled broadly and shook his head. "Yeah, I think I might be able to talk the Captain into that. It would make things a little easier. Not much parking by headquarters. It'll be a little chilly though. There's no room in the cab and it's wide open where I sit."

"Don't worry," he reassured Frank with a playful smirk on his face. "I can tough it out with the firefighters."

Mrs. O'Brian watched from the front porch as her son climbed onto the fire truck. The two men sat in the jump seats directly behind the Captain and the driver. The sliding doors separating the truck's cab from the seats were pulled closed. A speaker hanging from the middle of the roof allowed any firefighters riding in these seats to hear radio broadcasts. There was little radio traffic tonight.

"Your mom looks great," Frank said cheerfully.

"She's doing better," the young man replied. "How's that Asian beauty of yours doing?"

The firefighter's expression changed at the mention of his wife. "Lately, she's been having a hard time adjusting. The girl gets nervous about my job," he said forlornly. "It doesn't matter how much I reassure her. She's sees what is possible and assumes that's going to happen."

"Even after this stalker character has been cleaning up the streets, she's still nervous?" the young man said trying to get a true feel of what the firefighters thought of his work.

"That character took a shot at firefighters last night."

"I'm sure if you boys backed off, there would be no problem," he responded. If this message could get back to the firemen, the crusade would succeed. Frank was the perfect messenger.

"That wouldn't solve my problem, Dan," Frank said without much hope. "It comes down to a very basic difference between the sexes. Women get nervous about what is possible. Men are cautious about what is probable. The trick in a relationship is to bridge that gap. I haven't figured out how to do that." The firefighter then cursed under his breath.

"It will work out, Frank," the young man said. "I think things are going to change for the better in this city very soon. When I complete a little project I'm doing, you'll be able to tell her there's nothing to be nervous about and she'll trust you on it."

The rig pulled up to fire headquarters as he finished encouraging his old friend. "When I become mayor," he thought, "your wife won't have to worry about a thing." The two men stepped down from the rig as the Captain opened his door. Frank walked over to the cab door and spoke quietly with his skipper. Then he turned and walked toward his old friend.

"Dan, the Captain says they'll stay out here and mind the rig," he said with a smile. "We can go in and listen to the tapes. After that we'll drop you back home."

"Sounds good to me, Frank," the young man replied as they both started walking toward the side entrance to fire headquarters. "I didn't know dispatch was up here."

"Dispatch?" the firefighter said nervously. "No, the operators aren't in fire headquarters. We're going to the Arson Squad."

"The Arson Squad? Why would they have tapes from dispatch in the Arson Squad?" he asked sensing his friend's tension. Why would Frank be tense? Remembering what the firefighter had said about his wife, the young man relaxed. Being involved with a woman can turn a man's life upside down. There was no need for him to think any further on why his friend would be tense.

"Well, the Arson Squad's official name is the Bureau of Investigation. Any investigations done by the Fire Department are done out of Arson. There's no need to get the police involved."

He should have realized that. If the police were brought in, then the corruption which permeated that department could seep into the fire department. It made all the sense in the world that the Fire Department would have its own investigative arm. The two men entered a side door and weaved their way through desks in a dark outer office, the young man walked behind Frank toward a door in the corner of the room. They stepped into the light of the arson office. The walls of the room were lined with metal lockers. Desks were arranged in a seemingly haphazard manner around the office with typewriters and phones stationed on each desk top. Paint was peeling from the walls, but very few flakes were on the floor.

The young man scanned the room with a smile until he noticed an investigator seated behind a corner desk. His heart began to pound instantly. The man behind that desk had taken the police exam with him. There was no doubt. Every time the young man saw him, he wanted to shout, "You have my job!" The pretender seated at that desk was the first cop in his family. He did not deserve to be a police officer. A cop's presence meant the crusade had been sold out and Judas was walking next to him. Any fraternal feeling for Frank Helms was now supplanted by rage.

He reached into the side pocket of his trench coat and wrapped his fingers around the old police revolver. Then he turned to Frank and said bitterly, "Don't you want to kiss me on the cheek?" The firefighter looked puzzled for an instant, but only for an instant. "Move decisively and there will still be a chance to salvage this crusade," he thought.

The gun was drawn out of the trench coat pocket smoothly. Rage flowed down the young man's arm and into the finger squeezing the trigger. How dare he interfere with God's crusade. The thunder of a gun discharging indoors shocked his ears.

A bullet pierced the firefighter's turnout coat at the heart and drove him back into a locker. His helmet flew off with the concussion of the bullet. The force of his body slamming into the locker showered the assorted items stored on top of it down onto him. The thunder created by the gun discharging did not die down. It grew louder instead. The wrath of God was now being unleashed against all in the room. Even the young man felt pain.

Pain was suddenly all there was to his universe. Now he would meet God. His father's voice came to him as his body lost the strength to stand. "You disgust me," the cop's voice said hauntingly. "Your little mission failed and now you've killed a fellow uniformed civil servant. You are no longer my son!"

The young man wanted to shout, "Was I ever really your son?" but did not have the strength. It no longer mattered what his father said. Now the only reality was pain, all-encompassing pain. He could laugh at his father now and acknowledge he was a bad cop, a wife beater, a bastard. With this realization came a strange release as the pain began to ease. But if his father was a bastard, then his crusade was for naught and the crusader was nothing more than a murderer! Was that the answer he had been looking for when he began? The sound of the cop laughing assaulted his mind. So be it, the young man thought as the pain faded, faded, until it was gone.

Chapter Thirty Five

"Chief, can you explain to us why a firefighter was involved?" Kathy asked.

"Frank Helms is not just a firefighter, Miss Stanley," Chief of Police Smith answered. "He was trained as a police officer and was a veteran of the force before he transferred to the Fire Department."

"But why was he used?" a reporter from the Star Ledger asked.

"We had concerns for the suspect's elderly mother. It was felt that if he could be arrested away from home, there would be less chance of her being injured. Since Firefighter Helms was acquainted with the suspect, he was the logical person to lure him out of his house. We feel this operation avoided a hostage situation and exposed the public to the least amount of danger."

"You are sure this suspect was the firebox stalker?"

"Yes, the results are back from the revolver used. He also kept a diary of sorts. It details his efforts to 'cleanse' the city; I believe is how he put it."

"What is the condition of Firefighter Helms?"

Ray reached up and shut the television off when he noticed Frank was sleeping soundly. His friend was now the lead story on every channel and all he wanted to do was sleep. How could he get hold of whatever it was the hospital was feeding Frank? There would be no more sleepless nights, that was for sure. The detective walked out into the hall, closing the door quietly as he left the room. Thank God he had won the last argument they had.

"You have to wear the vest, Frank," Ray had insisted.

"Look, I'm just going to be walking next to him," was the stubborn reply. "I get him there. You arrest him. How is there going to be a need for this thing? I'll be hot and look like I put on twenty pounds. That will make him suspicious, if nothing else does."

"You can take your firefighter attitude and shove it!"

"What are you talking about?" the firefighter asked defensively. "You sound like the girls, always accusing us of pushing too far because of our pride."

"Oh. I've seen more than one thick headed fireman, too proud to wear the proper equipment into a building, staggering out with soot all over his face, heaving his guts out," the cop replied.

"Not from Six Engine on my tour you didn't."

"Well, if you're so damn safety conscious, why are you giving me a battle over wearing the vest? This guy's been blowing people away for weeks. I prefer him being suspicious to burying you. Wear the vest or go sit in the firehouse and we go in with a SWAT team."

Frank had taken a deep breath before he relented, but not before getting Ray to take the oath again. "I swear, Chingli will know nothing of your involvement." That vow got blown out of the water when Dan O'Brian turned on his old friend.

Gloria and Jack were sitting in the hall waiting. None of the three had slept for the past day. There had been a steady steam of visitors. Firemen, cops, and news reporters from the papers and television had all stopped by to see how "broken ribs" was doing. Frank was probably more exhausted from the visitors than from his injuries. When the boys from Six Engine had found out that he was still in the hospital because a typewriter had fallen on his head, they were merciless. But there was not a happier group of men in the world after they were told Frank would be all right. Ray smiled to himself as he sat down next to friends.

The three sat quietly for a minute before the detective voiced something that had been bothering him. "You know who hasn't been here yet?" he asked.

"We're working on Chingli," Gloria said with a tired smile.

"I wasn't thinking about Chingli. There have been no politicians, no mayor, no councilmen," the cop said indignantly. "I mean the man almost got killed for this city and none of the elected big wigs bother to come, thank him, and see how he's doing."

"Please," Gloria replied. "With everything he's been through over the past few weeks, he doesn't need any publicity hounds bothering him."

Jack came in on Ray's side when he heard his girlfriend's comment. "That's not the point, Glor," he said adamantly. "He went beyond what the city pays him to do, put everything on the line. The least these guys can do is come out and see if he's okay. Just acknowledge the effort, that's all."

"If you say so," she said with a sigh.

"What did your folks say when they came?" Ray asked her. He had missed Frank's parents because Stacey had wanted advice on driving to Queens.

"Oh, at first they were concerned. Then after Mom saw he was none worse for the wear, she lit into him," Frank's sister said with a laugh. "She told him in no uncertain terms that she felt it was time for him to move on. Reminded him that he worked very hard for his degree and that he should use the skills he acquired in school. There was no need for her to continue worrying about him being a fireman."

"How about your dad?" Jack asked.

"He was sympathetic, said he remembered his time in the army, the camaraderie of his unit and all, but when the war was over everyone knew it was time to move on," Then she lowered her voice and imitated her father "'You can always get together with the guys.' Frank wasn't impressed. When they left I gave him my own opinion."

"And what little bit of advice did you have for brother?" Ray asked sarcastically, knowing her ability for biting comments.

"I leaned over and whispered sweetly in his ear that I thought he was a flaming asshole. Then I walked out."

"Ah, kick a man when he's down," Jack groaned.

"Why not, it's easier than hitting him," she laughed.

"You know, before he fell asleep, Frank told me he was resigned to leaving the job. Or as he put it 'Being forced off the job by the women in his life.' Now I know why you and your mother were included," Ray said, chuckling to himself.

"Being forced off the Fire Department?" she responded indignantly. "You guys are so melodramatic. It's not like he didn't plan this all along."

"The boy is not getting any sympathy from his family, that's for sure," the detective said to himself while shaking his head.

"I empathize with his injuries," Gloria said defensively. "But I can't really sympathize with his plight. He made his bed. Now he has to sleep in it."

"Jack, are you paying attention? You're not going to get any sympathy from Miss Helms."

"Don't bother yourself with Miss Helms' reaction," Jack countered. "I'd suggest you figure out who is going to investigate what happens to you if you wimp out on my sister."

"I am not going to wimp out," he insisted. "I just have to get together with her and go shopping for a ring."

As the three sat silently, Ray began to think about his future with Stacey. How had he been backed into this corner? There was no doubt he loved her, but marriage had not been in his immediate plans. Of course, her pushing had made asking much easier. By the time he "asked", there were no longer any doubts about her answer. Even then, he thought they would set a date sometime in the next couple of years. Stacey staying at his mother's house had not been in those plans. The two women had only spent a night together and already there were plans being laid. Suddenly the date was being moved up. Before he and Stacey had a chance to sit down and discuss it, his mother and fiancé had pushed the date up a year and a half. The question of marriage had moved from "if" to "when" to "Can we get it done sooner than that?" within a week.

A major change was coming to his life. If Frank's experience was a harbinger of modern married life, then it was going to take a lot of adjustment. The detective smiled to himself. In the end, he did not mind this type of change. There was no denying it was time and Stacey was the girl.

Where his fiancé was now was the question. It should not have taken her this long just to pick up Chingli. She had been strangely secretive when asking for advice. Since she had already dropped Chingli to Kathy's place once, he was suspicious of her asking again. When questioned, Stacey had replied that it was dark and Chingli had read the directions to her. The focus of her questions had implied she wanted to go to JFK airport. At one point, the cop had stopped answering because he thought Chingli might be trying to fly back to Taiwan. Frank would be devastated if she fled the country. Ray was not about to make it easier for his friend to be miserable. After Stacey had sworn that she was not helping Chingli fly home, he had relented and given her the directions requested. Apparently, Kathy Stanley lived around JFK, but something still did not feel right. Maybe he could get something out of Gloria."Glor, why was Stacey asking for directions to JFK?" he asked, deciding on a frontal assault.

"What gave you the idea she was asking for directions to the airport?" was the innocent sounding reply.

"Because she wanted to know where to get off for the airport," he said, trying to sound casual.

"Then I guess Kathy lives around the airport," she said with a smile on her face. "I told Jack last night, Chingli wrote the directions in Chinese. I haven't the slightest idea where Kathy lives."

Seeing it would be futile to continue, he changed the subject to expected visitors. "I think Kathy should be here shortly. The press conference was winding down. It actually put Frank to sleep," he chuckled.

"The press conference had nothing to do with him sleeping," Jack pointed out. "I don't know what they're giving him, but it must be good."

Gloria shook her head when she heard this. "You guys talk about me not having any sympathy. He's been fencing with firemen and cops all day. That's more than enough to knock him out."

Ray had to admit she was right. The guys came in with a lot of energy, trying to cheer Frank up. They probably wore him out.

As far as sympathy for his buddy was concerned, he had plenty of that. Since Stacey had pried a proposal out of him, Ray had become more understanding of how difficult it was to change. He knew Frank's change was the hardest to take.

Ray looked up after he heard Jack mutter something under his breath. He saw a small Chinese woman walking toward them. There was something familiar about her regal gait. It was not until noticing

Stacey and Chingli walking behind her, that Ray made the connection, Chingli's mom! What was she doing here?

Instinctively, both he and Jack stood up. Mrs. Chiu smiled and bowed her head to them.

"Fa-ran-ke?" she asked, slowly pronouncing each syllable.

Jack smiled and pointed to the door of Frank's room. Mrs. Chiu turned around to find her daughter and said something to her before walking toward the door.

Chapter Thirty Six

Chingli walked a few yards behind her mother, feeling numb from the events of the past two days. The arguments of the last weeks echoed through her mind.

"You can't make up your mind. Are you a fireman or a cop?"

"I'm a civil servant, but it would be illegal for me to do a cop's job."

Maybe it was illegal for her husband to perform the duties of a police officer. It was not illegal for him to be a decoy, a target walking into a volatile situation beside a madman! When Kathy had called to tell her what had happened, Chingli had felt her world collapse. The tactic of waking Frank up by fleeing had backfired. If she had stayed home, he would not have volunteered to help the police.

Her mother had said little on the drive from the airport. There had been no need for her to voice an opinion of her daughter's actions. Chingli knew what she would say if asked. Mama had been right. It would have been better to stay with Frank and try to influence his action than to leave him to make decisions by himself.

After the general's wife called to her, Chingli quickened her pace. The two women met beside Frank's door. Mama began to tutor her daughter on the tactics she should use.

"Remember, you are now negotiating for your future. You will go in first. Control yourself and do not mention that I am here. Try to get a commitment from him before I come in."

"You talk about my future, what about my past, Mama?" Chingli asked, still not sure what she should say to her husband. "What about that stubborn man lying in there?"

"Your past? It will always be a part of you, but do not let it control. The present is all that really exists," her mother advised her calmly. "That stubborn man is your present. The future is what can be influenced by your decisions today. You cannot change what has happened. That is reality. How can you use it to achieve happiness?"

"Happiness?" she asked bitterly. How could she think of happiness now? Her husband lay in a hospital bed with two broken ribs and a concussion. A madman had tried to kill him. If she had had the courage to stand by him, maybe he would not have been injured. The bitterness of this guilt tainted everything.

That was not the problem that most concerned the Taiwanese woman now. She would have to persuade Frank to accept the position offered by her uncle. If he did not, she was determined to accompany her mother back to Taiwan. That resolve did not sit easily with her. Returning home would expose her to the shame of abandoning her marriage, but it was her only weapon. Frank would have to keep his word to her or she could never trust him again. He had said their future was beyond the Fire Department. The firefighter would either walk away from his profession or she would walk away from any chance for happiness.

Her mother smiled as she reached up and put her hand on Chingli's neck. The older woman leaned close to her daughter and said, "Don't you realize that is all your old mother wants, your happiness?"

Chingli began to cry quietly. She had never given any thought to whether or not her mother cared for her personal happiness. Since she had been a small child, all her energy had gone into pleasing her parents. If Mama had not fallen in love with Frank, Chingli doubted she would have had the strength to cut all ties with her family and marry him. It seemed so tragic that she had taken the love expressed in Mama's last words for granted all her life.

"I've spent my entire life trying to please you, Mama," she whispered. "I never thought that was all you wanted for me."

"Someday you will have a child and then you will be able to understand how I feel, Chiu Chingli." Her mother then switched to Mandarin, "*Yang zi fang zhi fu mu en.* Until you raise your own child, it is not possible for you to understand. Do you think I am happy that I must fly a day to see my child? The least you could do is help me to help you be happy," she finished in a voice choked with emotion.

"I love you, Mama," Chingli whispered.

"*Sanba*, so Americanized," her mother said with a laugh. "We Chinese don't need to say such words. It is actions that say it for us. Now go my daughter, your future awaits you beyond that door."

Chingli raised her head and dried her tears. She knew if Frank did not agree to resign and accept her uncle's job their marriage might fail. There could be acceptance of his job if he had no other options, but that was not the case. Frank had planned this change in occupation, had worked hard to earn his degree, and now had an opportunity to achieve his dream. Why was he being so stubborn? Was it because of his pride and determination to do everything on his own? Damn all men and their pride! The Taiwanese woman reminded herself to negotiate and then pushed the door to her husband's hospital room open.

Frank was lying on his back with a bandage wrapped around his head. The room smelled of flowers, disinfectant, and rubbing alcohol. Sunlight was streaming in through windows on the other side of an empty bed. There were bruises visible on Frank's face along with a cut on his cheek, but he seemed to be resting comfortably.

Chingli tried to control herself, but the emotions she felt overwhelmed her. With tears flowing freely and her heart feeling like it would burst with joy, she leaned over and kissed his head in an opening of the bandage.

The firefighter stirred and then woke to see her smiling down at him. All thoughts of confrontation were driven from Chingli's mind for an instant. Then her determination returned with renewed strength. She would win this battle with her man's ego and he would thank her for it.

"I told you at the valor dinner that I did not want you to receive any more awards," she said softly. "Now everyone says you are a hero."

"Does my wife think I am a hero?" he asked doubtfully.

"Your wife thinks you are a fool," she said with a smile.

"This is not the way it was supposed to happen. Did you talk with Mama?"

"Mama knows and asked what you are going to do."

"Well, since this stalker is no longer around," Frank began drowsily. "I thought the pressure for a decision would be off."

Chingli instantly changed. As far as she was concerned, what her husband had just said was a declaration of war. There would be no quarter given by her in this fight. "No!" she said firmly without raising her voice. "The decision will be made before you are off sick leave or I may not be around when you get home."

His wife's reaction seemed to pull Frank out of his lethargy. "There is no more danger of getting shot now. The quack with the gun is dead," he repeated as he sat up slowly. "When I get back to the firehouse, it will be business as usual. Nothing extraordinary is going to happen. Why can't we take some time to think everything over?"

"Because I will not put up with this anymore," she shot back. "We have been thinking everything over for a long time. You promised when we got married that you would leave this job."

"I will, but first I want the MBA."

"For what? Uncle has already offered you a job."

"Look, this was part of the deal all along," he said changing tactics. "You married a firefighter. Why does it bother you that I will be one a little longer?"

"No, I did not marry a firefighter," she replied sternly. "I married a student of China."

"What would you have done if I hadn't studied Chinese?"

She calmed down a little and took a moment to digest his question. "I would not have met you in Hong Kong if you had not studied Chinese," she said thoughtfully. "And I would not have married you if you had not promised to leave the Fire Department." She emphasized the "and" in her final sentence.

Frank winched as he lied back and rested quietly for a heartbeat. Then he asked softly, "So where does this leave the two of us now?"

"It is time to make a decision my husband," she said quietly, determined not to let his obvious discomfort distract her. She was proud of the control she had maintained throughout the discussion. "I want a commitment from you to leave the Fire Department before you have to go back to the firehouse"

"And what will we live on?" he asked in a last ditched effort to sway his wife.

"Mama will give you an offer," Chingli said with a smile, sensing victory. "She will give the details to you personally."

"As soon as she gives me something concrete we can talk about it," Frank replied with a little more energy. Was his sudden enthusiasm based on the impending offer or the mistaken impression that the offer could not be made in the near future? It did not matter. A commitment is what she wanted. That she got it on a mistaken impression did not bother her. "Then you agree. As soon as Mama gives you a viable offer you will leave the Fire Department?"

"I don't want to resign with only a telephone assurance, Chingli," he said in an attempt to avoid being pinned down. "We need a paycheck to live on. Food has to be bought and rent paid. I need something concrete."

"If Mama handed you a check from uncle to cover the start up cost of this business, would you commit yourself?" she asked, leading him on. This was going to be easy. She would take advantage of his male sense of honor. Frank always spouted proudly that a man was only as good as his word. Women were so much more practical. After all, had not her mother-in-law said that in the West it was a woman's prerogative to change her mind. This contrast allowed women to shift with changing situations, while men were constantly ensnared by their word. He would give his word any moment. She laughed inwardly while closing the trap on her unsuspecting husband.

"The day we have a check to start this venture, I swear to resign my position on the Newark Fire Department."

"You told me a gentleman's handshake is legally binding in America. Are you a gentleman?" she asked with a smile.

Her husband smiled back. "That you would have to ask my wife, but I would prefer we seal it with a kiss."

Chingli leaned over and gave her husband a peck on the cheek and then began to walk toward the door.

"Couldn't you give me something a little more passionate than that?" he asked. "We're concluding a business deal that will affect us for the rest of our lives."

"That is all you get," she said with a coy smile. "You are an injured man. We don't want anything to happen while you're recuperating." When she opened the door Frank knew he had been Shanghaied by his China girl. Mama walked in with a smile.

Chapter Thirty Seven

Frank pulled into the lot beside Six Engine and parked his car. It was hard to believe that half a year had passed since he had resigned from the Fire Department. He had found it gradually easier to visit over the past months, but, for some reason, it was difficult tonight. Maybe it was because this would be his first meal in the firehouse without Chingli accompanying him since leaving his second home.

Over the months, things in his old company had slowly changed. Wagon had died quietly about a month after his resignation. The City had finally broken down and purchased a few new rigs. Six had been assigned one of these after the pumps on register forty-seven had died from overuse. The guys had promptly nicknamed the new truck the "Tonka Toy" because of its short wheel base, but anything was an improvement over the pig it replaced. New firefighters had been appointed over the summer. How the City had swung that after pleading money problems and closing companies over the winter remained a mystery. One of these new firefighters had been assign to Six as his replacement. Now Jack had a "red ass" under him.

These changes had been observed on infrequent daytime visits. The former firefighter had not been in the firehouse at night since the shooting, but tonight was special. It would be Matt's last night. The veteran firefighter was retiring to South Carolina. Was that why he felt so melancholy? Frank was happy for Matt, whom he considered a mentor and friend for life. Why would he feel down? There were no answers in the car, so he picked up the cheese cake and opened the door.

Before going into the firehouse, Frank stopped at Firewagon's grave. This had been chiseled out of the concrete in a corner next to the side door. After the body of the little mutt had been laid to rest, her grave had been covered with cement. Etched into the top of this covering were the words "Firewagon, R.I.P." He smiled to himself and then took a final step toward the firehouse door. "Someone had better be home," he thought as he reached for the door knob. Jack had been given his key when Frank resigned. Presumably, the probie had that key now. The door knob turned easily, relieving one small worry.

Don was sitting at the kitchen table, peeling shrimp.

"You made it!" the chief's driver shouted.

"You didn't doubt I would, did you Don?" the former firefighter asked. "As I told my wife, this is an obligation, not a party. I owe Matt too much."

"That's why we miss you, Frank," Don laughed. "You take life so seriously."

"As opposed to the laissez faire attitude of your average fireman?"

Before Don could respond to this, the sound of Six's siren came from Springfield Avenue. Frank walked onto the apparatus floor and started the overhead door up. After the door completed its ascent, the "Tonka Toy" began emitting a high pitched beep as it backed into quarters. "That sound must go over big with the few neighbors still in the area," he thought while ducking back into the kitchen. As soon as the beeping stopped, the shouted banter of firefighters returning from a run replaced it.

"I'm telling you," Matt said as he walked in through the overhead door. "I saw him running back into the kitchen. He probably didn't want the world to see he still associates with the likes of us."

"Then he must have parked in the side lot," Al replied. "Cause his car wasn't parked out back or on the side of the building."

"Of course he parked in the side lot," Captain Wagner laughed. "The boy spent more than enough time in this house. He knows where it's safe to park."

An empty feeling filled the pit of Frank's stomach when he heard the shouts of his old crew. His mind could now put into words what his heart had been telling him. The blue haze which had covered the day was from a realization that he was now an outsider. This firehouse and the men who worked in it had once been his life. This had been home, but he had moved on and given it up. Everything about the place played on his emotions, leaving a void that seemed impossible to fill. Before these thoughts could drag the former firefighter down any further, Matt and Al came crashing through the double doors from the apparatus floor.

"Here he is!" Matt yelled with a grin. "Did you bring that lovely bride of yours to cook for us again?"

"Are you kidding?" Frank shot back. "She came here to cook my last meal in the firehouse because of an unvoiced fear that you boys would kidnap me. Chingli won't set foot in this firehouse again if she can help it. You should hear her description of this place. It starts off with the fly strips hanging from the ceiling and moves onto cockroaches, diesel fumes, and the fragrance of freshly burned wood."

"People pay good money installing fireplaces just to get that rustic scent of burned wood in their living room," Matt said with mocked seriousness.

"That's right," Jack shouted from the apparatus floor. "Besides, if we had wanted to kidnap you, you would have vanished long ago."

"Listen to the voice of reason calling from the wilderness," Frank retorted loudly, the void in his stomach filling with the warm welcome. He could forget the pressures of the office for one night.

Jack barged in through the watch room door and pulled up next to his old friend. "I already told them why the little China doll came to cook for us," he began. "It was her victory dinner. She came to gloat."

The Captain came in behind Jack and sat at the watch room desk. "What did you bring for dessert, Frank?" he asked while reaching for the company journal. "My old lady started me on a diet. How big a lie will I have to tell her tomorrow?"

"I picked up a chocolate covered cheesecake, Cap," he replied with a laugh. "The kind you turned me on to in your bad old days."

"You're trying to make me into a habitual liar," Wagner groaned.

"Habitual, Cap? I haven't offered you anything recently that would require you to bend the truth."

"No, but all these other bastards enjoy tempting me. It's not getting any easier around here, Frank. Those firehouse pounds are hard coming off."

"Cap, you gotta have will power," Al insisted.

"Will you listen to mister slim and trim," Jack laughed.

"Careful, red ass," the senior firefighter shot back. "That body won't stay slim once you settle down with Gloria and lose all your incentive for looking beautiful."

"Hold on," Jack said. "I am no longer the junior man around here. If you have a problem with junior, take it up with him. He's coming through the door now." Bob Brendler walked into the kitchen as Jack finished.

"Just because you're not the junior man anymore doesn't mean you're not a red ass," Matt laughed. "You're just the senior red ass."

"If you guys want to eat sometime tonight, you'd better pipe down and start getting dinner going," Don pointed out from his seat, the shrimp now peeled. "Frank, you going to perform your wonders with broccoli tonight or are we going to have to put up with Al's soggy vegetables again?"

"You're going to make a guest work for his meal?" Bob asked innocently.

"Guest?" Matt asked indignantly. "Careful junior, that boy was dragging hose through buildings when you were in high school. He's also the only man I know of who received two commendations after he left the job."

"Two?" Frank responding sounding genuinely puzzled. "I only received one and that was for being bait in a police operation."

"Oh, so you haven't seen this yet," Matt said while handing him a Fire Department notice.

Frank quickly perused an executive order dated the previous week. "This is from that job on Seventeenth Street where we got that little girl out."

"Where you got that little girl out, you mean," Jack laughed.

"If I had tried that alone, you would have buried me three days later."

"Yeah, yeah," Jack conceded. "They mention us in there too, but you have the starring role."

"I'm not looking for any role," Frank sighed remembering the carnival like atmosphere after Dan O'Brian had shot him. "I prefer to run silent and deep."

"Well, you might have to stand up in front of a bunch of partying firemen at the next valor awards dinner and explain yourself." Matt said with a smile. "And I'll have to come up from South Carolina just to enjoy the sight of you squirming."

"How could they do that?" Frank asked incredulously. "I'm not even on the job anymore."

"Stranger things have happened," Captain Wagner chuckled. "Now how about you get to work on that broccoli?"

Frank noticed that Bob had fallen quiet during this exchange and felt embarrassed for him. Remembering his first days in the firehouse, he had kept on eye on the newest member of Six Engine. Bob seemed so young and eager to fit in. Frank knew that enthusiasm well, never having forgotten the milieu of his first days in Six Engine or Matt's help. The kid knew little about what had happened before he was on the job. He was just trying to mesh with his new crew.

"These guys can be brutal, Bob," Frank said to the probationary firefighter. "Not only do I have to put up with their abuse, I have to work for my dinner."

"Oh, will you listen to this," Al shouted. "He's trying to convince the kid that he didn't expect to work tonight."

"I'm getting the impression, you expected him to cook," Bob laughed.

"You mean 'He expected to cook,' don't you Bob?" Jack asked.

Frank turned towards Bob and said, "They just want my broccoli."

"Damn right we want your broccoli," Matt shouted. "Now sit your ass down and get to work."

Frank, Al, Matt, and Bob sat at the table while Jack went to the refrigerator and took out the broccoli. This was placed on the table in front of Frank. "Don't do anything until I can watch," Jack shouted as he went to the cabinets to get plates. "You have to teach me how to do this or these guys will never have a balanced meal again."

"Oh, now you're mister health food himself?" Frank asked in surprise.

"Your sister wouldn't have it any other way."

The two laughed as Jack sat next to Frank. Don took the shrimp over to the sink and continued preparing that part of the meal. Al was in charge of the ziti while Matt put together a salad. Bob had appeared anxious to help with the broccoli, so Frank had sat next to him. He began to show the two young firefighters how to peel the vegetable.

Frank knew he was not in a position to help Bob, but the kid struck him as a natural. It would be up to Jack to train him. Everyone else would be gone within a year. Generations pass, but the job remains. Does the incentive to take the job remain the same? He laughed to himself. It's not the incentive to take the job; it's the incentive to remain on the job that counted and love of it had not sufficed for him. If he had followed his heart, Bob would not be sitting at this table and Chingli would not be sitting at home. Why do women always seem to win? That was question for the ages. Right now there was broccoli to peel and the last bit of camaraderie to savor.

Captain Wagner walked in from the watch room as the kitchen quieted down. "How's business, Frank?" he asked with a hint of concern.

"Business is growing, Cap," he answered with a sigh. "I'm sure Jack has kept you abreast of the deliveries he makes."

"Well, he comes in with all sorts of complaints about having to drive from Chinatown in New York to Short Hills Mall. Seems to be afraid one day he's going to deliver pieces of art to Chinatown and tourist souvenirs to the Mall."

"As long as the truck is packed right, that won't happen," Frank assured his former skipper.

"But you have a bunch of firemen packing the truck," Jack pointed out.

"Since when do you have a problem working with firemen?" Matt asked from the sink.

"I have no problem working with firemen. My problem is them getting it right after a night in the firehouse."

"That's my problem, Jack," Frank pointed out. "I check before you drive, don't worry."

Don checked the shrimp in the oven as Jack carried the broccoli to the sink for a final rinse. Frank took the wok out of the cabinet and placed it on the stove. They would be eating in a few minutes, so Bob and Matt cleared the table and put the dishes out.

By the time the Chief came down from his room, dinner was coming out. Everyone settled down, hoping the bell would not hit before they were through. Jack turned to his friend as the ziti was being passed around and said, "You know, we were talking about you the other night. Bob got a kick out the nicknames you picked up with your stupidity at one point or another."

"Is that supposed to make me feel good?" Frank asked, trying to sound insulted. "Which names and what acts of stupidity do I have to deny? I'll warn you Bob, they called me a lot of false names. It all depended on whether I gave them a shot at the tip."

The junior man seemed hesitant to join in the fun. Bob's mannerisms told Frank more than anything else that he was indeed a guest. Whoever said you can never go home was right. But it was more than just losing a place at this dinner table. "Firefighter" had once been his identity. Over the past six months, his inner struggle with change had replaced the feeling of being a part of something, of belonging. Would it be possible to substitute the fledgling company he managed in Port Newark for Engine Company Six? In order to stay sane, he would have to redefine himself. Sitting at this table having dinner with his old crew told Frank that accomplishing that would be one of the greatest challenges of his life.

Jack seemed to sense something of what his old friend was feeling. The firefighter pushed on relentlessly with his teasing. "We threw a couple of the old names at junior here, but didn't tell him how you earned them," Jack laughed. "Figured you should do the explaining."

"I already warned you about these guys, Bob. They are not the most reputable of people."

"Oh, I don't believe half of what they tell me, Frank," Bob said with a chuckle. "But I am curious. Why did they call you fifty nine ninety five?"

"That's a low blow, Matt," the former firefighter shot at the man most likely responsible for priming the kid with this question. Matt shrugged his shoulders innocently as he continued eating. "Well, Bob, it went like this. We were blown out of a building on, I think it was

Wolcott Terrace. Seventeen had gone in on the wrong side of a duplex so the fire got away from them. We pulled up and made the mistake of not stretching in because Eighteen had taken a hydrant. Well, Eighteen's rig died while we were on the first floor of this building, so we had no water. Everyone started to bail out because it became pretty obvious that the whole floor was going to flash over. I had the line, so ended up being the last one out of the first floor. Meanwhile there were some guys doing a search on the second floor. They came hauling down the stairs and one of them plowed into me as I came out of the first floor. I got knocked on my ass at the same time we got water. My helmet went in one direction, while the rest of me went in the other. Now, keep in mind, helmets at the time cost $59.95. Our line is the only water on the fire for like half a minute, so I can't just shut down and search for my helmet."

"At the time he's working this line, which only had a piss stream anyway, the flames are inches above his head," Matt interjected having emptied his mouth. "He's leaning into them trying to find his helmet. I had to go up and throw him down the front stairs of this place or he was going to burst into flames."

"I thought I was supposed to tell the kid this story," Frank interrupted. "First you tell me you wanted him to hear it from me then you start throwing in your half truths. And you wonder why a guy might think of divorcing you." Everyone laughed at how Frank described his resignation. It was the first time he had been able to mention leaving the department lightheartedly.

"Why did you leave, Frank?" Bob asked. "I mean, it sounds as if you liked the job."

Frank put down his fork and turned to the junior man. "Bob, this is the best job in the world, but nothing goes on forever. I had an opportunity that was very difficult to pass up and that I had been working toward for a number of years. It wasn't the best timing, but . . . . " His voice trailed off as he ran out of words.

"It wasn't because you were shook up from the shooting?"

This question brought out a howl of laughter from everyone around the table. "You mean the typewriter?" Al shouted.

"Typewriter?"

Frank put his hand on the probationary firefighter's shoulder. How could he explain in a few short sentences the struggle to complete his studies while working out of this firehouse? There was no time to tell him about Chingli or the opportunities that Asia offered. What of his need to challenge himself intellectually and his fascination with the Chinese language? Anything more than a few short sentences would put a damper on the evening. "Bob, what happened the last few weeks I was on the job had nothing to do with my resignation. As I said, years of work were put in to prepare for the opportunity I took. No matter how much you love this job there is a time when you have to move on. It's a young man's job, Bob. Just ask Matt."

"Why are you bringing me into this?" Matt asked.

"How can you ask why I brought you into this?" Frank replied. "It's your last night, not mine. I've been through this. We should be peppering you with questions."

"Fire away, my boy, everyone else has already heard the explanation."

His dinner was getting cold, but Frank knew the bell could hit at any moment, leaving his questions unanswered. "I'm really curious. You're on the captain's list. Why not hang around until you get promoted and up your pension?"

"Well, Frank, I sat down with the old lady and discussed it," Matt said reluctantly. "Seems your wife inspired her to accept it was time to move on. Especially after she realized it would take five years to reach full grade. Those salary increases the first few years didn't impress her. We're at the stage of life where time means more than money, so I'm calling it quits."

Frank knew from what Jack had said that Matt's wife had given him an ultimatum, retire or visit her on the holidays. Chingli's determination had encouraged many of the women who heard of it to push for what would make them happy without regard to how their hubbies felt.

"Okay, so why South Carolina?" he asked, not wanting to reopen a discussion on something that no longer mattered to either of them. "You could stay in Jersey. I've got plenty of work for retired firemen."

"No, thank you," Matt laughed. "I'm going to take advantage of all that Mediterranean cooking I learned in the firehouse and open an Italian restaurant to service all these Yankees retiring down there."

"I can't wait to visit this place," Al interjected. "He's going to have to get all his ingredients shipped down there from Jersey. Either that or serve frozen food."

"I'll just make sure when you come to visit, you drive a tractor trailer."

Laughter filled the room as they all responded to the give and take of friends sharing a meal. Frank felt himself caught between his past and his future at this table. The camaraderie that was once his somehow eluded him. Accepting the fact that he was now a guest became easier after Matt spoke of his plans. Had he not told Bob that there comes a time to move on? Matt's time came after he weighed the cost and benefits of waiting for a promotion. Frank's own decision to leave the department had been predicated on the same type of analysis.

"So, Frank," Al began. "Do you miss us?"

"I don't miss you walking out of the shower," he laughed while feeling a return of the inner turmoil that had eased for a moment. "But, yes, I miss this insanity."

"What do you miss the most?" Matt asked expectantly.

"What I miss most is being able to talk out my problems," he answered spontaneously, surprising himself. It was an answer from the heart. "If you guys hadn't been there when Chingli went off the deep end, I don't know what I would have done." The men around the table sat quietly, listening intently. "I miss the adrenalin. Sometimes when things get crazy in the office and I doubt how successful this whole deal will be, I hear a shout in the back of my mind. 'Give me more line!'" They all laughed.

"You always were a demanding S.O.B.," Jack pointed out.

"It gives me a little comfort, tells me I was part of something that counted, that I was at the top of a profession."

"You already said it, Frank," Matt said quietly. "We all have to move on sooner or later. You just retired a little sooner than average."

"Sometimes I feel like I bailed out on you."

"No, you would have been a fool not to jump at that opportunity," Al reassured him. "Besides we got a new kid to replace you, nothing like fresh meat."

"That opportunity is not as rosy as everyone seems to think," Frank replied seriously. "You don't exactly get a feeling of security out there guys. The Chinese would call this job an 'iron rice bowl.' You might drop your bowl, but it won't break. You'll always have something to eat from. My iron rice bowl is gone."

"I was thinking about you last night," Al began. "There are different types of people in this world. Some like to hunt and then sit close to the fire to enjoy its warmth and light. They roast meat and eat it leisurely. Others kind of hover just outside of the circle of light and warmth. They trade wood they've gathered in the dark for a few scraps of food. You're a hunter. You would never have been content to settle for an iron rice bowl. You want more out of life than that."

"You are one crazy bastard!" the Captain shouted at his friend, howling. "You must have been watching Channel Thirteen again."

"Look," Al replied defensively. "I'm trying to make the kid feel better. Anyway, the gist of what I said is true. You'd never be happy settling for an unbreakable bowl, Frank. That's just the way you are.""Thanks, Al," Frank said with a smile. "You're probably right. I just have to get used to the nine to five life, that's all."

"Alright, alright," the Chief interjected, "enough of this nostalgia. Three more of us are going to be leaving by the end of the year. Let's save some of the 'good old days' talk for then. You know Frank, Chingli's little performance was admired by more than one wife on this job. I suspect the subject of retirement was pushed forward a little in my wife's mind by your tenacious China girl. I know she's going to ask me how Chingli is when I get home tomorrow, so give us an update. Has she calmed down?"

Frank smiled at the Chief's description of his wife. As far as he was concerned, tenacious was just a polite way of saying stubborn. Chingli would prefer to describe herself as persistent, but all these words said the same thing. His wife was a woman who knew what she wanted and strove hard to get it. When she showed up at Seton Hall looking for him, alarms should have gone off. How could he have fallen so easily?

The former firefighter knew the answer before the question crossed his mind. Chiu Chingli was an exceptional woman who gave him everything a man could want, but it came at a price. Don't all men pay a price for their relationships with women? Gloria would say all women suffer the same fate. Poor Jack, he would not believe what awaited him. Frank looked at the Chief and gave a concise report of his wife's recent preoccupations. "She's in Stacey's bridal party, Chief," he began. "Stacey insisted, saying something about owing big time. When I asked Chingli about that, she just smiled. She spends a lot of time with me in the Port office, dealing with Taiwan. Then there's the foursome and their nights out."

Jack groaned when the foursome was mentioned. Frank turned to him and asked, "You want to tell them about the girls and their nights out?"

"No, no, you're doing a fine job," Jack answered with a smile. "I don't want to contradict what you say."

"You mean you don't want to admit that there's something going on that we aren't allowed to know," Frank said with a laugh. Jack just put his head in his hand and waved his fork at Frank. "It seems that Stacey, Gloria, Chingli, and Kathy Stanley have formed a little women's club. They go out maybe once a month. Then Ray and Jack start bitching to me about some subtle change in the way their ladies deal with them. But neither of them wants to believe me when I say the girls are conspiring against them."

Frank got the response he expected from the guys finishing their meal around the table. The laughter seemed to make Jack want to say something in his own defense, but he appeared to think better of it. Instead he stood up and carried his plate to the sink. "How about some of that cheese cake?" the senior red ass asked, changing the subject to something more palatable.

"Break it out!" Captain Wagner said enthusiastically. "If I'm going to be bad, I might as well go all the way."

As they all sat down, each with a slice of cake in front of him, the radio sprang to life.

"Engine Twelve to quarters, emergency!"

Frank instantly felt the familiar surge of adrenalin go through his system. Everyone became quiet as they waited for Twelve to complete their broadcast.

"Last unit calling quarters, come in."

"Engine Twelve, give me the box for Turner and Avon. We have a working fire in a three story frame!"

All the men around the table stood up except Frank. Bob and Jack took one last bite of their cake while waiting for the Captain and the Chief to move out of the way. The guys from Six Engine went out the double doors onto the apparatus floor while Don and the Chief exited the kitchen through the watch room. Frank rose and walked to the double doors.

"Don't eat all the cheese cake, Frank," Matt shouted from the side of the rig. "We'll be back soon."

Pushing one of the doors open slightly, he shouted back, "Soon? You boys have a working fire. What do you think? You're going to just walk in and blow it out?"

"Damn straight!" Al shouted back. "This is the Newark Fire Department boy!"

"If it gets out of hand, don't even think of cleaning up. Just go home to that little woman of yours and tell her we said 'hey'," Matt shouted from the rig.

The sound of the overhead doors going up followed this exchange. Doors slammed and engines started while Frank watched from behind the door. The rig pulled out with warning lights and siren on. Six Engine inched forward until the traffic on Springfield Avenue had stopped, then the rig shot across the avenue and down Hunterdon Street. Chief Gregor started the overhead doors down and then hopped in his gig. The car quickly followed Six Engine down Hunterdon Street. The guest was now alone; his hosts had a job to do.

Frank went back to his seat at the table. As he sat down he realized that the most satisfying years of his work life were probably behind him. Al was right about his needing more than an iron rice bowl, but that was an intellectual need. His need to feel close to the edge of life would never again be met. Responsibilities would only grow and he would have to reshape his inner life to meet those responsibilities.

Chingli had seen right through him. When he had left for the firehouse she had told him to enjoy himself because after tonight he would have to grow up and leave the Fire Department behind. Frank found it unsettling that his wife knew how he would feel before he did. The radio came to life as these thoughts passed through his mind.

"Deputy One on the scene. Deputy One to quarters, emergency, second alarm!"

As the bells began to come over the circuit, he swore softly to himself, stood up, and looked around the kitchen. The firehouse would always be a part of him. This realization somehow gave a little relief to the ache of having become a guest in it.

"Time to move on," the young businessman said quietly. A shipment was due in port tomorrow and preparations had to be made for a trip to Asia next week. Frank picked up his coat and walked toward the side door. The sound of the Chief giving instructions to incoming companies filled the room as the door was pulled closed.

www.ingramcontent.com/pod-product-compliance
Lightning Source LLC
Chambersburg PA
CBHW020838030726
47496CB00001B/260